D0900244

BLOOD ATONEMENT

A DAHLGREN WALLACE MYSTERY

BLOOD ATONEMENT

JIM TENUTO

The Lyons Press
Guilford, Connecticut
An imprint of The Globe Pequot Press

To buy books in quantity for corporate use
or incentives, call **(800) 962–0973, ext. 4551,**
or e-mail **premiums@GlobePequot.com.**

The Lyons Press is an imprint of The Globe Pequot Press.

10 9 8 7 6 5 4 3 2 1

Printed in the United States of America

Designed by Mimi LaPoint

Library of Congress Cataloging-in-Publication Data

Tenuto, Jim.
Blood atonement : a Dahlgren Wallace mystery / Jim Tenuto.
p. cm.
ISBN 1-59228-613-5 (trade cloth)
I. Montana—Fiction. I. Title.

PS3620.E58B58 2005
813'.6—dc22

2005040842

FOR LYNN

ACKNOWLEDGMENTS

My sincere thanks to all of those who helped this book become a reality. Inspiration came from three quarters—my friend Chuck Johnson, author Gerald Hammond, and the enigmatic Argentinean guide, Bartolo Martínez.

Thanks to those who read the book in its many previous forms: Blue Fogg, Betty Watson, Jerry Warren, Justin and Liz, Ed Bastarache, Connie Bastarache, Chris Britton, and Susan Schwartzwald.

I want to recognize the contributions of the late Sara Anne Freed, Edgar Award–winning editor, Greg Smith, DVM, and one of my best friends, John Lovasz.

Thanks to Alan Russell, a great friend and a wonderful author, and my tenacious agent, Don Gastwirth. Thanks to my editor, Lilly Golden. Her suggestions have made *Blood Atonement* a much better book.

And finally, my wife, Lynn. First reader, first critic, first fan.

AUTHOR'S NOTE

The events in this novel occur in May and June 2000.

While Bozeman, Big Sky, and Gallatin Gateway are real cities in Montana, the rivers described in the book are purely fictional, as are the characters. The only exceptions are those historical characters who did and do make their way in our world.

CHAPTER 1

A MOMENT OF PERFECTION

I neared a moment of perfection.

My definition of perfection involves moving water, solitude, a fly rod, a dry fly, and a trout. Building new memories to replace the old. The slow-moving water of the spring creek was icy, stained a peat green. No other angler spoiled the morning. The bamboo fly rod was one of my favorites, a Granger Victory half a century old, which the previous owner had purchased as a boy for five dollars out of a bin at a hardware store. I had tied the fly myself. An Adams. The one fly to carry if you carry only one fly.

The trout fed steadily, rising to take insects from the water. A trophy trout. Not the fish of a lifetime, but close. Two feet long, fat and healthy.

On my first cast the fly drifted over the trout. The fish rose, taking another natural, and this time the rise was flashy. I picked my fly and line from the water and made another cast. Again the presentation was classic, textbook. The fly dropped softly into the feeding lane and again it drifted drag free past the trout.

The third cast brought me incrementally closer to that moment of perfection. This time I cast the fly so that it dropped nearly on the trout's head. This would produce one of two results. Either I would put the fish down or the trout would take the fly in an instant, an instinctive feeding response.

The trout took the fly.

The beeper in my pocket vibrated and buzzed and perfection crumbled.

The trout was off.

There was never any question about who had called. The telephone numbers might be different, I could find myself returning the summons to just about anywhere in the world, but Fred Lather always waited, always impatiently, at the end of the line. When Fred called, I jumped. Reluctantly, but I jumped.

I reeled in the line, attached the fly to the hook minder near the cork handle of the old rod, and waded to shore. With some effort I pulled my boots from the silted shallow water near the creek's bank and clouds of silt, iridescent in the sunlight, drifted downstream. Cradling the rod under my arm, I dug my right hand into my waders and fumbled around until I found my right pants pocket. Fred, of course. The display flashed his number at the Carved L Ranch, followed by his emergency code.

"Where the hell are you?" Fred asked, without preamble.

"Standing in a phone booth," I answered. "Near Armstrong's."

"Didn't you see the emergency code on the page?"

"Yes, I did. What I didn't see were any phone booths on the creek."

"Change of plans," he said. "Need you back at the ranch like, right now."

As I drove into the courtyard in front of the ranch house, Fred was pacing on the lawn, gnawing on a cigar. He walked over to my truck.

"You look like shit," Fred said. "In fact, I would go so far as to say you look like hammered shit."

"Tough night," I said, rubbing the stubble on my chin. "I didn't expect to be working."

"Let's head down to the river. The Elderberrys are impatiently waiting to go fishing.

"I had this guy figured as the original alpha nerd," Fred said. "No hobbies, just work. Then he decides that he and his wife are going to become fly fishers."

We walked toward the river.

"Double-E Squared!" Fred gushed.

"Huh?" Tough night, dull mind.

"Elden Elderberry's nickname," Fred said, shaking his head in admiration. "The first double E represents his initials, and the second his degree from MIT, electrical engineering.

"Smart cuss," Fred continued, pausing to admire his cigar. "He's built a terrific business. The man has unlocked the secrets to video compression. Holds a number of key patents. Treat 'em like royalty."

"Fred," I protested, "I always treat your guests like royalty."

"Not true," Fred countered. "You weren't particularly affable to the senator from California. I'm just giving you a warning is all. You see, Elden's a Californian, born and raised."

I grimaced. I don't particularly care for Californians, invaders of the land and as pernicious as locusts. Instead of plants gnawed to the roots, Californians leave a trail of empty Starbucks cups and inflated real estate prices.

"So," Fred continued, "like I said, the Royal Fucking Treatment."

I usually receive "the Royal Fucking Treatment" speech whenever guests fish Fred's ranch. We don't see many regular folks at the Carved L.

"Susi, now she's actually the second Mrs. Elderberry," Fred said. "The first died in childbirth along with the child. Double-E Squared was one of the richest widowers in the world, and he stayed that way for nearly ten years. Then when he decides to marry it's to a former Miss Utah."

"Trophy wife?" I asked.

"Careful, Dahlgren," snarled Fred. "You're wading in treacherous water there." Fred and his divorce attorneys have more than a working knowledge of trophy wives.

"However, if a man is searching for a trophy wife, then it's best if she comes with her own trophies."

When I first saw him, Elden Elderberry was practicing his casts. He had the barest of basics down and he had worked himself into a sweat as he energetically heaved line back and forth. When he saw Fred and me, he stopped, a bit self-consciously, a sheepish grin on his flushed face.

When I first saw her, Susi Elderberry was watching the river, her back to us. It is no small feat to look great in a pair of waders. She did. When she heard Fred call out their names, she turned. A beautiful woman who looked great in a pair of waders.

"Elden, Susi," Fred said, suddenly oozing southern gentility and charm. "This here's Dahlgren Wallace. He's my river keeper for the ranch and he's a terrific guide." I shook hands with the Elderberrys.

"Dahlgren," Fred said, "I had Cook fill the cooler for you. You're all ready to go." He turned to the couple. "I'll see you at dinner."

"Looks like you know a thing or two about casting," I said.

"We took a lesson last Sunday," Elden said. "At the Golden Gate Fly Fishing Club."

"Let's see what you remember."

Elden and Susi made some casts for me and we worked for about half an hour on the mechanics. With conventional fishing tackle, spinning or bait-casting rods, the weight is in the lure. The thin monofilament fishing line flies off the reel as that weight is cast forward. With a fly rod, the weight is in the line itself, and a nearly weightless fly is usually tied to the end of the leader. With a fly rod, the cast is about moving line through the air.

The Elderberrys came with all the baggage of novice fly fishers. Their loops tended to open, backcasts fell into the water, forward casts slapped line into the water, and they worked hard, confusing muscle and strength for energy and efficiency.

"You don't need to make fifty-foot casts on this river," I said. "Actually, you don't need to make fifty-foot casts on most rivers. Let's concentrate on putting the fly out about twenty feet or so."

Susi sat in the bow of the McKenzie boat and Elden sat in the stern. At our first stop neither of the Elderberrys had a take. I had tied two nymphs onto their terminal tackle, pinched a bit of lead onto the leader, and attached a scrap of yarn as a strike indicator.

Because the river receives relatively little fishing pressure, the trout are, well, innocent. They don't see as many flies or artificial lures as the trout in public water do, so they come to these artificials with relish. For the beginning angler Fred's property is a dream come true. For the experienced angler it is nirvana.

At our second stop that afternoon both Susi and Elden landed their first fish. The river splits into two channels, the main channel and a side channel separated by a gravel bar densely covered with brush and a few trees. After I beached the boat I walked the Elderberrys into the side channel.

"Susi," I said, after she had made half a dozen casts, "let me see your rod."

She handed me the outfit, a beautiful Thomas & Thomas rod with a Hardy reel. I clipped off the nymphs, lead, and strike indicator, tied on a three-foot section of tippet, and tied on a streamer. Whoever outfitted the Elderberrys had enjoyed a great day at the cash register, the retailer's equivalent of a fifty-trout day.

"A Mickey Finn," Elden said.

"Yes," I answered.

"Elden studied and memorized all the flies in the Orvis catalog," Susi said.

"You did?" I asked.

Elden nodded, and beamed. "And you should see his fly boxes," Susi whispered, though intending for her husband to hear. "Arranged by type and color. He bought so many flies."

Elden's vest bristled with every gadget imaginable. Hemostats, stomach pump, clippers, dry-fly floatant, stream thermometer, a drying pad, and a Ketchum release hook remover. The vest pockets bulged with fly boxes.

"One thousand flies," Elden announced.

"That's more than I carry," I said.

"When Elden decides to do something," Susi said, "he spares no expense."

"Strip," I instructed, after she had made her first cast.

"Right here?" she said, laughing. I explained that I wanted her to strip line through the water, giving the fly the appearance of life.

Susi caught her first fish on her second cast with the Mickey Finn. She listened to every word of advice and we netted a fifteen-inch rainbow trout. Elden whooped and hollered and dutifully took photographs with a digital camera.

"You're up, Elden," I said, after releasing the fish.

"No," he said. "I'm content to watch Susi fish this water. I'll wait."

Susi caught several more fish, absorbing information and improving her technique with nearly every cast. Most guides will tell you that they prefer guiding women and children, both of whom come to fly fishing without what I call the "Daniel Boone Syndrome." Most men, even those who never have held a fly rod in their hands, think they are born with a gene that makes them natural hunters and predators.

Elden fished the main channel and fished it effectively. He displayed absolute focus as he watched the bit of yarn bounce along the water, watching for a telltale tug that would indicate that a fish had taken one of the nymphs. He beamed with each take. His hands shook when he held his first trout, now dutifully posing for photographs. When we had thoroughly fished the run we waded back to the boat.

"Beer?" I asked, as I opened the cooler.

"No thank you," Elden answered.

"You sure?" I asked. "It's way after twelve. Sun over the yardarm and all that."

"I'm fine."

"Coke?"

"No thank you." Elden was grinning. "Do you have any noncaffeinated drinks?"

"Sprite OK?" I asked. I handed them the soft drinks.

"We're Latter-day Saints," Susi said.

"Mormons," Elden said. Elden was still grinning. He had an expressive, open face where every feature took part in the smile. Mischievous, childlike eyes, an impish nose. "Fred told us that you hate Mormons."

"That's not exactly true," I stammered. "Hate's a pretty strong word. Dislike. Dislike's more accurate, and I came by my dislike honestly. Unless you played football at Brigham Young University there's a better than even chance that you'll make it off the river alive."

"Fred says you don't like Californians either."

Fred.

"That's true enough," I replied.

"I'm a Mormon from California. Two for the price of one, the hate exacta."

"Fred told you to say that, didn't he?"

"He did."

"Why do you hate BYU?" Susi asked.

"My left knee."

"Your left knee," Susi repeated.

"I left the better part of my left knee in Provo," I said, taking a long pull from a beer.

"At this point in my life I expected to be considering retirement from a mediocre career in the National Football League," I said. I certainly hadn't figured that I would be guiding the guests of a billionaire media baron.

I had attended Montana State University on a football scholarship and developed into a respectable tight end. During my senior year a number of professional football teams expressed interest in drafting me, more than likely in the late rounds. A few scouts attended our games and the team fielded requests for game film.

Our offensive scheme was mainly "three yards and a cloud of dust," straight ahead between the tackles running with short passes added for variety. Our quarterback, Rusty O'Neill, whom everyone called "Tatum," appeared incapable of tossing the pigskin beyond twenty yards. The perfect offense for a tight end.

As one local sportswriter put it, the Bobcats' offense was small, but slow. Somehow we got the job done, winning more than we lost, and we had a legitimate shot at the Big Sky conference title. Granted, that doesn't have quite the cachet of a Big Ten or Pac Ten conference championship, but a championship is a championship.

We only had a few games remaining in the season when we faced our biggest challenge, an away game against the Division I BYU Cougars. With the buzz of a possible professional career surrounding me, the Provo city newspaper sent its sports reporter to get my thoughts on the upcoming contest.

"There was a reporter named Hyrum Delvecchio," I said, emerging from my reverie. He was most certainly a Jack Mormon, since I could smell the Colorado Kool-Aid wafting from his rather large body. Delvecchio outweighed me by at least fifty pounds and he sweated more during our interview than I did in most practices. He told me that his father, a miner of Italian descent, had converted to the Church of Jesus Christ of Latter-day Saints so that he could marry. Delvecchio was slovenly in appearance and, as I came to learn later, in his reporting skills as well.

"I remember clearly what I said. I was answering one of those inane questions that sportswriters always ask. 'We know we're going to face a tough defensive line in tomorrow's football game.'

" 'Yes,' Delvecchio said. 'Actually, both lines are rather big.'

" 'The Mormon mission advantage,' I said."

"That's a curious comment," Elden said.

"Funny," I said, "that's exactly what Delvecchio said."

"Now, here's what I told Delvecchio. 'Let's look at the facts. Every Catholic kid wants to play for Notre Dame and every Mormon kid wants to play for BYU. A kid shows up and he's red-shirted the first year. That's a fairly common practice at most college football factories. But at BYU he's shipped off for two years on his mission and when he returns, he's twenty-one years old and he's still got four years of eligibility left. Half the guys we'll line up against tomorrow should already be playing pro ball.'

"And that's what I said, no less and certainly no more."

What appeared in the *Provo Herald* the next morning put me in the same league as Zane Grey. My observation, highly accurate by the way, was twisted into an anti-Mormon diatribe that painted me as a latter-day rider of the purple page.

"Delvecchio quoted me as saying that the players received special training and diets during their mission, that steroid use was rampant in the BYU program, and that the leaders of the Church of Latter-day Saints were hypocrites because they allowed Steve Young to play football on Sundays.

"I never said any of it, and for the life of me I could never figure out why Delvecchio had penned such rubbish."

"You know something?" Elden said. "I remember this. Homecoming game, about a dozen years ago."

"Fred said you went to MIT," I said.

"I got my postgraduate degree at MIT, undergrad at Brigham Young. Yes, I definitely remember this incident. You were the talk of the town that morning."

WALLACE RIPS LDS, the headline blared. The subtitle read, TIGHT END ACCUSES REVERED COACH OF CHEATING. Long before my 7:00 A.M. wake-up call I was "taking a meeting" with the Bobcats' head coach and the sports information director. Needless to say, the three of us were not pleased.

As luck would have it, our offense was introduced during the pregame ceremonies. When the announcer brayed, "At tight end, number eighty-one, Dahlgren Wallace," I felt the wrath of the assembled multitude. I had been booed before, but never like this.

We won the toss and elected to start on offense. After a kickoff return to our own twenty-five we lined up for the first play. I squared off against the left defensive end.

"Wallace!" he snorted. "I am going to fuck you up."

I wasn't normally a trash talker, but Delvecchio, the *Herald*, and the crowd had put me in a surly mood. The whites of my ignoble opponent's eyes were yellow, and a few drops of blood had already seeped through the back of his jersey.

"Hey ass clown," I countered, "if you keep taking the juice, your balls are going to shrivel up and you won't be able to have your fifteen kids."

With the assistance of the right tackle we turned the end outside and our running back scampered for eight yards. For my efforts I received a poorly disguised punch to my kidney.

The next call was a play-action pass. Tatum faked to the fullback, who dove into the line. I released from the line and caught a wobbly dump pass over the middle. I cradled the ball into my body with both hands, lowered my shoulder, and drove into the middle linebacker. As I hit the ground I felt about half of the BYU defense pile on.

A miscreant worked his hand through my face mask and tried to gouge my eyes out. I turned my head sharply and buried my face into the ground. I also received a few more rabbit punches. This, I thought as I jogged back to our huddle, was going to be a long day.

Depending on your perspective that prediction was either appallingly off the mark or spectacularly accurate. The next play made the lowlights reel on ESPN and the troika who hold down the college football desk even managed to express an appropriate amount of chagrin.

On the third play of the afternoon I lined up on the left side of the line. At Tatum's first bark I went into motion, coming down along the line. At the snap I turned and again went after my new best friend, Mr. Yellow Eyes. He reached under my shoulder pads and held me upright while the nose tackle hit me low. I felt my left knee give way and I felt the pain an instant later.

I received the penalty. Fifteen yards for unsportsmanlike conduct. I think what I said was "Fuck you, you juiced-up proselytizing cocksuckers!" I directed the comment toward a pair of behemoths who were standing over me, laughing, as I writhed on the turf.

The line judge whipped out his penalty flag and dropped it on my chest. "That's fifteen yards, Number Eighty-One."

"What? You got to be shitting me, you Mormon bun boy!"

My teammates began to circle the wagons around my prostrate form.

"That's it," the line judge said. "You're out of the game!"

"Great call, Einstein. I'm already out of the game. I'm probably gonna be a fucking cripple."

I took that last ride off the football field on the cart, the ride that every player dreads. Mine came under a continuous chorus of boos. And I'll swear to this day that the cart driver intentionally drove over the pothole. We lost the game 49–0, and our head coach was suspended for a week following an attack on the "Revered Coach" of the Cougars. He took exception to BYU attempting an onside kick when they were up 42–0. Yeah, Mormons.

An athlete knows his body, and I knew the verdict even before the ortho doc let fly with the three worst initials in sports. "ACL." Anterior cruciate ligament.

I was not drafted that spring. I rehabbed and worked hard but I had, in the vernacular, "lost a step," and it was a step I couldn't afford to lose. I had a tryout up in Canada but I didn't make it past the first cut. I was, however, fast enough for the United States Marine Corps and the Gulf War.

"What I couldn't figure was why Delvecchio wrote the story that way," I said. "With the exception of my rather trenchant observation on the age and size of the offensive and defensive lines, the rest of the story was outright lies and fabrications."

"Lying for the Lord," Elden said.

"What?" I asked.

"Yes," Elden said. "Lying for the Lord. You see, when we feel that we are doing the work of the Lord, it's not a sin to tell a lie. There are two important institutions in Utah, Dahlgren—the church and BYU football, sometimes even in that order. BYU was ranked that year, Top Ten as I recall. According to the coach, he felt that the Cougars had practiced poorly all week, taking the game against MSU rather lightly. That newspaper article gave the boys a different slant on the game."

"So, Delvecchio was doing the work of the Lord?"

"Absolutely," Elden said. "He covered the BYU Cougars. If that's not the Lord's work in Provo, I don't know what is."

We fished until late in the afternoon. Elden fished hard, asked questions, and concentrated on his casts. Elden even enjoyed wind knots, a euphemism for tangled wads of line. With impatience in his backcast, a not uncommon failing for a novice, he was adept at creating them. He was simply masterful at untangling them. Elden carried a wine bottle cork, two needles, and a pair of magnifying eyeglasses. He had the supreme patience and the dexterity of a skillful surgeon. He often paused from this task to watch his wife fish.

I've fished with men who take any measure of success on the river by a wife or girlfriend to be a direct challenge to their manhood. Not Elden. He relished his wife's success as much as his own.

Elden wouldn't let go of my hand at the end of the day. He kept pumping it throughout a *Guinness Book of World Records*–length handshake. "I had a great time," he gushed. "I can't wait to do this again tomorrow. How early can we head out?"

"Eight o'clock?"

"I thought fishermen got up in the wee small hours of the morning."

"Not fly fishermen," I explained. "We keep more gentlemanly hours."

"Then eight o'clock it is."

At the takeout point I used the winch to pull the McKenzie boat into the trailer. We climbed into the truck and drove back to the ranch.

"I'm curious," I said, glancing over to Elden. "Did you wake up one day and decide that you would become a fly fisherman?"

"No, I have wanted to do this for years," he said. "Hemingway."

I groaned.

"You know," Elden continued. "Nick Adams? 'Big Two-Hearted River'?"

"Nick Adams," I said, "was a bait fisherman."

CHAPTER 2

HOW I CAME TO WORK FOR FRED LATHER

"Are the Elderberrys sleeping in?" I asked as I walked into the dining room of Fred's ranch house.

Fred, reading glasses perched on his nose, rattled the pages of the sports section of the newspaper. "Nope," he said, "they already ate breakfast." He glanced at his watch. "In fact, I believe that they are waiting for you down by the river."

"I told them eight o'clock," I said, checking my watch. Seven-twenty.

"Elden wore his waders to breakfast," Fred said.

Cook stuck her head into the dining room and I gave her my order. I eat breakfast at the ranch whenever Fred is in residence, especially after the divorce of the most recent ex-Mrs. Lather. It serves a secondary purpose, meeting the guests that I take fishing on the private water.

"You shaved," Fred observed, his eyebrows arched over the frames of his glasses, "but frankly, son, you still look pretty ragged."

"Up late," I muttered.

"Drinking?"

"Well, that, yes," I answered slowly. "I also ran into Maureen."

"You didn't?"

"We did."

"Really, Dahlgren, there's nothing as depressing as pity fucking."

There was some truth to that observation. Maureen and I had dated for six months and at present had not been dating for six months. You tend to run into folks in Bozeman, and we had. When last night's brief tryst ended, we both jumped out of bed scrambling for our clothes and mumbling excuses on why we had to leave, especially embarrassing for me because we were at my cabin.

Cook rescued me with a steaming plate of fried eggs and sausages.

"I take it that Elden and Susi are having a good time," Fred said.

"They are," I said. "You should see them watching the strike indicator. Wonderful powers of concentration. Elden wades the river like he's been fishing for years."

"No pressure, Dahlgren, but Elden's visit is really important. The Royal Fucking Treatment."

"I know."

"You know he's a Mormon?"

"Yes, Fred, I do," I said, "and I want to thank you for telling him about my dislike of said Mormons."

"Got to keep you on your toes, son," Fred replied. "One of my rules of negotiation, always keep folks a little off balance."

"We aren't negotiating, Fred."

"We are always negotiating."

Fred is also always competing. When Fred and I fish the river he immediately turns it into a contest. First fish, biggest fish, smallest fish, most fish. Money bets on the side to keep things interesting. Fred will cast from the boat while I'm rowing, arguing that this extra time with a fly on the water evens the odds. "Seeing as how you're a professional and all," he argues.

After my failed tryout among the Canadians, I was suddenly without prospects, unless I wanted to join the family business. I had earned a degree in Fish and Wildlife Management, a degree that absolutely qualifies you for a tour of duty with the Marine Corps. After completing The Basic School, I was commissioned as a 2nd lieutenant with an Infantry Military Occupational Specialty. By the time I pinned on the silver bar of a 1st lieutenant, I was a Force Recon-trained Marine, commanding a fourteen-man platoon. Operation Desert Shield turned into Desert Storm, and I eventually ended my brief military career in Twenty-Nine Palms.

When I returned to Montana and applied to the Department of Fish & Game and the U.S. Forestry Service, both gave me the thumbs down. My knee and some lingering health issues from the war. Someone at Fish & Game, a diehard Bobcats fan, suggested that I give a call to a fly shop in Bozeman. And that's how I became a fishing guide.

These were the days before "The Movie." The sports were more genteel, mostly men, mostly middle-aged, and primarily easterners. The pay was modest, the tips vastly appreciated, and for three years I guided the rivers around Bozeman, learning how to maneuver a drift boat, paddle a canoe, and handle a raft. I also had escaped into the cash-and-carry world of the Free Territory of Montana, where it hardly matters who the president is or what the talking heads on the evening news have to say.

During the season I worked nearly every day and found odd jobs during the winter. I lived in a modest cabin, dated a few women, and unwound with a few beers at more than a few local watering holes. During the months that professional football fills the screens, it may have been more than a few beers.

A lodge owner in Alaska called, saying one of his clients had recommended that he hire me as a guide for the upcoming season. On the fly-fishing circuit Alaska is the equivalent of the NFL. I immediately accepted. Plush lodges, expensive trips favored by well-to-do sports, and generous tips.

A bush pilot in a floatplane dropped me off at the Big Stone Lodge in early June. Many people considered the lodge owner, Buckminster Wright, the meanest man in Alaska. A tough, cantankerous bastard in his sixties, Wright had served two terms in prison, one for assault in his younger days, and a more recent visit to a federal facility for violating game laws. Something about illegally hunting polar bears. When I asked him how he chose the name for his lodge, he answered, "I passed a big fucking kidney stone the day I closed escrow. Took it as a good sign."

His fourth and current wife, Chantilly, looked and dressed like a hooker. The Capri pants, stiletto heels, and leopard scoop-neck tops revealing ample cleavage somehow didn't match the ambience of the rustic lodge. Wright had met her at her last place of employment, the Great Alaskan Bush Company.

"Figured it'd be cheaper to marry her," Wright said, "than to keep shoving twenty-dollar bills into her G-string."

In mid-August I received a message to call Fred Lather. The area code was 406, a Montana number, so I suspected one of my friends of playing a practical joke. In the months before I left for Alaska rumors about Lather purchasing one of the largest ranches in the state swirled around every bar, every real estate office, every grocery store and diner.

Fred earned his celebrity with several shrewd business moves that eventually made him a billionaire. He launched LNN, a twenty-four-hour news channel that evolved from laughingstock to the paragon of electronic journalism. He bought entire studio film libraries long before cable television's insatiable demand for product was recognized in the marketplace. Fred enhanced his celebrity with a penchant for living large; his horses had run in the Triple Crown, he owned professional sports teams, and his third wife was an Academy Award–winning actress, the daughter of Hollywood royalty.

Fred and Sally Lather sightings became a popular diversion in Bozeman.

After my four-month stint in Alaska I was happy to get back to my cabin. Dust covered the few pieces of furniture and the rooms were musty with stale air. I threw open the windows and played the messages on my answering machine.

"Dahlgren Wallace," announced a smooth southern-accented voice in the middle of the tape, "this here's Fred Lather. I need to talk to you. Call me at . . ." and this time the number had an Atlanta area code.

I paused the messages and called the number. Lather answered on the first ring.

"Mr. Fred Lather?" I asked.

"Yes."

"This is Dahlgren Wallace, sir, returning your call."

"You mean calls. Returning my calls, you pissant. I called twice and had to wait six weeks for you to call me back. Is this how you're going to act when you work for me?"

"Who said I was going to work for you?"

He laughed. A sugary, genuine laugh. "Son, you'll work for me. I can pretty much guarantee that.

"I bought a place in your neck of the woods that's got seven miles of river and a bunch of streams on it. I asked three folks who I should hire as my river keeper and two of them gave me your name. You see, you hardly got any choice in the matter.

"Be at the airport tomorrow, general aviation. I'll send the Lear down for you. We'll discuss this tomorrow night over dinner. Bring a coat and tie, I dine like a gentleman.

"And Dahlgren, the next time I call you, son, I don't want to be waiting six weeks for a return call."

He hung up.

~

Elden again was practicing his casts. As I neared the McKenzie boat he turned to me, grinned broadly, and shouted, "Nick Adams *was* a bait fisherman!"

"Elden reread 'Big Two-Hearted River' last evening," Susi explained. "Aloud."

"Some consider it the best short story ever written," I said.

"Grasshoppers," Elden said. "Live grasshoppers. All these years and my inspiration for fly fishing turns out to be a bait fisherman."

"Nick did use a fly rod," I countered. "As a matter of fact, the purists would argue that the way we fished yesterday, with nymphs and streamers, shouldn't be considered fly fishing."

"I take it you're not a purist," Susi said.

"No," I answered. "I'm a pragmatist. Most of the people I take fishing want to catch fish."

Elden and Susi climbed into the boat. I pushed the boat off the river's bank, hopped in, and took the oars. Susi sat in the bow, facing me. She tucked her chin into the collar of her fleece jacket. May weather can be unpredictable in Montana. Snow is not unusual, nor are sweltering temperatures.

"Fred told us an interesting tale last evening," she said.

"Let me guess," I said. "It was about the morning I helped him spend a hundred thousand dollars."

"That's the one!" Susi said. "Except he said that you spent considerably more money that that."

"Storyteller's license."

"He is quite the raconteur."

"That he is," I said. "In a couple of years he'll have the collective price tag up to a quarter of a million."

As charming as he can be, Fred Lather also holds the copyright on how not to win friends and influence people. Immediately after buying the ranch he took out full-page ads in every major Montana newspaper. The simple message: Don't even think about asking to hunt or fish on the Carved L. Overnight Fred went from putative economic savior to enviro demon.

A knock on the ranch house door and politely asking permission are usually all it takes to hunt or fish on private property. Owners asked that you respect their land and most people did. Those who didn't usually received equally polite refusals when they knocked again. Generations of families had fished and hunted on the Carved L. A few of those families relied on an elk to fill a freezer with meat. They were subsistence hunters with no care for trophies.

The Carved L Ranch foreman, Mordecai Shames, sort of came with the property. He views his fellow humans as vermin, and he was delighted with his new instructions from Fred. He suddenly had permission to be misanthropic. He gets along quite well with horses, and a top-notch mechanic, he has wonderful relationships with the motorized ranch equipment. Even before Fred bought the Carved L, folks were smart enough to avoid Mordecai and find the owner to ask permission to hunt or fish.

Many locals blamed Fred's future ex-wife. In addition to stunning looks, an incredible body, and a razor-sharp mind, Sally brought decidedly liberal viewpoints to the union. Sally and Fred didn't discuss politics; they vehemently argued politics. Jim Lehrer should have moderated their dinners with ground rules set by the League of Women Voters.

She claimed credentials as an environmentalist, and with Fred's wealth and holdings she could act on her beliefs. Initially, Sally stubbed her enviro toe over the elk issue. She proposed feeding the migratory elk herd during the harsh winters. Fortunately, Fish & Game talked her out of providing fodder to what they calmly explained was the Yellowstone Park herd. Feed them, they warned, and you'll suddenly have over fifty thousand pet elk.

The woman was an enigma. She acquitted herself quite well with a shotgun and fly rod. She calmly shot her limit of pheasant and took great pride in preparing them for the table, and she was a thoughtful angler.

Fred had hired me on the heels of an announcement that struck fear into the hearts of every rancher in the state. The Carved L would raise bison. Most people view bison as a link to the West's glorious past when millions of the animals roamed the great grasslands. If they've seen bison at all it is in Yellowstone National Park. Ranchers, who tend to view the world through shit-colored glasses anyway, see bison as mobile brucellosis factories. Bison and elk carry this disease with no ill effects, but the disease can wipe out cattle. If a Yellowstone bison strays from the park, it can be legally destroyed, and usually is.

Then an enterprising reporter for the *Bozeman Daily Chronicle* discovered Fred had all his food flown into the ranch. In two months as a landowner, Fred—who made few missteps in business—managed to stomp on the toes of local hunters, fly fishers, ranchers, business owners, just about everybody. Many of these people felt compelled to write less than flattering letters to the editor of the *Daily Chronicle*.

On my first official day on the job, Fred invited me to breakfast, and a stack of those editorials sat on the table between us.

"I figure I stepped on my dick pretty good," Fred said.

"Yes, sir," I said. We were still in the "Mr. Lather" stage at this point.

"But you do it with such panache, Fred," said Sally.

"Well, we're just going to have to do something about this. I am nothing if not a pragmatist, Dahlgren. I know that I have fences to mend with my neighbors, and I think you can help, son."

"Who? Me?" I registered both surprise and panic.

"Yes, you," Sally said. "People like you, Dahlgren; you're a pleasant young man."

"And Mordecai's no help. He doesn't even talk to me let alone anyone from town," Fred said.

"Here's what I want you do," he continued. "You're going to be my link with the locals, a go-between, so to speak. Tell me what I need to do and I'll do it. What clubs to join, what charities to donate money to, things like that. But I am intractable on two issues. First, I'm raising bison. The land's perfectly suited for it. It's a business decision, pure and simple. The other ranchers sell beef to McDonald's. I'm going a little more upscale.

"Second, I'm adamant about the hunting and fishing. Nobody hunts and fishes the ranch except my guests. Other than that, knock yourself out."

"When do we start?"

"Now would be fine, before the Bozemaniacs decide to tar and feather me."

"Then grab your checkbook and let's head into town."

"Who? Me?" Now it was Fred's turn to register panic.

We drove the oldest and most battered ranch vehicle, a 1968 International Harvester Travelall, into town and went on a buying spree the likes of which Bozeman had never seen. Our first stop was the local fly-fishing shop. We bought, or rather, Fred bought, half a dozen rods and reels, vests, waders, boots, fly boxes, tools, a Renzetti vise, tying material, and hundreds of flies. By the time Fred removed the checkbook from the back pocket of his jeans a small crowd had gathered inside the shop.

"That'll be 12,163 dollars and seventeen cents, Mr. Lather," the shop owner said. A communal gasp greeted the tally. Fred never even blinked.

"Call me Fred," he said as he bent over the counter to write the check. "Tell you what, I'll make the check out for 13,000 dollars and we'll leave the rest on account. I'm sure Dahlgren will have a need for more gear later."

When we loaded the purchases in the back of the Travelall, Fred whispered to me, "I could have got this stuff wholesale from Leigh Perkins. He's a pal of mine."

"We're buying goodwill, Mr. Lather."

"You spend money faster than Sally, son. You better start calling me Fred. If I'm getting fucked I prefer to do it on a first-name basis."

By the end of the morning we bought two trucks, half a steer, piles of Carhartt overalls, coats, gloves, and shirts, two shotguns, a target launcher, five cases of shells, Montana resident fishing licenses for Fred and Sally Lather, a big-screen television, a DVD player, and twenty movies. Fred also signed a contract with the owner of the Mail Boxes Etc., to handle all his shipments and parcels.

We stopped at The Mint for lunch.

"Why did we buy half a steer?" Fred asked.

"For the barbecue you're hosting on Saturday," I replied.

"I'm not hosting a barbecue on Saturday."

"Yes, you are. A small affair, about one hundred and fifty people or so, that's including children. I think it would be a nice touch if you personally called everyone to invite them over."

"Excuse me." A waitress stood near our table. "The bartender would like to buy you both a drink."

"We'll take a couple of Sierra Pale Ales," I answered. When she left I said, "You see? Word's already getting around."

"I'm not partial to ale," Fred complained. "I'll be farting all afternoon."

"I doubt they carry what you drink," I said. "By the way, what do you drink?"

"Laphroaig. Single malt scotch."

During lunch four other people came over to our table and thanked Fred for all he had done for the town. He became more effusive as he absorbed the praise, even inviting the last two well-wishers to join us. We enjoyed a long, leisurely lunch.

Before returning to the ranch, we visited two of the area's leading large-animal veterinarians; both specialized in bovine medicine. Fred left each a blank check and instructions that he would pay for brucellosis vaccinations for any rancher who wanted to inoculate his herd.

Back at the ranch I loaded a case of Laphroaig into my truck and delivered a few bottles to a number of Bozeman restaurants. I made it clear that this was not to be treated as Fred's private stock; he just wanted to be certain that his libation of choice would be available if he came in for a meal. I kept a bottle for myself. Purely for research.

The barbecue on that Saturday nearly five years ago was a huge success. Sally charmed everyone, though Fred drew a circle with a heavy hand on the drinks and reckless distribution of expensive cigars. The children rode horses under the steely and disapproving eye of Mordecai Shames.

"Do you find Fred a difficult man to work for?" Elden asked.

"Now there's a dangerous question," I said, laughing. "Why don't we say that it has its moments."

"Any opinion of him as a businessman?" Elden asked.

"Honest, tough, loves the game. Fred enjoys keeping people a little off balance, business and personal."

We fished a deep pool about half a mile down from the ranch. Elden and Susi fished nymphs and both of them caught a couple of decidedly average trout. Yet each hookup, each battle, each landed fish brought whoops of delight from Elden. His face, burned from his afternoon in the sun, reflected childlike joy and wonder. Everything was new for Elden, every experience.

We leaned against the boat watching Susi fish. She had the grace of a natural athlete. Elden told me that her family had been avid outdoor sports enthusiasts. Camping, hunting, fishing, and snow skiing.

"Did you ever fish before?" I asked.

"Never," he replied. "My parents were the quintessential San Francisco urbanites. Nob Hill, operas, theater, symphonies, and political fund-raisers. The Elderberrys are seventh-generation Californians and seventh-generation Mormons. Many times over Great-Grandfather Elderberry knew the Prophet personally. He was one of the first converts to the church."

At the mention of Mormons I reached into the boat and removed a small flask from the wading jacket I kept folded under my seat.

"Care for some?" I asked Elden.

"Dahlgren, you are a corrupting influence!"

I took a short nip. "Sure?"

"Positive. Anyway, isn't it a bit early in the morning to be imbibing?"

"A wee dram, Elden. Keeps the parts lubricated."

Susi's rod bent deeply. Elden shouted.

CHAPTER 3

THE SHORT, UNHAPPY DRIFT OF DOUBLE-E SQUARED

I had never seen a fly rod broken so completely. The last time I had seen a man broken so completely was on the battlefield.

I waded to the rocks and looked down at Elden. He lay between a pair of boulders, the hydraulics of the river pinning him into the crevice. One leg was bent at an unnatural angle and his left shoulder was out of its socket. The current pushed water over his face. His sunglasses and hat were gone. Blood seeped from the back of his head, creating an ever-diminishing line of red in the swift water. I reached down and gently lifted his head and felt the back of his skull. It was soft, and I felt bone fragments and tissue. Panicked, I released his head, which splashed back into the water. Elden's startling blue eyes were wide open. Gulping air, I quelled a strong urge to vomit.

I'm familiar with death. You can't spend any time on a farm or a ranch without death becoming familiar. Hunting often ends in death. I had seen the bodies of Iraq's vaunted Republican Guard in Kuwait. I had seen the bodies of men I had killed, or caused to die. Elden's death, though—sudden, immediate, oppressively present, personal—drained the strength from my legs.

I was frightened, nearly paralyzed. Suddenly I heard everything—the rush of the water, birds, the wind. I was taking in great gulps of air and began to feel light-headed.

Just to have something to do I bent down and examined the rod. My knowledge of fine fishing gear exceeds my knowledge of gross anatomy. The beautiful rod, the work of a proud and able craftsman, had probably come with a lifetime guarantee. A moot point now.

The fly line kept the pieces of the rod somewhat intact. The upper section of the rod broke about six inches below the tip-top. The ferrule that joined the two rod sections looked as if it had exploded. The cork grip was nearly shorn from the rod, and the reel had been torn away from the reel seat.

The Hardy reel was another work of art. English and expensive, the finish polished to a mirrored sheen. The line from the reel ran downstream, pulled taut by the current. The spool had separated from the frame, so I put the two pieces back together. When I tried to reel in the line that lay in the current, the line on the reel spooled out. Odd. About ten feet of the line had been wound on the reel in the opposite direction. I stripped those ten feet off the reel and then reeled in the line.

There was no hook on the end of the leader.

I heard Susi shout, "Fish on, Dahlgren! Fish on!" I had left Susi upstream and around the bend, casting into the river's main channel. I did what any guide would have done given the circumstances. One sport clearly did not require my expert services and another one did. I placed Elden's broken equipment on the bank of the river and waded upstream to help Susi.

When I had pulled the boat into the gravel bar that separated the main and side channels, Elden had asked if he might fish alone. "I think I can release a fish by myself," he said.

"Got to catch one first," I said. "I'll put you in the side channel. The water's a little tricky, but you're an excellent wader. Let me have your rod. I'll put on a Gray Ghost."

"Isn't that an eastern pattern?" he asked.

"Yeah, but don't tell these western trout." Elden and I waded into the side channel and I positioned him so that he would be fishing downstream. He practiced with a few casts. "When you strip, vary the speed and how much line you bring in. Keep giving the fish a different look at the streamer."

"I think I got a tap!" he said. He made his backcast, the loop expanding until the fly slapped the water behind him, and then he muscled his forward cast. The streamer whizzed by his ear. His eyes widened. "That was close."

"Make sure you don't hook yourself," I cautioned. "I pinched the barb down, but you'd look kind of ridiculous with a Gray Ghost earring."

"I'd feel ridiculous with a Gray Ghost earring."

"I'll go get Susi set up and then come and check on you."

"No hurry."

I had then waded back into the main channel and helped Susi.

"How's Elden?" she asked.

"Having a great time," I answered.

"Fred's invitation was just so timely," she said. "I sense that Elden's a bit bored with the business. He's devoted his entire life to his company. Poor Elden needs a hobby."

That chapped my ass a bit. Poor Elden? Those two words in any proximity insulted my intelligence. Like Fred, Elden was a bona fide member of the billionaire's club. And a hobby! Fly fishing's not a hobby. It's a passion. And "Poor Elden" looked like he might have promise on that front.

Now, as I waded into the river's main channel, Susi's rod was nearly bent double. Her cheeks were flushed and her forearms were taut with effort. Once again I fought to keep down Cook's eggs and sausage.

I walked to Susi's side.

"I think it's a lunger," Susi said.

"A lunker," I corrected. I carefully placed a finger on the rod. It thrummed. For a brief moment I considered allowing her to play the fish. Fly-fishing guides understand that the opportunity to land a trophy trout rarely presents itself. I was in no hurry to impart the tragic news and I rationalized that at least Susi could cling to this last pleasant memory of the river.

I took the rod from Susi's hand and threw slack into the line. The fish was off.

"Why did you do that?" Susi asked.

I didn't, couldn't, answer.

She snatched the rod from my hand and reeled in her line. She attached the fly to the hook minder and tightened the line until the rod bowed slightly.

"Where's Elden?" she asked, looking over my shoulder.

"There's been an accident," I said.

Her entire body tensed. Her jaw tightened and her eyes flashed with fear, darting from me to the side channel. "What kind of accident?"

"The worst kind, Susi." Big swallow. "Elden's dead."

Fear became anger. She punched me. Her right hand still clutched the rod and I felt the reel slam into my jaw. Susi slipped, and fell forward. I tried to hold her, but she pushed me away.

"I am sorry," I repeated.

"What did you do to him?" she asked.

"Nothing," I answered. "Nothing. I told you, there's been an accident."

"What did you do to him?" she repeated. Then she said, "I want to see him." Her voice hardly above a whisper.

"I think we should get back to the ranch," I suggested, ignoring her last request. "We'll leave the gear here and hike back upstream."

I stood in the river, blocking Susi from walking downstream. She stared at me for a long moment. Then she began to sob. Her shoulders relaxed and she handed me her rod. I took her by the elbow and we walked back to the McKenzie boat. I put the rod in the boat, gently wedging the reel under the center seat. I gave the anchor a tug, burying the flukes deeper into the river bottom and further secured the boat by tying it to a tree.

Susi made a last attempt to enter the side channel. She charged upstream, arms windmilling. When I caught her by the arm she shrugged free, stumbled, her right knee buckling. I pulled her to her feet. "No. Don't," I said. She allowed me to help her back to the boat.

I shrugged off my vest and dumped most of the contents into the bottom of the boat. The trappings of a guide, fly boxes brimming with countless flies, lead, tippet material, a thermometer, strike indicators, and a leader wallet. I removed two bottles of water and stuffed them into the back pouch of my vest, where I keep a small first-aid kit.

I spit blood, washed my mouth with the ice-cold water from the river, and took more than a wee dram from the flask.

"Take off your vest, we're walking out," I said.

"Wouldn't it be faster to drift down to the takeout point?" Susi asked.

"We've only got a mile or so to hike. Besides, the truck and trailer won't be there yet. No one is expecting us at the takeout until five o'clock."

Hiking in wading boots is no treat, although a hint of a path remained, testimony to the large number of people who once fished this stream. With Fred's restriction on fishing the Carved L Ranch, nature has begun to reclaim the paths. We've had our share of poachers, especially for elk, the most recent former Mrs. Lather's wilderness pets. But fishing the river is nearly impossible.

The law states that anglers have access to all Montana rivers and streams between the high-water marks on each bank. But take one step above that high-water mark and you're trespassing. Fred owns nearly seven miles of the river. We occasionally see some hard-core trout bum slogging through the property. If they see us we usually receive the one-fingered salute.

Susi hiked behind me. I could hear her breathing and checked her frequently with brief glances. Susi acted quite stoically. She hadn't cried since I had first delivered the news, nor had she exhibited any signs of shock. Instead she seemed stronger, somehow more determined. Pioneer stock, generations of tough western women.

We stopped once and I drank some water. Susi just shook her head when I offered her a bottle. We didn't talk.

The circumstances of the death of Elden Elderberry bothered me. I've seen my share of klutzes on the water, folks who have trouble walking on a sidewalk let alone a rock-strewn, gravel river bottom. Elden had managed quite well. The side channel, though somewhat swollen with snowmelt, wasn't particularly treacherous. His injuries seemed . . . well . . . a bit overdone. The rod's damage also seemed excessive. The condition of the reel bothered me.

When we came into view of the ranch house Fred appeared on the porch. He knew something was wrong, had to be with me walking along with only half of the party.

"Elden hurt?" he shouted.

I shook my head, and then raised my right hand, as if to ward off any further questions.

"I said," Fred shouted, "is Elden hurt?"

"Call Horace," I shouted back. "Call him now."

CHAPTER 4

WADING THE CRIME SCENE

Chief of Police Horace Twain looked like central casting's idea of a small-town law enforcement chief. Mystery surrounded the buckle of his Sam Browne belt, hidden by a large, hard stomach. Horace, as my mother would put it, was a husky man. His arms were rock solid, heavily muscled with Popeye-like forearms. Presently, he wore a khaki uniform, most of it hidden by a pair of Red Ball waders. He favored a crew cut, his gray hair stiff on his scalp.

In addition to Horace, the McKenzie boat I rowed downstream held Officer Buttram Andrew and the county coroner, Dr. Ignatius Cord. You can squeeze four people into a McKenzie boat, though not comfortably, and fishing from the boat becomes nearly impossible. Both Andrew and Cord were lean men, but Cord had an Ichabod Crane look about him. He stood nearly six and a half feet tall and had a prominent Adam's apple. He looked like he was perpetually on the verge of coughing up a golf ball.

Fred remained at the ranch offering solace to the Widow Elderberry. He was upset and angry, and I could understand that. In these parts it's considered bad form to have an invited guest die on your property. Frankly, though, I felt I had a slight edge over Fred when it came to the anguish department. Guides don't lose sports, guides don't allow their charges to get injured, and guides don't normally take their clients off the river in body bags. I know a guide who drank himself into a self-pitying stupor because he had fallen into the Madison River during spring runoff. The woman he was helping across the river went in to her neck and spent an uncomfortable, though uncomplaining, day nymph fishing. What would he have done if he had lost his grip and her body had popped up in Ennis?

"You don't think this was an accident," Horace said. Not a question, a statement of fact.

"No, Horace," I answered, "I do not."

"So we're talking, what then, murder?"

"Well," I said slowly, "yes."

"See anyone else out there on the river?"

"Nope."

"Another fly fisherman?"

"Nope."

"Somebody who might be poaching?"

"No one, Horace."

"So it was just you, Mrs. Elderberry, and the corpse?"

"He wasn't exactly a corpse when we left Fred's boat ramp this morning."

"Again, it was just you, and Mr. and Mrs. Elderberry?" Horace placed an unnecessary emphasis on the "Mister."

"Yes, but someone else must have been out here."

The river cuts through a heavily wooded valley, remote but not altogether inaccessible. In addition to the footpaths that parallel the river, a number of paths lead to an old fire road.

"Let me tell you what's troubling me about your theory, Dahlgren," Horace said. "Life'd be a whole lot easier for you and Fred if somebody murdered this Elderberry fellow."

"How do you figure that?" I asked.

"There's a liability issue here. An accident where an extremely rich guy dies? I can see the attorneys lined up to prove wrongful death and negligence.

"Then there's your reputation. How would all those fancy Dan buddies of Fred's feel about fishing with a guide who had one of his clients die while out fly fishing?"

I could see the other boat.

"Almost there," I said. I concentrated on the oars and drifted the boat into the gravel bar. I anchored and tied our boat to the other.

"Before we wade to the body I want to hear about what went on this morning," Horace said.

"This was our second stop. We had fished upstream in one of the pools."

"Catch any fish?" Horace asked.

"Actually, both the Elderberrys were doing quite well. I had them working a two-nymph rig, Prince with a green Serendipity."

"They take the Serendipity?"

Cord harrumphed. "Gentlemen, are we filming an episode of *Fly Fishing America*, or are we here to examine and retrieve the remains?"

"Christ, Iggy," Horace replied, "I need to know what went on beforehand. Continue, please."

"When we pulled in here I changed out Elden's terminal tackle. Put on a Gray Ghost."

"Why?"

"Susi did very well in that side channel yesterday. She fished a streamer and it made sense to try it again today."

"Do you always stop here to fish?"

"Yes. Like I said, we've got the side channel that's usually productive and there's a nice long run here in the river. That's where I had Susi fishing."

"She was still fishing the nymphs?"

"Yeah. First I got Elden set up in the channel. Watched him make a couple of casts and retrieves. He thought he might have had a take. He was stoked. Couldn't wait to get a fish on."

"All right, you've got Elden fishing in the side channel and then you come out here. What happened next?"

What happened next? I paused and tried to remember the sequence. That's the problem when you've done something hundreds, perhaps thousands of times. You do things so automatically that they don't even register. I took Susi by the elbow and led her to the tail of the run. We reviewed the high-sticking technique I had taught her the day before and watched her as she lowered the rod after the strike indicator floated past her. She then fed line into the rod as her flies drifted downstream. Then she slowly took in line and used the surface tension of the water to toss her line upstream to repeat the whole process over again.

"She snagged her line and lost her flies. Cleaned her out."

"Lost everything?"

"Everything, up to the strike indicator. Tippet, both flies, the split shot."

"What possible relevance does this have?" Cord asked.

"We ever gonna see this here corpse?" Officer Andrew asked.

Horace ignored the two questions. "Blood knot or double surgeon's knot?"

"Chief Twain, I strongly protest," Cord grumbled. Color actually rose into Cord's face, giving him a slightly human look. "You are merely indulging yourself by asking these absurd questions."

"No, Iggy," Horace replied. Horace did not wear those Red Ball waders only to wade crime scenes. They were much used, well worn, and frequently patched, all come by honestly. Horace Twain was damn near a trout bum. In the nearly arctic-length summer days, Horace's cruiser could often be found streamside during the evening hours. Horace, armed with a fiberglass Fenwick rod, normally caught the evening hatch and a few trout.

"I am conducting an investigation," Horace said. "Dahlgren here says that he left the deceased in that side channel and returned to help the wife." Turning to me he said, "Where were you standing?"

"Over there, at the tail-out."

"Let's go," he ordered. As we walked to the tail of the run, Horace continued. "Mrs. Elderberry gets cleaned out and Dahlgren adds new terminal tackle. That means marrying at least two sections of tippet material, tying on a couple of flies, and then pinching on split shot. For a guide, all that'll take three to four minutes. You see, Iggy, a blood knot is a fairly intricate knot to tie while the double surgeon's relatively easy. By using the blood knot, Dahlgren added another minute or two to the operation."

"Oh, I see," said Officer Andrew.

"You don't see shit, Buttram. You can barely tie your shoes. What I'm trying to determine here is how long Elderberry spent alone in that channel. Now, Dahlgren, let's continue. You replaced Mrs. Elderberry's flies and she starts casting again?"

Susi had cast again, and in the downstream drift, as the flies came across the current, the indicator suddenly dipped. When nymph fishing, many anglers let their minds wander, they get distracted and stop watching the indicator, or their reaction times are slow. They see the indicator dip, but it's like their neural paths are covered with gumbo. Susi's concentration was extraordinary. She raised her rod and was into a fish. She quickly played the fish, a ten- or eleven-inch rainbow. I removed the hook—the fish had taken the green Serendipity—revived the trout, and in a flash it disappeared back into the deep pool.

"Susi caught a small 'bow, I figure about another five minutes," I said. "I had her cast a few more times and then I went to see how Elden was doing."

"Buttram, make yourself useful," Horace said. "Time how long it takes us to walk over to the side channel."

Officer Andrew owned one of those Ironman Triathlon watches and he bent to the task. A few beeps and he said, "We're on the clock."

"Try to walk over at the same pace you did this morning," Horace ordered.

That nearly had the effect of stopping me dead in my tracks. This reconstruction business was perplexing. I had surely walked over to the side channel at my "normal pace," but now I fought two simultaneous inclinations. The first was to run over there and the second was not to go at all. Once again I was disturbed by the fact that so much of what I do is repetitive and ordinary that these separate actions blur and become indistinguishable. Suddenly I felt like a short-order cook who, after frying five pounds of bacon, has been asked to describe one particular slice.

As we neared the channel Horace asked me to recount "to the best of your recollection what had transpired."

I stopped.

"What?" Horace asked.

"I didn't go right to the channel. I stopped at the drift boat."

"Why?"

"I left my net with Susi, clipped it to the back of her vest. I didn't remember if Elden had his net, so I went over to the boat and checked."

"OK, let's do that."

We waded to the McKenzie boat. I looked into the boat, as I did that morning. My gear was strewn around, but something was wrong. When you spend as much time in a boat as I do there is a particular order to things, and that order was out of kilter.

"Anything the matter?" Horace asked.

"Yeah, but I can't put my finger on it just yet."

"Was Elderberry's net in the boat?"

"Huh?"

"Pay attention here, Dahlgren. Was Elderberry's net in the boat?"

"No," I answered, "it wasn't."

"Then let's get back to the business at hand."

"All right," I said. "When I didn't see the net I walked to the side channel. As you can see, this gravel bar and the brush hide the channel from view. Now would be about the time that I would expect to see Elden."

"Buttram, stop your watch," Horace said.

"Four minutes and seventeen seconds."

"Double it to include leaving the channel, so that means the deceased could have been alone for twenty-five to thirty minutes. Does that seem right?"

"Seems right," I answered. Half an hour? That seemed like forever.

"What happened next? Did you see the deceased right away?"

"I didn't, not at first." The channel runs about seventy-five yards and I should have seen Elden immediately if he was fishing. When I didn't I searched both banks, expecting to see him sitting down, dealing with a wind knot.

"I think I saw his line first." When I failed to see Elden on either bank I looked downstream and studied the water. I saw a flash of green and recognized it as fly line. My eyes followed the line back. "And then I saw him."

The others were already staring at Elden Elderberry.

"Hard to believe you missed that," Officer Andrew observed. I had to agree with him. Elden, or the deceased, or the corpse, was hard to miss. I closed my eyes for a second.

"The light," I said, "the sunlight."

"What about the sunlight?" Officer Andrew asked.

"Horace, you know what I'm talking about. Early morning, late evening, the angle of the sun, how it puts a glare on the water?"

"I do."

"That's why I saw the fly line first and not Elden. I remember that even as I got closer to him, with the reflection off the water it was like he wasn't really there."

"You would only see part of him?"

"Exactly."

We waded to the body. I described finding the rod and how I examined Elden, lifting his head to feel the back of his skull. I pointed to the bank and Elden's shattered rod.

"Start taking your pictures, Buttram," Horace ordered.

Officer Andrew removed a battered Pentax 35 mm single-lens reflex camera from his shoulder bag and he began to take the crime scene photos. Cord also removed a camera, a Polaroid, from his backpack.

"You don't use digital cameras?" I asked.

"No; with a digital camera, a computer, and a teenage kid, I can put Jimmy Hoffa into the picture," Horace said.

After the photos, Cord bent to examine the body. Officer Andrew walked to the bank and unfolded the body bag, made of a heavy-gauge plastic. I nearly jumped when he opened the zipper, the noise magnified over the gentle sounds of the river. The sounds of moving water are always present for me, forming a foundation for all the other sounds. I am usually not aware of the river's noise, but acutely attuned to everything else. Why hadn't I heard anything this morning? Not a cry, not a splash.

Cord's examination took nearly twenty minutes. He then asked us to help him carry the body to the bank. Dead weight made heavier by the water. Elden's net hung from the back of his vest, a vest bulging with every gadget imaginable and assorted fly boxes. The wooden frame of the net was broken.

As we placed Elden on the bag, Horace asked Cord, "You taking a body temperature?"

"No, that would be useless," Cord replied. "First of all, we've got a fairly accurate time of death, around ten-thirty if Dahlgren here is to be believed. Second, the water will have quickly cooled his core temperature."

"Do you have an opinion on the cause of death?"

"Massive trauma to the back of the head. The current left the wound relatively clean. I didn't see any evidence of any foreign objects or nonorganic matter. Tissue, brains, and bone only. No wood, no stone, and no metal seen in the preliminary investigation of the wound. He also has a broken left leg, just below the knee, and his right shoulder has been dislocated. Can't tell now, and may never be able to ascertain, if those injuries were postmortem.

"This is curious though," Cord said, as he bent and pointed to Elden's face. "There's a deep laceration across the bridge of his nose, more than likely caused by his sunglasses. He also has a contusion on his forehead and several abrasions to his right cheek."

"What's curious about these specific injuries?" Horace said.

"If we assume that this is still an accident, that the deceased tripped and struck his head directly against a large stone or boulder, that accounts for the trauma. But I'm at a loss to explain how he received these relatively minor facial injuries. Wallace claims to have found the body in the same position that we did, on its back. The current is not strong enough to tumble a body. Let's say that I have some questions."

"Then it could be murder?" I asked.

"Now don't go jumping the gun, Dahlgren," Horace chided. "Questions don't exactly add up to murder. You see, if they did then I would be asking you some questions about that fat lip of yours."

"Horace," I said, "I told you back at the ranch that Susi hit me in the face with her reel."

"Are you sure that you and Elderberry here didn't have a set-to?" Horace asked. "Maybe he sneaked in a lucky punch before you thrashed him. Wouldn't be the first time you coldcocked someone."

"Yeah, that's it. He wouldn't switch to a dry fly, and you know how that really pisses me off."

"Shouldn't you be reading Wallace his rights?" Officer Andrew asked.

Horace glared at the policeman. He didn't dignify the query with an answer. "Questions, my boy, merely questions. I'm still inclined to list the preliminary cause of death as an unfortunate accident. Iggy?"

"I wouldn't vehemently object to that, pending the results of an autopsy, naturally."

"Naturally," Officer Andrew mused.

"Then what about the rod?" I countered.

"What about it?" Horace asked.

"Just look at it, Horace. Broken in three places. And check out the reel seat and the grip. I've seen my share of broken rods and this one looks like it's been mauled. Then there was the reel. I found the rod wedged against Elden's body. When I picked it up I noticed that the reel had come off and was lying in the water, spool off the frame. I put it back together and when I reeled in the line some of it spooled off."

"How was the reel lying on the bottom, crank up or down?" Horace asked.

I thought a moment. "Up," I said, "yes, up. I remember turning it in my hand and then starting to reel in the line." I pantomimed each action.

"Is this significant?" Cord asked.

"Left-hand wind?" Horace asked. I nodded. "Could be significant. This reel was set up for a left-hand retrieve. That means the crank is on the left when it's mounted into the reel seat. The fisherman uses his left hand to reel in the line, holding the rod in his right. When Dahlgren tried to reel in the line, the line spooled out. That means that there was line on the reel that had been wound on backwards, so to speak."

"Couldn't Elderberry have done that himself?" Officer Andrew asked.

"Could have," I answered. "When I got the line in the hook was gone. Elden could have tied into a huge trout, or snagged himself on the bottom, and he could have fallen, smashing his rod. When he started winding the line back on the spool he could have fallen again."

"Plausible," Horace said. "How much line was wound backwards on the reel?"

"About ten feet. The placement of the rod bothered me, Horace. It was too pat; you know, perfect, staged."

"But you moved the rod."

"I did. But I remember exactly how it lay in the water."

"Motive, means, and opportunity," Horace mused. "We've got not a one. Who would want to kill a California businessman all the way out here in Montana? And the opportunity? Too narrow a window; someone would have to know that the victim would be here at an exact moment. I'm leaning towards an accident.

"Now, let's walk the scene, in the channel and on the bank."

"What're we looking for?" Officer Andrew asked.

"First, a handwritten and signed letter addressed to the Bozeman chief of police saying, 'I killed Elden Elderberry,'" Horace said. "Shit, Buttram, the usual stuff—footprints, a place where someone might have been lying in wait, any trash or unusual objects."

Horace enlisted my services in the search, but we discovered nothing, except a piece of waxed paper with cookie crumbs that Officer Andrew "bagged and tagged." He acted as if he had discovered evidence from the Lindbergh kidnapping. Then, with each of us holding a corner of the body bag, we carried the corpse of Elden Elderberry back into the main channel of the river and placed him in the boat we had used early that morning.

"Here's the drill," Horace announced, after his breathing returned to normal. "Dahlgren, you take Elderberry downstream to the take-out point. We got the meat wagon waiting. Also, please try to touch as little as possible in the boat. I've got a trailer waiting as well and we're going to take the boat in for the crime lab folks to go over. Just a precaution.

"I'll take the second boat. Nothing tricky about this water as I recall, right?"

"No, if you've handled a drift boat before it shouldn't be too difficult."

"OK, you take off and we'll follow."

So, with only the earthly remains of one of the world's richest men for company I moved downriver. Only then did I realize what had bothered me when I examined the boat during our reconstruction. We had left Susi's rod and vest in the boat before beginning our hike back to the ranch. Both were gone.

CHAPTER 5

THE BLACK HELICOPTER

Each year I endure the various and sundry probing into my personal life by the Secret Service for the dubious privilege of guiding Bobby Lee Cash, the best ex-president of the United States. I consider it a tune-up of the Top Secret clearance I held as a Marine Corps officer. On the advice of his protection detail President Cash abruptly canceled his annual assault on brown trout. Fred, faced with the prospect of allowing me an idle day on the Tuesday following Elden's death—anathema when he found himself in residence at the ranch—quickly substituted a trio of "local" writers. All were well known and each provided cachet value to Fred's ranch parties.

Jon, Leo, and Mel, the self-anointed Spam Brothers, complete with ball caps sporting the Spam logo, were bad boys who drank and ate much more than they fished and hunted. I never knew which version of the three men would show up to fish Fred's private river. They were either on the wagon, enrolled in a variety of twelve-step programs, or bent on bouts of hedonism that were astounding even to me.

As I loaded two enormous coolers into the drift boat, Leo uncorked a bottle of red wine and announced, “Merlot, the perfect breakfast wine!” We had our morning “eye-opener” before we pushed off into the river.

Mel, who insisted that he was almost a native Montanan because he had settled in Livingston before Peter Fonda, was the best fly fisherman of the bunch. A lean man, who also took ranching seriously—he owned a thousand acres—Mel kept his fly on the water while Jon and Leo were content to sit back and punish the Merlot.

“What’s in the coolers?” I asked, as I rowed downstream.

“A fine spread,” Jon answered. “We’ve got smoked duck, an elk stew, quail marinating in my special Italian dressing, some excellent cheeses, a couple of loaves of bread, chili, menudo, a salad, and a few other odds and ends.”

“And that’s just Jon’s food,” Leo said. “Into the size 42s yet?”

“I’m well beyond that,” Jon said. “Christ, a forty-two-inch waist and I’d be a sylph.”

“Dahlgren, if you’re planning on killing one of us,” Leo said, “make it Jon. It’d lighten the boat.”

“I didn’t kill Elderberry,” I protested.

“Come on, you can level with us. Did you do him?” Jon asked.

“Do him?”

“Yeah,” Jon said. “Did you off him? Kill him.”

“No. Of course not.”

“Jon, don’t be an asshole,” Mel said.

“Hey, it’s taken me fifty years to become the asshole you see before you today. I’m proud of my asshole chops. Not nearly in the same league as our esteemed host.” Jon slurped a generous swig of Merlot. “How is Fred?”

“Fred is Fred,” I said. Jon frequently baits me with these types of questions, hoping for a slip of the tongue.

"Nearly a Zen koan, 'Fred is Fred,' " Jon said. "You can let your hair down with us, my young apprentice. Leo, don't you think that Dahlgren has the makings of a world-class asshole?"

"No," Leo answered. "I see him more as a curmudgeon in training."

I opposed the oars and brought us hard into a gravel bar. I jumped out and secured the anchor.

"Just make certain we fish the side channel where he died," Jon said.

"Jon," Mel said, "you are a true pain the ass. I'm sure that Dahlgren has some simply dreadful memories of that place."

"Dahlgren here is a stout fellow," Jon said, "he can cowboy up."

Mel turned to me, stepping out of the boat with his fly rod. "He possesses the morbid curiosity of a young boy who pokes dead critters with a stick."

"That's not true," Jon protested.

"Yes it is," Mel said. "The last time we went elk hunting, Jon just came along for the hike."

"I don't kill mammals anymore," Jon said. "No qualms about birds, but I'm done with bigger game."

"Cried over the elk," Mel said, shaking his head. "Howled some mumbo jumbo bullshit."

"That was a very spiritual moment," Jon said.

"No qualms about eating the elk, however," Leo said.

"Jon has no qualms about eating anything," Mel added.

With Leo and Jon content to sit in the boat, feet propped on the gunwale, Mel and I waded into the tail of a run. Mel had an unusual method of fishing. He tied his own leaders, usually sixteen to twenty-four feet in length, and used a short, 5-weight Fenwick fiberglass rod. He caught more fish than any other sport I guided on the river. And he had the most unusual style of releasing fish I had ever seen.

On Mel's second cast a pan-sized rainbow took his fly. Mel played the fish quickly, leading the trout downstream. He reeled his line in until the hook and fish were nearly at the tip-top of the rod and then he gave the rod a shake. The fish was off, without Mel ever handling the fish. I've seen him catch over twenty fish in an hour using that technique.

Mel's method flies in the face of conventional wisdom. I advise and practice the technique of reeling in the fly line only, never allowing the leader to go past the tip-top and into the guides on the rod itself.

"Dahlgren," Mel said, as we waded back to the McKenzie boat, "for the record, I don't subscribe to either assessment offered by my fellow Spam Brothers. You are neither an asshole nor a curmudgeon in training."

"Thanks."

"Don't thank me just yet. What you are is angry without anything to be angry about."

I started to answer, but Mel held up a hand to silence me. "Don't play the Gulf War card with me," he said. "Fucking four-day war. Try flying Hueys for two years."

I didn't bother to answer. Mel's perspective was not unique. Everyone thinks that the Gulf War was a four-day conflict. They forget the six months in Saudi Arabia and the thirty-nine-day air war that presaged ground combat. For my Deep Reconnaissance platoon, Desert Storm started long before the first smart bomb found its target.

When we started downstream again, Jon bragged about how manufacturers sent him truckloads of free fishing gear. "The bastard has not purchased even so much as a fly since the first Woodstock," marveled Leo. "I swear, Jon's got more rods than Orvis." Before he turned to fiction, Jon had been an outdoors sportswriter. His latest stick was a gadget rod, an effete little 6 1/2-foot, 1-weight.

"Jon," I cautioned, "you might want to use a different rod."

"And why would I want to do that?" queried Jon.

"Well," I began, "it's a fine rod and all, don't get me wrong, but better suited for an eastern brook trout stream."

"I've seen photographs of big fish taken on this rod," Jon argued. "I think it has enough spine to take some big browns and rainbows."

In the hands of an experienced, able angler it might indeed have enough spine. While Jon was experienced, measured strictly by time on the water, and enthusiastic, he was far from able.

"I'd recommend a 6-weight today."

"Dahlgren, there are days you remind me of publishers, always wheedling for something bigger and longer." Jon was the master of the novella. "A thinking man uses less to achieve more. The 1-weight it is."

As I do on every trip down the river, I ran the boat into the gravel bar near where Elden had died. Leo leapt from the McKenzie boat into the water and stumbled, putting down most of the fish.

Anglers employ an element of stealth when pursuing the "noble trout." Trout are wary creatures, given their relatively low standing in the food chain. A mere shadow over a pool will send trout to the relative safety of an undercut bank or the deep recesses of the pool. Hawks, eagles, and ospreys smash into the water and then fly away with a trout firmly gripped in their talons. Raptors do not practice catch-and-release.

Even if you're unintentionally too clumsy and you stumble while wading or crash through the water without a care, the results are the same. Good-bye, Mr. Trout.

That got me thinking. Whoever killed Elden Elderberry—and though officials still ruled it an accident I was certain that it was not—would have made a superb fly fisherman. He displayed the traits necessary for success on the water: patience, stealth, decisiveness, swift action, and acute judgment.

"Are you with us, Dahlgren?" Jon asked.

I retrieved Jon's gadget rod from the boat and reached into my vest for a fly box. I scanned the water, hoping for an early morning hatch of insects.

"You're studying that box like it was the holy scriptures," Jon said. "Thought you said the Serendipity was working."

"Well, Jon, we should use dry flies only. I would never use a weighted nymph, a beadhead, or any split shot with this rod. All you need to do is tick the rod and it'd break. I'm thinking about a small Royal Trude, a sixteen or eighteen."

Flies, in most cases bits of fur and feather held to a hook by some thread, are available in a variety of sizes. Countless patterns imitate the trout's food sources, from small baitfish to tiny insects. The higher the number the smaller the fly. A #16 or #18 was small, but not tiny.

Jon, naturally, took the contrary position and lobbied hard for the nymph. I responded by tying the #16 Trude to some fine tippet. Nonverbal, yet effective. I have never been able to understand why someone would bother to work with a guide and then argue every point with him.

"Leo," Jon said, "are you going to join me in the side channel?"

"No," Leo answered. "I have no interest in viewing where that poor man passed. I'll stay right here in the main channel and fish with Mel."

Mel already had a fish on. In contrast to Leo's inelegant escape from the McKenzie boat, Mel had used stealth to move into the tail of the run on the main channel.

Jon shrugged his shoulders and invited me to lead him to the promised water. We nearly retraced the steps I had taken only a few days before with another excited angler.

"Where'd you find him?" Jon asked.

"Right over there, Jon, near that boulder."

Jon unleashed an anemic cast into the water just ahead of the boulder where Elden's corpse had lain. Improbably, a large trout inhaled the fly.

I wonder if all ex-outdoors sportswriters are as pigheaded as Jon. I suspect so. Most people involved in the fishing and hunting industries are out to please them and cater to every whim and desire. Trout are not people, despite the claims of the animal rights crowd, and they have a way of humbling even the great and powerful. You find true equality on a trout stream.

I tried, I really did. I never wanted to be accused of being an "I told you so" sort, but in my profession it's inevitable. When you're in the business of dispensing advice to stubborn clients steeped in their own ways of doing things, you often have the opportunity to utter those words. Usually I never have to utter them; they hang in the air like a thick cloud of evening caddis.

The rod shattered in Jon's hands. The advice I had offered just prior to hearing the sharp crack was for him to throw line into the rod and ease the deep bow in the rod. The rod broke in the upper section, a few inches above the ferrule, the joint where the two sections are joined.

Jon handed me the now useless rod. "Can it be repaired?" he asked.

"No."

"I think it comes with one of those lifetime guarantees. Damned defective rod."

"Too much fish for too little rod."

"Isn't it more sporting to use lighter tackle?"

"No, Jon, it is not," I replied. "I think it's more sporting when an angler has enough rod for the job. That way you bring in the fish more quickly and release it faster. Less stress on the fish and you don't play it to exhaustion."

Jon immediately descended into a funk. Catch-and-release purists hate to face the fact that not all of the fish they release survive being caught. Despite every effort to revive them some swim off only to die minutes later. Some are hooked so deeply that they bleed to death. A large percentage does survive, but some don't.

We trudged back to the boat, pushed off, and continued our float. Jon refused to touch a rod for the rest of the morning, though I repeatedly offered him the use of my 5-weight. Instead, he began to empty the contents of one of the coolers and another bottle of Merlot. Mel and Leo fished with gusto and great success. Mel took advantage of a late-morning hatch to switch to a dry fly. Using perhaps that most generic and universal fly, the #16 Adams, he caught several trout. He had a trout on when the black helicopter appeared.

The black helicopter threw me into a funk. First of all the damned thing was nearly silent; I heard the *whump, whump* of the blades at about the same time the helicopter hovered over us. Second, the mere presence of a black helicopter jarred me. Friend or foe? No heart-warming USA emblazoned on the fuselage. Third, when six black-fatigue-suited and heavily armed men rappel into your trout stream, you wish you had more than a landing net and a Leatherman to defend life and liberty.

The initials ATF covered the backs of the black fatigues. The weapons were at the ready but not pointed at anyone. Leo's face wore a shell-shocked expression and Jon was passed out and snoring loudly. Only Mel, still keeping modest pressure on his trout, maintained any level of calm. "Fucking Feds," he said, shaking his head. "Boys and their toys."

Four of the black-fatigued men slowly approached the McKenzie boat and the other two waded toward Mel and me. "Mr. Wallace!" one of them shouted, "please keep your hands where we can see them. Sir, please step toward us."

"I'm sorry, boys, but I can't do that at the moment," Mel replied. "I have a fish on." He turned his back to the ATF agents, took a few steps downstream, and began reeling in the line.

Meanwhile, the black helicopter had landed in a clearing. Chief of Police Horace Twain and a man wearing dark blue suit pants, a white shirt and tie, and a windbreaker that sported the initials FBI emerged from the helicopter.

No fewer than three law enforcement organizations, two federal and one local, had invaded my river. And you'd have to go to a gun show to see as many weapons in such a relatively small area. A helicopter, a black helicopter, had just landed in an idyllic field more suited for a streamside lunch, and a man had just instructed me to keep my hands in plain sight.

Horace and the FBI agent walked to the edge of the river. The FBI agent took careful steps, as if searching for a stealth cow pie that would soil his highly polished black shoes. Whatever the occasion, he was not dressed for it.

"Dahlgren," Horace bellowed, "you were right. Elderberry was murdered!"

"And Mr. Wallace," the FBI man said, "you are under the arrest for the murder of Elden Elderberry."

CHAPTER 6

BRINGING IN THE FEIB

A ride in a helicopter and having a federal agent read you your Miranda rights—does life get any better than this? The handcuffs were a bit of overkill. What was I supposed to do, attack five silent ATF agents and hijack the helicopter? Even if I was successful, where would I go? "Take me to Great Falls," rings a bit hollow. And once in Great Falls what could I possibly do? Get drunk and wait for the reinforcements to come and do it all over again.

Once they shed their face masks and helmets, the agents from the Bureau of Alcohol, Tobacco and Firearms could have posed for a diversity poster. The six men turned out to be five men and a woman. The team included an African American, an Asian American, and a Hispanic. Each one was impossibly fit; these folks were no strangers to gyms and long runs. The woman agent, much to the delight of the Spam Brothers, had been tasked to row them to the takeout point.

Chief Horace Twain sat next to me, and every time he looked in my direction he chuckled. I hate the word "chuckle" and I don't particularly care for people who chuckle. Chuckling reeks of superiority. "Goddamn it, Horace," I said, "if you want to laugh, laugh."

Horace chuckled. "Ain't no laughing matter, Dahlgren. The Feds are fixing to question you about the Elderberry murder."

"I told you it was a murder," I said.

"They not only agree with you, but they think you did it."

"That's bullshit."

"My words exactly, but nonetheless, here you are, handcuffed and chained to the floor of a helicopter."

Chained into an eyehook bolted into the floor of the helicopter. "What happens if we crash?" I asked the FBI agent, who was sitting to my right. "How am I supposed to get away from the wreck?"

"You won't," the agent said. "You would probably die."

"Well, that puts my mind at ease."

Our brief flight took us back to the Carved L, where we landed at Fred's helipad. A squadron of black Suburbans with heavily tinted windows were parked nearby. Fred waited in the camp Jeep, driven by the taciturn ranch foreman, Mordecai Shames. When the rotors stopped turning the FBI agent and Horace escorted me to one of the waiting SUVs. Fred leaped from the Jeep and trotted alongside.

"Don't say shit, Dahlgren," Fred said, "I'll get you a lawyer."

"I don't need a lawyer, Fred."

"You may think you don't need a lawyer, but in my dealings with the federal government I have found it's always best to be represented by legal counsel. I've already called Sherman and he'll be on the next flight out of Atlanta."

"Sherman's a mergers and acquisitions guy," I said. "I don't think I'll be buying or selling any businesses in the near future."

"Sherman is world class when it comes to the fine art of obfuscation," Fred said.

"Now there's a winning strategy. I'll just confuse these guys until they let me go."

I endured further ignominy when the FBI agent put his hand on the top of my head as I bent to enter the Suburban. Sober, I have never hit my head getting into a car or truck. He then slid into the middle row of seats and we settled in for the ride into Bozeman. We cruised downtown with the bubble lights flashing along with an occasional chirp of the sirens. This ensured that anyone with a shred of curiosity would follow this cortege to its final destination, which happened to be police headquarters.

I removed my boots and waders, was handed a pair of paper slippers, emptied my pockets, surrendered my belt, and walked over for fingerprinting. I shuffled into an interrogation room. The FBI agent sat in one of the battered chairs testing the tape recorder. He sounded like a roadie checking the microphone before the headlining act comes onstage.

Horace sat in another seat and had his feet propped up on the scarred table. Forty years of drunken cowboys had carved their initials, hearts, the names of their sweethearts, and pithy western aphorisms into the oak tabletop.

"Any chance I could get something to eat?" I asked. "You took me off the river just before lunch and I'm so hungry now I could eat the ass off a bear."

"I can get you a soda pop and a candy bar," Horace said.

"No chance for a steak sandwich and an ale?"

"You already smell like you've had a few," Horace said. I heard a hint of condemnation in that remark.

"Christ, Horace," I replied. "A couple glasses of Merlot. I'm told it's a breakfast wine."

Horace snorted and called to Officer Andrew, who was standing by the door, gave him a handful of change, and told him to buy some sodas and candy.

"This is Special Agent in Charge Sully Feib, Bozeman field office," the FBI agent said into the tape recorder. He gave the time, date, and location. "We are interrogating Mr. Dahlgren Wallace, a suspect in the murder of Mr. Elden Elderberry. Mr. Wallace has been read his rights. Mr. Wallace, do you understand your rights?"

"Yup."

"Please answer with a yes or a no," the agent said.

"Yes."

"Do you wish to have an attorney present?"

"Nope . . . no."

"Did you murder Elden Elderberry?"

"No. I guess I can go now." I stood.

"Let the tape reflect that the suspect rose from his chair. Please be seated, Mr. Wallace. You obviously think this is humorous."

"Ridiculous, perhaps. Ludicrous, certainly. Humorous? No. Agent . . . what was your name?"

"Feib, Sully Feib." Did this guy think he was Sean Connery playing 007? "Bond, James Bond." The name sunk in. I know that the local police always refer, pejoratively, I might add, to the FBI as "Feebies" or "Feebs."

Officer Andrew came in with the sodas and candy bars. I selected a Dr. Pepper and the Reese's Cups.

"You forget your manners, Dahlgren? You never even asked if I wanted the Dr. Pepper or the Reese's Cups."

"Tough shit, Horace."

Horace, a man of gargantuan appetites, selected a Coca-Cola and the Nestle's Crunch bar. He finished his candy bar and was knocking off the soda in the time it took me to open my Reese's Cups. Feib stared at Horace and not in admiration. He was truly among the savages. I wolfed down the candy, licking chocolate off my fingers, but my eating habits are downright dainty when compared with Horace's.

During the days of J. Edgar Hoover, Montana was the backwater for the FBI, the equivalent of being shipped to Siberia. Agents weren't assigned to Montana, they were banished to Montana. Things began to change around the time of the Kari Swenson kidnapping. Two mountain men, Don and Dan Nichols, snatched the young Olympic biathlete while she was out on a training run. The plan was for Kari to be Dan's mountain woman. This turned into a high-profile case, capturing the attention of the nation. It ended with a more or less acceptable outcome and put a bit of glitter into Big Sky country. With the rise of domestic terrorism, militia groups, and the arrest of Montana's most famous hovel dweller, the Unabomber, assignments were suddenly career making, not career breaking. Hard to say in which camp Feib rested his feet, the banned or the ambitious.

A knock and another blue suit half-entered the room. His only contribution to the dialogue was a shake of his head, and then he withdrew and closed the door.

"Can you explain this facial laceration?" Feib asked, sliding a photograph across the table. I stared at a rather unflattering portrait of me taken on the day of Elden's murder. I sported a split lip and a shadow of blood streaked my chin.

"Susi . . . Mrs. Elderberry reacted violently to the death of her husband," I said. "She sort of hit me in the chops, accidentally, of course."

"Would it surprise you that Mrs. Elderberry has no recollection of this alleged assault?"

"No. Like I said, she was angry and confused."

"Are you still claiming that you didn't murder Elderberry?" Feib asked.

"Are you claiming I did?" I asked.

"Yes or no, please."

"Yes."

"Yes, you did kill him?" Feib was visibly shaken; he had clearly not expected to hear what he thought he heard.

"No, yes as in 'yes' being the answer to the question you asked me: 'Are you still claiming that you didn't murder Elderberry?' Don't they teach you how to ask questions in FBI school?"

"The Academy, the FBI Academy," Feib said, correcting me and recovering his poise. "You are trying my patience, Mr. Wallace."

"And you have already tried mine, Agent Feib. I've been accused of a murder I did not commit, arrested in front of my three clients, deprived of a luncheon feast that can only be imagined, paraded in handcuffs in front of my boss and half the citizens of Bozeman, and then subjected to your asinine questions." I turned to face Horace. "What the fuck is the FBI investigating a murder for anyway? Ain't this your turf?"

"We are liaising with the local authorities on this matter," Feib answered, "though there are some federal aspects to the case."

Horace belched loudly. "Dahlgren, the sooner you answer these questions the sooner you can leave."

"Who says he's leaving?" Feib asked indignantly. "Wallace, we completed a thorough search of your home, your automobile, the drift boat you used the morning of the murder, and your vest. Guess what we found?"

"Now I know you've got the wrong guy," I answered, a bit indignant myself. "I live in a cabin, drive an F150, and if you can find anything in my vest you're a better man than I."

"Wrong answer. We found the murder weapon."

Now it was my turn to be visibly shaken.

Feib slapped a thin, foot-long black object on the tabletop. I jumped. I really did. Horace's boots never even twitched. Through the clear plastic was a nasty-looking device. Whatever it was, it looked lethal.

"Have you ever seen this before?" Feib asked.

"No. I have not. What is it?"

Feib pulled on a pair of plastic gloves and opened the bag. With a flick of his wrist the foot-long object expanded to over twice its size. "This is a telescopic steel baton. It was found in the storage compartment underneath the center seat of your drift boat. Have you ever seen this before?"

"Do you always have to ask the same question twice?"

"Do you always have to answer my questions with another question? Well?"

"No."

"How do you account for it being in your boat?"

"I don't."

"You don't?"

"You just did it again. I have no earthly idea how this got into the drift boat."

"Let's review your actions on the morning in question . . ., " and once again I told my story. How at first I didn't see the body, only the fly line. How I found both Elden and the rod and reel. What I thought was unusual about the damage to the rod, and the line that was wound the wrong way on the reel. Horace nodded his head, affirming each of my answers.

"When you left the corpse in the side channel and before you helped Mrs. Elderberry, did you stop at the drift boat?"

"No."

"When you emptied your vest and got the water from the cooler, did you perhaps take a moment and hide this weapon in the storage compartment?"

"No."

"Chief Twain, when you rowed downriver, following the boat that carried Mr. Wallace and the victim, did you at any time lose sight of them?"

"Maybe for a few seconds, around a bend or two," Horace answered.

"So, Mr. Wallace could have hidden the weapon in those moments."

"Not hardly. We'd have seen something like this either in the boat or on Dahlgren's person."

"He was wearing waders."

"True," Horace said. "Chest waders. Could he have hidden that thing down a leg of the waders? Sure. Could he have retrieved it and hidden it during any time we were together? No way. Doesn't make sense, Sully. Assuming it is his, he could have ditched it in any number of places. Why carry the thing around and hide it where even a moron knows we'll find it?"

"Somebody was around the boat after Susi and I hiked back to the ranch." I blurted this out. I actually felt a twinge of panic.

"Why do you say that?" Horace asked.

"Her rod and vest were gone."

"What in the Sam Hill you talking about?" Horace thundered, sweeping his feet from the table and replacing them with his elbows. His face was now only inches away from mine. I could make out the veins in his ruddy cheeks.

"Remember when we stopped at the boat during the reconstruction and I told you something didn't feel right?"

"Yeah."

"That's what wasn't right. As I was rowing downstream I noticed that Susi's rod and vest were missing. I left them in the boat. No sense in having her lug that stuff back to the ranch."

"Why didn't you tell me this before?"

"I forgot."

"You forgot? That's pretty thin."

"I'm telling you, I forgot. First you tell me not to touch anything in the boat. Then when we get to the takeout your men almost snap the boat in half winching it into the trailer. And then you had me help carry Elden's body to the ambulance. Plus we discussed when I could get all my stuff back, you know the gear I had taken out of my vest that was scattered on the deck. Thousands of dollars' worth of flies. Hell, Horace, with all that shit going on, I just forgot, plain and simple."

"Gentlemen," Feib said, "we need to establish a time line. How long did it take you and Mrs. Elderberry to walk back to the ranch?"

"About an hour. We stopped to rest halfway."

"What's the distance?"

"Mile and change."

"Slow pace, wasn't it?"

"Not really. We were wearing wading boots and waders, not exactly your ideal hiking gear. And it's not like we were walking on a sidewalk."

"Then, when you got back to the ranch, how long until Chief Twain and his men arrived?"

"About forty-five minutes."

"That was rather leisurely, wasn't it, Horace?"

"What's the hurry?" Horace answered. "The guy was already dead."

"You had a possible homicide. You should have made every effort to examine the crime scene when it was fresh."

"Sully, there's an old adage that you never stand in the same river twice. In this case, you never stand in the same crime scene twice. Besides, we weren't thinking homicide, we were thinking accident."

"How long until you were back at the scene?"

"Thirty-five minutes," I answered. "I sort of hauled ass, no messing around."

Feib thought. "Two hours," he mused. "All right, Mr. Wallace. Let's discuss your well-documented history of violence towards Californians."

"What well-documented history of violence?"

He picked up a folder and opened it. "Three years ago you had an altercation . . ." He looked down and read the report, "near Ennis. Would you care to discuss it?"

"The peckerwood was pulling on his damn waders on the put-in ramp. I mean, how ignorant can you get?"

"And what's so bad about that?"

"It's pretty much common knowledge that you put your boat in the water and haul your trailer out, all as quickly as you can. You got a lot of people waiting their turn, and like me, some of them earn a living on that water."

"The man was a Californian."

"It figures, but it wouldn't have mattered if he was a Martian."

"And this bothered you?"

"Damn straight. I shouted down to him that maybe he ought to have his mother dress him before he comes to the river."

"Then what happened?"

"We got to shouting back and forth. Then he really pissed me off, pulled some passive-aggressive shit. He makes a big show of putting on his wading boots. Kneeling down, snugging up the laces through each eyelet, looking at his boots like a monkey studying a math problem. I lost it. I walked down the ramp, picked him up, and threw him in his boat. I launched the boat, jumped in his truck, and pulled his rig into the parking lot. Got a standing ovation from the other folks."

"So he swore out a complaint?"

"Yeah, and the sheriff was waiting on me at the takeout. A few of the other guides attempted to intercede for me, but I still had to go in and answer a few questions. Let me off with a warning. Hell, I should have gotten the key to the city."

"I understand that you might be suffering from Gulf War Syndrome," Sully said.

"Not exactly true. I just felt a bit punk when I returned from the war."

"Isn't one of the manifestations of GWS an unexplained and uncontrollable anger?"

"I don't suffer from either."

"Really? What about the incident that occurred a month ago?"

"How you know about that?" I asked.

"Chief Twain filed a report."

"Horace, you wrote me up?"

"Yeah, Dahlgren. Sorry. Padding the statistics. We're looking for some extra funding in next year's budget."

"The report said that you punched a man in the jaw, knocking him unconscious. Furthermore, the report states that you committed this battery without provocation."

"That's not true; I had my reasons."

"Ordering a margarita hardly qualifies as provocation," Horace said.

"It wasn't a margarita, it was a tropical drink with a fucking paper umbrella."

"Still—" Feib said.

"And he ordered it with Bacardi Carta Blanca Light-Dry Rum. Light-dry rum, for Christ's sake! Even then I kept my temper."

"You consider this mitigating evidence?" Feib asked.

"When he pulled out the cell phone and announced that he was going to check his e-mail and see how the Dodgers were doing, then, yeah, I coldcocked him."

"Were you drunk?"

"No."

"Your Breathalyzer results were point eight."

"Horace," I said. I was disappointed with my friend. After I had dispatched this particular L-Alien, the bartender bought me a drink and then called the police. Horace himself walked down to the bar and we returned to the police station. Sure, Horace made me wheeze into the Breathalyzer, but mostly we played two-handed gin and talked about fishing until he felt I could safely drive back to my place.

"Chief," Feib said, "there's a long history of Montana law enforcement turning a blind eye towards offenses committed by locals. Here we have two cases of battery that were merely swept under the rug. Frankly, I think it's sloppy police work."

"That may be true, Sully," Horace said. "I won't argue with you—but look on the bright side. Ain't that many locals left anymore. We're being invaded by the Californicators."

"So I roughed up a couple of California dudes; both of them had it coming," I said. "How does that make me a murderer?"

"Elderberry was from California," Feib replied.

"It's not as if there's a bounty on Californians, Agent Feib."

"This is moving into the realm of the absurd, Sully," Horace said. "Formally charge him or kick him loose."

"You mean I'm not under arrest?"

"Not technically," Feib said.

"So I can go?"

"Yes, though I will caution you not to leave Gallatin County. We may have follow-up questions." And without even a thank-you or a fare-thee-well, Feib gathered up his folder and the evidence bag holding the steel baton, and he left the room.

"Statistics," I muttered, shaking my head.

"Said I was sorry, Dahlgren. You still hungry?"

"Hungrier'n a bitch wolf."

Horace stood and stretched. "Good. Let's go get us some Jew food."

CHAPTER 7

MY RABBI

The best place, and nearly the only place, to get authentic pastrami sandwiches in Bozeman is at The Cowboy Vey Deli. When Horace made his coarsely worded recommendation for our very late lunch, I knew our destination.

If I had to describe my emotions as I left the interrogation room, I'd say they were a combination of pure anger and calm befuddlement. The arrest, I now knew, was a sham, though elaborately orchestrated.

I collected my waders, boots, vest, and belt from the property cage. I bent down to remove my paper slippers. You don't have to get all dressed up for lunch at The Cowboy Vey Deli, or just about anywhere else in Bozeman, but a pair of damp, felt-soled wading boots made a rather bizarre fashion statement.

"Leave them slippers on a spell," Horace said. "Fred had your truck driven into town. Think I saw your Jesus shoes in the back of the cab." Horace meant my Tevas, formerly the exclusive footgear of choice for rafting guides, river rats, and hard-core outdoorsmen. Once, like Henry Ford's Model T, you could get them in any color you wanted, as long as it was black. Now every Californicator and outdoors *poseur* has a pair, usually with little dinosaurs or lizards on them. They're nearly as chic as a Wolfgang Puck pizza.

We walked out of the police station and into the parking lot. I stowed my gear in the cab, tore off the paper slippers and my damp socks, and pulled on my Tevas. Still a mite brisk to be traipsing around in air hose, but hell, I'm a tough fishing guide. I leaned against the hood of my truck as I changed my footgear.

"How long has the truck been parked here?" I asked.

"Fred had it driven up here this morning, about nine, I think."

Before I had been "arrested," given an e-ticket ride in a black helicopter, et cetera, et cetera, et cetera. Something smelled rotten in the state of Montana.

"Horace," I said, using my best Ricky Ricardo impersonation, "you got some 'splaining to do."

"C'mon, let's go eat," Horace said. "Ain't all that much I can tell you. The Feebs, and Feib, tell me what they want to tell me, and they don't tell me much."

I hardly knew where to start; a dozen questions lay tangled in my mouth. We walked. A few people stared at us and I knew that they weren't focused on Horace. Whatever grist had been ground in the rumor mill must have been downright tasty. Dahlgren Wallace was the center of attention.

The Cowboy Vey Deli is nearly as eclectic as its owner and proprietor. The building's facade is old Bozeman and the lettering reminiscent of a nineteenth-century drugstore and soda fountain. THE COWBOY VEY DELI, and just underneath that, PROP. S. SCHWARTZWALD, and just under that, EST. 1998. This conveyed the sense of a long-established, solid business, though the shop and its owner were newcomers.

People come to Montana to reinvent themselves, to start a new life without the baggage of the old. One of the best bird hunters and hunting-dog trainers I know grew up in San Francisco, the son of a wealthy plastic surgeon. He anointed himself with his own nickname, Slim. He's more native than the natives. Sy Schwartzwald didn't so much reinvent himself as polish a work in progress.

"I grew up in the days of the great horse operas," he once told me. "Imagine, a Jewish kid from Brooklyn who wanted nothing more than to be a cowboy. First the radio, then the serials in the movie houses, and finally, television. With me, everything was cowboys and Indians and horses."

For thirty years, Sy headed west during the summers, and when he retired as a professor of comparative religion from Columbia University, he and his wife moved to Bozeman. "My claim to fame," he boasts, "is introducing a decent bagel and a schmear to the state of Montana. That, and klezmer music. You think any of these cowboys ever heard klezmer music before The Cowboy Vey Deli opened?" The Cowboy Vey Deli was a bagel shop, a delicatessen, and what passes as a literary salon. Inside, the western motif gives way to Greenwich Village ambience. Books and magazines surround the sofas, overstuffed chairs, and coffee tables. A few scattered tables and chairs and a pair of wonderful display cases round out the furniture. In one case the baked goods tempt the patrons: bagels, bialys, knishes, and freshly baked breads. The other holds the luncheon meats and salads. In front of that case is a large crock with a pair of wooden tongs, where the customers fish for their own thick kosher pickles.

"*Oy*, the erstwhile fugitive from justice," Sy said when we walked into his shop. A bell tinkled as we opened the door, a delightful bit of kitsch and nostalgia. Sy is a small man, wiry and with a shock of gray hair that reminds you of Albert Einstein, and a voice that retains its full measure of a Brooklyn accent. He had learned the business as a young boy, working for his father and uncle who owned a deli in Brooklyn so famous for the amount of meat they put in their sandwiches that they refused to sell extra bread. He pushed his reading glasses into his forehead. "The way people are talking, you're the hottest item since O.J."

"Sy, all I want right now is a hot pastrami sandwich," I said wearily.

"Corned beef and tongue, some horseradish," Horace said. "Make it two."

Sy hand-sliced the rye bread and made our sandwiches. We served ourselves at the fountain and I selected a pickle, half-wrapping it in a slice of waxed paper. Sy served our sandwiches, went to the door, locked it, and flipped his sign from OPEN to CLOSED. He joined us at the table. "Eat," he commanded. "Food first and then conversation."

My pastrami sandwich tasted so good that it was almost worth getting "arrested." Sy brought us some extra napkins. I finished eating, long after Horace inhaled his brace of sandwiches and made three additional trips to the pickle barrel. He was probably dreaming of dinner, or high tea, or his midnight snack.

"I think it's time for you to do the talking, Horace," I said. "Why don't we start with the baton?"

"We found it as soon as we went over the drift boat. Opened the ice chest and there it was."

"The ice chest? I thought Feib said he found it in the compartment under my seat."

"He did. We can lie during interrogations," Horace answered. "Feib ain't exactly sure of your complete innocence, so maybe he was trying to trick you into admitting something. Crime lab found hair, blood, and some brain tissue on the weapon. Matched Elderberry. As soon as we found the baton we knew it wasn't an accident."

"How did the FBI become involved?"

"We asked the FBI crime lab to do some DNA analysis for us, and the next thing I know I've got Special Agent in Charge Feib sitting in my office. Like he said when he was questioning you, there are some federal aspects to this case."

"Like what?"

"Don't know. But you might ask your boss."

"Fred?"

"Better it comes from him. In fact, Feib's first request was for me to arrange an interview with Fred. Some amazing shit going on is all I can say."

"Why was Dahlgren arrested?" Sy asked. He had been following our conversation like a spectator at a tennis tournament, his head swiveling to follow the exchange.

When Horace answered he looked at me, addressed the answer to me. "I told Feib that you didn't kill Elderberry. But he does think you might have something to do with it."

"Why?" I asked.

"The timing. Whoever killed Elderberry knew that he would fish that channel and what time he'd be there. Damned lucky coincidence."

"Hell, Horace, it's common knowledge that I fish there with nearly every sport I take down the river."

"Feib's suspicious is all. And you certainly didn't help your cause when you so politely informed us that the woman's rod and vest went missing."

"I told you, I forgot."

"You still haven't answered why Dahlgren was arrested," Sy said.

"I'm not too clear on that myself."

"Allow me to make a conjecture," Sy said. "I assume that the murder will be widely reported?"

"Safe assumption. Elderberry's death is already big news. Caused quite a stir on Wall Street. Now being a murder, we're right in the middle of a media feeding frenzy. Brokaw and Rather could show up for the news instead of the fly fishing," Horace said.

"Will Dahlgren's arrest be part of the story?"

"I don't rightly know."

"Trust me, it will," Sy said. "There's your answer, Dahlgren. The FBI wants it known that you were arrested and questioned, that you were or are a suspect."

"For what purpose?" I asked.

"For their own purpose. Horace, does this make sense?"

"It's plausible."

"That also explains the drama surrounding the arrest," Sy said. "The helicopter and the procession through town."

"How do you know about the helicopter?" I asked.

"You're the toast of Bozeman, my friend," Sy answered. "If we took a poll right now, half the folks in town would say you did it. They offer the most amazing rationale. 'Did you hear about Lather's guide?' they ask." Sy attempted the local patois. " 'Kilt a feller, some sorta rich Mormon. Beat him to death. Word is he doesn't particularly care for Mormons.' It's quite entertaining."

"You can always count on more than just great food at The Cowboy Vey Deli," I lamented.

"I'm leaving," Horace said, pushing his bulk away from the table. "Crime never sleeps. Dahlgren, if I were you I'd stay out of the bars tonight. Spend a quiet evening at home. Sy, take care now."

Horace left before I realized that he stiffed me with the check for lunch.

"I believe that Horace is guilty of the sin of omission," Sy said.

"Damn straight; he just beat me for lunch."

"No, I mean he was less than totally forthcoming with information."

"Do you know that they searched my cabin, my truck, even my fishing vest?" I asked. "Horace said that Fred had the truck driven into town early in the morning, while I was out fishing."

"As I said, the FBI and the police are going to great lengths to make certain that your involvement is well known."

"But why?"

"The murder is connected to Fred in some way. Do you agree?"

"You are the master of the obvious, Sy."

"Does he have any enemies in the community?"

"It'd be a helluva lot easier to round up his few friends," I said. "Fred has pissed off nearly every civic organization, club, businessperson, and politician in a fifty-mile radius."

Following my infamous shopping spree when I began working for Fred, I settled into a long-term approach to improving neighborly relations. By far the easiest group we had to deal with were the Hutterites, and the most intractable were the Montana Patriots.

Unfortunately, Fred's high-water mark with the ranchers was the offer of the brucellosis vaccine. Members of the Gallatin County Cattlemen's Guild always had a bone to pick with Fred. While the vaccine offer alleviated some concern, the deep-seated fear of the American bison could not be eased. The bison also subtly changed the economics of ranching in the valley. Ranching is a tough business, always has been, always will be, but ranchers have a peculiar way of seeing enemies when they should see friends.

Fred also refused to sign the guild's petition protesting the reintroduction of wolves into Yellowstone Park. The cattlemen were willing to risk imprisonment and $100,000 fines by "removing" predators through their own methods. They reserved their loudest wails, however, in lamenting the upward spiral of property values, making it difficult to escape inheritance taxes when the ranches passed to the next generation. They didn't seem to blame those ranchers who had sold their properties to developers. The developers carved those vast holdings into small parcels, purchased by out-of-staters, mostly Californians. Suddenly Montana was the in place to own a second home, and Hollywood stars began gobbling up ranches at inflated prices. Somehow, all this was Fred's fault.

The most enigmatic group we dealt with was PETEM, the international animal rights group. At first, People for the Ethical Treatment of Every Mammal lauded Fred's stands and plans. They roundly endorsed the bison breeding program, until they discovered that some of the animals were raised for slaughter. PETEM enthusiastically greeted the hunting and fishing ban until they learned that the Carved L's guests would be extended these privileges. "There's no pleasing these weenies," Fred grumbled. "The only mammals they don't treat ethically are humans. If they had their way they'd throw me off my own land."

And we never made any inroads with the local outdoors sportsmen. Among the most strident was the African Brothers Club. Think of the Safari Club meets Robert Bly and you get an idea of what the African Brothers are all about. To become a member you have to first be a man, then have made an African safari—photo safaris don't count—and finally, be sponsored by an existing member. You will not find an African American brother in the African Brothers; white men only need apply. These men were big-game, big-rifle hunters, obsessed with Boone and Crockett trophy animals. Their "Chief Bwana" or "Headman," C. Brewster Duff IV, claimed a world-record dik-dik, a dwarf antelope just a tad larger than a barn cat. Duff was also president of the Cattlemen's Guild, so he had multiple reasons to loathe Fred.

After he owned the ranch for a year I was able to convince Fred to allow a handful of elk hunters on the property during each season. First, I argued, it made sense in terms of game management. Second, it might discourage poaching. Third, the folks Fred opened his ranch to needed the meat to feed their families. None would ever be invited to join the African Brothers Club.

Fishing proved to be a tougher task. Fred, who had no interest in hunting mammals, truly felt he owned every fish in the river. He acted paternalistic, the overbearing steward of the land. He hired river experts to improve the river, deepening pools, improving spawning beds, and planting along some denuded banks. Fred was like a child who owned the ball and wouldn't let anyone else play with it. After two years he relented. Twice each season he allows forty local children to fish the river, under the supervision of nine other guides and me. I have no difficulty in finding guides to donate their expert services for those days. The only problem is keeping them focused on taking charge of their little charges instead of indulging their own respective fishing jones. Spin fishing, bait casting, or fly fishing, it doesn't matter. Fred allows the kids to harvest a few trout for the fry pan.

All this had helped, but a level of resentment and envy still colored Fred's relationships with his neighbors. His popularity also suffered when Sally divorced him. Though the locals usually got tight jawed regarding her political views and causes, to them she was a real person, genuine and friendly.

"Who would benefit if Fred sold his ranch?" Sy asked.

"Fred will never sell the ranch." Fred bought, he never sold.

"Perhaps, but the question is who would benefit?"

"Even that list is a long one." Four years ago, when Fred bought the ranch, he aced out two other purchasers—Duff, who dreamed of owning the largest ranch in the state, and PETEM, which wanted to return the land to nature. The Montana Patriots have a long-running feud with Fred over water rights. Even the Hutterites make frequent offers to purchase portions of the Carved L.

"You mentioned Wall Street earlier," I said.

"Front page article of *The Wall Street Journal*. Elderberry was president and chief executive officer of VideoComp. He owned over fifty percent of the outstanding shares. In terms of employees it's a surprisingly small company, but highly profitable and the leader in its field. The price of the stock fell by a third yesterday, based on the news of Elderberry's death."

"Fred said something about video compression; do you know what that means?"

"The VCR in my house reads twelve o'clock. I know *bupkis* when it comes to technology. I have trouble with the credit card machine. Enough already; a game of chess?"

I was less competition for Sy than I normally am, and our game ended in under half an hour. Sy could do *The New York Times* crossword puzzle—the Sunday puzzle—while he plays, and still beat me. He claims that because I am a naturally aggressive player I have great instincts for chess. "You lack focus and perspective, you substitute anger for cunning," he said, "and you play the game literally with no feel for the nuances and subtleties."

After I paid the check I decided to take Horace's advice and head home. I walked back to the police station and climbed into my truck. I noticed that it was both cleaner and more orderly than usual. When I opened the glove compartment to retrieve my keys, I saw that everything was stacked by height. I could actually find things among the stuff I stored in the center console. When I lowered the sun visor I discovered that my CDs had been alphabetized by artist. That made me check out my vest. All the boxes containing dry flies were in one pocket, the wet flies in the other. The tippet material was arranged by size. Lead, strike indicators, and sink tips were stored together. I marveled at the warped, anal-retentive evidence technician who had searched through my truck and vest and felt compelled to organize my life.

I found Dave Matthews, between Incubus and Radiohead, and slipped the disc into the player. I idly wondered if my radio stations had been reprogrammed in ascending order by frequency.

I drove at a leisurely pace, raising a hand in greeting at the drivers of the cars and trucks coming from the other direction. That's one of the reasons I love Montana. People always find the time to smile and wave. In California the only time people bother to raise a hand when they're driving is to give someone the finger or empty their pistol in a fit of road rage.

I guess I had reinvented myself as well. Locals have more tolerance for transplanted midwesterners than they do the sun worshipers from the left coast. Perhaps it's the common bond of harsh winters, or a shared work ethic, or an innocent friendliness. Sy once said that those in the East judge each other by their families, who your people are. On the West Coast your status is measured by who you know. In the great middle of the country you judge a person by who he is.

When the Gulf War ended the 1st Force Reconnaissance Company rotated back to Camp Pendleton to begin a postdeployment phase. Three months designed to wind down from the ever-present stress of combat operations. At first I wrote off my constant lethargy to the natural letdown. My platoon had penetrated deep into Iraqi-held territory to plant sensors, map possible attack routes and landing zones for helicopter assaults, and for intelligence gathering.

But the lethargy persisted, and my next duty station was Balboa Naval Hospital. My diagnosis, chronic fatigue syndrome. I thought that malady was unique to overweening yuppies who worked long hours on Wall Street. In time I got better, though I still have joint pain and swallow ibuprofen like candy.

The more full my days, my life, the better. I don't have flashbacks. I'm not one of those wretched stereotypes of the post-traumatic stress veteran. But I do have a memory, and my memories of the Gulf War I wish to keep memories. Each year these memories fade, become less distinct and certainly less visceral. While I recuperated at Balboa those memories crowded my mind. I couldn't stay active; I could barely concentrate on a magazine article or a television commercial, let alone a book or movie. Elden may have unlocked the secrets of video compression, but my mind experienced it long before his first patent.

In this case idle hands weren't the devil's workshop, they were the satanic theater. Broken, smoking bodies, the smell of burned flesh, the utterly black midday sky—the result of over six hundred oil well fires—all collapsed and intruded into my mind. Even the mundane memories, the daily life in the converted warehouse, the persistent sand flies, bottle after bottle of Evian water, all spooled to a never-ending reel that played on my own private screen.

With activity I crowd them out.

By the time my four-year tour ended, the Gulf War Syndrome, a vague collection of maladies suffered by large numbers of Desert Storm veterans, was an open secret. Using the Agent Orange playbook, the government initially denied that the "toxic soup" of inoculations, depleted uranium ammunition, the oil well fires, the primitive living conditions, and the possibility of chemical warfare contact had anything to do with the poor health that some of my brothers and sisters in arms endured.

Disgusted, I drove back to Bozeman and stepped off.

For me Montana represents a more vigorous life, a life spent outdoors. Action versus inaction. I couldn't bear to be locked up in an office where you can't even open the window.

Someone had left the lights on in my cabin, and as I walked up the three steps to my porch I could see through the windows. I'm sure I frowned. I'm fairly certain that I even muttered a few expletives aloud. When you live alone it's acceptable to talk to yourself, as long as you don't answer. The place was a mess. Whoever searched my cabin had not approached the task with the same level of care I had now come to expect from federal evidence technicians. Hell, I was half expecting that someone would have dusted and vacuumed the place for me. Maybe even done the laundry and folded my clothes. As I walked through my unlocked front door I intended to march right over to the telephone and call Special Agent in Charge Feib and register my—

And that's the last thing I remember before the room exploded, first into dazzling spots of light and color and then utter darkness.

CHAPTER 8

I AM THE VERY MODEL OF A MODERN MILITIA GENERAL

I returned to consciousness in stages. My first attempt to regain my senses occurred in complete darkness. A rank-smelling cloth covered my head and I was aware of only darkness. On the next attempt I felt as if I were moving, though I could not make my legs work. The third and ultimately successful try came in a brilliantly lit room. I heard martial music played softly. The room brightened in steps and my vision sharpened like a lens pulled into focus. My head pounded and the most acute pain centered above my right ear. I felt nauseated.

I awoke with an eerie sense of déjà vu. I had suffered a couple of concussions during my football career at MSU. The first, severe enough to cause short-term memory loss—fortuitous since it also prevented me from taking midterm exams. I spent the days wandering in a fog, with no sense of time and incapable of concentration. I remember that all I wanted to do was sleep.

The second and milder concussion in its way remains in my memory as the more frightening. I knew that I was injured yet I remained in the game, masking my injury. On some primal level the survival instinct had kicked in with a vengeance. I had one of my best games and could not remember the second half.

I slowly became aware of my surroundings. I sat in a straight-backed wooden chair. My hands were tied to the arms of the chair. A man sat in a chair next to me. He stood, stepped in front of me, and pointed a penlight into my eyes. My brain registered slight ripples of explosions. I gagged. The ministering angel leaped backward.

"He's all right," the man said. "There should be no permanent damage. He's probably still a bit disoriented." His voice had the lilt of a Cajun accent.

"Thank you, *Herr Doktor*." The voice came from very far away, but as the doctor returned to his seat I saw, as if in the distance, a large desk, flanked by two bright spotlights that shone in my face. Carved into the front of the desk, with the quality of a high school shop class project, was a swastika. A man sat at the desk, and as my vision cleared, he drew closer. Behind him stood the flags of the United States and Nazi Germany. I also saw framed photographs of Adolph Hitler and Timothy McVeigh.

"Howdy, Colonel," I said.

A hand slapped me hard across the back of my head. I controlled another wave of nausea.

"It's General Ferris to you, you race-mixing piece of shit," grunted a voice behind me.

I had been in this office—affectionately dubbed the Bunker—before, arguing over property rights and water rights with the self-appointed leader of the Montana Patriots, General Dalrymple Ferris. Tied to a chair, the room looked more sinister than during my previous visits. This was all taking on the shape of a very bad movie.

"Avoid any further blows to the head," the doctor instructed.

I turned my neck to attempt to see my assailant. "The Major and I are old pals." This time I received a punch to the shoulder.

"Dahlgren, I am profoundly disappointed in you," said Ferris. He wore a khaki uniform with a matching khaki tie. Four gold stars adorned his epaulets. With a Sam Browne belt, the one that sports a strap that crosses the torso, he looked vaguely military. Ferris tips the scales at well over three hundred pounds and his face displays a perpetual sheen of greasy sweat. Large perspiration rings darkened the armpits of his shirt.

"Pardon me, Captain Ferris, but my goals in life do not include winning your approval or admiration." Ferris quickly raised a hand, stopping the retaliatory blow that accompanied each of my verbal reductions in rank.

Why do all these militia types fancy themselves as great generals? Most of them never spent a day in the service, and if they did, most of them probably wet the bed and received Section 8 discharges. The people who successfully overthrow sitting governments are never generals; they're colonels like in the South American juntas, or Gadhafi in Libya. Sometimes, like in Liberia, they're mere sergeants. And here I was, privileged, I suppose, to be sitting in front of a four-star general whose command included a cadre of sixty or so malcontents and ass clowns.

"And we are not old pals," The *Generalissimo* corrected. "But until today I had respected you as a fellow Aryan."

Ferris had filed a number of lawsuits against Fred, claiming the Carved L's riparian improvements severely altered the river's drainage on the ten-thousand-acre parcel owned by the Montana Patriots. Ferris's proposed remedy was always the same. He would settle for ten thousand acres carved from Fred's property, a prime ten thousand acres, I might add. Though foolish in appearance, Ferris was no fool. Those who underestimated him did so at their own peril. He had earned a law degree from Stanford University and had served as a deputy district attorney in Los Angeles. He was disbarred following a well-publicized hearing in which was alleged to have systematically manufactured evidence and suborned witnesses in cases where the defendants were black or Hispanic. At the hearing, Ferris proudly confessed to membership in a number of extreme right-wing groups, espoused the incarceration of all "mud people," and said he was actively working to overthrow the duly elected government of the United States.

He learned the militia ropes in Idaho during the 1980s. I guessed they wouldn't make him a general in Idaho, so he moved to Montana to raise his own band of merry pranksters. The Montana Patriots were more of a nuisance than a legitimate threat. They march in a parade on Hitler's birthday, celebrate the anniversary of Waco and the Oklahoma City bombing, and generally make pests of themselves. When Sy first opened The Cowboy Vey Deli his windows were broken twice. Horace pulled Ferris in on a bogus traffic violation and had a private discussion with the General. According to Horace, the General morphed into a "quivering piece of shit" while seated in the back of the police cruiser. He hyperventilated while being fingerprinted, and had to ease his bulk into a chair until he got his breath back.

The window breaking ceased and Horace earned himself a place of honor on the Patriots' "Removal List." When the Montana Patriots succeeded in taking over Montana, they planned for the death of a number of the local citizenry. Chief Horace Twain topped the list. "I'm more worried about stepping on a rusty nail and dying of tetanus," Horace said.

I had yet to earn a place of distinction on that roster, though I felt that today might be my lucky day.

"And what's so special about today?" I asked.

"Your actions today may have seriously jeopardized the security of the Montana Patriots," Ferris replied.

"This I've got to hear," I said. "You know, Lieutenant Ferris, I've had a really shitty day. I spent a good part of this day handcuffed and restrained." I tried to lift my hands by way of demonstration. "I can only assume that one of your Aryan asswipes coldcocked me—"

"Silence!" roared Ferris. He has a wonderful speaking voice, stentorian, precise. He stood up and walked to the front of the desk. He crossed his arms over his chest and leaned against the desk. "You were duly arrested in accordance with laws of our brotherhood. You have been detained for questioning and I will determine, based on your replies, whether I will let you go or turn you over to a military tribunal."

I might have been taken down a peg here. On Ferris's Sam Browne belt was a black nylon case that held a telescopic steel baton. I twisted in my chair to view the man who stood behind me, surprised to find two men and even more surprised to discover they each had a steel baton on their belts. Obviously the Montana Patriots had a volume discount for these nasty devices.

"What did the FBI and ATF ask you about the Montana Patriots?" Ferris asked.

"Nothing."

"I find that hard to believe."

"I'm telling you, not a word."

"And I'm telling you, Dahlgren, I find that utterly astonishing." Ferris returned to the chair behind the desk.

"We could use the sodium pentothal," the doctor suggested.

"Who are you?" I demanded. "I've never seen you here before."

"The doctor is a recent volunteer, providing much needed medical care to our cadre," Ferris said. "His identity is of no matter to you."

"Back-alley abortionist?" I asked.

"You know that we consider abortion murder! We believe in the sanctity of the white, Aryan fetus," Ferris shouted.

"Fat chance that any of those will be conceived on this compound," I said. A handful of postmenopausal women lived with the Montana Patriots. "I've got twenty dollars says the medico here no longer has a license to practice medicine."

No one said a word.

"Pushing pills? Selling steroids? Human growth hormone?" I offered.

Ferris realized that I had taken over the "interrogation" and signaled to the men behind me. This time, however, my assailant walked in front of me and punched me in the stomach.

"One day, Bruno, or whatever your name is," I gasped between waves of nausea, "I'm going to catch you outside of this compound."

"What will you do then, race mixer?" he snarled. The man in front of me obviously thought he was tough. Early twenties, a skinhead, well beyond the starter kit when it came to tattoos. He had swastikas tattooed on the flesh between his thumb and index finger on both hands. His biceps and triceps were impressive, but the rest of him was soft.

"First I'll kick your balls up into your throat. After that, who knows? I'll play it by ear."

"Stop, that's enough," Ferris barked, stemming any further retribution. The skinhead returned to his position behind me, stepping on my foot in the process.

"Bush league, Bruno," I said.

I must admit that I was impressed with Ferris. He knew that positioning two thugs behind me would create fear. Every one of my answers could be met with physical violence. The threat of violence alone was enough to weigh heavily on me. He knew his business; these lessons learned in the interrogation rooms of the LAPD. I regained some of my lost aplomb. This was poker. He had raised the stakes by kidnapping me, physically assaulting me, and imprisoning me. How far would he go? I doubted that I would be put before a military tribunal and shot at sunrise. This melodrama had gone on long enough. Ferris wanted something, but so far he had been coy.

"Sergeant Ferris," I said, "if you have any questions you want answered, why not ask them? I'd like to get at least some sleep this evening."

A nod by Ferris and a punch to the back of my head. Fuck it, I thought. I was weary of battling the nausea, so I puked. I heard one of the storm troopers behind me gag in sympathy.

"You see, Dahlgren," Ferris said, ignoring my recent contribution to the decor of the Bunker, "I find it difficult to believe that the FBI did not question you in detail about the Patriots. We are, and I have this on good authority, considered by the federal police to be a highly disciplined and well-armed militia group, capable of achieving our stated goals. I cannot fathom that they would pass up an opportunity to closely question someone who has been inside our secret compound."

"The FBI seemed preoccupied with a murder, Corporal Ferris," I answered.

"Ask yourself, Dahlgren, why would the FBI be involved in a local murder?"

"You know, great minds think alike, Private Ferris. I asked that very same question myself."

"What was the answer?" Ferris leaned forward, his hands folded on the desk, shaking slightly.

"The agent said that there were federal aspects to the case."

"Of course," Ferris snorted, and leaned back in his chair. He folded his hands across his ample belly. His smile was beatific. "That federal aspect is possible domestic terrorism. The FBI is concerned about our involvement. They know we are capable of political assassination to further our noble aims. They know we have the means and the will to do this. Yes," he mused, "the FBI is quite correct to claim federal aspects to the murder.

"They spy on us. Because of the Zionist influence over our government, because of the New World Order, they spy on us and they fear us.

"There are some who consider us mad, even delusional. We have warned the American people about the thousands of NATO troops illegally stationed in America. We have warned the American people about the squadrons of black helicopters and the secret bases located in remote areas of the West. Many still are blind and deaf to our message, but you have personally seen the dark fruits of our government's capitulation to the Zionists. You have seen with your own eyes the depths of this conspiracy against White America."

"I have?"

"You were taken prisoner this morning and transported against your will in a black helicopter."

"Yes, I was. I was also taken prisoner and transported against my will to your little slice of heaven."

Ferris ignored my comment. "Did you see any markings on the helicopter, any identification marks or numbers that would indicate that the helicopter belonged to the U.S. military or a federal police agency?"

"Well, no. But the people in the helicopter were ATF agents."

"Oh," Ferris said, snorting in satisfaction, "how did you determine that?"

"They all had the letters ATF stenciled on the back of their uniforms."

The four members of the Montana Patriots laughed at my answer. Ferris waved his hand in a gesture that meant, "You see?" When he sufficiently recovered his serious mien and his sense of history, he continued.

"You are so naive. Like so many your mind refuses to comprehend the facts even when they are placed in front of your very eyes. How many of these 'agents' were mud people?"

I didn't answer.

"Did they even speak English?" Ferris asked.

"Yes, one of them told me to keep my hands in plain view. Yeah, they spoke English."

"I'm curious—did you hear all of them speak?"

As a matter of fact, I had not. Ferris must have read that realization in my face. "You were captured by members of a multinational NATO army, an army bent on the subjugation of the United States of America. The Zionist bankers and the Trilateral Commission have sold us out. I ask you, was it not a coincidence that our president during the Gulf War was a member of Skull and Bones? As is his son, who may be our next president. The day nears, Dahlgren, and we are the last hope for White America. We are the last lines of defense. You have seen, yet you refuse to believe.

"Did it occur to you that we have abandoned our passive, defensive role? The time is near. We are on the march!"

"Did you kill Elden Elderberry?" I asked.

"We could have."

"But he was the whitest man I ever knew," I feebly protested.

"Collateral damage, Dahlgren. A few white men may be sacrificed to forward our goals, to begin the revolution. Even you."

"Collateral damage," I repeated. I pointed my chin at the photograph of McVeigh. "Isn't that what that coward called the children he killed in Oklahoma City?"

"We will brook no disparagement of Timothy McVeigh," Ferris said, quietly, reverentially. "He is a true American, a patriot, a hero."

"He's a psychopathic, weak, feeble-minded little prick."

"He is a political prisoner, sir. Believe me, if the government had incarcerated McVeigh in Montana, the Patriots would have mounted a rescue mission to free him. He avenged the tragic massacre at Waco and the struggle at Ruby Ridge. Like you, McVeigh is a Gulf War veteran. Unlike you he saw the true purpose behind the coalition forces. The New World Order and the Zionist takeover of America. It will be a sad day indeed when he is executed." Ferris opened a drawer in the desk and removed a dog-eared paperback. "Do you have a copy of this book?" he asked. He held the book so that I could read the title, *The Turner Diaries*.

"Yeah," I said, "I do."

"What are your thoughts about this book?" he asked.

"I find it a little rough."

"Many do the first time they read it."

"Read it? No, I haven't read it. I tear pages out of the book to wipe my ass when I run out of toilet paper."

I expected corporal punishment for my outburst. None came.

"You should read this book, Dahlgren. You should study and analyze this book. Some of what McDonald predicted has come to pass. He wrote about brownouts, and now we have an energy crisis in California and New York. All around the country the infrastructure is crumbling. Poor roads, long delays at airports, sewer system failures, and impure water. These are symptoms of a government ruled by mud people—idiots and incompetents all. Look at how our Second Amendment rights have been trampled upon. Registration leads to confiscation! The federal government has replaced the welfare state, hiring nothing but niggers and spics and yids.

"America is a powder keg. Timothy McVeigh was God's instrument to provide the spark for the revolution. If only he had waited. Another Oklahoma City and the militias would rise and we could begin the long, arduous process of reclaiming America for the Aryan race."

I kept my mouth shut. Ferris had worked himself into a frenzy. Spittle flew from his lips; his eyes had a distant look. He saw a world of his own making, a world populated by Aryans, a White America devoid of "mud people."

"Unfortunately, as a certified race mixer you will have no part in this new America, Dahlgren."

"Can't say that I'm disappointed, Ferris." There's nothing lower than a private.

"Your choice of companions repulses me. How can any self-respecting white man patronize a shop with the name The Cowboy Vey Deli?"

"Best bagels in Montana. But don't take my word for it. Try one for yourself. You know where it's located."

"I don't eat bagels," he said. "On principle. Jew food does not pass my lips."

Horace had used almost the same words when he suggested Sy's place for lunch. Coming from Ferris, however, the words were sinister, evil.

"When you order your first bagel, ask for the one that comes with strychnine in the cream cheese. My treat."

"Our intelligence shows that you not only ate at the yid's place, but you remained and talked with him for over an hour. Do you think this Jew is your friend?"

"Yes. I count Sy as a friend."

"The Jew is no friend to the Gentile. They are a conniving race. They pretend to worship God, but they worship only money."

"This is all very interesting. I'm learning such new and fascinating things, but I'm still at a loss as to why I am here."

"Again, I must say that I am disappointed in you. You are worse than a race mixer, you are a traitor to your race. You are a dupe, another mindless automaton who fails to accept the cold facts placed before you. Today you were a prisoner of the New World Order. Where is your outrage? Where is your vengeance?" Ferris paused, expecting an answer. "Well?"

"Oh, I'm sorry. I thought those were rhetorical questions."

"How will you make the Zionists pay for their sins?"

"Right now I'm too busy figuring out how to make you pay for your sins."

Ferris laughed.

"As far as I'm concerned," I continued, "any discussion regarding water rights or property rights between us is over. Through. You know, *kaput*!"

"I couldn't agree with you more," Ferris said. "There can and will be no further discussions. There are only our demands. Tell Lather that we expect him to deed over to us, by the end of next week, the ten thousand acres we have discussed. That should give him sufficient time with the legalities."

"The land is not for sale."

"We have no intention of buying it, sir. Lather will give us the land."

"I wouldn't hold my breath."

"Please inform Lather that we are willing to escalate our campaign. In return, we shall let him live. The death of a second billionaire is of no consequence to us."

Again I asked, "Did you kill Elderberry?"

"Let's say that his death is not at cross-purposes with our goals. The battle is joined, Dahlgren. Sides must be chosen. Lather will deed that land to the Montana Patriots or we promise that he will come to regret his decision."

"I'll carry your water, Ferris, but I can already tell you what his answer will be. Fuck you and the horse you rode in on."

"That is an unacceptable answer to a reasonable request. Please make it clear to Lather how serious we are."

"Oh, I will."

"Himmler!" Ferris snapped. From a dark corner of the room I heard the rattling of chains. A black, menacing Rottweiler walked to the side of Ferris's desk. The animal yawned, displaying an impressive set of choppers, and then sat heavily.

"Himmler, meet Dahlgren Wallace."

The dog growled, a rumble deep in its throat.

"We come now to the last order of business before we release you. You are to tell no one about your visit this evening. Am I understood?"

"Visit implies that I came here of my own free will, Sea Cadet Ferris," I said. I was sure that a private outranked a sea cadet.

My luck ran out. Bruno leaped into action. Again he stood in front of me, but this time he removed the telescopic steel baton from its nylon sheath. One flick of the wrist and the sections extended. The second flick of his wrist brought the baton crashing into my leg just below the knee, my bad knee. A white-hot bolt of pain shot through my torso into my brain. My leg was numb.

"Listen to me, Wallace," Ferris said. "You will tell no one about being in this compound. Not your friend Chief of Police Twain, not the FBI, not the ATF, and not your Hebe buddy. No one. If you tell anyone that we've brought you here and questioned you—all within our rights as a sovereign nation—then two things will happen.

"We will, naturally, most vociferously deny everything. In fact, none of us are here. We are at a recruiting meeting in Missoula. Believe me, our Aryan brothers in Missoula will vouch for us.

"If you reveal our little secret you will have to deal with Himmler. If you force us to take you as a prisoner again, to interrupt our critical timetable, then your punishment will be swift and sure. I will allow Himmler to eat your genitals."

Ferris stood. "Get him out of here." Bruno and his companion removed the ropes that held me to the chair and lifted me to my feet. I still had no feeling in my left leg, so they half-dragged me out the door. Ferris, with Himmler on a short leash, and the doctor followed. They pushed me into the backseat of a van, with Bruno sitting to my right and the other Patriot to my left. Another man sat in the driver's seat and he started the van.

"Anything else you'd like to say, Dahlgren?" Ferris asked.

"Just one thing, if you don't mind, General," I answered.

"Please." In victory, like all great generals, he displayed magnanimity.

"I wonder if I may offer some advice to make your task easier?" I said.

"Of course, please do."

"When you capture me again and feed my Johnson to old Himmler over there?"

"Yes?"

"I thought it'd be polite to mention that I've got a really huge dick. In my estimation, this would be a two-dog job."

Ferris laughed. "Dahlgren, I truly like you. I admire a man who can maintain a sense of humor in the face of danger. You would have made a fine Montana Patriot. Nevertheless, I am quite serious. You would do well to keep your own counsel."

He backed away from the van. "Take him back to his place. No further beatings. Those are my orders."

"Yes, sir!" the three men in the van shouted. Ferris slid the door closed.

I slept. Or tried to sleep. The evil twins did not speak, nor did the driver, and without sparkling conversation I started to drift off. Excuse me, I had had a trying day. My head, shoulder, stomach, and right knee pained me in varying degrees. I was hungry and thirsty. My sleep was fitful, interrupted by the bumps in the road and an occasional prodding elbow from Bruno, who took it upon himself to introduce a bit more discomfort into my life.

The van stopped on the main road in front of my cabin. Bruno opened the door and said, "Get out, race mixer!"

"What?" I asked, as I hobbled out of the van. "No door-to-door service?"

Bruno jumped out of the van and pushed his chest against mine. "I'm outside the compound," he said. "Think you're up for kicking my balls up into my throat?"

"Do I look dim? Give you mighty Patriots an excuse to gang up on me? I'm a patient man. I can wait."

"Patience, right," Bruno said. "You're just another faggot Marine."

Bruno jumped back into the van. The door closed and the van sped away, kicking up dust and gravel.

I hobbled down the driveway and made my way back to the cabin. I rested on the second step. The lights were still on, and as I peered through the window I saw that order had been restored. First someone tossed the place and then someone cleaned it! I picked a piece of firewood from the pile I stored on the porch and stepped through my door.

Special Agent in Charge Sully Feib sat sleeping on my couch.

CHAPTER 9

WASTED DAY AND WASTED NIGHT

My cabin is my refuge, a sanctuary. I'm not one for entertaining. I don't receive many visitors, and I'm between girlfriends. No poker games, lodge brothers, old college chums. I'm not a hermit; I've been described as a hail-fellow-well-met. After living in Saudi Arabia in a converted warehouse with 156 of my closest friends for half a year, I've just got an extreme possessive feeling about my cabin.

The cabin is a real log cabin. Sure, it was built from a kit, but it's a real log cabin. About a thousand square feet spread over three rooms: a bathroom, a bedroom, and the great room that takes up most of the space. Kitchen, eating area, living room, all in one. I wish I owned the place and maybe someday I will. I've lived here since I first worked as a guide.

I don't own a lot of stuff. A big easy chair and an ottoman, a sofa and a coffee table, an old oak table and four chairs I bought out of a restaurant liquidation sale. There's a library table I use for tying flies, and a pair of bookcases. CD player and speakers. In the early days, before Fred, I did not own a television. Bed, dresser, and nightstand, and that's about it.

Feib slept on my sofa. He had neatly folded his suit jacket and draped it over an arm of the sofa. He had taken off his shoes and they were perfectly positioned next to his feet. His hands rested in his lap, fingers interlaced. His shirt collar was buttoned and his tie still snug, not loosened at all. Feib's white shirt looked as if it had just come out of the laundry and off the hanger. He did not strike me as the kind of guy who rolled up his sleeves when he was at work. I'll bet he wears pajamas. Hell, I'll bet he irons his pajamas.

I dropped the piece of firewood I had drafted as a weapon, and in keeping with my sudden descent into a Neanderthal-like mood, walked to the refrigerator and grabbed a Black Dog Ale. I washed my face and hands at the kitchen sink, gently probing the egg-sized lump above my right ear. The skin wasn't broken but it felt hot and tender to the touch. I filled a plastic bag with ice and limped to the easy chair.

Feib was now awake. He had put his shoes back on, tied them, and was even wearing his suit jacket. He watched me as I crossed the room.

I decided that I would not say anything, not a word, until Feib spoke. Fred taught me a few of the tricks he used in business negotiations. "The first guy who talks loses," he cautioned.

They must teach that same course at the FBI Academy, because Feib also did his best impersonation of the Sphinx. We stared at each other. He had the edge, because I was doing something. He sat unmoving on the couch, providing little in the way of entertainment value. In contrast I moved the ice bag to various body parts: my head, my knee, and my forehead above the right eye. And I was drinking. I finished the beer, struggled to my feet, and got another one out of the fridge. Feib had certainly observed I was much the worse for wear. Did he think I had battled in a bar or lost a first-round match in a World's Toughest Man competition?

When I stood to get a third beer Feib bolted from the sofa. "Sit down," he said. "Same?"

"Why yes, Special Agent Sully," I said, "Thank you."

"Mind if I have one?"

"Knock yourself out."

I heard a cabinet door open and watched Feib first study and then select a glass from a shelf. He held the glass up to the light and decided that it passed his hygiene inspection. He poured his beer into the glass, rinsed the bottle, opened the cabinet beneath the sink, and put the empty bottle into the trash. He definitely knew his way around the place.

He handed me my beer and took his seat. He studied the coffee table. I'll bet he was searching for a coaster. Finding none he resigned himself to holding his glass. Again we sat in silence.

"Tough night?" he asked.

"No," I answered. "Average night for me. Kidnapped, beaten, threatened with mutilation and death. No biggie."

Feib did not register any surprise, not even a raised eyebrow. I might have told him that I had gone shopping at the grocery store and found a wonderful price on hamburger.

"Special Agent Feib," I said, placing the empty bottle on the floor near my chair, "I'm really enjoying your visit and I can't remember the last time such a sparkling conversationalist has graced my humble cabin, but I think it's time for you to ride into the sunset."

"Montana Patriots?" Feib did not look like he planned on leaving any time soon. He removed a notebook and pen from the inside pocket of his jacket.

"Yes. Actually, I think I cracked your case."

"Really," Feib said.

"Yes. Means, motive, and opportunity. Every swinging dick in the Patriots' compound is carrying one of those telescopic steel batons. They threatened to kill Fred if he doesn't hand over a ten-thousand-acre parcel they want."

"And to think that I gave away my last Junior Special Agent badge yesterday to a sixth grader at Sacajawea Middle School," Feib said, shaking his head. "You can buy those steel batons through the Internet on fifty sites. You can probably buy one at a gun shop in town."

"Maybe, but they were also spouting a bunch of conspiracy bullshit, or maybe New World Order. They practically admitted that they killed Elden Elderberry."

Feib sipped his ale. "The Montana Patriots did not kill Elden Elderberry."

"How can you be so sure?"

"We're sure. They are perhaps the most inept militia group in Montana. Whoever killed Mr. Elderberry executed a well-timed, militarily precise assassination. Not unlike a Force Recon Direct Action mission." Feib smiled. "The Patriots are strictly amateur hour."

"Can't prove that by me," I said. "Those amateurs whacked me on the head, tied me up, considered shooting me up with sodium pentothal, and then knocked me around for a couple of hours. You could arrest them for that, I assume?"

"We could," Feib answered, slowly drawing out the "could." "But we won't."

"I thought you FBI types were sort of the go-to guys when it comes to kidnapping."

"We are. I'm sure that you've told me the truth, and I believe that you spent a very painful and unpleasant evening in the hands of some truly wretched human beings. We also know that they searched your home, but we're at a loss to say why. We know they assaulted you. We also knew that the assault would not escalate. I must admit that this little operation was their most ambitious. Way beyond tossing bricks through the plate-glass window of a bagel shop. But arrest them? No. Not right now."

I resorted again to silence, this time to do some thinking. Feib baffled me. I presented clear evidence of a series of crimes that would lead to the arrest and conviction of members of a militia group bent on revolution. Also, he had not been surprised when I gave him my report on the evening's activities.

"You knew I was at the Patriots' compound," I said.

"A brilliant deduction, my dear Wallace," Feib said, "but forgive me if I neither confirm nor deny your speculation."

"Do you have a man on the inside?"

Feib took a deep breath. "In a manner of speaking. Would you mind telling me exactly what went on during your questioning?"

For the next hour I talked. Feib asked a number of questions, and when I finished he asked me to identify the Bunker from an aerial photo of the compound. He circled the building I pointed to with a red marker and returned to the sofa.

"You mentioned when you first came to, you felt that your head might have been covered."

"Yeah. Total darkness, and I remember a foul smell; then I went out again."

"That doesn't make any sense. You know exactly where the compound is and you said that you've been in the Bunker before, talking with Ferris. Why the hood?" Feib thought for a moment. "Describe the smell."

"I can't. Never smelled anything like it before. Smelled bad."

"You mentioned a doctor. Our files don't list a doctor as an active member of the Patriots. Local doctor?"

"No, definitely not a local, and I never saw him around the Patriots' property until this evening. Ferris said something about him being a new recruit. Had a Cajun accent, and when I said something about betting that he no longer had a license to practice medicine the room got quiet."

"That's helpful. We'll check with the medical boards in Louisiana and see if they've recently suspended any doctors. Back to the smell. Think—was it organic, food, alcohol, dirty laundry, chemical, or medicinal?"

"Rank, but that might have been just the cloth. Maybe a little chemical smell too."

"My guess, ether. That would explain why you went out again and why you vaguely remember walking from the van to the Bunker. They wanted you unconscious, docile, until they could tie you into the chair. You ever had a fight with any of the Patriots, or did your reputation precede you?"

"No, no fights—yet—but there's one prick I'll be looking for."

"The one you called Bruno?"

"Yeah."

"Describe him." I did. "Tattoos here?" Feib pointed to the area between thumb and index finger on his own hand. I nodded. "Axel Jackson, aka, Action Jackson. Juvenile records are sealed, but he was an active young man. He's from your favorite part of the country, California. Sacramento, California."

"I'm impressed," I admitted. "Do you know every Montana Patriot?"

"Even Himmler." Feib smiled.

"Do you happen to know if Himmler's partial to pecker?"

Now Feib laughed.

"What the hell is the Triathlon Committee?" I asked.

"Trilateral Commission?"

"Yeah, that's what Ferris said. Trilateral Commission."

"Among the conspiracy buffs and the militia groups the Trilateral Commission is the bogeyman of bogeymen. David Rockefeller formed the commission in the early 1970s, and its charter was to bring private, but influential, citizens together to build unofficial bridges between democracies. Members include Paul Volker, the former chairman of the Federal Reserve Board, and Tom Foley, former Speaker of the House of Representatives."

"In other words, I shouldn't be checking the mail for invitations to join."

"Correct. Many of these private citizens are chairmen or board members of some of the largest multinational corporations in the world. True global corporations with global business interests. Our friends who worry about the black helicopters and NATO troops and the New World Order argue that these interlocking corporations represent the de facto world government, master puppeteers who hold the strings and control the elected leaders, the president of the U.S., and Britain's prime minister.

"Your hosts also mentioned Skull and Bones. That's a secret society at Yale University. Each year fifteen members of the upcoming senior class are tapped for membership. The roster reads like a Who's Who of American politics and finance. A large number of Skull and Bones society members also found their way into the OSS and the CIA. Once again you'll find the name David Rockefeller. The society was founded in mid-1800 as a chapter of a German secret society. One of the founders was Alphonso Taft, whose son, William Howard Taft, not only served as president of the United States but also chief justice of the Supreme Court.

"Some people believe that Skull and Bones is the first step that the sons of the rich and powerful take on a long path that introduces them into the secret governance of our entire planet."

"This is bizarre," I said.

"And it gets more bizarre each day. The Internet has become a breeding ground for conspiracy theorists, militia groups, and neo-Nazi cells. One frightening aspect is that a kernel of truth becomes the foundation for the lies. Yes, there is a secret society at Yale, and the Trilateral Commission exists. Facts.

"We have always been a country suspicious of secret societies. Suddenly a group of fraternity boys and private citizens are morphed into a cabal bent on making America kneel at the altar of the New World Order. People believe this, Wallace, and some believe it enough to kill."

"Who were the people in the helicopter this morning?" I asked.

"All ATF agents, including the pilots. It was their bird. They all speak English, but that's exactly what I mean. Ferris takes this shred of truth and weaves his own convoluted conspiracy. NATO troops and secret bases."

"You said that a number of these groups believe these theories enough to kill. Why not the Patriots?"

"Because they're idiots. Our local domestic terrorist agents have covered this group for years, and we've assigned them the lowest threat category. Additionally, Ferris has serious problems within his own organization. Other, younger, true believers are challenging him for leadership of the Patriots.

"The group is almost out of money, and it costs a small fortune to outfit, feed, and clothe an army of almost sixty people. The indolent life of the modern militiaman is about to end. These guys are going back to work. Ferris had money; he had a trust fund, and he made good money while he worked as an ADA in Los Angeles. Some of his members also had a measure of personal wealth. Most of the rank and file are losers who have always stood on the lowest rung of the economic ladder. Poorly educated, unskilled, and they waste no time blaming the minorities for taking their jobs.

"What have they done to move their own revolutionary goals forward? They march in a parade and throw bricks through a storefront in Bozeman. They distribute hate literature. An army that does not fight gets restless.

"So Ferris seizes the day. He orchestrates a plan that can keep him in power and just might solve their money woes.

"He takes advantage of Elderberry's murder. He enhances his standing within the Patriots by claiming responsibility for the murder. Naturally, he'll stop short of being indicted and tried for the crime. The younger members of the Patriots, demanding a call to action and grumbling about Ferris's ineffectiveness as a leader, are suddenly knocked off track. Ferris swears you to silence, promises retribution if you tell anyone about the events of the evening, and still he's a winner either way."

"I see where he's suddenly the fearless leader with his men," I said, "but how does he win if I talked to the authorities and they got off their bureaucratic arses and actually did something about it?"

"He has an alibi, remember?" Feib answered. "Recruiting in Missoula."

"You just about admitted that you have someone on the inside."

"We are not ready to compromise our resource. Even if we did arrest Ferris, his stature increases in the compound. He would be in the clutches of the federal government, his sworn enemy. Who knows what tales he would concoct about his stay with us, and I promise you that at this point, the stay would be brief.

"Despite his bluster, Ferris has a severe phobia about being arrested. Horace Twain confirmed that. We want to avoid bringing him in too early. It actually suits our purposes to have him remain the undisputed leader of the Patriots."

"Better the devil you know than the devil you don't?"

"Exactly. The Patriots conducted a rather amateurish but clean search of your cabin. I had my team in here and they dusted. No fingerprints, no physical evidence beyond a few fibers. Could I get your plat map of the Carved L? You can show me the land that Ferris wants."

"How do you know I have a plat map of the ranch?" I asked. I immediately answered my own question. "I forgot; you've spent more time in my cabin today than I have. Anything I should know?"

"It's probably time to do laundry," Feib said. "You have a message from your father. He caught your perp walk on LNN, and you should think about ordering more dry-fly hooks before the summer."

"Get the map."

Feib rose, disappeared into my bedroom, and returned with the plat map I stored in my closet. He opened the tube, removed the map, and spread it on the coffee table. I lowered my feet from the ottoman and leaned forward.

"You said that Ferris wants Lather to deed him a ten-thousand-acre parcel. Do you have any idea about what specific parcel he wants?"

"Sure," I answered. "He's been after the same land for years. It's right here."

"That's odd," Feib said, studying the map. "It's not contiguous with their existing compound."

"No, it isn't, but it's one of the best parcels on the ranch. Look here, access to an old fire road that connects to a paved road. There's river frontage. Own the property and you own the land on the river to the high-water mark. Because the Carved L owns the property both upstream and downstream, this water would remain nearly inaccessible; legally, that is."

"What's this land?'" Feib pointed to a parcel crosshatched with fine blue ink.

"That land is owned by the Hutterites."

"The Hutterites?" Feib asked.

"You ever hear of the Anabaptists?"

"Heard of them, don't know what they are."

"They believe that baptizing babies has no biblical foundation. They're also avowed pacifists and they shun the modern conveniences. They don't own cars or telephones or televisions."

"And they own this property?"

"Yes. The McDougall family originally owned the Carved L. The family patriarch, Laird McDougall, donated the land to the Hutterites. At the time this represented the southwestern boundary of the ranch. Later generations of McDougalls acquired the surrounding property."

"A religious group, in effect, owns this land in the middle of Lather's ranch?"

"Accurate enough."

"What do they do, these Hutterites?"

"They're farmers. Organic produce and hay. We buy whatever hay they don't keep for their own use."

"Why would Ferris want the land next to a pacifist religious group?"

"Based on what you told me about their money problems," I said, "probably to sell it to the Hutterites."

"That makes sense."

"Before I thought the Patriots wanted the land because of the river access. I've had dealings with the Hutterite elder, Luther Schlager. They would like to buy more land and expand their farming operation. This parcel would be ideal, though expensive because of the river access."

"Over a million dollars?"

"Multiples of that, I'm sure."

"Ferris extorts the land from Lather, sells it to the Hutterites, and his money problems are over. Can they afford to buy the land?"

"Many times over," I answered. "They run a very profitable operation. And they don't spend much on clothes."

Feib rolled up the map, slipped it back into the tube, and replaced it in the bedroom. He returned to his seat on the sofa, still showing no intention of leaving. I looked at my watch: 1:30 A.M.

"I am curious about something," I said. "Why have you been so . . . garrulous?"

Feib considered his answer. "You know that the arrest was a farce?"

"I've gathered that, yes."

"Lather asked me to talk to you, to explain our actions. He's a bit nervous because most of what we did this morning we did with his permission. I think it would be better if you talked to him about all this."

"I plan to."

"Lather also told us that you know everyone and you move in many different circles. We'd like your cooperation. If you hear anything, have any suspicions or thoughts, we'd like you to share those with us. Like the information about the doctor in the Patriots' compound. That's helpful."

"And for this cooperation, I get . . . what?"

"The thanks of a grateful nation," Feib said, smiling. "Same as you got when you returned from the Gulf War. Who knows, you might even find a little purpose to your life again."

"What makes you think my life lacks purpose?"

"I've read your service record," Feib said. "I know the training you endured. I know what you did in Kuwait. I know what you and your team did in Khafji. I know about the Navy Cross. What I don't know or understand is why you decided to become a glorified fly-fishing guide. Maybe it's time to rejoin the world.

"Officially I can't give you specific details about the case, like the fact that we found water in Elderberry's lungs. Officially I can't tell you that when we do move on the Montana Patriots, we'll be in a position to shut them down. Officially it will have to be a one-way street. Perhaps you could discover a few more details by staying close to your circle of friends."

Feib glanced at his watch. "Look at the time!" He stood and walked to the door. I heard a car coming down the drive. "I must be going. Thanks for the beer. I'll be in touch." He neither waited for nor wanted a reply as he walked out. I heard a car door slam, the gravel under its tires crunch, and the noise recede as it moved toward the road.

CHAPTER 10

SHERMAN'S MARCH TO THE RANCH

I awoke that morning sore, stiff, and still tired. I swallowed two Advil before I attempted to rise from the bed. The shower was painful; the warm water intensified my pain while the cold water merely made me uncomfortable. My right arm, my casting arm, felt heavy and tight. The left leg was rickety. The lump on my head had gone down, though the first hints of discoloration had begun to appear around my right eye.

Feib's warning about the laundry had been accurate. Before I left for the Carved L, I put a load of wash into the machine. My laundry skills have waned since my first days on campus at MSU. I remember walking into the laundry room with a pocketful of quarters and my mother's advice written on a three-by-five index card. Once I sorted my dirty laundry into whites, light colors, and darks, I read the labels on the clothes to determine the recommended washing temperature. I usually brought a book down to the laundry room. I wasn't concerned about someone stealing my clothes; I was interested in taking the clothes out of the dryer as soon the machine clicked off and stopped tumbling.

Over a decade later I approach the task with more nonchalance. I wash by weight, not by color. Unfortunately this results in some whites taking on a utilitarian gray hue, and once a pale pink when I included a new red shirt in the laundry. I don't measure the soap with any precision. I grab a handful of laundry detergent, toss it in, and clean my hand by sticking it under the water filling the washing machine. I've made the bachelor's compromise—some tasks require attention to detail, precision, and concentration, like tying flies. Laundry does not.

The telephone rang.

"It's me. Are you now in the habit of not returning calls?"

"Good morning, Dad. How are things in Grosse Pointe?"

"Delightful. Your mother and I had a most enjoyable evening at the club explaining your appearance on the national news."

"The arrest was a sham," I said.

"Not unlike your life, Son."

"We really don't need to get into this now, do we?"

My father is the Paper King of Detroit. Wallace Publishing, Inc., prints every automobile owner's manual, every annual report and quarterly statement for the major automobile manufacturers and their suppliers, as well as most of the industry magazines. His dream was for me to be the third generation of Wallaces to head the company.

"I blame your grandfather," my father said, sighing deeply.

"He built the business. I am merely the caretaker for our family. He ruined you with those Huckleberry Finn summers. You should have been toiling in the plant, working your way up from the bottom, just like I did."

My grandfather had filled my days with fishing and improving the upland bird habitat, tracking deer and other game at his hunting lodge in the Upper Peninsula. Trade those days on streams or in the field for the yet-to-be air-conditioned warehouse stacking and shipping boxes of printing material? No thanks.

" 'It is impossible to please all the world and one's father.' "

"That's rather deep for a fly-fishing guide," my father said.

"Agreed. I'm quoting Jean de La Fontaine."

"And who says you're pleasing anyone, let alone the world?"

"I'm pleasing myself." We said our good-byes.

I made coffee, waited for the first load of wash to finish, and reconsidered the previous evening's events. I had neglected to thank Feib and his team of anal-retentive evidence technicians for bringing a semblance of order to my cabin. Before my Patriots-assisted trip to the land of Nod, I had noticed the militia's search of my property had been conducted with a bit less care. Like Feib, I was at a loss to figure out what they had been looking for.

Feib's comment implying that my life had no purpose bothered me, simply because it struck too close to home. Mine has been a life lived by accident. Somehow things just work out. In my senior year at MSU I accepted that I might play professional football, but it had never been a dream. Even joining the Marine Corps had an element of serendipity. Guiding, my summer in Alaska, even working for Fred had more or less just happened.

I played football with a smoldering anger and somehow made it work. Too often anger on the field translates to stupid mistakes, penalties, lost games, or senseless violence and injury. Witness my treatment at the hands of the unfriendly horde at Brigham Young University. I held that anger in check when I served in the military. Too often anger on that field ends in death.

I know that I have the capacity for violence, lethal violence. My anger remains tamped down, but I know that it lurks just under the surface.

Now I'm too busy living to think about what has happened in the past. I have never worshipped at the altar of regret. Occasionally, Sy will get all metaphysical on me and quote one of the Greek philosophers—"An unexamined life is not worth living"—and I counter with

"The unlived life is not worth examining." Or, if I'm feeling erudite I might answer with a bit of Henry David Thoreau: "Live your life, do your work, take your hat."

Ask me what I plan to be doing next month or next year and I can honestly say that I don't know. And I don't care. I've never had a plan, or set goals.

I transferred the damp, clean clothes into the dryer, turned it on, and put a second pile of clothes into the washing machine. When both machines were merrily chugging along, I took my hat, left the cabin, and climbed into my truck. I sipped coffee, waved to the driver coming the other way, and headed for the ranch.

Since Sally left last year, I make it a point to join Fred for breakfast. Half the time I then proceed from breakfast table to drift boat, ranch guests in tow for some fishing. I expected that it would just be Fred and me at the table, so I was modestly surprised to see William Thayer Sherman, Esq., half-glasses perched on his sharp nose, peering at *The Wall Street Journal*.

An Atlantan who can hire someone named Sherman must have juice. Fred does. Lawyer Sherman even bears a resemblance to the more infamous General William Tecumseh Sherman. Both were small, wiry, bearded men. Hard, predator's eyes stare out of disapproving faces. Atlantans remember with palpable outrage the Civil War general's March to the Sea, a swath of destructive fire trailing his brutally effective army. Never mind that none of the Atlantans who so vividly recall the firestorm was actually alive during these trying days of our nation's history. The South possesses a rich sense of history. Many children of the South accurately recite facts about obscure battles fought by their ancestors. Many children of the North are hard pressed to tell you the decade in which the Civil War was fought.

Lawyer Sherman shares General Sherman's strategy and fondness for scorched earth. His battlefields are boardrooms, courtrooms, and stock exchanges. In the game of mergers and acquisitions, sometimes a polite euphemism for a hostile takeover, Sherman attacks with single-mindedness. He plays the game to win, and if he doesn't, the target company is but a scorched shell of its former public entity. I suspect that if you somehow could transport William Thayer Sherman, Esq. to 1864 and put him at the head of an army, the other Sherman would suffer by comparison.

I recalled that the morning before, as I was being led away in handcuffs, Fred had advised me to dummy up until Sherman flew in from Atlanta. He had hardly been summoned solely for my benefit, if at all. Sherman's steel-gray eyes rose over the reading glasses to watch me approach the table.

"Police brutality?" he asked, in his gravelly, flat voice. "If those goddamned Feds—"

Feeling surly, I interrupted. "No, I had a late-night meeting with our favorite militia general and some of his Aryan brothers.

"And a fine good morning to you, Billy," I said. Sherman believes that you can cling to your youth by affecting diminutives when talking with your acquaintances. Everyone was Billy or Johnny or Bobby or Jimmy. As far as I know, he's the only human being who can get away with addressing Fred as "Freddie."

"Steak and eggs this morning, coming right up," Fred said.

I sat at the table and sipped from a large glass of orange juice. I hadn't consciously meant to, but evidently I had employed Fred's negotiating technique of silence before all.

"Dahlgren, I feel terrible," Fred said after breakfast had been served.

"Fred, I feel terrible, period."

"I feel I owe you an explanation."

"Wonderful," I said, "because I feel you owe me one as well."

"What do you know about video compression?" Sherman asked.

"What does video compression have to do with anything?" I replied.

"Maybe everything." Sherman folded the paper and removed his reading glasses. "In the early days of cable television, Freddie recognized and understood that content, software, programs—all would have value. You couldn't go from three networks and a couple of local UHF stations to forty channels without content to fill the airwaves. Now it's hundreds of channels, specialized to a fine level. Turn on a television set today and you can choose from four ESPNs, the Food Network, Animal Planet, Home and Garden Television, several different music stations, the History Channel, and a number of twenty-four-hour news channels. Programs fill airtime. Freddie understood this and that's why he bought the film libraries. Nearly sixty thousand hours of movies.

"That's nearly seven years of viewable content. Each year, more movies, television shows, documentaries, and short films are produced, adding to the macro library.

"The advances in technology continue to offer consumers choices. Look how people have viewed movies in their own home. Beta, VHS, laser disc, and now DVD. On-demand purchases from either cable or satellite. TiVo to pause, record, and save live television. Each new advance means more control over content and timing. I want to see this movie when I want to see it, down to the minute. Not when it happens to be shown on HBO or because it's due at Blockbuster before noon tomorrow.

"Imagine a physical store whose inventory is everything that has ever been put on film or videotape. Every episode of every television show, every news broadcast from every station in the world, every movie—from Academy Award winners to independent films to pornography. Even home movies on video."

"You see, Dahlgren," Fred said, "you could never build an actual store like that. You could never bring all the video into a single location, and it would have to be single location because a significant percentage of the video would be unique."

"What do you know about computer telephone and cable modems, DSL, or T1 lines?'"Sherman asked.

"The basics," I answered. "I know that download speeds are based on the type of connection you have."

"Exactly," Sherman continued. "The better the connection, the bigger the pipe, and the faster your download or 'throughput.' With some Internet connections, streaming video is nearly seamless, and you can download an entire movie in minutes. But you still lack the quality and consistency consumers expect to see on their televisions.

"Enter Elden Elderberry and VideoComp. Elderberry's technology compresses video, crams it down to a manageable size. The video can be stored digitally and accessed by the individual subscriber. The video file is opened, decompressed at the point of viewing—on the television."

"How?" I asked.

"Think of it as a cable box on steroids. In truth, a computer. Video compression is the realization of a dream, the true marriage of computers and television."

"Dahlgren," Fred said, "this is the ultimate pay-per-view. A consumer would subscribe to the service, much like your current cable or satellite user, but your options would be limitless."

"Anything on film I could order up and watch?" I asked.

"Anything," Fred replied.

"Why would I want that?" I said.

"You wouldn't," Fred said. "Dahlgren is a television snob," he explained to Sherman. "But for the couch potato this is the ultimate fantasy realized. The average child spends more time watching television, playing video games, and surfing on the Internet than he or she does in school. Adult Americans watch nearly five hours of television a day. Hard-core videophiles spend thousands on home theaters. Early adopters always own the latest developments in video technology, like flat-screen, wide-screen digital televisions connected to sophisticated audio systems."

"Great," I said, "but how does this have any bearing on what happened to me yesterday?"

"We're getting there," Sherman answered.

"Spoken like a man who charges an hourly fee," I said.

"Only chumps charge an hourly fee," he said. "I've watched Elderberry since his senior year at MIT. I am aware of nearly all the developments in the world of video technology and broadcasting. We study promising technologies and conduct detailed surveys on the practical applications of these technologies. We even have an ethicist and a philosopher on staff to study the social implications.

"Fifteen years ago Elderberry was just another whiz kid engineer, but his vision was laser-focused. About five years ago he began filing a series of patents for video compression hardware and copyrights on intellectual property. He had constructed the architecture for true video compression at about the same time he took his company public.

"VideoComp is unique in that Elderberry controlled about fifty percent of the stock. He built the company without the aid of venture capitalists. You know what a VC is?"

You can't work for Fred without picking up a thing or two about finance. I even have a 401(k). "Yeah," I answered, "venture capitalists identify promising companies and invest money in them."

"Correct," Sherman said, "usually for a significant equity, or ownership, position. It's rare to find an entrepreneur who, by the time his company is ready for the public issuance of stock, owns a large percentage of his own company.

"Elderberry received his start-up funds from an unusual source, and he negotiated an unusual deal. His only investor is the Mormon Church. It owns ten percent of VideoComp. All of this is public knowledge, published in the company's annual reports and proxy statements."

"I invited Elden to the ranch to talk to him about buying a controlling interest in his company," Fred interjected.

"We started buying stock in the open market several months ago," Sherman said. "We used a number of brokerage houses and a variety of different accounts. We currently own about two percent of the company, though that represents a larger percentage of the float."

"The float?" I said.

"The shares in the public's hands. Between the church and Elderberry's personal holdings just over sixty percent of the stock is not liquid and doesn't trade. So our two percent is nearly five percent of the float.

"A month ago I flew into Salt Lake City and offered to purchase the entire block of stock held by the church. We were ready to file the appropriate reports and disclosures with the Securities and Exchange Commission. The church's holdings have a market value of approximately five hundred million dollars. We offered them just under a billion."

I still have fourteen payments left on the truck. Sherman and Fred live in a world where billions are tossed into the game. A big chip, but in the end, still a chip.

"They refused," Fred said. "Never even made a counterproposal. We knew that they would immediately contact Elden. Long before Billy flew into Salt Lake, I had already invited Elden to the ranch and he had already accepted. He knew why I invited him, laughed about it over the telephone.

"We talked after dinner the night before he was killed. Elden kept an open mind. These weren't negotiations, more like general discussions. I had a sense that Elden was at an interesting crossroads in his life and I felt that we might have worked something out."

"Our strategy was to own a majority interest in VideoComp," Sherman said. "We wanted control, but we also wanted Elderberry on board."

"I talked with Sy yesterday," I said, "and he said VideoComp stock dropped by a third on Monday. How does that affect your deal?"

Fred and Sherman exchanged a glance. I had touched a nerve.

"There was a perception in the marketplace that Elderberry *was* VideoComp," Sherman explained. "No Elderberry, no company. That was true five years ago, but it's no longer true. In fact, yesterday the stock price recovered and closed higher than it did on Friday."

"A wild ride," I said.

"That, my dear Dahlgren, is an understatement," Fred said. He walked over to the drinks table and poured himself a generous dollop of Laphroaig. Fred, while a championship tippler, has one sacrosanct rule. He never drinks before noon, and he's not one of those fellows who winks and rationalizes that it must be noon somewhere. I looked at my watch. Somewhere in the mid-Atlantic Ocean it was noon.

Fred inhaled half his drink and he took no pleasure from it. "I might have stepped on my crank on Friday," he said. "I called Billy and I told him what had happened. We discussed how the markets might react to the news of Elden's death, and we agreed that the perception was VideoComp was a one-man band." Fred finished his drink with a second swallow.

Sherman continued. "We took steps to protect our investment. We employed a number of strategies that, in effect, bet that the stock price would drop. We closed those positions on Monday, before the price recovered yesterday."

"I guess you made money," I said.

"Yes, about twenty-five million dollars. There is a gray area here. Freddie knew that Elden was dead about an hour before it was announced in the media. We may face an SEC investigation to determine whether we violated securities laws by acting on insider information. I argued that we are on solid ground. Freddie merely was in a position to make an observation about the company that no one else could.

"The FBI, in the person of Special Agent Feib, visited Freddie on Sunday. Freddie had the good sense to call me, and I remained on the speaker phone during the interview."

Rich guys are interviewed, guys like me get interrogated.

"At this point," Sherman said, "the authorities knew they were dealing with a homicide. Feib also discussed how poorly things looked for Freddie; how he, above many others, would benefit from Elderberry's death."

"That much money would be enough of a motive for murder," I said.

"For most people that would be, but not in Freddie's case," Sherman argued. "Freddie's worth well over three billion, so twenty-five million is more or less pocket change. You're also forgetting that we hedged the original investment. We were protecting the value of the shares of VideoComp that we already owned."

"The dust settles and you're up by twenty-five million dollars, because you said the price of VideoComp is higher now than where it closed on Friday, when Elden was alive. Do I have it right?"

"Yes, and with Elderberry's death the company is in play," Sherman replied.

"In play," I said. "It really is a game to you, Billy."

"Mere semantics, my young friend. The president of VideoComp, a fellow named Brigham Briggs, was named interim chairman of the board, but the company will be sold, and it would have probably been sold if Elden were still alive. Yes, the technology exists, but the implementation will be extremely costly. Fortunately for Susi Elderberry, there is no pressure to sell, so it won't be a fire sale."

"Why?"

"She controls Elden's stock. California is a community property state, and federal estate tax laws allow for an unlimited marital deduction."

"I hate to flog the deceased equine, but again, gentlemen, how did all this lead to my arrest yesterday?"

Fred coughed. "Feib intimated that if I were to cooperate, then perhaps the SEC investigation might be derailed."

"I lobbied against cooperation," Sherman said. "I think the SEC threat is a bluff. I contend that Freddie did nothing illegally."

"Feib countered that we operated in a gray area of the law," Fred said. "In any case, it would be embarrassing. Given my interest in VideoComp, literally and figuratively, he further argued that I enjoyed a unique benefit in having Elden stroll out of the picture. My invitation, my ranch, my guide, death occurs on my property, and then I short the stock using every strategy known to man. The scales didn't exactly line up in my favor."

"There are, however, additional mitigating factors," Sherman said. "In the last few months the ranch has lost a number of bison. Most have been shot and butchered for the meat. In the last few weeks the ranch lost three calves to poison."

"During the same period," Fred mumbled, "I received a number of death threats."

"Warning him off the Carved L," Sherman said. "The threats have come in the regular post and once by e-mail. The e-mail was sent through a computer owned by a student at UC Santa Barbara. The investigation determined that his computer was a Trojan horse."

"A Trojan horse?" I asked.

"A common hacker tactic. They use other computers to send e-mail. Usually it's used in Smurf attacks. That's when corporate e-mail systems are overloaded with millions of incoming messages, launched by a single hacker using thousands of other computers. The regular mail came from Wyoming and Idaho.

"And if that's not enough, Duff has made three offers to buy the Carved L. With each succeeding offer he lowers the price. The most recent one came today, hand-delivered to Freddie's real estate agent in town.

"We made Horace aware of the death threats immediately, and he called in the FBI. People like Freddie get harassed all the time. Freddie gets sued nearly once a week, and he receives any number of threats with some frequency. Two years ago both an Israeli right-wing group and an Islamic fundamentalist sect threatened to kill him."

“So why take these recent threats seriously?” I asked.

“Because these threats came with photos,” Sherman said. He slid a file across the table. Inside were copies of an original letter and photos. The letter was brief:

> We do not want your kind in Montana. If you leave now we will let you live. If you stay here you will die here. Sooner than you think.

A series of black-and-white photographs showed Fred in a variety of Bozeman locations. Leaving his private jet, eating breakfast at Gateway Café, having dinner at The Mint, walking around town, buying books at Borders, sitting on the porch of his ranch house, even fishing. The implication was crystal clear: If we can get close enough to you to shoot these photos, we can get close enough to shoot you. The Gateway Café photo was especially disturbing to me because I was caught passing Fred the hot sauce. I closed the folder and slid it back across the table.

“The FBI crime lab results were not helpful. The letter was printed off an ink-jet printer. The paper is Hammermill, sold everywhere and anywhere. The photographs were not processed commercially and again the paper was generic. No fingerprints on the letter or the photos, no other fibers, and the envelopes were a forensic cesspool. The postmarks were from central post offices. Nothing unusual.

“Freddie has been the victim of a carefully crafted, well-orchestrated, and persistent campaign to get him off this property. The murder of Elderberry demonstrates how determined his adversaries are.”

“You think that Elden’s death leads back to Fred?”

“You can’t come to any other conclusion, and it appears that the authorities share that conclusion.”

“Dahlgren, we still haven’t answered your question,” Fred said, “and I’m fixing to do that sooner rather than later. Have you seen this morning’s *Daily Chronicle*?”

I shook my head. Fred passed me the front section.

I've been in the newspaper in the past, but always on the sports page. Scoring a touchdown or making a block. I've had the occasional quote or feature article. And who can forget my infamous interview with the *Provo Herald*?

This was decidedly different. The banner headline and an above-the-fold photo. Horace was to my right and Feib to my left, though most of Feib had been cropped out of the photograph. And me in the middle, handcuffed, being led into police headquarters. Even to myself I looked guilty. I read the article. Every word reeked of ambiguity. The reporter must have worked entirely from a list of clichés: "local man questioned in murder of wealthy California businessman . . . questioned for several hours regarding his involvement . . . last to see the victim alive . . . A spokesman for the Bozeman police and the FBI said that physical evidence pointed to Wallace as a strong suspect," and, "Wallace has been ordered to remain in Gallatin County."

"Freddie's clipping service reported that the story is national," Sherman said. "Television news is also running a clip of you being escorted into the police station, usually over the news about the murder."

"I know," I said, "my dad saw it on LNN. Thanks again, Fred."

"When Feib interviewed me on Sunday," Fred said, ignoring my jibe, "he asked a lot of questions about you. He wanted to know if you had money problems or a drug habit. He dug hard for reasons on why you might want to kill Elderberry, like, were you having an affair with his wife? Could you somehow be partners with the people who want me off the ranch?"

"Freddie steadfastly maintained your innocence," Sherman said.

"Feib said that Elden couldn't have been alone in the side channel for long," Fred said. "He asked why he was even left alone in the side channel. He was quite convincing. He said that they found the murder weapon in your boat, and I must admit that shook me. He made it sound like you must have had something to do with it.

"Feib called me yesterday morning and said that he was going to stage an arrest. He's convinced that you must cross paths with the real murderer. I told him that you had just left to go fishing.

"That's when he asked my permission to use my helipad and the ranch as a staging area. I asked him what he was going to do, and he said he would send a helicopter in to take you off the river.

"I argued against that. I told him to arrest you at the takeout point, but he was adamant. What if you really were involved, he said. How would it look for both of us if something happened to any of the other guests while fishing my river with, arguably, a murder suspect?

"You can see I had no choice."

A patsy. A pawn of the rich and powerful. Or bait. I felt ill-used, but slightly guilty. I had a secret that I hadn't told. On the night that Elden died, I slept with the Widow Elderberry.

CHAPTER 11

TWO MOMENTS OF WEAKNESS

When I need to think I head to a river or a stream. I don't fish while I'm thinking, or do much thinking while I fish, except about fishing.

I don't golf. The excuse I offer is that I'm not old enough yet. They say that your mind must be focused on the game. Thinking about a business deal or a gift for your spouse or the last episode of *The Sopranos* while driving a ball usually results in a slice or hook into the woods.

Fly fishing requires total concentration. You're not sitting around watching a bobber. You're observing, stalking, making choices and decisions constantly. What fly to present, what cast to use, how to approach the water; it takes all my concentration to fish well.

After breakfast with Fred and Sherman, I decided that I needed to attempt cogitation. I stopped in a small market and bought a sandwich, fruit, and a couple of beers and drove to a small creek that I like to fish. My favorite time of the year to fish this creek is summer, when I can wet wade. I love feeling moving water on my legs, cold water running into my boots. A truly wonderful and invigorating sensation, after the initial breathtaking shock. In May the water and ambient temperature are not conducive to wet wading.

I parked the truck in the empty lot. I pulled on waders and boots, loaded the food and beer in the back pouch of my vest, and put up a 3-weight rod. I threaded the fly line and leader through the guides, tied on a small Royal Wulff, and hiked along the creek.

If you are willing to hike you can find water that receives little fishing pressure. Many anglers start casting five feet from the parking lot and succeed only in spending a frustrating day on the water. After I walked for nearly an hour, covering two miles and working up a sweat, I stopped and listened.

I've heard that there is nowhere on the planet where you can experience absolute silence. If that's so, then I prefer to pick my noise. In New York City you can always hear a siren blaring. The traffic roars, horns, tires squealing, the hum of some motors and the staccato rumble of others, the heavy thump of trucks. These distinctly urban sounds energize some people.

As I stood next to the stream I could hear my own breathing, still labored from the hike. And I heard the stream, the soft rush of moving water. And I heard the wind soughing through the trees, the leaves rustling. And I heard birds singing and tiny scuttling feet in the ground cover.

After I placed the two bottles in the river to keep them chilled, I watched the stream. Water bulged over submerged rocks. The freestone stream bottom glimmered in rainbow colors in the bright sunlight. I slackened my line, applied Gink to the fly, stripped line from the reel, and made a cast. Gink is a dry-fly floatant, a dressing that helps the fur and feathers repel water. The Royal Wulff danced in the water, then began to drag in the current. I retrieved the fly and cast again. I repeated the process several more times and then took a few steps upstream. I lengthened my cast and felt pain in my arm and shoulder. I dwelt on the pain rather than on watching the fly, and I missed a strike.

I cast again. And again. And yet again, slipping into a rhythm that felt perfect. I paused on the backcast to allow the line to straighten behind me and then threw a tight loop forward. The line unfurled and the fly dropped into the water. This time I did not miss the strike.

I raised my rod and set the hook. Instantly a rainbow trout leaped from the water, flexing its body. I lowered the rod and then brought it back up when the trout's body slammed into the stream. I brought the fish in quickly and reached down to release the hook without touching the trout. The rainbow flashed back into the depths of the pool.

I've always had luck with the Royal Wulff. Like most attractor flies it's flashy; peacock herl, red floss, brown hackle, and white wings, and it imitates exactly nothing in nature. Books, serious books, have been written about the feeding habits of trout. Thousands of pages devoted to outwitting a creature whose eggs are larger than its brain. What spark ignites the trout's instinct to feed? Those who are devotees of matching the hatch tie on specific imitations to the insect life hatching on the river. They pay particular attention to size and color. Others suggest that the presentation of the fly is the critical success factor. Still others subscribe to the school of thought that puts their fate into the hands of curiosity. What's that? I think I'll eat it!

Fish don't have that internal dialogue. The whole anthropomorphic Disney thing bugs the shit out of me. A friend of mine once said that if Bambi had been a trout, fishing would be banned in America, and he might be right. I've already spent more time on the water than most people do in a lifetime. I've caught or helped others catch thousands of fish. Not one fish has ever communicated so much as a single thought to me. It says more about us than the trout when the animal with the most highly developed cerebral cortex devotes so much ink and paper to the capture of an animal with one of nature's tiniest brains.

I continued to fish, never glancing at my watch. When my stomach began growling I pulled the bottles of beer from the stream and found a place to sit. I finished a beer and ate the sandwich and fruit. I drank the other Black Dog. I took a nap. I take the art of cogitation very seriously, approaching it carefully, sort of sneaking up on it like I would a trout.

I woke and stretched. Some body parts felt better than others did. I drank water, made a little of my own, and walked to the stream. I sat down and placed my feet into the stream, watching the water glide over the tops of my boots, a hypnotic effect.

A gentleman does not discuss a dalliance with a lady, so I will avoid the details of the evening I spent in Susi's company.

I had helped Horace, Officer Andrew, and Dr. Cord carry Elden's body to the waiting ambulance and somehow avoided interfering as the drift boat was inexpertly winched to a police trailer. I remember urgency in all the activity. My stomach felt tight and I was nervous. When Horace and his crew left, I winched the second drift boat to the trailer attached to the ranch vehicle that had been left for me. The trailer bounced and banged on the gravel road, the ride smoothing out when I pulled on to "the oil," as the locals call a paved road.

I drove to the ranch and tended to the gear. Dusk turned into complete darkness. Fred walked down from the ranch house to keep me company.

"Think you can stay tonight?"

"Don't see why not," I answered. "Any particular reason?"

"Propriety, Dahlgren. I think that it would be bad form for Susi and me to be alone in the ranch house this evening."

"She's not leaving?"

"Not tonight," Fred said.

"Why not put her up at the Gallatin Gateway Inn? One of the suites."

"I can't very well send her into town to a hotel. Think about it; her husband dies on my ranch, and I throw her out."

"Yeah, I see your point. That's callous even considering your standards."

"Funny," Fred said. "I'm letting her use the Gulfstream to return to San Francisco late tomorrow. She's taking Elden's body back with her.

"And, she's acting, well, sort of strange."

My turn to remain silent. Fred, recognizing the ploy, glowered before he continued.

"One minute she's quiet, so still it's like she's a statue. The next time I see her she's damn near bouncing off the walls, like she's jacked on speed or something."

"People react to grief in different ways," I said.

"What are you, a fucking expert now?"

"One of my former clients owned a chain of funeral homes in Chicago."

"A fly-fishing undertaker?"

"Said he saw reactions that ranged from the stoic to the inconsolable. Some folks needed sedatives and others a strong drink. Some went quiet, others chatty. Said he saw wakes where the mourners told jokes and laughed in front of the casket."

"Susi's running the table on the emotional front. So plan on staying for dinner and the evening." Fred turned on his heels and marched toward the house, very much the laird of the land. I had my doubts that Susi would even show for dinner, but I never pass up an opportunity to tuck into the ranch's generous supply of food and drink.

Fred kept a room for me in the ranch house, and I use it frequently during the summer. In July and August I'm not off the river until 9:00 P.M. By the time I get the gear ready for the next day, it doesn't make sense to drive back to my cabin to sleep for a few hours only to stumble out of bed to repeat the process.

In turn, I kept clothes and toiletries in the room, including one of my two blue blazers and half of the four ties I own. Fred insists on a measure of formality at dinner. I showered and dressed. After only three attempts I had a decent knot in my tie.

Fred sat alone at the head of the dining room table, nursing a man-sized ration of his favorite. As soon as I walked into the room he began peppering me with questions. When you rub elbows with the likes of Fred, you do become accustomed to the finest things in life, like single malt scotch. I poured an equally impressive snort of The Macallan and settled into a chair. Fred wanted to know every detail. We spoke in hushed tones. He shared my opinion that Elden's death had not been an accident.

Susi entered wearing the "little black dress" and a string of pearls. The little black dress seems to hang in every woman's closet. This particular dress had not been designed with mourning in mind. The former Miss Utah, though more than a decade removed from her title, still looked ready for the runway.

Fred and I both rose to our feet when Susi entered. Fred, holding her elbow, gently led her to the chair opposite mine. He poured Susi a glass of nonalcoholic white wine.

Fred and I were suitably somber. In addition to somber, I was surprised she had made it down for dinner. Maybe F. Scott Fitzgerald was right about the rich being different. Given Susi's mien, they sure mourned differently. I also had trouble shaking the recurring vision of the body bag in the drift boat that I had stared at for the better part of six miles. That body bag brought to mind others, of my brothers in arms, ravaged by the sandstorms of Kuwait. The Susi who sat down to dinner, however, was, as Fred mentioned earlier, the positively high-voltage version. She spoke incessantly about the late Elden. At times her eyes clouded with tears, and she sniffled, but she did not cry.

"Elden was fascinated by the Mormon forgeries," she said, the words tumbling out in a rush. "I'm sure you remember the bombings in Salt Lake City in the mid-eighties? Two people were murdered with pipe bombs in an attempt to cover up one of the most elaborate forgery schemes in the history of American letters.

"The forger, Mark Hofmann, was a dealer in historical documents. He was raised a Mormon but he seriously questioned his faith. The document that shook the church was the Salamander letter. The letter, written by Martin Harris, claimed that the Prophet used a seer stone to locate the Golden Plates. These were plates from which Joseph Smith translated the Book of Mormon.

"Hofmann seemed to have an uncanny ability to discover rare and important documents, and not only those that had significance to the church. He also forged a missing poem by Emily Dickinson and he nearly sold a forged copy of the 'Oath of a Freeman,' a document printed on the first Colonial printing press.

"Many of Hofmann's Mormon forgeries cast the church and its early history in a rather unfavorable light. The First Presidency is rumored to store controversial and embarrassing documents in a secret vault, and that only a limited number of Mormon historians are granted access to these documents. Hofmann duped the church leadership into buying documents that were truly explosive, that could have caused many believers to question the very origins of their religion."

"In what way?" Fred asked.

"In the teachings of the church, Joseph Smith is led to the Golden Plates by the Angel Moroni," Susi said, "while Hofmann's forgery claimed that the Prophet located the plates with a seer stone. In his youth, Joseph Smith was a money digger, a not-uncommon profession in nineteenth-century New England. These people professed an ability to find buried money and treasure using seer stones and other divining devices. Using this well-known fact about Smith, Hofmann created a controversial document guaranteed to catch the attention of the church leaders.

"When his house of cards collapsed, Hofmann killed two people. He also became a victim to one of his own pipe bombs."

"He blew himself up?" I asked.

"Yes, but the blast was not fatal," Susi explained. "Eventually he was arrested. He's now in jail, serving a life sentence. Elden's hobby was locating and purchasing Hofmann forgeries. Ironically, some of them are now quite valuable."

"I understand that the Mormons also maintain one of the best genealogical resource libraries in the world," Fred said.

"We do," Susi said. "You would be accurate to say that many members of our faith are obsessed with their own roots, though Elden's interest in genealogy waned in the last few years."

"Why this universal interest in genealogy?"

"Are either of you familiar with the tenets of the church?" Susi asked.

Both Fred and I shook our heads.

"Each man in the church may be a priestholder. Our vision of the afterlife is a Celestial Kingdom where each man reigns over his own universe. The church's overall interest in genealogy assists the members in locating ancestors and relatives who can then be sealed in a temple ceremony. Wives are sealed to their husbands in a temple wedding ceremony.

"When I die, Elden can invite me to his Celestial Kingdom. In the wedding ceremony we enact this ritual. I have a secret name that only Elden knows. In this way I can join him in eternity."

"In theory, the more folks I have sealed to me, the larger my universe?" Fred asked.

"Yes," Susi said. "We can baptize our ancestors, even though they have passed on before us, and have them sealed to us."

"What's with the whole underwear thing?" I asked.

"We call them garments," Susi said, laughing. "When a man is ordained into the priesthood and when a woman marries in the temple, they are given their garments, special underclothes. The devout continuously wear their garments. We are allowed to remove them for sports and other activities, but frankly, the California Mormons have never wholeheartedly embraced that tradition. If I were wearing my garments now, you would see them. I'm curious; how do you know about the garments?"

"I played football at Montana State, and we had a few Mormons on the team. Their underwear seemed kind of funny, embroidery and the kind of shape you don't find in a three-pack at J. C. Penney's."

"No, you won't," Susi said. "Devout Saints believe that no harm can come to them while they wear their garments. Mormon soldiers in battle have sworn that bullets altered their trajectories to miss them."

After dinner Fred led us into the library and we sat drinking coffee, and, for Susi, decaffeinated herbal tea. Susi continued to talk about Elden. Our contributions were the occasional question or comment.

I started to hear only part of what Susi said. Despite the verve and nervous energy in her words, the accumulated weight of the day began to take its toll on me. Sitting in the overstuffed leather chair, feet propped up on the ottoman, the weight of good food and better drink in my belly, I drifted in and out, barely able to stay awake. I felt heavy and lethargic. Somehow I struggled to my feet, made my apologies, and climbed the stairs to my room.

I barely had the energy to hang my clothes in the closet and brush my teeth. I fell asleep instantly, a heavy dreamless sleep.

The next events I remember as if in a fog, or as if I had layers of gauze over my eyes. These memories are not sharp and they remain only impressions. I heard the click of someone carefully closing the door to my room. I heard soft, quiet footsteps cross the wooden floor to my bed. I heard my name whispered. Then I heard, "I don't want to be alone tonight." What Susi said next I am not quite sure of; it was either "I need to have a man in my bed" or "I don't need to think of the dead." Then Susi was in my bed and I instantly felt the heat from her body and she moved next to me. All I'll say is she wasn't wearing her garments.

Were my actions in the least way admirable? I could argue that she came to my room and joined me in my bed. I could plead that I only offered solace and comfort, that for a time I helped someone who grieved—OK, she was the former Miss Utah—escape an oppressive sadness. But afterward I felt guilty and uncomfortable. I slept fitfully through the remainder of the night until sometime before dawn I realized that Susi was gone. I then slept the sleep of the unrighteous.

We saw each other at breakfast. We even sat in the same chairs that we had the night before, across the table from one another. Susi appeared fragile. Her face revealed a hint of fatigue, as if she was only now realizing the enormity of what had happened the day and night before. The energetic, frenzied monologue of last evening's dinner gave way to a halting reluctance to speak this morning. If she weren't so devout, I might have suspected her actions of the previous evening as the result of better living through chemistry. Power by cocaine.

Susi and I politely shook hands on the ranch house porch as she left. Fred drove her to the airport.

As I watched the water flow over my boots I still felt guilty. I knew that this particular confession would not be good for the soul. Who could I tell? Fred? Hardly. Horace or Feib? That would introduce an interesting dimension in the investigation. Sy? Maybe. In the end I knew that I would tell no one, and that in this instance I would keep my own counsel.

A man had died. A man whom I had come to like, a man well on his way to sharing my passion for fly fishing. I had slept with his wife on the day that he died. Since then I had been arrested for his murder, kidnapped, beaten, and had dominated the front page of the local fish wrapper as well as the national news. I learned that Fred had sacrificed me to play a role in the FBI's artifice. And I had eaten a wonderful pastrami sandwich.

Elden's killer knew that I had nothing to do with the murder. If I were the killer I'd be feeling secure and smug. The arrest charade would not smoke out a deliberate and careful assassin. The fallacy in Feib's logic was that I cross so many paths, eventually I would cross the murderer's. He assumed I would continue to deliver little gems and nuggets like the doctor in the Patriots' camp, but I had my doubts. People were more likely going to keep me at more than an arm's length.

I did not feel restored or refreshed. Instead I felt enervated. I had not sorted things out, and I had a two-mile hike ahead of me.

I walked without the energy of the early morning. I walked with confused thoughts bombarding my brain. I walked with a distinct sense of uneasiness.

Dusk. When I walked from the path onto the gravel in the parking lot I paused to look at my watch, surprised at the time. It's always later than you think.

I should have been more observant and more cautious. A Volvo was parked next to my truck. Coming back I hadn't seen anyone on the river, and I am sure that no one had gone farther upstream than I had all day. The Volvo's windows were tinted, though I was able to make out a couple sitting in the front seat as I approached. Two women engaged in what seemed to be an earnest conversation. I smiled. They did not smile back.

I broke down the rod. I cut the fly from the leader, hooking it to a square of sheepskin I have pinned to my vest. Then I reeled in the line and removed the reel from the rod. I placed the reel in its case. I separated the two pieces of the rod, slipped each piece into a flannel bag, and put the bag in the aluminum tube.

I walked to the passenger's side of the truck and opened the door. I removed my vest and laid it on the seat. I kicked off my boots and peeled the waders off. I felt the chill of the cool air on the sweat-soaked pants I wore under the waders. I strapped on the Tevas and tossed the waders and boots into the bed of the truck. When I walked to the driver's side of the truck I noticed that the Volvo was parked very close. Close enough that I would need to be a contortionist to squeeze into the driver's seat. Close enough that I had to turn and sidestep between the two vehicles. A parking lot with all the room in the world to park and the only two vehicles in the lot were inches apart. Go figure.

I gently rapped a knuckle against the tinted window on the Volvo's passenger side window. The woman in the seat deliberately rolled down the window.

"Evening," I said. I might have even raised a finger to my ball cap.

No answer.

"I was wondering, if you don't mind, that is," I stammered, "well, maybe you could please move your car so that I can get in, ma'am?"

"Fuck off, you Neanderthal!" the woman barked.

"Pardon me?"

"You heard me," she snarled. "Can't you see we're involved in a serious conversation here? Big macho asshole! Did you kill enough fish to prove your manhood?"

Over the years I've learned to hold my tongue. Once I might have entered into a philosophical discussion, calmly marshaling the facts about how those of us who participate in outdoor sports are the true stewards of the land and wildlife. Not anymore. They don't listen and they only see their side of the issue. So I said nothing. She continued to rant but I mentally switched off her station. I turned my back to the woman, my backside pressed to the side of the Volvo, and I began to carefully open my door.

The shock exploded in every cell of my body. I jolted in the air and the next thing I knew, I was lying on the gravel, conscious but unable to move a muscle. I wasn't even sure that I was breathing.

CHAPTER 12

PETEM IF YOU'VE GOT 'EM

I was utterly paralyzed, physically incapable of moving a muscle, yet I also could hear well and see everything in my field of vision. Two women stood over me, both holding what appeared to be radios. One woman raised the radio to her lips. "Clear!" she said, keying the transmitter twice. I heard a squeal and two clicks in reply.

"Can he, like, hear us?" she said, lowering the radio away from her face.

"He's supposed to be fully conscious," the other woman, late of the passenger's seat and the surly attitude, said. "Think I ought to hit him again?" She bent down and brandished her radio-shaped device in my face. Instead of an antenna it sported two metal prongs. She clicked a switch and a tiny blue bolt of electricity leaped between the contact points. I smelled ozone, the clean, slightly metallic scent that follows thunderstorms.

"No," the other woman answered. "He looks pretty much, you know, out of it. How long did you like, zap him with that thing?"

"The full five seconds. I buried it in his ass and kept it there." She looked at me. "Prick," she said. She kicked me in my ribs. I felt the sudden dull pain.

"How long will he be parasitic?"

"Paralytic . . . about fifteen minutes."

I heard the sound of tires on the gravel and allowed myself to feel a brief glimmer of hope. The vehicle stopped and three men, wearing ski masks and dark clothes, joined the women. They all said "Hey" to each other. Annoying.

"He looks weak as a baby," one of the men said.

"Fucking-A right," said my malefactor. "I hit him with all 625,000 volts."

"It's best for you to get out of here," the man said. "Give me the stun gun."

Two of the men lifted me into a sitting position. I felt dizzy, disoriented. I had no sense of balance and my spine felt like jelly. My head lolled. I managed to see the front license plate of the Volvo in the fading light. Montana plates.

"Dude, he's bleeding," another of the men said.

"How badly?" asked the man who had appropriated the stun gun.

"Bad—he might need stitches, dude. He must have cracked his head when he fell."

"I'll get the first-aid kit."

I heard footsteps retreat and return. I could faintly feel someone applying pressure to the left side of my head. Then I saw an arc of gauze pass four times in front of me.

"I just saw his fingers move!" a shrill, high-pitched voice shouted.

"Chill, dude. We still have the stun gun."

The trio more or less dragged me to a van. Another van, another kidnapping. This shit was getting old.

"This guy's huge," said the man with the high voice.

"Just get him into the back."

They pushed, pulled, and levered me into the van. Sensation returned to my hands and feet but I had no control over my arms and legs. My lips felt numb, as if I had returned from a visit to the dentist. The side door of the van slid shut. The carpeted floor of the van smelled of dogs. In the few seconds that the interior lights were on, I saw that a metal mesh grid separated the front row of seats from the empty compartment in the van's back section.

Over the next few minutes I regained feeling. New pain joined the now familiar aches I carried from the previous evening's misadventure. I pulled myself into a sitting position against the sliding door. No door handle, no visible lock. I touched the bandage that had been wound around my head. The bandage was damp and sticky with blood. My misshapen noggin was fast becoming a phrenologist's nightmare. My ass hurt. Not my entire ass, but two distinct points on my right buttock ached with burns.

"Oh. My. God!" The high voice sang in three distinct words. "He's awake!"

"He's always been awake, dude," said the driver. "Hey dude," he shouted over his shoulder, "you OK?"

I tried answering him, but I still lacked total control over my tongue, fine motor skills still beyond my capabilities. I grunted what I hoped would be taken for an answer.

"Sorry, dude," the driver said. "We figured this was the only way to get you to come along. You're kind of a burly fucker and we didn't want to, like, do the whole violence scene."

I grunted again.

"You're welcome, dude!" the driver joyously replied. "We're off to see the wizard, man."

What wizard? A Ku Klux Klansman? The Wizard of Oz? Merlin?

"Do we get to zap him again?" the man with the high voice asked.

The driver laughed. "Yeah, little man. Why don't you climb back there with him and try to whack him. He'd take that stun gun away from you and stick it up your ass and play shock the monkey."

"Good . . . idea," I managed to say.

"Great, dude, you can, like, conversate, which is mostly quite excellent." The van turned off the oil and we bounced along a dirt road. I heard pings as stones bounced in the wheel wells and I smelled dust. The van stopped.

"Dude," the driver said, turning in his seat to face me, "we can do this a couple of different ways. You can be a good boy. That way we open the door, you walk out and have your sit-down. Or we can do it the hard way. There are some nasty motherfuckers out here who love to open a can of whoop-ass on dudes like you."

"Dudes like me?" I asked.

"Yeah, man, dudes who torture, kill, and oppress other species."

I still felt weak. I doubted that I could have won an arm-wrestling contest with a sixth grader. "I'll be a good boy."

"Excellent!" the driver said. "A wise choice. Now move away from the door, go sit with your back to the other side of the van."

The three men abandoned the front seat of the van. The cab light robbed me of my night vision. The side door slid open and a flashlight blinded me. Squinting, I slid along the floor of the van, dangled my legs out of the door, and stood. I wobbled, but my equilibrium and balance had returned. Two men flanked and supported me, leading me into an abandoned barn. A man sat at a small table in the center of the barn. A Coleman lantern burned; a soft circle of light glowed around the table.

Like the others he wore a ski mask and dark clothing. His clothing was baggy and he also wore gloves. I could not judge his height or his weight. And when he spoke his voice sounded computer-generated, synthesized. A man who obviously valued security and anonymity.

"I am Zed."

PETEM, People for the Equal Treatment of Every Mammal, vehemently disavow any connection with Zed and his provisional wing of animal rights warriors. Zed and his devoted followers have no compunction in resorting to violence to achieve their goals. Zed strikes and claims credit in PETEM's name. A spokesperson for PETEM issues a lukewarm denial and further explains that while the organization supports Zed's goals, it does not approve of his methods.

Zed earned the distinction of being the first animal rights activist to be honored with a spot on the FBI's Ten Most Wanted List. Zed began his actions by throwing paint on New York City women who wore fur coats. He then graduated to forcible entry at a number of animal testing labs. He released thousands of animals from a mink ranch, at the same time committing his first felonious assault. The actions escalated. He mailed a letter bomb to the owner of a cosmetics company, who lost his hands and then his life in the explosion. He torched a pharmaceutical lab. Two people died in the blaze. He sank a Zodiac boat carrying hunters bent on killing baby harp seals. Three died of hypothermia.

Inspectors at the FDA apprehended radical PETEM members aligned with Zed attempting to smuggle into the country antigens carrying hoof-and-mouth disease and mad cow disease. They confessed that they had been willing to introduce the devastating diseases in the hopes that America would throw off its nasty habit of consuming beef. Zed once threatened to bomb a McDonald's every week until the fast-food chain mended its ways, whatever that could be.

Their views extended beyond merely culinary concerns. PETEM also seeks the end of horse racing and dog racing, the dissolution of 4-H, banning the use of draft animals, and instituting codified animal rights that begin with changing the title on mandated licenses from "owner" to "guardian." They had also asked the Indianapolis Motor Speedway to stop serving milk to the winning driver of the Indy 500.

I am wary of zealots without regard to what side of the aisle they preach. Pro-lifers who think God directs murderous hands against doctors, the Buffalo Commons folks who want to tear people out of the heart of the country and return the grasslands to the bison, and enviros who spike trees or decide to live in them for a year—they all give me pause. Hell, I get tight-jawed when I'm accosted at the supermarket to sign a petition when all I want is to buy groceries. When Zed's name arises, fear replaces wariness.

What do you say after "I am Zed?" Nothing.

We sat in silence. Just when I thought I'd have to talk to Fred about maybe teaching me a new negotiation tactic, Zed spoke.

"You are a fortunate man, Wallace. Because we need you for our purposes, we will allow you to leave alive and intact."

"Something smells good," I said. "You guys barbecuing burgers?"

Nobody laughed. That's another thing about true believers, they don't laugh. Life for them is so grim, so many wrongs need to be remedied, and the world is such an awful place that they have no time to develop a sense of humor.

"You find that humorous?" Zed asked in his eerie techno-voice.

"Actually, no," I confessed.

"What you find humorous is the torture and murder of animals."

"Absolutely not, Zed. Don't pretend that you know me. You haven't the slightest idea about why I hunt and fish. Let's keep the preaching to a minimum and get on with business."

"I find you and your kind repulsive."

"And I find you and your kind hopelessly deluded. You kill people to save animals. You're a terrorist."

"We are freedom fighters!"

"You're no different than white supremacists, it's just that your vision of nirvana is different. They want to rid the world of blacks, Hispanics, and Jews. You want to rid the world of hunters, fishermen, and meat eaters."

"Not rid, reeducate."

"Great. That comforts me to no end. How will you do that, Zed? Concentration camps where we all learn the wisdom of eating tofu and sprouts? You are Pol Pot and Mao rolled into one."

"People must be saved from their own ignorance. Even the Bible supports our vegan lifestyle."

"God said, 'See, I give you all the seed-bearing plants that are upon the whole earth, and the trees with seed-bearing fruit, this shall be your food.' Genesis, chapter one, verse twenty-nine."

"I'm impressed, Wallace."

"Don't be. I've heard the argument before. But you conveniently ignore the preceding verse. After God creates Adam and Eve he says, 'Be fruitful and multiply, fill the earth and conquer it. Be masters of the fish of the sea, the birds of heaven and all living animals on the earth.' "

"We interpret those words as instructions to become stewards of the earth, protectors of all fish and animals, not their devourers and enslavers."

"But why are we debating the Bible?" I asked. "Even the devil can quote scripture. You, however, seem to have forgotten a rather important verse in Exodus."

"I believe you refer to chapter twenty, verse thirteen. 'Thou shalt not kill,' " Zed answered.

"My turn to be impressed." I nodded to Zed.

"A verse that countries and governments ignore in time of war, or conquest, or dispensing their versions of justice. We consider ourselves at war, Wallace. We are at war against those who eat the flesh of other animals and fish."

"News flash, Zed—we're carnivores."

"News flash, Wallace. Anthropologists have documented tribes and entire civilizations where only grains and fruits were consumed."

"Is that a fact? I heard that they recently discovered another."

"Really?"

"Yeah, scores of anorexic Hollywood actresses. This vegetarian trip is a lifestyle choice, an affectation. Homo sapiens are meat eaters. Way down deep in the collective unconsciousness we are hunter-gatherers."

"Then we must reprogram the collective unconsciousness."

"And if you succeed, what's next? Cats? The world's purest carnivores. Will you reprogram their instincts so that they prefer muesli to mice?"

"Nature will make its own way."

"Exactly my point. It's my nature to hunt and fish. People like me do more for nature and the environment than head cases like you."

"That's absurd."

"No, that's a fact. Over thirty million people purchase fishing licenses and eighteen million buy hunting licenses. Those fees are used to buy new habitat and improve existing resources. Ducks Unlimited has done more to preserve wetlands than the Sierra Club.

"And since we're into news flashes, let me give you another. Nothing dies of natural causes in the wild, Zed. In forests, jungles, rivers, and the oceans very few animals die of old age. They're killed and eaten by other animals.

"But you didn't go to all this trouble to debate me about our respective belief systems, did you?"

"You are correct," Zed said. "We did not." He remained silent for a moment, though I could hear his breathing through the device he used to disguise his voice. "I see that we would face an insurmountable challenge reeducating you, Wallace."

"Never happen, Zed. You'd have to kill me," I said.

"You are probably correct."

For the second time in as many days my life had been directly threatened. I never realized that so many different people wanted me dead.

I studied Zed intently. He remained still, his hands folded on the table, his feet flat on the ground. I did not observe any tics or mannerisms.

"To business then," Zed said. "We have a list of demands that we want you to present to Fred Lather."

"Fred doesn't do well with demands," I said. "No, that's not true. Let me rephrase that. Fred doesn't do well when people make demands of him. He's excellent in making demands on others. I think it's a rich-guy thing."

"Our first demand," Zed said, ignoring me. "The Carved L Ranch is to cease the slaughter of bison or the sale of bison for slaughter.

"Our second demand. The Carved L Ranch will no longer permit elk hunting or the hunting of any other mammals.

"Our third demand. The Carved L Ranch will no longer permit the hunting of birds."

"It's called wing shooting," I interjected.

"The fourth demand," Zed said. "The Carved L Ranch will no longer permit fishing in any fashion, including catch-and-release, which frankly we find even more cruel than other types of fishing.

"Our fifth and final demand. As punishment for the vast accumulated crimes against animals, because he has not given these fellow creatures equal treatment, Lather will donate fifty million dollars to PETEM."

"Let's see if I got this right," I said. "Stop raising bison for the table, no hunting, no wing shooting, no fishing, and write you happy warriors a check for fifty million?"

"You are correct."

"I know Fred quite well. I believe that I can answer for him, or at least tell you what I am quite certain his answers will be."

"Educate us, please."

As I answered I raised the fingers on my left hand. "No, no, no, no, and fuck you and the horse you didn't ride in on."

"Those are unproductive and foolish answers, Wallace. At present, because I do not believe you have the authority to speak for your employer, I choose to accept those as the ravings of a man who has a chemical imbalance brought on by a toxic diet."

"There's no need to get personal," I chided. "And to think we've gotten on so swimmingly to this point. That is, if I ignore being shocked into paralysis with a stun gun, receiving a head injury, and being kidnapped to hear you rant and rave in front of your fellow travelers. I'm going to give you a bit of advice, gratis. You can't make ridiculous demands on Fred Lather because you have nothing to negotiate with. You have no leverage."

"We do," Zed said. For the first time his hands unclasped. With his left hand he reached under the table and when it reappeared it held a telescopic steel baton. With a flick of his wrist, Zed extended the weapon to its full length.

I swiftly came to the conclusion that I was the only person in Montana who did not own a telescopic steel baton.

"Did you kill Elden Elderberry?" I asked.

"Forgive me if I choose not to incriminate myself. I will only state that Elderberry's death suits our purposes. He was executed while pursuing a barbaric and violent blood sport. Others who pursue these pastimes could be executed with just as much ease."

"Zed," I said, "forgive me if I'm not ready to buy into this particular charade. It's a big step going from throwing stones into pools to actually killing an angler because he's fishing."

In the last few years, one of PETEM's favorite tactics was the organized harassment of fly fishers. PETEM members threw stones in pools or waded noisily nearby to spoil the fishing. Their logic was if you're already not killing the fish, then maybe they could convince you to stop catching them at all.

"Not if you've killed before," Zed replied. "We will win, Wallace. You and I might not live to see it, but we shall succeed. Mankind will embrace an ethos that does not condone hunting or fishing. Once we accomplish the banning of blood sports we will work to cleanse everyone from eating animals and fish.

"You speak eloquently about your millions of fishermen and hunters. Our ranks pale by comparison, but we are well funded, focused, and quite organized. We will win the war.

"Please relay our demands to Lather."

"How will he communicate his answer?"

"Have him make the announcements through the media."

"I wouldn't hold my breath."

"In that case, let us hope that you or another person on the ranch is not taking the last of his."

My two escorts appeared next to me. I rose, and saying nothing, left the barn. They led me to the van and I climbed into the rear compartment. The sliding door closed behind me. Only the driver sat in the front.

"The Zedster is such an awesome dude," said the driver.

"A true humanitarian," I answered.

"He sure, like, cut you down to size, dude."

"Not hard to do when you've surrounded yourself with little toadies incapable of even hearing the other side of an argument. Tell you what, dude. Why don't you shut the fuck up and drive me to wherever it is you're supposed to drop me."

The driver stopped talking, or conversating, or whatever else he called it. We drove for only a few minutes.

The driver turned in his seat. "There's a screwdriver somewhere back there. When you find it you can unscrew this metal screen." He rattled it with his fingers. "I was supposed to leave you the key so that you could drive to your truck, which is about a mile down the road. But you were rude to me, so like, walk, dude." The driver opened his door, stepped into the night, and then slammed the door.

Removing eight large screws in total darkness is no easy task. By the time I finished I had barked and bloodied my knuckles and I had a pounding headache. I was hungry and dehydrated. When I finally did remove the last screw and pulled the metal mesh screen away, it was well past eleven. I walked the mile down the road to the parking lot.

A cloudless sky filled with stars eased my effort. I saw my breath in the chilled, damp air. Bright moonlight fell on the road.

I vowed that from here on I would exercise caution, so I didn't blunder into the parking lot and leap into the truck. My stealth paid off. I saw someone sitting in the passenger's seat of my truck. I searched for a weapon and selected a piece of deadfall, a couple of feet of spruce. I crouched and crept toward my truck. In the moonlight I saw Special Agent in Charge Sully Feib, once again asleep.

CHAPTER 13

MORDECAI SPEAKS

Tom McGuane's book *Some Horses*, hot tea, a slice of pie, and a blazing fire in the hearth. After two late evenings as the honored guest of a brace of psychopathic cult leaders of sorts, a quiet night in the cabin was literally what the doctor ordered.

Apple pie, my favorite. Though when it comes to pie I have two rules. It's all good. And it's always the right time for pie. Breakfast, lunch, dinner, and snack times at any hour of the day or night.

I sat at the kitchen island and pushed the fork through that first bite of pie when the telephone rang. I momentarily debated the wisdom of answering the phone. After 10:00 P.M. I never answer the phone, because only tragedy or emergency waits on the line. But it was only a little after eight so I felt safe. I placed the fork on the plate and answered the phone.

In the background I heard shouts, a slide guitar solo from a popular country-and-western song, breaking glass, and heavy breathing.

"Hey, Dahlgren!" a voice shouted over the noise. "It's Rusty!"

My college teammate, the weak-armed Tatum O'Neill, tended bar at Stacey's, the closest thing to a genuine cowboy bar in these parts.

Tatum worked a number of odd and minimum-wage jobs to supplement his equally meager salary as the quarterbacks and receivers coach at Montana State. He once entertained visions of roaming the sidelines as a head coach of a perennial Top 25 powerhouse. He had labored since we graduated in the relative obscurity of the Big Sky Conference, the prospects of a six-figure contract fading with each miserable Bobcats season.

Three nights a week he tied an apron around his waist and dispensed medicine to the patrons of Stacey's. The finely honed skills of a mixologist were not prerequisites for employment as a barkeep at Stacey's. Pull a tap lever and pour a shot. Occasionally you might actually be called upon to use tonic or ginger ale. You won't find any umbrellas or pineapple slices behind the bar, and nobody would dream of ordering a drink with Light-Dark rum.

"Hiya, Tatum!" I shouted back.

"Jeez, Dahlgren, there's no need to shout," Tatum shouted. "We got us a situation here. Think you ought to drive on down."

"Mordecai?" I asked. Stacey's reserves a special table with one chair for the foreman of the Carved L Ranch. Twenty years ago Mordecai must have ordered his usual, a draft and a shot of Old Bootstrap or some such appropriately named rotgut. Now, whenever he enters Stacey's, the bartender knows exactly what to serve, and as long as there is money on the table, to keep on serving it. Mordecai walks in, drinks to his heart's content, picks up his change, and staggers out of the bar, all without the benefit of uttering a single word.

"Yup!" Tatum shouted in reply.

"Passed out?" I asked.

"Lordy, Dahlgren, if you give me a chance I'll tell ya already!" Another loud crash drifted over the line. I faintly heard Shania Twain belting out a pre-Mutt Lange number. "Mordecai got into an argument with Brewster Duff and all hell's broke loose."

An argument requires at least two people yelling back and forth about whatever bone of contention they happen to be chewing over. And the possibility of C. Brewster Duff IV gracing Stacey's with his presence was equally astonishing.

"Horace is here with Buttram and they've got Mordecai and Ebon Jones in handcuffs! They're fixing to arrest them!" Ebon worked for Brewster and what he lacked in intelligence he more than made up for in brute strength.

I stared at my pie. My stitches itched and I avoided scratching them. I folded over the corner of a page of *Some Horses* to mark my place. "I'll be over in half an hour." I hung up.

I drove to Stacey's and pulled into the half-full parking lot. Not bad for Thursday evening. On Friday and Saturday nights Stacey's offers live music and the place is packed. In the old days, the real old days, the bar was known as Mae Ping's and enjoyed a reputation as a spot for those who wanted hard drinking interrupted by frequent fisticuffs. Old-timers say that on any night you could usually fish a tooth out of the sawdust on the floor.

I walked in and no one turned to see who had come through the door. Most of the patrons sat huddled at the bar, hunched over glasses of beer, a few halfheartedly watched wrestling on the television. A few others sat at scattered tables. Mordecai's usual table had been reduced to a pile of splinters, and Tatum, wielding a broom, pushed together wood, broken glass, and sawdust.

"Leave me finish up here and we'll set a spell," Tatum said. I found a table and "set" down.

Tatum finished his chores with the push broom. He stepped behind the bar and ministered to the needy and then came back around to my table.

"A regular old donnybrook is all I can say," Tatum said, still without dispensing any of the niceties of civilized conversation like "Hello" or "Can I get you anything?"

"Mordecai came in about six-thirty or so and ordered up his usual the way he does. He had three, no . . . four rounds, I bought him back his last shot and beer. He sat there minding his own business. And then Brewster Duff comes strolling in."

"Brewster a regular?" I asked.

"Not hardly! I tend bar at them African Brothers Society meetings is how I know him. He's a tiny little feller, you know."

"I know."

"Got the tiniest little feet I ever seen on a growed man. 'Course, he has those lift things in his shoes to raise him up some. Tiny little feet, I swear."

Tatum likes to tell a story and I knew better than to rush him. If he suspected you didn't want the unabridged version he would get huffy and omit the most important detail in the tale.

"Anyways, Brewster comes in and slaps a fifty-dollar bill on the bar and says drinks for everyone, in that voice of his. Like he's president of the damned chamber of commerce or something."

"I think he is the president of the chamber of commerce," I said.

Tatum thought for a moment. "Now that you mention it, I think you're right. Well, you know what voice I mean, all happy and like ain't it wonderful, old Brewster's here, and what a great guy he is, that kinda voice. I'm sure he expected everyone to thank him and clap him on the back and toast him. He got a few grunts, maybe a belch or two in thanks. Mordecai, he throws down his shot as soon as he sees Brewster walk in, the one I bought him, and he chases it with his beer. He reaches down for his money. He's fixing to leave, no doubt about it.

"Brewster grabs hold of a chair and swings it to Mordecai's table. He says to me, 'A glass of your finest.' Finest what, I ask? And he says, 'Scotch.' I pour him a Chivas, which is the best we got. Darn bottle's been around nearly as long as I have. I carry the glass over to the table 'cause it's apparent that Brewster isn't going to get off his duff . . . oh, no pun intended . . . and save me the trip. I hear him say, 'Why

Mordecai, won't you allow me to buy you a drink? I came in here especially to see you.'

"Mordecai, he's got his arms folded across his chest and he's pushed his chair back away from the table. He's got his hat on, he never takes it off, don't even know if he's got hair under that hat. Does he?"

"Yes," I said, "full head of hair."

"He's got that hat on and he's staring daggers at Brewster. Pure hatred. 'Course, Brewster don't see it or pays it no mind and keeps right on rattling away. He's got his arms and hands flapping while he's talking, so it's hard for me to put the coaster and the drink down in front of him. We usually don't use coasters here but seeing as how he ordered a Chivas and all, I figured what the hey, be civilized, use a coaster.

"Excuse me, got to take care of some fellers." Tatum dove behind the bar and dispersed shots and beers to the faithful. He returned, wiping his hands with a towel, but neglecting to bring along anything to wet my whistle.

"Did you know that Mordecai once worked on Duff's ranch? Didn't think so. Worked for Duff Three, actually, and the day they planted him and the present Brewster became the head honcho, Mordecai hitched up his Airstream and drove it over to his new job on the Carved L. Seems like he never cared for Brewster.

"I mention this because while he's flapping his arms and preventing me from serving him the finest, he's trotting out a line of bullcrap the likes I never heard before.

"Where are my manners? Can I get you something to drink?"

"No, I'm fine."

"Wouldn't be any trouble," Tatum said.

"Naw."

"Really? You look parched."

"Really." I exercised every shred of willpower I possessed to refrain from reaching across the table and choking my former teammate.

"Where was I? Yeah, right. Brewster's spouting on about how he intends to buy Lather out, buy the Carved L Ranch. Says Lather's going to sell, how they never wanted his kind in Montana, rich boy and his rich liberal friends, bunch of tree huggers and faggots and such like. Brewster says he knows the Carved L's been losing livestock on account of Lather's poor management. Knows it's not Mordecai's fault, no reflection on Mordecai, everybody knows he's a top hand. No sir, Lather's spending too much money on the river to pay any attention to the important business of ranching. 'When I own the Carved L,' he says, 'by God, when I own the Carved L, thing's are going to be different.'

"Dahlgren, you know how some people fall in love with the sound of their own voices? How they just talk on and on?" He paused and waited for my answer.

"Yes," I said, "I know. Annoying, isn't it?"

"Darn straight! That's Brewster. Thinks when he talks the wisdom of Solomon spills forth. Never heard a man yammer so much and say so little. 'Course, he not only rambles on, but he's ignoring what's going on right across the table. Mordecai's getting some color in his face, a terrible color. Red as a beet, like one of them Looney Toon fellers. I expected to see steam come pouring outta his ears and shirt collar, I swear. Them eyes of his squint down. He's working on a powerful anger.

"Then Brewster pops the question, only it's more like a statement, really. 'Mordecai, my old friend,' he says, 'when I buy the Carved L, I'd like you to stay on as foreman, yes, sir.' "

Tatum paused, shaking his head and smiling, remembering and savoring the moment.

"Mordecai, he unfolds his arms and he grips the table, veins standing out on his hands. He stares at Brewster and for the first time maybe Brewster figures he stayed in this poker game one card too long. Mordecai spoke. Been here nearly since we graduated from State, Dahlgren. Seen Mordecai hundreds of times, maybe thousands. Never once heard him speak a single word. Most closed-mouth sumbuck I ever seen. Didn't even know he could speak. Pardon me 'cause I don't use this kind of language but I ain't gonna sugarcoat what he said. Needs to be quoted accurate.

" 'Fuck you,' he says, 'you little pisspot.' "

Five words. A filibuster for Mordecai. He might need to put his lips in traction.

"Then he stands up, pushes past me, and picks Brewster right up out of his chair. Picks him up by his collar and his belt and carries him to the door and throws him out into the street. I never even served him his Chivas.

"Mordecai, he walks back to the table, reaches into his pocket, pulls some money out, smooths a few bills, and sets down. I know what's good for me so I pull him a draft and pour him a . . . all right, Chester, hold your water."

Tatum rose again and returned to the bar. I looked around and counted heads. About twenty hard cases. "This round's on me," I said. "Give everybody a drink."

A couple of the men almost fell off their stools. For the second time in a single evening an angel had landed on their besotted shoulders. Could this be heaven? Tatum lined up the drinks, counted them, and slid them across the bar. "That's mighty generous of you, Dahlgren. Be twenty-nine dollars when you're ready to square up. I'm sure the boys appreciate it, don't you, boys?"

At the far end of the bar someone lustily broke wind.

"Back to my story. I pull Mordecai a draft and pour out a snort and put both on his table. Ebon Jones comes flying through the door. He couldn't have looked more like a bull if he'd been blowing snot. Huffing and puffing and his arms swimming like he can't hardly wait to get to Mordecai and tear him apart. Mordecai waits until Ebon's about five feet away, and Mordecai throws the entire beer into Ebon's face. Beer, glass, the whole thing.

"Ebon's blinded like and he tries to stop but he's got momentum working against him. Arms still windmilling, trying to wipe blood and beer outta his eyes, and he crashes into the table. Breaks it like it were kindling.

"Me, I'm dialing nine-one-one, calling out the cavalry. Then I called you. Somehow Mordecai managed to stay out of Ebon's clutches, but they continued to bust the place up. Behind the bar I got one of them steel baton things, like a high-tech blackjack, slick little thing, but I ain't in no hurry to break it out, no sir. Figure somebody grab it and violate me with it.

"Horace comes in with Buttram, Buttram wearing one of them clear plastic riot helmets and slapping his billy club in his hand and talking all high like Barney Fife. Horace, he just unbuckles his holster, takes out his pistol, and slides one in the chamber. 'Ebon, Mordecai. That's enough,' he says. And they stop. Magic, I tell you, pure magic. Had Buttram cuff 'em and arrested the pair. Like watching an episode of *Cops*, I swear."

"Where's Brewster through all this?"

"Once he flew out the door I never saw him again. I'm sure he sent Ebon in to kick Mordecai's butt, but he's too smart to stick around and watch."

I handed Tatum two twenty-dollar bills. "Keep the change, Tatum," I said, "I owe you one."

"You don't owe me anything," Tatum said, "we were teammates."

I paused. "You know a guy named Axel, has swastikas tattooed here and here?" I asked.

"One of them militia types, right?"

"That's the one. He come in here?"

"Ever' once in a while. Real jerk if you ask me."

"Could you call me if he comes in?"

"Sure thing, Dahlgren."

I drove to the police station and parked. The desk sergeant nodded and buzzed me through. "Horace is waiting on you," he said. "You know the way."

I hadn't seen Horace since he stiffed me for lunch at The Cowboy Vey Deli. "Christ on a crutch, Dahlgren," he said. "What's happened to you?"

"Doesn't Agent Sully keep you up to speed?"

"He told me about your visit with our favorite general, but I haven't seen him all day. He called in late last night and had the graveyard shift run a pair of plates for him."

"I know. I was with him when he called."

"Sit down. If I had any liquor in here I'd offer you a snort."

"I'm on the wagon, doctor's orders."

"Are those stitches?"

I touched the side of my head. "Yeah," I said. "I fell."

"Likely story," Horace grunted.

"It's the truth. I fell after a little wisp of a girl who happened to be an animal rights terrorist stuck a stun gun in my ass and zapped me."

Horace narrowed his eyes and drummed his fingers on the top of his desk. He sat back in the chair, rubbed the bristles of his short hair, and then clasped his hands behind his neck.

"Maybe you better tell me what went on," he said.

I did. I told him about my conscious but paralytic trip by van to the abandoned barn, about my chat with the delightful Zed, and my walk back to the truck where I found the sleeping federal policeman.

When I saw that it was Feib sleeping in wait rather than another PETEM guerrilla, I tossed the spruce branch to the ground and knocked on the window. Feib awoke. I hadn't startled him. His eyes opened and he slowly turned his head toward me, a paragon of nonchalance. The eyes widened when he saw the bandage wrapped around my head.

He held a Glock in his right hand, index finger resting outside the trigger guard. He unlocked the door and stepped into the chill air. He holstered the Glock, reached into the rear cab, and retrieved his suit jacket.

"This is getting to be a habit, Agent Feib," I said.

"What is?"

"Whenever I return from an unpleasant evening I seem to find you asleep."

"I was not asleep."

"Resting your eyes, perhaps?"

"What happened to you?"

"I spent an evening with another psycho," I replied. "This time PETEM sponsored the evening's entertainment, and the master of ceremonies was Zed."

"Zed."

"Yes, Zed. I was fishing and when I came off the river I found a green Volvo parked close to my truck." I gave him the details up until I was unceremoniously loaded into the back of the van.

"Did you happen to get the license plate on the van?"

"I can do better than that, I can take you to the van."

"First let me have a look." He took a tiny flashlight from the inside pocket of his suit jacket. He unwound the bandage and examined my scalp wound. "Head wounds bleed quite a bit, but this time things are as bad as they look. Give me the keys, I'll drive you to the hospital."

"I don't think terrorist assaults are covered by my HMO."

Feib held out his hand. "The keys are under the driver's seat," I said.

Feib walked around to the driver's side of the truck and then had to wait until I climbed in and unlocked the door. He drove to the van, parked behind it with the headlights illuminating the license plates. He made a call on his cell phone.

"Sergeant, this is Special Agent Sully Feib, FBI. I'd like you to run two sets of plates for me. A green Volvo and a Dodge Econoline, both

Montana plates . . ." He gave the numbers. "Thank you, yes, as soon as possible."

I finished my story as we drove into town.

"The driver of the van, the man who kept calling you 'dude' is Dustin Rhodes. We've nicknamed him the Silver Surfer," Feib said. "Born and raised in the San Fernando Valley. Parents are still stuck in the sixties. The driver of the Volvo could be his sister, Wanda. They have worked with Zed since the beginning."

"So who is Zed?"

"We don't know. Even in his spray-paint days he always wore a ski mask. In the last few months he has become obsessed with security. You have helped us more than you know."

"How?"

"We now know that Zed is left-handed and can quote scripture. That will help the profilers. You also confirmed our suspicion that he is operating in Montana."

"What's he doing here?"

"Montana offers a number of targets of opportunity. The Federation of Fly Fishers holds its annual convention in Livingston in August. Zed also threatened to dispatch anyone who kills straying bison in a similar fashion. And he wants to free the bears at the Grizzly Discovery Center."

"He gets no argument from me on that one."

"That is what makes our job more difficult. Most people agree with an aspect of Zed's agenda."

Feib's cell phone rang. He answered and after a yes or two and a thank-you, he hung up.

"The Volvo is registered to Straw Fields and the van belongs to a veterinarian, Monica Jackson," Feib reported.

"Fields owns one of those New Age shops in Big Sky," I said. "Crystals, candles, aromatherapy, massage oils. He's also the local PETEM bigwig. I've had dealings with him. Don't know the vet."

"In the last half hour both of them reported their vehicles stolen. A remarkable coincidence. Tell me about Fields."

"Fields shows up a couple of times a year at the main gate to the ranch, protesting something or another. Fred invited Tom Brokaw to fish the ranch last October, and sure enough, Fields and his true believers are out there doing their thing, arms linked together, singing songs, chanting, waving signs.

"The Carved L has been a favorite target of theirs since Fred bought the place. PETEM hates Fred. Zed could have killed Elderberry, it does fit."

Feib sighed and slowly shook his head. "You are determined to earn that junior agent badge."

"Zed showed me one of those telescopic steel batons, the murder weapon. Makes sense in a bizarre way."

"The fact that he knows what the murder weapon is does bother me; however, PETEM and Zed did not kill Elderberry."

"How can you be so sure?"

"Because it doesn't make sense. Look at their demands. No hunting, fishing, and write us a check. Opportunistic to be sure. Imagine if they are successful in getting Lather to agree. They not only advance their agenda but they send shock waves throughout the western states. Landowners think that if PETEM can get to Lather, they can get to anyone. PETEM could effectively stop hunting and fishing on millions of acres of habitat, all done in a low-risk, high-reward campaign. Tonight has all the earmarks of a hastily executed operation requiring minimal effort."

We pulled into the hospital parking lot.

"Maybe you should explain how you ended up resting your eyes in my truck," I said. "You guys following me?"

"If we had been following you we would have seen what happened. We would have arrested Zed. That is a very high priority for the bureau.

“No, we are not following you. We did, however, attach a sensor to your truck after we searched it yesterday. An off-the-shelf commercial product, the same sensor we use to monitor our own vehicles. We can track your location, tell whether the engine is running, even if the doors are opened. We became concerned this evening when you opened the doors and never started the engine.

“I sent an agent to check and he reported that he found blood near your vehicle. You had us worried.”

“How touching,” I said. “Did you ever think to ask how I feel about all this?”

“No, and I also did not have to tell you anything. I could just as well have fed you a line about how we happened to come by your vehicle. I chose to tell you the truth.”

A sedan pulled into the hospital parking lot and stopped behind us. Feib got out of the truck, but before he closed the door he leaned in. “Get that wound examined. Everything has been taken care of, courtesy of Uncle Sam.”

CHAPTER 14

JOLLY RANCHERS

Horace opened a desk drawer and removed a deck of playing cards. He shuffled and dealt me eleven cards to his ten. Two-handed gin. I continued recounting a day in the life of Dahlgren Wallace.

The emergency room nurse had ordered me to take my shirt off, don a sleeveless hospital gown, open in the back, and then lie down on the examining table. She reminded me of the gruff waitresses you find in diners named "Mom's."

The emergency room physician, Dr. Raj Patel, greeted me with an "Oh, my! Are you going to be telling me now that I should be seeing the other gentleman?"

"The other gentleman was a not-so-gentle woman."

"A big woman?"

"I think she went about 115 pounds."

"She must have been a hellion, oh dear," Patel said. "I will be irrigating this wound, then I will be shaving the area around it and then closing it with many stitches."

Unlike the nurse, Patel had a pleasant bedside manner. He clucked while sewing the wound, muttering "This is truly a nasty cut." He had numbed the left side of my head with a local anesthetic, but I could still feel each tug as he closed the wound.

"Eighteen stitches," he pronounced. He stepped back and admired his handiwork. "I am like a tailor," he said. "Beautiful stitches. You need not concern yourself about a scar, though; with the hair, when it grows back, everything will be covered."

Patel insisted that I remain in the hospital overnight. A precautionary measure, he said. "Repeated head trauma is definitely not what this doctor ordered, oh, no!" He gave me an antibiotic and a topical cream to prevent infection. "I suggest that you take the wagon for the next few days. No drinking," he said, "and if I were you I'd stay away from that woman." He laughed. "Who knows what she will do if she gets more angry with you."

When I was discharged from the hospital I still felt like the left side of my head weighed more than the right. I drove to the cabin, took the pills, did not operate a motor vehicle or heavy equipment, and slept most of the day.

"I'm going down with two," Horace said.

I counted my cards. "Seventeen," I said. Horace wrote down the score and I collected the cards and took my turn as dealer. "Those pills knocked me out. I woke up around four and went to eat at Sy's place. Then I drove back to my place and I had just sat down to eat a slice of apple pie when Tatum called me. By the way, any chance I can take Mordecai back to the ranch?"

"You bring along a ranch check?"

"You know I always carry one."

"Five thousand ought to do it."

"Mordecai been charged?"

"Absolutely. The belligerent drunk's trifecta—public intoxication, disturbing the peace, and assault. If he'd been singing 'My Way,' he'd've hit the superfecta. Goddamn song's the national anthem of drunks.

"I expect the judge will be amenable to tossing everything out if the parties agree to pay for damages. I don't think Ebon or Brewster will be pressing any charges. Embarrassing enough what happened to them."

Horace beat me soundly. My aching head wasn't in the game. I kept thinking about something Tatum said that Brewster said. In my experience, raconteurs—and Tatum qualifies as a bona fide raconteur—have the uncanny ability to remember conversations nearly word for word. Brewster told Mordecai "how they never wanted his kind in Montana," referring to Fred. Almost identical to what I had read in the death threat letter Sherman had shown me the morning before.

Duff not only wanted to buy the Carved L Ranch, he might be willing to go to extralegal lengths to do so. I never figured Duff to be that ruthless or stupid. Also, in my experience most people with a Roman numeral after their names lack ambition. By the time III or IV wets his nappies, the trust funds bulge with cash.

And I also kept reviewing my meeting earlier with Sy. When I had walked into The Cowboy Vey Deli earlier that day, the entire room went silent. Only a few early diners, Sy, and one of the college kids he employs were in the deli, but they all stopped talking to stare at me. With part of my head shaved and bathed in Betadine, assorted bruises visible on my face, and a slight limp, I cut quite the figure. That and my recent appearance on the front page of the *Daily Chronicle* lent additional drama to my entrance.

"Chicken soup," Sy said. "No arguments." He turned to the thin, bespectacled young man who wore a knitted yarmulke. "Aaron, please bring it in the back." Sy took my elbow and led me to the back of his shop.

"You are looking more like a murder victim than a murderer," he said.

"I feel the way I look," I said.

"So, how does a nice *goyische* boy like you collect all these battle wounds?"

I told Sy about my late evenings with the Montana Militia and PETEM.

"Your government at work," Sy pronounced when I completed my monologue.

"How do you figure that?" I asked.

"You mentioned the FBI agent felt that you could be useful to their investigation. You run in so many circles, you know everyone in town, everyone loves Dahlgren."

"Ferris and Zed? I can feel the love."

"You have been used. Ill-used, I might add."

"I couldn't agree more."

Aaron knocked and delivered the chicken soup, pausing to stare at my various wounds.

"Then what do you intend to do about it?" Sy asked when Aaron returned to the front of the shop.

"What do you mean?"

"I mean, what do you intend to do about it? You know who the malefactors are, yes?"

"Yes."

"What is it that all those football coaches say before a big game?" Sy asked. "When they want to sound like they have an IQ larger than their hat size? A good offense is the best defense, right?"

"A variation of that." I said. "They might also say a good defense is the best offense."

"You're exasperating," Sy snorted. "You need to work this investigation like you play chess."

"Whoa. Slow down, Sy. Who said anything about an investigation?"

"*Oy*," Sy said, rolling his eyes toward the ceiling and raising his hands in supplication. "It's like talking to a block of wood. The only person who doesn't know he's part of an investigation is you. The FBI arrests you in an extremely public manner. Front-page news. Film at eleven news. Where did they print the story that you were released? On the same page as the animal shelter adoptions. The Nazi cowboys think you're involved. The animal rights group thinks you're involved. Who else would make the same conclusion?"

"I see your point."

"Do you? If so, then you must go on the offensive. You bring the battle to them. Attack, attack, attack. Time for you to plant your boots into someone else's *tuchis*."

I remembered the words of Mel, one of the Spam Brothers. I now had something to be angry about.

I wrote the check to bail out the ranch foreman and followed Horace into the holding cells. Mordecai sat on the bunk, bent over at the waist, staring at the floor, still wearing his hat. Horace unlocked his cell and Mordecai rose and walked out.

Ebon occupied the next cell over and one closer to the exit. Ebon sat on the floor, a real jailhouse pose. When he saw the ranch foreman, who had bested him at Stacey's, he began to bellow. "Shames!" he shouted. "The next time I see you I'm gonna fucking astigmatize you!"

Horace barely got out his admonition for Ebon to shut up when Mordecai punched the bars of the cell with the side of his hand. Ebon leaped to his feet and grabbed the bars with his meaty hands.

"Goddamn you, Mordecai," Horace said. "Stop teasing the animals."

"Ebon," I said, facing him. Horace and Mordecai continued walking toward the exit. "Could you do me a favor?"

"Huh?" he grunted, his eyes darting from Mordecai to me.

"Need you to pass along a message to Brewster."

Ebon squinted at me.

"Tell Brewster that the proctologist called. They found his head."

Horace laughed, Mordecai wheezed, and Ebon stared at me, certain that his boss had been insulted but not understanding how.

Horace walked Mordecai out of the station and he told the foreman that all the bars in the county were off-limits. Mordecai was to head straight home. "Conditions of release," Horace said. "Don't make me come out again." Mordecai nodded. I drove him back to Stacey's so he could pick up the ranch Jeep.

Naturally we drove in silence. I pulled into the parking spot next to the Jeep. "Mordecai," I said. The ranch foreman's hand paused on the door handle and he turned his head slowly. The brim of his hat was pulled low so he had to raise his chin to see me.

"You think Duff has anything to do with the bison being shot?"

He pursed his lips and raised an eyebrow. I read that as noncommittal.

"How about the poisonings?"

Mordecai paused for a long moment. He drew in a deep breath. He shrugged.

"One last thing," I said. "I heard about what went on in Stacey's. Wish I could have seen it is all. Better yet, wish I were sitting right here when Brewster flew out of the door. And Ebon Jones! You kicked his ass and never laid a hand on him."

I saw Mordecai smile the first smile I had ever seen on his face in the four years we had worked together on the ranch.

" 'Preciate it," he said, and he got out of the truck.

That made seven words in an evening. Mordecai would be mute for weeks to come.

The next morning I drove to the Carved L for breakfast.

Even before I sat down to breakfast all I could think about was lunch. On the third Friday of every month the Gallatin County Cattlemen's Guild meets for lunch at the Gallatin Gateway Inn. The railroad hotel enjoyed its heyday in the 1920s and '30s. Airplanes and interstate highways reduced rail travel to the phobic and hopelessly sentimental. Convenience in the form of Howard Johnson's motels and Magic Fingers replaced luxury and the inn fell into disrepair. A recent restoration resulted in a charming, purely American hotel.

Forty or fifty stalwarts, more titular than actual ranchers, wallowed in the delightful beef dish created by the inn's chef. Most of the guild members knew only the business of ranching, eugenics, yields, feed specifications, land leases, commodity trading, hedge accounts, and laptop computers. The actual breeding, calving, castrating, branding, and mending fence remained necessary evils performed by men in love with the idea of being cowboys. And because they loved it, the wealthy lairds need not pay them a princely wage when a minimum one would do.

If I didn't know any better I might have assumed that Sherman hadn't moved in the last two days. On his visits to the Carved L he wore what he considered appropriate ranch attire; a tailored denim shirt, Polo blue jeans, and Bally loafers without socks. He had his newspapers arrayed in front of him as he avidly checked the scores in his sports page, the stock market reports.

"Heard we had a little excitement last night," Fred said, as he looked over a true sports page, probably reading the box score of his baseball team. "I'm feeling southern today, Dahlgren, biscuits and gravy. The Big Guy pitched a two-hitter." He folded the newspaper and looked at me. "Goddamn! Are those stitches?"

"Eighteen of them, to be precise, compliments of your favorite animal rights group."

"Straw Fields did that to you?" Fred asked. "Why, that herbal-tea-sipping pissant must have used the biggest fucking crystal in his shop!"

"No, it was a bit more serious than that," I said, "but that story can wait. I had to write a good-sized check for Mordecai's bail."

"Tore up Stacey's, did he?"

"Stacey's has seen worse. Few tables, several glasses, and a chair. Mordecai felt obligated to defend the honor of the Carved L."

We were served the biscuits and gravy. Real biscuits and real gravy. That means both made from scratch. Nobody pours gravy like this out of a can. Pork sausage and grease, evaporated milk, cayenne pepper, and flour to thicken it. I stared at that plate and heard my arteries harden.

"Ain't this special?" Fred asked, his accent nearly as thick as the gravy. "He's not normally a mean drunk. Do you know what got him going?"

"Brewster Duff got him going," I said. "Seems like Brewster wants to buy you out."

"I told you that yesterday morning," Sherman said, still not bothering to tear his eyes away from *Investor's Business Daily*.

"You certainly did," I answered. "However, I sensed that you thought Duff's offer was a joke. You're not taking him seriously."

"I ran a complete set of financials on Duff," Sherman said. "He doesn't have the kind of money to buy Freddie out."

"He's the second-largest rancher in the county," Fred said, "and it galls him to no end."

"It's an ego thing with him," I said. "I don't know anything about his financial wherewithal, but I know that if he buys the Carved L he becomes the single largest private landowner in Montana. Combine the Lazy D and Fred's ranch and you've got one of the largest ranches in the West."

"I know that," Fred said.

"You might be ready to sell the ranch once you hear about PETEM's plan for the Carved L," I said.

I asked Sherman if he planned on eating his biscuits and gravy. He said no and slid his plate across the table.

I relayed PETEM's absurd demands. I told Fred and Sherman about the depths of Duff's desire to own the Carved L.

"Well fuck me!" Fred exclaimed. "You know, it's getting so a guy can't enjoy being rich anymore. Everybody lined up wanting something. The Nazis want ten thousand acres, PETEM wants me to turn the ranch into an animal sanctuary, and Duff wants to steal the place. Least Duff doesn't want me dead."

"Don't know if you can say that with absolute certainty," Sherman said. "If what Dahlgren says is accurate, then Duff could very well be behind the death threats."

"You never met Brewster Duff, right?" Fred asked. Sherman shook his head. "I've taken shits bigger than Brewster Duff. He lacks physical courage. No way he sent me those letters or that e-mail."

"He may lack physical courage," Sherman agreed, "but he has enough money to hire courage. What about this Ebon Jones character?"

"The only thing Ebon could do with a computer is lift it," I said. "The man has a room-temperature IQ."

"And it's a cold room," Fred said. "Naw, Ebon is strictly muscle, somebody to help Brewster into his booster seat. Besides, Brewster's smart. He may write threatening letters, but he would address them to the *Daily Chronicle*. This sure is a funny situation."

"How so?" Sherman asked.

"All these bloodsuckers and bottom-feeders making demands and threats and all of them taking advantage of Elden's death. Seems like everyone wants me to think they done the evil deed."

"That's what Agent Feib thinks," I said.

"You and that FBI boy getting to be asshole buddies, huh?" Fred asked.

"And to think I have you to thank for the introduction, Fred."

"Ouch!" Fred said. I was pleased that he still had a shred of guilt regarding his less than honorable decision to throw me to the federal wolves. "All I'm telling you is that you got to be careful with the federal government. You may think he's your friend, but he's got his own agenda."

"Fred, we're not dating," I said, "and I haven't introduced him to my folks yet. But I think he really cares about me. After someone beats the living shit out of me, he's right there to offer moral support."

"Be careful," Fred repeated. "That's all I'm saying."

"I intend to be less careless," I said, "especially around green Volvos."

"How do you feel?" Sherman asked.

"Brittle." I had not felt like this since my football days at Montana State. After a particularly punishing game, and at my position that meant most games, I would be creaky, sore, bruised, and brittle until the middle of the next week. That was years ago. My recuperative powers had only waned.

Then it struck me. Why was Sherman asking? Soliciting information about anyone's general welfare was out of character for him. The next thing you know Sherman would be defending indigents pro bono.

"Why do you ask?" I asked.

"I wondered if you thought you would be up to snuff by Tuesday?" Sherman said.

I turned to Fred. "Did I miss the memo? Is Billy running the ranch these days?"

"No," Fred said, "we're just a bit anxious. We invited Brigham Briggs out to the ranch. He's the interim chairman of VideoComp."

"Fisherman?"

"Degenerate fly fisherman," Fred said. "He fishes all over the world. Argentina, New Zealand, Christmas Island, even Kamchatka. Boy's got some chops."

"We are proceeding with the purchase of VideoComp," Sherman said. "Briggs's trip is an important step in our due diligence process. If we like what we hear—"

"And there's no reason to expect that we won't," Fred interjected.

"—then we will proceed with a formal offer to Susi to purchase half of her holdings."

Fred had been willing to pay one billion dollars to the Mormon Church for its 10 percent stake. What would he offer Susi for more than twice that much stock?

"We've continued to purchase shares in the open market," Fred said. "My interest in VideoComp may be Wall Street's worst-kept secret. VideoComp is also attracting other suitors."

"We know that Disney and Time Warner have acquisition teams assigned to explore a possible buyout."

"And I'd be flabbergasted if Murwell's acquisitive fingerprints weren't discovered in the near future," Fred said. "Imagine shelling out a billion to buy a soccer team."

"Time is of the essence," Sherman said. "This deal is going to be compressed. Briggs flies in Monday evening. We're planning dinner and informal discussions. Tuesday you take him fishing. That evening and Wednesday we start the serious arm wrestling."

"I take it that with a first name of Brigham, he's a Mormon?" I asked.

"Yes, but what's that got to do with anything?" Sherman asked.

"As a rule, Dahlgren doesn't like Mormons," Fred said.

"I asked because I need to know what to place in the cooler," I replied, ignoring Fred's comment.

"What do you mean, the cooler?"

"Mormons, as a rule," I said, now looking right at Fred, "drink only decaffeinated beverages. And they do not drink alcoholic beverages. So it's out with the Cokes and Coors and in with the Sprite. Just Briggs?"

"For the fishing, yes. He's bringing his chief financial officer and the company's investment banker. While you're fishing the two of them will be working with Billy. And, Dahlgren—"

I raised my hands in mock protest. "I know, Fred. The royal treatment." I stood to leave. "Actually, I'm looking forward to taking Brigham fishing."

I spent the remainder of the morning going over the gear. I washed and polished both boats and re-covered them with tarps. Briggs would probably bring his own outfit, but I checked the rods and reels. I stripped about twenty-five feet of fly line from each reel, checking for nicks and breaks. I took a quick inventory of flies and made a note to order grasshopper patterns for the late summer and early fall. I would need to buy new tippet material on my next visit to Bozeman.

Using my room at the ranch, I showered and changed into khaki pants, a button-down blue shirt, the blazer, and cowboy boots. I drove to the Gallatin Gateway Inn to attend the monthly ranchers' get-together.

Fred is actually a member of the Gallatin County Cattlemen's Guild, though not one in good standing. He pays his dues, donates prizes for the annual fund-raising event, and makes a few outrageous bids at the auction. His schedule prevents him from making most of the meetings, and common sense precludes attendance at the others. The last time he attended one of the luncheons Fred said, "I feel like the proverbial turd in the punchbowl."

Fred raised bison in the land of cattle. And that wasn't all the GCCG members held against him, despite his offer to pay for brucellosis vaccinations. Nearly all the members owned ranches that had been in their families for four and five generations. Over a hundred years on the land. In their minds Fred was a nouveau riche southerner playing at ranching.

As I did in many local associations and organizations, I acted as Fred's proxy and I usually made it a point to attend the Cattlemen's Guild luncheon at least once a quarter. I came for the food.

I ordered a glass of ginger ale at the no-host bar and surveyed the room. Knots of men, drinks in hand, engaged in animated and hearty conversation. You need a stout back to work this room because someone is always slapping it. You couldn't smell the testosterone, but the room had the air of a high school locker room.

Most wore western suits, string ties, and cowboy boots made of exotic fauna. Even the associate members, a handful of attorneys and a pair of accountants, dressed the part. Every third Friday of the month was a great day to be a cattleman.

I made my move as the members took their seats for lunch. I worked my way near the circle of men buzzing around Brewster Duff, and with a few apologies and pushes I managed to sit next to him at the table.

"Why, Dahlgren, what a pleasant surprise," Duff said.

Pretending that I didn't know where the sound had come from, I searched the room at my eye level, and then dropped my gaze to Duff.

"Brewster," I said, clapping him on the back and driving his chest into the table, "I didn't see you down there." I put out my hand, and Duff, a cool customer, laughed and shook it.

"You boys all know Dahlgren Wallace, right? He works for Buffalo Fred," Duff said. The other six men around the table dutifully laughed. "That's what we call Fred Lather, Buffalo Fred."

"How clever," I said.

A waiter placed a plate in front of Duff. I was next. A large filet the size of my fist sat in the center of the plate. Green and black peppercorns, onions, and bacon covered the beef. Garlic mashed potatoes and fresh green beans surrounded the filet.

"Excuse me," I said. The waiter paused. "By any chance, do you have this cut in buffalo?" Duff guffawed and clapped me on the back, allowing everyone at the table to laugh along.

"Dahlgren has a wicked sense of humor," Duff said.

I pointed to Duff's drink, a smoky scotch. "What are you drinking, Brewster?"

He covered the cut-glass tumbler with his hand. "No thanks, Dahlgren, I've had my fill. Restrict myself to only a short one at lunch. Business demands, you know."

"You misunderstood me, Brewster. I didn't ask because I wanted to buy you another. I'm just curious. What are you drinking?"

"Glenfiddich."

The rest of the table gave a collective "Ooh!" in appreciation.

"Would you happen to know if they pour Glenfiddich at Stacey's?" I took a bite of the filet. It was so wonderful that I almost closed my eyes.

"How would I know that?" he asked.

"I heard on good authority that you were in there last night, trying to hire Mordecai Shames. Word is that you left in a hurry."

It got quiet at our table. Fork-poised-in-midair quiet. Stop-cutting-the-meat quiet. Mangled-Dahlgren-walks-into-The Cowboy Vey Deli quiet. Ranchers abide by an unwritten code that includes not hiring hands off a neighbor's ranch. If what I said was true, Duff was guilty, at least, of a breach of etiquette.

"As a matter of fact," I continued, looking around the room, "I was wondering about Ebon? Heard he had a rough night. In fact, I saw him in jail last night and asked him to pass along a message to you."

"Never got it," Duff said. "Maybe you would feel more comfortable discussing this somewhere else?"

"Actually, you might, but I wouldn't."

Duff chewed his first bite, and from the expression of his face it looked as if he had filled his mouth with the sole of an old shoe.

"We've had a bit of trouble on the Carved L," I said, now taking in the rest of the table. "Nothing we can't and won't handle, mind you, but an annoyance nonetheless. Seems that someone's developed a taste for buffalo meat. Shot and butchered some of our stock. We've also lost calves—poison, we think. Any of you gentlemen facing similar issues?"

A few heads shook, one rancher coughed, and the man wearing the HELLO, I'M EUSTICE name badge said, "Lost two calves to those damn wolves."

"More than likely it was feral dogs," I said. "There haven't been any confirmed sightings of wolves in the valley yet. You order a necropsy?"

"I don't need a necropsy to let me know my calves were killed by wolves."

"Sure you do, Eustice," I said. "When the last wolf was shot in the valley your grandfather hadn't been born. Next you'll be telling us that extraterrestrials are abducting your cattle for scientific tests.

"Reason I asked, we're having necropsies performed on our bison. The ones where we suspect poison, that is. You gentlemen know Fred, more money than brains sometimes. When he gets something in his head he's tough to dissuade. He'll spend thousands to get to whoever is doing this to him."

"Goddamn buffalo are a pestilence in the valley," Duff said.

"Glad to see that you've recovered your powers of speech, Brewster. I was afraid you had been struck dumb."

"There's no call to be rude, Dahlgren."

"Me, rude? No sir, not me. I wasn't the one poaching my neighbor's foreman. And I'm certainly not lacing another rancher's land with poison. Tell you what, though. I'll bet you that someone in this room—hell, maybe even someone at this table—is behind the poisonings. I'm so confident that I'll buy the entire guild a round if I'm wrong. Any takers?"

"I'll take that bet," Duff said without hesitation.

"I heard you've got practice buying rounds, Brewster. This time it's going to cost you more than it did at Stacey's. But look on the bright side; at least I'll let you stick around to finish your drink."

CHAPTER 15

BACK IN TIME

Once again Tatum O'Neill thwarted my plans for a quiet evening and an attempt to obey the orders of Dr. Patel.

"Hey, Dahlgren!" he shouted into the telephone. I heard the unmistakable sound of live music and the persistent hum of a large crowd. Friday night at Stacey's.

"Evening, Tatum."

"Did you say something?"

"Evening, Tatum!" I shouted.

"I can hardly hear you, but at least I know that I got you and not an answering machine. We got us a crowd tonight. Guess who's here?"

"Brewster Duff?"

"Ain't hardly likely. We got Led Tailings playing here tonight. Country-and-western metal band. Guess who else is here?"

"Mordecai?"

"Brewster Duff'll show up before Mordecai. Mordecai ain't partial to live music. Come to think of it, he ain't partial to no kind of music. Give up?"

"Axel," I said.

"See you around," Tatum said and hung up.

The chances of a country-and-western metal band making the charts are remote. Then again, a few Christian heavy metal bands have cracked Casey Kasem's Top 40 countdown. Led Tailings was loud; their singer shouted nonsensical lyrics and the instruments throbbed with an atonal lack of precision.

The crowd loved it.

Incongruity ruled the evening. Men in cowboy boots, Stetson hats, and Wranglers held up with platter-sized belt buckles slam-danced, while the women looked like Goth versions of Dale Evans. Denim skirts, tight white blouses with colorful bandanas, and black eye make-up and lipstick to achieve that somber, despairing, haunted look. I noticed a few interesting piercings.

The quartet of headbangers that looked most at ease in Stacey's were the four Montana Patriots. They pounded their beer glasses and sang along lustily, though I'm sure no one, the band included, knew the words. Two pitchers of beer rested on their table and they energetically bobbed their heads to the driving bass. One leaned back and took some licks on his air guitar. Our men in uniform enjoying an evening away from the base—heartwarming.

Axel Jackson wore biker boots, black Levi's, leather-studded wristbands, and a black leather vest that showed off his well-developed arms and nascent beer belly. As Sy might say, a beer hall *putz*.

I sat at the bar, my back to the tables that surrounded the dance floor. I could see the action reflected in the mirror. Tatum brought me a ginger ale. Stacey's was slam-dancing room only, so my former teammate kept busy slaking the insatiable thirst of the metal crowd. We had only a few seconds to talk, and in that brief time worked out a signal. When Tatum saw Axel go into the men's room he would bring me a bottle of beer.

"What are you fixing to do?" Tatum asked.

"I promised him that I would kick his balls up into his throat," I said.

"Am I going to have to call the police?"

"I doubt it."

"You want to borrow the steel baton? I'll need it back when you're through."

"No, thanks."

The band covered "Wasted Days and Wasted Nights," though it took half the song for me to recognize the Freddie Fender standard. They performed a metal parody of mullet-head Billy Ray Cyrus's "Achy Breaky Heart" that had everyone in the bar roaring with laughter.

Axel proved to have a prodigious capacity for holding his water. He drained glass after glass of beer and seemed immune to the biological need to offload any. His fellow militiamen were made of weaker stuff, each tottering off to the restroom at least once. I saw Tatum sprinting down the length of the bar, fumbling with a bottle of beer. He stared at Axel, tried to twist off the bottle cap and appear coolly nonchalant as he placed the beer in front of me.

Axel stood and loudly announced during an unexpected lull in the music, "I'm going to drain the dragon!"

When Axel pushed through the door of the men's room I slid from the stool and followed him. He stood at the first urinal, eyes closed and head raised in blissful relief. Grunts came from a locked stall and a man stood at the sink wetting his comb, running it through his slicked-back hair, and admiring the results. I stood next to him, keeping him between Axel and me.

"Hey, aren't you . . . uh . . . ?" I said, pretending to recognize him, and trying to remember his name.

"Marvin."

"Yeah, Marvin," I said. "I thought so. There's this hot gal asking for you, waiting just outside the door."

"Yeah?"

"Yeah. Great big tits. Blonde hair."

Marvin pocketed his comb, checked his look in the mirror one last time, and left. Axel was staring down at his feet. He took a step back from the urinal and zipped up his fly. I walked behind him and drove his head into the wall.

His forehead and face made a damp crunch against the tile. He exhaled loudly and staggered backward. I grabbed Axel by his shoulders and led him over my outstretched foot. He fell heavily to the ground. I delivered one kick between his legs and whatever wind he had left him. His hands, hovering around his face, immediately dropped to his crotch. A spasm of pain left him in the fetal position, his head writhing on the damp floor near the urinals.

Axel had a gash on his forehead and his nose was broken. Blood ran freely from both. I crouched down next to him. Through his pain I could see that he recognized me. "I always keep my promises," I said.

I walked out of the men's room and into the bar. I stopped at the table where the three other Montana Patriots sat. I leaned over, lowering my head to their level. "I think your friend could use a little help," I said, jerking a thumb over my shoulder to indicate the men's room. "He asked some guy if he could blow him and the other guy kicked the shit out him."

The three still shared confused glances and sat frozen with indecision when I left Stacey's. Tatum would find a soggy twenty under my glass of ginger ale.

I stepped outside into a cool May evening. When the door closed I could hear only the deep bass of the music. My ears throbbed as the normal sound of the world replaced the din of the bar. I drove back to the cabin and slept like a baby, though I did sleep with the front door locked.

Saturday morning I drove to the Bozeman Trail Colony and made my monthly visit to the Hutterites.

Religious persecution in Europe drove the Hutterites to the not-so-New World. They arrived in the late 1800s and settled in the unforgiving Great Plains, concentrating in the Dakotas and Montana. From four hundred immigrants they now numbered over forty thousand, yet still remain almost invisible to the outside world.

The Hutterites live in a colony, a true commune where everyone shares. They own nothing as individuals and everything on a communal basis. They are among the best ranchers and farmers in Montana. Other similar-sized farms and ranches support a family and a few hands while a Hutterite colony usually supports one hundred people.

Like the Amish, they are Anabaptists. They do not baptize children at birth. Hutterites choose to be baptized into their faith, usually in their teens or early twenties. Unlike the Amish, they use the modern implements and tools of farming and ranching. Tractors, automated milking equipment, even computers. Each colony owns a van or large SUV used to ferry members into town. You won't find a radio or television or telephone in a Hutterite colony, but they subscribe to magazines and a local newspaper, and so are aware of what is happening in the world and their community at large.

The ten families who live in the Bozeman Trail Colony reside in a single rambling series of manufactured housing components. Meals, like church services, are taken communally. The modern farm buildings are models of efficiency. They raise their own chickens, ducks, turkeys, hogs, and cattle. Twenty-five of the chickens walking around this morning could be the guests of honor at lunch.

I drove into the yard in front of the barn and even before I turned off the engine, Luther Kleinsasser, the colony's farm boss, lumbered across the expanse, his blunt, squared right hand raised in a casual greeting. Luther's English, like every Hutterite's, is accented. The first language the Hutterites speak is German.

"*Guten Morgen*, Dahlgren," he said.

"Good morning, Luther," I said, stepping out of the truck.

He gripped my hand in his, his powerful, calloused hand crushing mine.

"These are terrible events I read about," he said. "For more than four centuries no Hutterite has killed another. I read about murder and I see my friend's photograph in the newspaper. Very sad."

"You know that I did not kill this man."

"I knew before the newspaper tells me. We have death here. We live with death every day. The animals we slaughter for food. The old folks passing, and sometimes the younger ones, too. Ranching and farming, these businesses are not without danger. But to purposely end another man's life? This is senseless. This we do not understand."

Luther wore, as always, black trousers and work boots. His plaid shirt, with the traditional two-button collar, was soiled from work. He wore a plain, black cowboy hat. He was a barrel-chested, stout man made solid from work. Like all married Hutterites he wore a beard, his flinty gray. His features were broad and weathered. Though only fifty-three, he looked older.

"Let's walk," he said. We did, initially in silence.

"I am deciding whether I should be angry with you," Luther said.

"Because of the murder?"

"No, I told you, I always believed that you did not raise your hand against that man. It is about the land that I have anger. I have prayed about this anger, but *Gott* has not lifted this burden from me."

"I am confused, Luther."

"Herr Lather is selling land to *Der Milizmann*, the land we have asked him to sell us for a new colony."

"Fred isn't selling land to anyone."

"That is not what *Der Milizmann* says to me. He visits and tells us that he will own this land that we want and he will sell it to us."

Der Milizmann. I thought for a moment, turning the phrase over in my head. "Ferris? General Ferris was here."

"General, hah!" Luther sneered, using a hard *G* when he said "general." "General of what? How can one man rule another, how can one man judge another, or ask a man to forfeit his life? *Ja*, Ferris. He is . . . *fett* . . . obese. Comes to see us and he tells us soon he own some land from Herr Lather's ranch. Do we wish to buy this land? He will make a fair price, he says. Two thousand dollars each acre. Ten thousand acres. Two millions."

"When did he come to you with this proposal?"

"Early this week. I forget the day."

"Before you read about me in the newspaper?"

Luther stopped walking, his hands clasped behind his back. He bent, deep in thought. "*Ja*," he said and resumed walking. "I think perhaps the day before. He comes in the late afternoon, just before our supper."

And a few hours before he sent his storm troopers to the cabin to drag me to our confab. The former assistant district attorney certainly could seize the day.

"Luther, I had breakfast with Fred yesterday. We talked about the ranch. Ferris pretends that he killed the man on the river."

"Lunacy! Why would he make such a claim if it is not true?"

"Ferris is trying to scare Fred into selling, no, giving him the land."

"Give him the land? He pays nothing for it?"

"That's what he asked."

"Madness. I have never heard such nonsense."

"So, you see, Fred won't sell the land to him or give it to anyone."

"He will not sell to us?"

"No," I said. "We've discussed this many times. Fred won't sell because of the river access. He wants to control the water rights."

"For his *Fischers, ja*?"

"Yes, for his fly fishers."

"We don't fish."

"You don't fish, true. But what about Sarah?"

Luther laughed, a deep belly laugh. "Sarah, *ja*. She would fish that river until there were no fish left."

Sarah Kleinsasser is an unreconstructed fishing fanatic and poacher. On a trip during my second season working for Fred, the drift boat silently floated around a sharp bend in the river. On the far shore, I saw a young girl, dressed in an ankle-length skirt, a brilliantly colored blouse, and a bonnet that resembled a World War I leather aviator's helmet. In her right hand she held a department store fishing pole. When she saw the boat she bent down and pulled a stringer of trout out of the river with her left hand. She ran like a deer through the woods. By the time I beached the drift boat and jumped to the bank she had a quarter-mile lead on me.

The couple I guided that day couldn't wait to tell Fred about the little imp who poached his river with impunity. "Damned thievin' Hoots," Fred had barked.

I caught her the next season, and strictly by chance. I floated alone that day, conducting some initial survey work for the river improvement project. Around the bend I heard the *zip* of a spinning rod cast and the soft plunk of a spoon splashing into the water. I crept into the woods, paralleled the river, and cut in. I watched the little girl. She methodically covered water, and she was deadly. If a stretch of water failed to produce, she took a few steps upstream and began casting again. In the time that I watched her she caught three fish. She released the largest one, a fifteen-inch brown, but the two smaller trout went right on her stringer.

I coughed. She jumped and spun around. Her eyes darted about, searching for an avenue of escape. Her clothes were similar to what she had worn when I first saw her. A long skirt covered her legs to her ankles. She wore sensible shoes, more suited to the feet of a spinster than a young girl. Instead of the bonnet she wore a black scarf decorated with white polka dots. Her hair, yellow as corn silk, was parted in the middle and woven into two intricate braids that started at her brow and disappeared under the scarf. Her arms were tanned nut brown.

"You're not supposed to fish here," I said.

"Good morning, kind sir," she said, in a junior Greta Garbo voice.

"Yes, good morning."

"Fishing is *verboten*?"

"Yes."

"I see you fish here."

"I do fish here. I work for the man who owns this river."

"One man owns this river?"

"One man."

"And he allows you to fish, with your friends?"

"Yes."

"You think this man would allow me to fish?"

"I don't think he would."

She was quiet, thinking. "You do not fish well."

I raised my eyebrows.

"The fish take your lure, but you never hold them. They always swim away. I could teach you how to hold them."

"Ahh," I said. "We catch the fish and release them."

"On purpose you do this?"

"Yes."

She giggled. "So silly. I eat the fish." She lifted her stringer from the water. Perhaps a dozen trout. She lowered the stringer back into the water.

"I saw you put one back."

"He was too big for the frying pan," she said.

"What is your name?"

"Sarah Kleinsasser. What is your name, sir?"

"Dahlgren Wallace," I answered. "You came from the colony?"

"*Ja*." This meant she had walked at least four miles over some unforgiving country.

"Do you know Luther Kleinsasser, the farm boss?"

"*Ja*, he is my *Grosvater*."

"Tell your grandfather that I will come to speak to him, to talk to him about the fishing."

She removed her stringer of trout, curtsied, and walked past me. I turned and watched her. Without turning she said, "You should eat the fish."

Sarah, now eleven years old, all elbows and knees, is the apple of her grandfather's eye. When I first spoke to Luther about Sarah's trespassing and poaching he said, "These are *Gott's* fish."

"I am sure that Fred would agree with you," I said. "He frequently mistakes himself for God."

Luther laughed at the blasphemy. He promised to speak with Sarah. During the last two years we have reached an accommodation. I bring Sarah some Panther Martins and Rapalas to replenish her meager tackle box. She has a strict five-fish limit and keeps nothing over twelve inches. She does not and can no longer fish every day. Like the other members of the colony she has responsibilities and chores.

A bell rang announcing lunch.

"Come, eat with us," Luther said.

You need a hearty appetite to eat lunch with the Hutterites. We entered the communal dining hall, men and women taking seats at their segregated tables. The men removed their hats and hung them on pegs. The women ate with their scarves covering their hair. They sat at a long table, not unlike what you might find in a high school cafeteria. The Hutterites do not hold conversations while they eat. Eating is another job, necessary to provide strength for their other work. Only a few words pass between them.

They are trenchermen, tucking in and consuming a startling amount of food in the fifteen minutes or so they allow for lunch.

Platters filled with fried chicken, fat sausages, thick slices of ham, bowls of mashed potatoes, carrots, broccoli, and pitchers of ice-cold milk and pots of scalding coffee covered the tables. The sounds of utensils against plates, of men and women eating with gusto echoed in the hall.

"Dahlgren," Luther whispered.

I turned to him and he looked me in the eyes. His lips betrayed a small smile. I jumped in pain as something hot pressed against my left hand. The circle of men around us laughed.

Luther had left a teaspoon in his coffee and then touched my hand with it. "Luther thinks this is great fun," the man to my right said. "He has done it to all of us. Each time again we are surprised!"

When we finished lunch we waddled outside and made our way to my truck.

"I hope I convinced you that Fred will not sell or give any land to Ferris."

"Nor to the *Lehrerleut*," he said, mentioning the name of his sect.

"I am afraid not."

"Then what of *Herr Runt der Sanfte*?"

"Who?"

"Herr Duff; we call him Mister Runt of the Litter."

"What about him?"

"He, too, says that he will soon own Herr Lather's ranch. Not part of it like *Der Milizmann*. All of it. Is this possible?"

"Brewster Duff has been out here, too?"

"*Ja*," Luther said. "He visits and buys some things from us. Now he tells us that he buys the Carved L Ranch."

"Not true."

"So many people lie out there in the world." We stood near my truck. He extended his hand and we shook. "Dahlgren, our colony grows rapidly. Already there are over one hundred and thirty people. We must buy land and start a new colony. That is our way. The older ones will be sad if the children and babies must leave to a farm far away from our colony.

"Please talk again with Herr Lather. We make him a good price."

"I will, but I don't think he'll change his mind."

"*Gehen Sie mit Gott*, my friend."

CHAPTER 16

JACK MORMON

For a guide, a day with a superb fly fisher always holds the possibility of a busman's holiday. Sure, experienced fishermen still rely on your local knowledge, what flies to use and how to approach water and what techniques or presentations are the most effective, but they are usually fiercely independent and self-reliant. They tie on their own flies, release their own fish, and through their own experiences, questions, and intelligence, often add to the guide's store of knowledge. The best of these sports insist that the guide grab a fly rod and fish with them.

Most of Fred's guests fall into the intermediate category. They are adequate fly fishers. They uncork casts with consistency if not technical perfection. They have a basic knowledge of entomology and they possess the rudiments of reading water. A few of them are rank beginners, not unlike the Elderberrys. At the other end of the bell curve are passionate fly fishers, men and women who are a step away from disconnecting with the real world to lose themselves in streams and rivers and creeks.

Brigham Briggs ate breakfast with his vest and Gore-Tex waders draped over the back of his chair. In addition to VideoComp's interim CEO, Fred, Billy, and two pale specimens with "bean counter" tattooed on their foreheads made for a crowd. We ate buffet style, loading our plates from a restaurant-quantity spread. Fred, the sensitive host, had a pot of decaffeinated herbal tea and another of decaf coffee prepared in deference to religious strictures. Briggs poured himself a cup of the regular, a dark French roast that curls your toes.

"Think we'll have a hatch?" Briggs asked.

"It could happen," I said. "I've seen a few bugs on the water the last few days. Blue-winged Olives and the Adams might work."

"My father's favorite fly, the Adams," Briggs said. "He always preached to me 'When nothing's working, tie on a #16 Adams.' "

While Briggs couldn't wait to discuss fishing, the others around the table were also anxious to talk. About numbers. We ate quickly, and I poured Briggs and me each another coffee in Styrofoam cups.

"Let's go wet a line," I said. "Fred, gentlemen, we'll see you when we see you."

"Dinner's at seven-thirty, Brigham," Fred said.

"We might make that," I said.

Briggs pulled on his waders and boots and put on his vest. The vest was well worn, an Orvis guide vest, the neck frayed, and the pockets dirty. He wore a Sage baseball cap and fished one of their more expensive two-piece rods.

"How do you like the rod?" I asked as Briggs threaded his fly line through the guides.

"This is my favorite," he said. "It's stiff enough to punch through the wind and the action is soft enough to drop a #22 on 8X tippet."

"You ever fish bamboo?" I asked.

"Yeah. Sweet, man, sweet. I had Kane Klassics build me a rod. You know the company?"

"From your neck of the woods, right?"

"Yeah, Oakland," Briggs said. "It's a frigging work of art is what it is. I'm afraid to fish with the damn thing. What should I tie on?"

"Here." I selected an Olive Soft Hackle and a Serendipity from a fly box.

"Dropper or tandem?"

"Tandem," I said. Briggs expertly tied on the flies, first the soft-hackle fly, an emerger pattern, and then, after attaching eighteen inches of tippet to the bend of the first fly's hook, the nymph. He tied double clinch knots and tied them quickly. He bit the tag ends of the tippet off with his teeth.

I had the feeling that this was going to be a good day.

It was a great day, from a number of points of view.

"Listen," Briggs said, as he spit a short length of tippet to the ground. "I don't normally do this, but at one I've got to make a phone call. Believe me, man, I never bring a phone when I'm fishing, but . . . well . . . you know."

"Good luck making the call."

"Why?"

"Nothing works out here."

"Mine will," Briggs said with a smile.

Briggs celebrated his first fish, a decent-sized brown trout, with a Coca-Cola. He watched me for a reaction. At eleven in the morning, after an hour and a half of hard fishing, he reached for his first beer.

He winked at me. "I may be a Latter-day Saint," he said, "but I'm also a present-day sinner."

When I started guiding, I learned most of the tricks of the trade from a friend of mine who works in Sun Valley, Idaho. Opening his cooler one day when we fished together, I saw a six-pack of Sprite. "There for the Mormons?" I asked.

"Let me tell you something about Mormons," he said. "When you guide two or more Mormons they walk the straight and narrow. Won't even sip a Coke. Take one Mormon out fishing and he'll drink every beer in your cooler. When they fly solo, they're all Jack Mormons."

Briggs did drink nearly every beer in my cooler. Six to my one, and I had two. He especially enjoyed the Black Dog ale. I brought two bottles for lunch and shared one with him.

"This is beautiful water, my friend," Briggs said. Briggs took off his vest and placed it on the ground. We sat with our backs to a pair of trees, devouring sandwiches, cookies, and apples. I took it as a rhetorical statement and continued chewing.

"You ever get spoiled? Jaded?"

"No," I answered. "I personally fish about seventy to eighty days a season and I make it a point to fish other water."

"I fish nearly that much!"

"It always surprises people when I tell them that. They think I fish every day of the year. Remember, I take people fishing about one hundred days each season, and I don't usually get to fish when I've got sports with me. You're the exception, and I thank you again. I appreciate fishing with you."

"I'm sure you've heard this one before," Briggs said, "but I'm thinking of chucking it all. Yes, chucking it all and just fishing. Maybe move back to Utah. We've got great waters in Utah."

"What about VideoComp?"

"What about it? The company is being sold. Let me clue you in on the world of corporate takeovers. Lather buys now, someone bigger comes along and buys us all out. All the shareholders, including yours truly, make a ton of money. Everyone hugs and swaps spit and makes beautiful speeches. They roll out every cliché in the corporate book. The company has a talented management team. We're committed to growing the business and we already have our team on board. Servicing the clients, shifting paradigms, empowering the employees, becoming more value-added, and evolving into a world-class organization.

"Here's the translation: If it weren't for us buying you guys out you'd be selling pencils on the street corner. Somehow you idiots got lucky and built a better mousetrap. Now step aside and let the real professionals take it from here.

"I'll sign an employment contract, two or three years with a big severance buyout clause. The day after I sign, whoever bought the company will begin easing me out and bringing in their own guy. That's the way of the world. Though I get to walk away a wealthy man."

"Doesn't sound very loyal."

"You want loyalty, buy a dog. Don't get me wrong, working with Elden was fabulous. He was a genius and we all had fun. I've been with VideoComp from the beginning. We built something, man, we were part of something. We took a dream and turned it into reality. Was I loyal to Elden? Absolutely. Loyalty to a nameless corporation? Never. Talk about loyalty to the thousands of middle managers and line employees who got downsized or deselected in the great reorganizations or reengineering initiatives."

He glanced at his watch. "Shit," he muttered. He reached for his vest, opened the back pouch, and removed a telephone.

"Ever seen one of these?" he asked.

"No."

"Elden didn't bring his on the river?"

"Not that I can remember."

"Hmmm," he said. He handed the phone to me. "Kyocera makes it. It's an Iridium phone, a true satellite network phone." He pointed to an attachment that resembled a flashlight. "That's the satellite attachment unit. I connect through one of sixty-six orbiting satellites. I can basically be anywhere and call anyone."

The entire unit weighed about a pound, the heft of a fair-sized trout. When my Recon team was dug in within spitting distance of the Iraqi army, we used a small satellite radio to send short bursts of targeting information. Our unit weighed twice as much and even had a small dish.

I handed the telephone back to Briggs. I rose. "Make your call, Brigham," I said. "Think I'll see if I can raise a few trout."

I then proceeded to break my rule about thinking and fishing. I cast and missed two strikes. My initial concern was that Fred would soon add this piece of intrusive electronics to my required equipment. Bad enough I had to endure his inopportune pages. Already at his beck and call, I rued the day when we would be totally "connected." But my mind also wandered to Elden and his waterlogged vest.

I false-cast to dry the fly and then sent my next cast close to the bank. A small brown trout took the fly. Eight inches long, its sides the color of burnt butter, the spots rich, vibrant, and pulsing with life.

"Took a dry, did he?" Briggs asked. He stood behind me, on the bank, vest on and ready to fish.

"Some bugs coming off the water," I said. "We might be a tad bit early, but go ahead and tie on the Adams."

"Yeah," he said, pumping his fist in the air. He began to change his terminal tackle. "Five X or 6?" he asked, questioning what size tippet to use. The higher the number, the thinner and more delicate the tippet, and the more difficult for the trout to see and the easier to break off. The perennial dilemma, strength versus stealth.

"Five," I answered. He clipped the flies and tippet from the end of his leader. He tied on a three-foot section of 5X tippet using a double surgeon's knot and then a #16 Adams to the tippet. He smudged the fly with Mucillin, a British variety of fly floatant. We climbed into the drift boat and I began moving downstream.

"So Elden had one of those gadgets?" I asked.

Briggs gave me a quizzical look.

"Iridium phone," I said.

"Oh, yeah! Elden's what you'd call an early adopter. If any new technology hit the market he had to own it. The man lived for the COMDEX show, you know, the big high-tech trade show? Plasma television, Sony Playstation, Palm Pilot, hands-free adapters, voice recognition software, MP3 players, it didn't matter. Real satellite telephones? Had to be the first kid on the block to own one. Wasn't shy about showing off either. Elden couldn't stand being on the off-ramp of the information superhighway. He was always connected."

"The only thing he connected to out here were trout."

"You're kidding, right?"

"No."

"Amazing." Briggs reached over the gunwale and let his hand drift in the icy water. He shook water from his fingers. "Tell me, what kind of fisherman was he?"

"He would have been a very good one," I said. "He enjoyed himself. He learned quickly. I don't think he would ever have had a great cast, but frankly, you don't need one to have a wonderful time."

"Still hard to believe he's gone. And murdered to boot."

"Tell me, what kind of man was Elden?"

"Recently, we were all a bit worried about Brother Elden," Briggs said. He opened the cooler. "You only had two of those Black Dogs, huh?"

"Yeah."

He took out another beer. "Want one?"

I shook my head.

"Are you a religious man?"

I shook my head again.

"You probably think I'm a hypocrite," he said, and took a long pull from the beer. "A Jack Mormon. But I am a religious man. I believe deeply in my religion.

"Does the Mormon Church have inconsistencies? Sure. Joseph Smith and some of the early church members were fond of the grape. They drank. So why can't I? Let's face it, all religions are fairy tales. Religions ask their adherents to suspend belief in what is scientifically improbable. Hell, hard-shell Baptists still believe the world is only a few thousand years old. They ignore the scientific fact of carbon dating, believe absolutely in the word of the Lord.

"We worried about Elden. He appeared to be questioning his faith and the church."

"In what ways?"

"Hey, man, you're a Gentile, I wouldn't expect you to understand."

"Anything to do with the forgeries?"

"How do you know about that?"

"The forgeries? Read about those in the newspapers," I said. "Susi told Fred and me that Elden had an interest in collecting the forgeries."

"He did." Briggs finished his beer and put the empty back into the cooler. "He bought Mormon historical documents, certified and authentic, and the Hofmann forgeries. Then he expanded his scope. Elden claimed he was on the trail of the eight Golden Plates. Just mentioning that sent shock waves through the church."

"Why?"

"After the Prophet translated the plates into the Book of Mormon, the Angel Moroni carried them back to heaven. So you see, if someone actually located the plates . . ."

"That seems sort of far-fetched."

"Does it? Is it any more far-fetched than Crusaders searching for the Holy Grail?"

"Guess not."

"Then there was the whole children thing."

"I thought Elden and Susi didn't have any children."

"They don't. Word was that Susi wanted them and Elden didn't."

"Marital problems?"

"Man, who knows what goes on in another guy's house? I knew this much. Some guys do and some guys don't. Elden definitely did not cheat on his wife. So that wasn't the problem, and I'm not saying there even was a problem.

"Her picture was always showing up in the society pages. Junior League shit. Auctions, fund-raisers, save this, preserve that. Elden couldn't be bothered with that stuff. He just wrote the checks."

"Divorce?"

"Very rare for a Latter-day Saint, my friend," Briggs said. "Not unheard of, but very rare. My gut feeling? No."

We fished through the afternoon and we did catch a hatch. Mayflies. Aquatic insect life begins at the bottom of rivers, when nymphs hatch. They struggle to the surface and emerge from the water as winged adults. Later the adults return to deposit their eggs on the water's surface. Spent, they fall back into the water. At this stage the insects are called spinners. Trout feed on insects at every stage of their development. To take a trout on a dry fly, either when the insect oviposits or struggles to break free from the surface tension of the water, has always been the paragon of fly flishing.

"*Paraleptophlebia*," Briggs said, identifying the insect.

"A man who knows his Latin," I said.

"And spouts it, too. Not bad for a Mormon boy who turned the corner on his second six-pack."

"You might want to go smaller."

"Twenty."

"Start there." He rapidly changed flies, tying on a #20 Blue-Winged Olive Dun. He cast, his loops tight, and dropped a fly in the foam line. He bent at the waist and slowly stripped line as the current pushed his fly downstream. I saw a trout rise, a slashing, darting rise to the fly. Briggs saw it as well, and raised his rod to set the hook.

"Man, I love it!" he shouted.

Briggs fished hard and drank hard. When we reached the takeout point he climbed into the truck and fell asleep. He didn't even bother to remove his waders or boots, but he did take down his rod. I trailered the drift boat. He woke as we bounced down the dirt road but slept again when we reached the paved road. I drove to the front door of the ranch house and nudged him awake.

"Thank you very much, my friend, thank you!" he beamed. He reached for his wallet. I raised a hand. "I talked with Fred and I know the drill. How often do you think I get to fish waters like this and get a snoot full at the same time?" He handed me three one-hundred-dollar bills. "It's only money."

Briggs took a deep breath, gathered up his rod case and his reel, and took a few unsteady steps toward the porch.

I cleaned and stored the gear, covering the boat, which I left on the trailer under a tarp. I drove into town and stopped by The Cowboy Vey Deli. Sy was wiping the tables, preparing to close for the evening.

"What do you know about the Mormon religion?" I asked.

"Enough to know that they prefer to be called the Church of Jesus Christ of Latter-day Saints," Sy answered. "Tell me, what is the extent of your knowledge?"

"Basically that they wear funny underwear, and that in the good old days the Mormons had more than a few wives."

"The good old days never passed. There are sects of Mormons who still actively practice polygamy. From what you read the polygamists are conservative, primarily rural throwbacks who cling to the early teachings and revelations of the Mormon faith. This is not true. There are rumors that some of the General Authorities are practicing polygamists."

"What are General Authorities?"

"The men who compose the hierarchy of the leadership of the Church of Jesus Christ of Latter-day Saints," Sy answered. "The head of the church is the president. He is the Prophet, Seer, and Revelator. He speaks for God on Earth."

"That's rather arrogant," I said.

"Is it?" Sy answered. "The pope speaks for God and even claims papal infallibility. The imams of the Muslim faith speak for Allah. Just as in the Catholic religion where the pope is the direct descendant of Saint Peter, the president claims his line of succession to Joseph Smith. The president has two counselors, who together with him make up the office of the First Presidency. Then there are the Twelve Apostles."

"Twelve apostles?"

"Were you raised a heathen, Dahlgren? Do you worship trees or salmon or some other pantheistic deity? Surely you understand the basic tenets of Christianity?"

"I grew up an Episcopalian."

"Ah, yes, the junior varsity Catholics. So you do understand the concept of the twelve apostles."

"I do," I answered.

"The apostles, as you can imagine, are very powerful men. And before you ask, they are always men. The brush of political correctness has not touched the Saints. Finally, there is the First Quorum of Seventy. These men are the true bureaucrats of the church, with responsibilities for all religious and secular aspects of running a huge business."

"You mean religion."

"No, I mean a business, as all organized religions are. The Mormons are a uniquely American religion. They believe in prosperity. They believe that God has chosen them not only to live as gods in the Celestial Kingdom, but also to live as successful, rich men while on earth.

"The Book of Mormon itself is a fascinating document. A work of fiction, of course, but then you may argue that all religions are based in myth. Adam and Eve? Noah? Are they any more real than Nephi and Laman in the Book of Mormon?

"Smith was a gifted man and an imaginative one. The Book of Mormon, a document purported to be thousands of years old, somehow provided answers to all the great philosophical questions and debates of the early nineteenth century. The detractors and critics of the church—and they coexisted with the Mormons from their earliest days—argued that Smith was a charlatan and a huckster endowed with a healthy libido. His revelation from God about plural marriages gave a sacred rationale to adultery under the guise of polygamy."

"And you say that polygamy is still practiced today, even in the highest levels of the church?"

"I said that it is suspected."

I spent another half hour with Sy, receiving a primer on the history and theology of the Mormons.

I left the deli and drove to my cabin. In the last few days I had taken to locking the door, something I hadn't ever done in the years I'd lived in Montana. I had stopped being careless.

I called the Bozeman Police and left an urgent message for Horace. He called back a few minutes later.

"Dahlgren, you are the only thing standing between me and a slab of ribs," he barked. "This better be good."

"Did Elderberry have a telephone in his vest?"

"You gotta be shitting me, Dahlgren."

"Horace, please."

"No, he did not have a telephone. Hell, with all the crap he had in that vest he couldn't have squeezed in one more fly, let alone a phone." Horace paused. "Something I should know about, maybe?"

"Maybe."

"Well?"

"You're the policeman, Horace," I said. "And those ribs are probably getting cold." I hung up.

CHAPTER 17

MORDECAI'S SILENCE

The best-laid plans and fly lines. Fishing streamers on the Madison River on a miserable Friday morning. Two weeks since Elderberry's murder. Away from everyone and everything. Miserable described only the weather. My grandfather, who taught me to fly-fish, dispensed wisdom guaranteed to take the chill out of a day like this. "You can't catch fish with spots on them unless your nose is running," he would say.

My nose was running. Only the coffee-colored water offered any contrast to a cold, gray day. Drizzle, not rain, blanketed the Madison valley, squeezing the color out of the dramatic landscape. Spring runoff from the snowmelt swelled the river, and only a few hearty souls braved the elements.

Streamers imitate baitfish and add to the ongoing "But is it fly fishing?" debate. The purists hold that only presenting dry flies to a sighted fish with an upstream cast constitutes the science of the angle. This rules out nymph fishing, especially with any type of strike indicator, or streamer fishing. The purists also eschew adding weight to the line, whether that is done using a sinking line, pinching on split shot, or using weighted flies. I'm not that highly evolved yet, so I fish to the conditions.

After probing several runs with scores of casts I finally found a nice seam. Trout took the streamer on every fourth or fifth cast. I wouldn't set any International Game Fish Association records with these fish, but they were all healthy, firm, and strong. Mostly rainbows, and none displaying any evidence of whirling disease, but once I found a cuttbow at the end of the line. Trout miscegenation, a hybrid of rainbow and cutthroat. A beautiful fish, the crimson slashes under the gills and the bright rainbow iridescence along the sides.

I was a happy man. Fred, Billy, and the trio from VideoComp concluded their business and departed the day before. Fred would return in two weeks' time and his guests would begin their pilgrimage to the ranch. On this upcoming swing I would extend the royal treatment to the Senate majority leader, one of the TV anchormen, a best-selling mystery writer, and several captains of industry. Unless the senator misspent his youth, the prospects of fishing again with an angler of Briggs's caliber appeared remote.

The SkyTel pager vibrated against my thigh. I had cast upstream, allowed the streamer to swing across the pool, and begun quick, short retrieves, stripping line into the water next to me where it floated in a loop. When the pager began its insistent thrumming, it broke my concentration. I felt a take through the line but reacted too slowly to set the hook.

As always, there never is any question about who will be on the other end of the page. Fred. The only question is, from where was he placing the call? I plunged my hand inside my waders and thrust it deep into a pocket. The screen flashed a 212 area code, New York City. Following the telephone number I read "911."

Fred and I had worked out this unoriginal code in the event of an emergency. Other than the page that summoned me back to the ranch to guide the Elderberrys, Fred had used the urgent message only twice before. Once to warn me of his unscheduled visit to the ranch and his burning need to catch fish. The other 911 page resulted in sending a 9-weight rod by Federal Express to Belize. Both legitimate emergencies.

I walked the half mile from the river to the road and another mile to the truck. Without bothering to remove my waders I climbed into the truck and drove toward Ennis. I stopped at the Grizzly Bar Restaurant, where I had planned to eat dinner and maybe watch the NBA playoffs. There was a pay phone on the back deck of the restaurant. I dialed the New York City number.

"Dahlgren," Fred said, "where the hell you been?"

Fred must imagine I sit in my cabin and stare at the pager waiting for it to go off.

"About thigh-deep in the Madison."

"The Madison."

"Yeah. I'm calling you from the Grizzly Bar."

"You need to haul ass back to the ranch."

"What's wrong?"

"Mordecai's missing. He took the Jeep out yesterday afternoon and no one's seen him since."

"Do you know where he was heading?"

"Hell, no. Mordecai doesn't need me to tell him how to run the Carved L. And he certainly doesn't give me his daily itinerary."

"So, we've got a foreman missing somewhere on a 250,000-acre ranch."

"About sums it up."

"I'm a fishing guide, Fred, not a bloodhound."

"Find him, Dahlgren. I'm worried."

"What about the other ranch hands?"

"What about them? They couldn't pour piss out of a boot if the directions were written on the heel."

"I'm on my way. You call the police?"

"Mordecai's free, white, and over twenty-one. You think the police are going to call out search and rescue on my hunch?"

"What hunch?"

"We lost four more calves this week."

"And?"

"The necropsy toxicology reports from the first three won't be ready for a few more days. But Mordecai's sure they were all poisoned."

"Fred, I'll call you later. I'm leaving."

I drove the 120 miles back to the ranch. When I pulled into the parking area in front of the barn, Grady, one of the young ranch hands, ran to the truck and started talking even before I opened the door. It was a few minutes before one. We had about six hours of daylight to search.

"Do you have any idea where Mordecai was headed?" I asked.

"Naw, he never tells us where he's going, especially lately," Grady said.

"What do you mean, especially lately?"

"With the problems and all? Kept everything to hisself like."

"What problems?"

"The speed butchering and losing the calves." Grady stared down at his boots.

"You know anything about that?"

"Naw, don't think so."

"Did you check Mordecai's trailer?"

"You crazy? Mordecai, he ain't never allowed nobody in that trailer. We was afraid to even knock on the door."

"I'm going to check the trailer. Get the rest of the hands together. I'll see if I can dope out where he went off to and we'll start searching."

"Aw, we was planning on knocking off early. It's Friday."

"I don't give a fuck if it's your birthday and Christmas all wrapped into one. You make sure you're around when I come out of that trailer."

Mordecai parked his vintage Airstream trailer behind the Carved L's barn fifteen years ago. As far as anyone could tell, it had never been moved. The outside of the stainless-steel trailer gleamed like it was new. The door to the Airstream was locked. Mordecai used a Master padlock to keep any unwanted visitors—essentially the entire human race—from entering his mobile castle. Using a hacksaw I found in the tool shed inside the barn, I cut through the lock.

Mordecai's personal appearance was always tidy and neat, never flashy. I don't believe that I ever saw him in anything but Wrangler jeans and cowboy shirts, but they were always pressed and clean. The inside of the trailer reflected his fastidious nature. Spare and spartan, orderly and neat. I've seen trailers that could be entered only by wearing a level-one biohazard suit. That was not the case here. The Airstream smelled antiseptic, a mixture of soap and furniture polish.

While the furniture was unremarkable, the rest of his stuff was not. An original Charlie Russell watercolor hung on a wall. On the coffee table a Remington bronze, *Coming Through the Rye*, was displayed. Books lined most of one wall, first editions of Zane Grey, Louis L'Amour, Will James, and Tony Hillerman. A Navajo rug dominated the center of the room. Mordecai also collected pottery, and he appeared especially fond of blackware.

A Dell computer sat on the rolltop desk. I sat down, pushed the tab bar, and the screen crackled to life. An Excel spreadsheet displayed the supplemental feeding program for the bison. Scrolling down to the last entry, I saw the location of the last delivery of hay. On the wall next to the desk was a plat map pinned to a bulletin board. He had fixed ten red pushpins at various locations on the ranch. Another seven blue pins marked other locations. From each pin a tiny scroll of paper hung, with a date written in tiny script. I stepped back and studied the map, trying to discern a pattern. Then I stopped, reminding myself that I had to locate the ranch foreman, not decipher his investigation of poaching and poisoning.

Once again I looked at the location of the last delivery of feed and located it on the plat map. I left the trailer and walked back to the barn. Grady and four other men sat on benches, doing their best to appear disconsolate.

"What vehicles are available?" I asked.

"Got us some ATVs, the pickup, and the Harvester," Grady answered.

"I want you and the boys to search the area around the little pond. I'll take the Harvester. If you find Mordecai, come fetch me." I told them where I would search. "In any case, let's all meet back here at six-thirty."

I'm not as familiar with the ranch as I am the rivers and creeks on the ranch, so I wasn't surprised that I got lost. Eventually I found my way to a sweeping vista that looked to me like most of the other sweeping vistas. A small creek ran along the far, northern edge of the meadow. Bison grazed in the meadow, ringed by a dense growth of pine trees. With a pair of binoculars I glassed the meadow. Away from the herd, near the west edge of the meadow, lay a single, unmoving bison.

I searched the meadow again and this time noticed two calves lying still. They were on the eastern side of the meadow, but closer to the main body of animals.

Bison are not domesticated livestock. Only an idiot would meander through a meadow in close proximity to bulls that weigh nearly a ton. I drove the Travelall to the northern side of the meadow, parked, and walked along the tree line until I could cut in and look at the calves.

Both were dead and covered with flies. Not knowing what I was looking at, I walked back to the tree line and passed the herd, turning in when I was on a line with the dead adult bison. This time I was certain of what I was looking at; the cow had been shot with a large-caliber rifle. The scavengers hadn't started in on her yet, though I could almost feel the eyes of the coyotes. If I assumed that the cow fell where she had been shot, then whoever had shot her had done so from the cover behind me. I glassed the opposite end of the meadow, the southern edge. I stared into the binoculars, focusing so hard that I felt as if my eyes were being pulled from their sockets. I saw a glint of metal, the front grille of the ranch Jeep.

Mordecai had figured something out. Somehow he had made sense of the pushpins and discovered a pattern. The three dead bison confirmed his deductions. Giving the herd a wide berth I returned to the Travelall made a three-point turn and drove back to the southern end of the meadow. The rough road through the woods was wide enough for the small Jeep, but not for the old International Harvester. I parked and hiked along the road.

Mordecai had parked the Jeep so that he could watch the meadow and the herd. As I neared the Jeep, approaching from the passenger's side, three smells hit me simultaneously. The heavy smell of radiator fluid and motor oil, and then the unmistakable copper smell of blood. The driver's door was partially open. I walked around the Jeep from the front, my boots slipping in greasy mud.

Mordecai lay sprawled on the ground. A large-caliber bullet had pierced the Jeep's small half door and that bullet had exploded into Mordecai's chest. Above his head, Mordecai had a death grip on a Winchester rifle. Strangely enough, I felt calm. I had no concern that whoever had shot the bison and Mordecai was still around, lurking in the trees on the northern edge of the meadow. I knelt next to Mordecai and looked at his face. His features registered surprise, but perhaps I read that into his expression. The skin was pale with a bluish tint. Bits of windblown dirt and grit adhered to his now dry eyeballs.

I made a quick search of the Jeep. A sleeping bag had been tossed into the backseat of the Jeep. On the passenger's seat I found a cooler and a thermos. Both were empty. Paper poked out from under the cooler. A single page, a printout of the Excel file that had been left open on Mordecai's computer. Mordecai had written notes in his tiny script: BTC and 5/20 and then LASS? I replaced the paper.

My first call was to Horace, the second to Fred. I made both calls from the telephone in Mordecai's trailer. Figuring that I had half an hour until the police arrived, I used the time productively. I printed a copy of the Excel supplemental feeding program spreadsheet and wrote down what I had seen on the copy I found in the Jeep. Then I studied the map. On the reverse side of the page I had just printed, I listed the dates associated with the red pins and in the next column the dates for the blue ones. At first I could not see a pattern. When I did, I took another look at the map and confirmed my suspicions.

Sitting back at the desk, I opened Explorer and then My Documents. Mordecai's computer files were as orderly as the rest of his life had been. You could run the ranch from this desk. Breeding records, feed schedules, and personnel records. I opened Quick Books Pro and found inventory lists, purchase orders, and payroll records.

At any point in time the Carved L might have anywhere from five to thirty ranch hands employed. A core group of five or six enjoyed year-round employment, while the others were hired on as the demands of the ranch dictated. I opened a recent payroll file for temporary hands and understood every note Mordecai had written on the feed schedule.

The 5/20 was easy. It corresponded to the date of the last entry on the spreadsheet itself, a delivery of half a ton of hay to the meadow I had just visited. I saw BTC under the address column next to a dozen of the temporary employees. The last names of these ranch hands were Kleinsasser, Wipf, and Hofer, all Hutterites. BTC was the Bozeman Trail Colony. Cole Lassiter appeared to be the answer for LASS? notation.

Horace arrived with bubble lights flashing. If he had approached Elderberry's death in a lackadaisical manner, he more than made up for it on this visit. Horace and Officer Andrew led a motorcade that included the county medical examiner's "meat wagon" and a black Suburban containing Agent Feib and two evidence technicians. Eight people climbed out of the vehicles, a show of force.

"Dahlgren," Horace said, "you ride with me." He looked around. "Where are the ranch hands?"

"Sent them off to the small pond to search for Mordecai. Told them to be back at six-thirty."

Horace glanced at his watch. "Two and a half hours. OK, we'll deal with them when the time comes. Let's saddle up."

Horace drove, following my directions.

"What was Mordecai doing up there?" Horace asked.

"I think he figured out who was poaching and poisoning the bison. Looks like he spent the night up there and was waiting this morning, sort of a stakeout, I guess. Mordecai was right, because someone shot a cow this morning."

"Not yesterday? Shot this morning, you're sure?"

"Relatively sure. Scavengers haven't started in on the carcass yet."

"Makes sense. What do you think happened out there?"

"I think that whoever shot the cow was set up on the northern side of the meadow. Somehow he discovers he's not alone. He sees Mordecai or the Jeep. Or maybe Mordecai took a shot at him—he's still holding a Winchester. Then the fellow sends a round through the Jeep and then one through Mordecai."

"What's the distance across the meadow?"

"Six, seven hundred yards, maybe. From tree line to tree line."

"Big caliber, you say?"

"Yes," I answered. "I'm thinking a Sharps."

"I'm thinking you're right. And Mordecai out there with a Winchester. No chance."

The three vehicles stopped where earlier I had parked the Travelall. The entourage, including Dr. Cord and his coroner's assistants, followed me as I hiked along the tree line. We all stopped about twenty yards from the Jeep.

"Chief," Feib said, "I'd like to send a technician in to secure the crime scene."

"Fine by me," Horace said.

"It didn't look like anyone else but Mordecai had been here," I said.

“Oh?” Feib said.

“I hunt, Agent Feib,” I said. “That requires that I possess at least a shred or two of woodcraft. Checking for sign, reading trails. All I saw were Mordecai’s footprints. Probably got out to stretch or take a leak.”

“Your footprints will be there, of course.”

I nodded.

“You touch anything else?”

“No,” I lied.

“Touch the body at all?”

“No.”

“Not even to check for a pulse?”

“Agent Feib, I can damn near put my fist through the hole in his chest.”

“I’m trying to determine whether or not you contaminated the crime scene.”

“I don’t think I touched anything here. In Mordecai’s trailer, now that’s a different story. I was on his computer. In fact, that’s how I knew to search for him in this meadow. He had a spreadsheet open that showed this was the most recent location for the delivery of supplemental feed.”

“I fail to see the connection.”

“You’ll find two dead calves on the eastern edge of the meadow. That makes nine lost to poisoning.”

“What does the feeding program have to do with the poisonings? Lather surely isn’t poisoning his own herd.”

“I didn’t say that. But whoever’s poisoning the bison knows the feeding schedule. Both where and when the supplemental feed will be delivered.”

“How do you know that?” Horace asked.

“While I waited for you I looked at the feeding program and a map Mordecai had posted to a bulletin board. He marked the location of each calf poisoning with a pin, along with the date. The calves all died within a day or two of the supplemental feed deliveries.”

"Explain supplemental feeding," Feib said. "I thought that bison didn't need to be fed."

"They don't. Mordecai distributes half a ton of hay on a regular basis until early June. This ensures that there's enough fodder at a time when the calves are young and vulnerable. Weather can make foraging difficult. The feed was also laced with vitamins. Basic animal husbandry."

The evidence technician shouted, "All clear!" and we moved toward the Jeep and Mordecai's body. Officer Andrew puked. My plan was to be as unobtrusive as possible but close enough to where I could make observations of my own.

One of the evidence technicians set up a device that looked like a surveyor's transit. "I can locate the shooter's position," he said. "Get us within fifty square yards. If I use the buffalo I can narrow the area, assuming that he didn't move between shots."

"If you're going to use the bison," Horace said, "you better get down there now. Critters'll be chewing on it this evening."

"I'll go down and get the measurements," the technician said. "I'll shoot a quick line and see if it gets us closer."

"How you going to do that?" Horace asked.

"Simple. Figure the buffalo was standing when it got shot. Measure the distance from the wound to the hooves. Throw in a fudge factor was its head lowered to eat? Was it moving? Could change the measurement, but we'll get it. I'll find the shooter's perch."

He did. Within an hour of arriving at the Jeep, the team had located where the shots had been fired, collected each item in the Jeep, taken hundreds of photographs, and placed Mordecai in the body bag. With all the activity I didn't hear the zipper close, the sound that had startled me out on the river.

Horace and Agent Feib discussed their preliminary findings, with me quietly eavesdropping.

"You first," Horace said.

"First shot, the cow is killed. Shames is sitting in the Jeep at the time, looking through the binoculars. Maybe the shooter sees a reflection off the binoculars or glare from the chrome or metal on the Jeep. Second shot hits the Jeep and pierces the radiator and the engine block. Shames gets out of the Jeep and takes shelter behind the door. Brings the Winchester with him, maybe even looking to shoot. Third shot kills him."

"Winchester wasn't fired?" Horace asked.

"No," Feib answered, "and it would have been ineffective at that range. A distraction for the shooter, and I don't think he would have been distracted easily."

"What's the distance?" Horace asked.

"Seven hundred and eighty yards," Feib said.

"Damn!"

"A great shot, but not an impossible one. Not even lucky. Plenty of people around who can make the thousand-yard shot these days."

I was one of them, having graduated from Scout Sniper School. While many can make the thousand-yard shot, not many can do it while aiming at a human target.

"Maybe with a telescopic sight," Horace said. "I'm thinking this guy made the shot with a Sharps. That means Creedmore sights."

"Know anyone who owns a Sharps rifle?" Feib asked.

"Plenty of folks own the reproductions," Horace said. "I only know of a couple who own the genuine article."

"Who?"

"Brewster Duff owns one, and so does another guy in that hunting club of theirs. They dress up as Jim Bridger and John Colter for the Fourth of July parade, playacting like they're real mountain men. Carry their Sharps rifles. Damn thing is bigger'n Brewster."

"You see things differently?" Feib asked the sheriff.

"No, I think we've got the sequence down. We'll call in the tracker and have him out here at first light."

"We'll head back and search Mordecai's trailer," Feib said. "I'll take the computer and have one of our forensic computer techs examine the hard drive. Also sounds like we can take the bulletin board off the wall, the one with the map. No question Shames figured this thing out. We will, too."

"Don't forget the ranch hands. I'll try to be down there when they arrive, but make sure you hold them there in case I'm not. And take Dahlgren down there with you. You hear that, Dahlgren?"

"Every word, Horace," I said. "Every word."

CHAPTER 18

BACK IN THE HIGH LIFE AGAIN

After a long telephone call to Fred, I drove back to my cabin. Still in a state of shock following my first, brief call, when I had reported that Mordecai had been shot, Fred proceeded to make a couple of less than brilliant decisions. The first was my elevation to ranch foreman.

"Just run the place until I find a real foreman," Fred argued. "Calving is done, just a matter of mending fence and keeping on top of maintenance."

"I don't know dick about ranching," I protested.

"First thing you do, take one of the ranch hands and knock him upside the head. From the rumors I keep hearing, you're perfectly capable of that job competency. The boys know what to do, they just need the occasional kick in the ass. A strong whip hand, Dahlgren."

The second poor decision was that Fred planned to fly in only for the funeral. "Let me know when the funeral's going to be held. Strictly an in-and-out trip for me. I'll stick around for the service, shake a few hands, and then it's back to New York."

"People are going to expect that you'll be here for the viewing. Show Mordecai the proper respect."

"I hate viewings worse than I do the funerals, and I hate funerals. Standing around and saying how natural he looks and he's in a better place and all that happy horseshit. Forget it!"

"What's so important that you can't leave New York?"

"We're lining up the financing to purchase half of Susi's stock. I've kissed so many bankers' asses, my lips have pinstripes."

"Mordecai have any family?" I asked.

"Widower, I seem to remember," Fred said. "Can't remember if he had any kids. Mordecai wasn't exactly the type to yank out his wallet and show you pictures, now was he?"

"What about the arrangements?"

"You handle all that."

"You got any other jobs for me, Fred? First ranch foreman, now mortician."

"I'm not asking you to embalm him, Dahlgren."

"Maybe I should fire the chef. Then I could start cooking for you."

"There's no reason to get pissy, Dahlgren. You've had a shock, son. We've both had a shock. Calm down."

Sitting on the couch I decided that I would send Mordecai off in grand style. I called the director of the largest mortuary in town. In a somber, respectful voice, rich with sympathy and empathy and concern, he promised that he would attend to all the details. He would arrange for the body to be delivered to the funeral home from the coroner's office following the autopsy. He would also make sure that the body would be presentable for viewing.

"Would you care to visit us and select an appropriate coffin?" he asked.

"No," I answered. "Go ahead and use the most expensive wooden casket you've got. Something with carving on it."

"Would you like us to select appropriate clothing for the deceased?"

"No, I'll bring something by tomorrow."

"Do you have a preference for the cemetery?"

"There's a graveyard right here on the Carved L. Can we bury him here at the ranch?" I asked.

"Oh, my," he said. "I don't believe anyone has been interred there since the 1950s. I'll have to check with the Department of Health."

"Money is no object. We'll pay whatever and whoever we have to pay, but Mordecai's final resting place will be the Carved L."

That evening I received two telephone calls and a letter. One of the calls and the letter contained death threats. Things were looking up. The first telephone call was from Brewster Duff.

"I'm sorry to hear about Mordecai," Brewster said. "I tried calling Fred, but it appears he's not currently in residence at the ranch."

"I'll pass along your condolences."

"If there's anything I can do to help, you let me know."

"Don't you think you've done enough already?"

"Whatever do you mean?"

"You know exactly what I mean. I'll bet that you called your real estate agent first. Should we prepare for another bid, Brewster?"

"My condolences and conducting sound business are separate actions, Dahlgren. Without Mordecai, without a strong foreman, a property like the Carved L could go down quickly. With all your problems, I thought it would be neighborly of me—"

"Don't think, Brewster. The Carved L is not for sale. Mordecai knew who was killing the bison on the property, and I suspect that the FBI will also know soon enough."

"I have nothing to do with your problems on the ranch."

"And I think you do."

"I warn you, sir," Brewster said, "if you go around town making base and insupportable accusations about me, slandering the Duff name, a name that goes back to the earliest days of the settlement of this valley, I'll . . . I'll sue you. I will ruin you."

He hung up.

The telephone rang again.

"It's Friday."

"Ah, General Ferris," I said. "Good day to you, or is it evening already?"

"It's Friday."

"And tomorrow it shall be Saturday. So what?"

"I believe that you were supposed to have something for me by today."

"Refresh my memory, it's been a hectic week."

"So I have heard. The deed."

"What deed?"

"Don't toy with me Wallace! I thought it was understood that we demanded title to ten thousand acres by today."

"Listen, Ferris. Fred's not going to give you a handful of dirt, let alone ten thousand acres. He'll sell first, and he's not selling."

"We have already taken action. Mordecai Shames was our last warning. Next time it could be Lather, or you."

He hung up. People were, on the whole, quite rude to me this evening.

When I opened the front door a couple of hours later, I found the death threat neatly tucked under my welcome mat. Thoughtfully, Zed had handwritten his note on recycled paper.

> Today the Provisional Wing of PETEM executed another enemy of animals and the environment. Our demands regarding the treatment of the animals and fish on the Carved L Ranch have not been acted upon. Unless Lather immediately agrees to our conditions and announces the same in the media, others will die. Perhaps you shall die. Zed.

I placed the note on the coffee table and left.

"You're getting to be a regular here," Tatum shouted as I climbed onto a stool at Stacey's.

"The place is growing on me."

"Some of them militia types are back," Tatum said, pointed with his chin to one of the tables. "Axel hasn't been back. You still on the wagon?"

"No," I answered. "Give me a Black Dog."

"What's a black dog?"

"Black Dog Ale."

"Dahlgren. You're at Stacey's."

"What kind of beer do you have?"

He rattled off a half dozen domestic beers and then stopped, snapping his fingers. "Got us a few of them Guinness stouts," he said. "Left over from the chili cook-off." He found the Guinness and poured the dark beer into a glass. "This gives me some mean gas, I'll tell you."

I sipped the Guinness and looked over the crowd. I topped off the glass, slid off the barstool, and walked to the table where four of the hands from the ranch sat. Grady looked up at me when I tapped him on the shoulder.

"Grady," I said, "why don't you grab your beer and we'll go outside. Like to talk to you about a few things."

"Maybe I don't want to," he said, sipping his beer. "Maybe I don't have to."

"Then again, maybe you do." I picked Grady's cowboy hat from the table and placed it on his head. "Maybe I'm the new foreman. Maybe I'll fire your ass right now, or maybe I'll just kick it here in front of your buddies."

"All right," Grady said. "No need to get shitty." He scraped the chair away from the table and followed me outside.

"I'm depressed about Mordecai," Grady said. He leaned against the wall of the bar, attempting to project a melancholy that I saw he did not feel.

"Yeah, I can see you're all broken up."

"I am. Mordecai weren't much for jawboning, but he was an all right guy."

"What did the police question you about?"

"Hey, they told me not to discuss what I talked about."

"Don't see any police around here," I said, looking around.

"They were all serious, like. 'Specially that FBI agent."

"Grady, you don't work for the police and you sure as hell don't work for the FBI. If you want to keep working at the Carved L, I suggest you start talking."

"No need to get your shorts in a bunch." Grady sipped his beer. "First thing they asked about was if we knew where Mordecai went off to yesterday. How stupid is that? If we knew where he lit off to we'da found him our own selves. No need to go gallivanting all over the ranch.

"Then they asked us about the feed schedule."

"What did they ask?"

"Like, who knew about the schedule?"

"Who did?"

"Anybody who could read. It's posted right in the barn. Schedule usually runs a couple of weeks in advance. Got to be flexible, though, 'cause the herd don't stand around in one spot very long."

"How do you get feed out to the herd?"

"Same question that agent asked. Flatbed truck, or we haul it out on a trailer with an ATV. Normally only half a ton or so."

"Bales?"

"Yeah. The Hoots still make up hay in hundred-pound idiot wads, the ignorant, backward Christers."

"What else did they ask you?"

"Asked if anyone was hanging around wasn't supposed to be there. 'Course not. Asked about the temporary hands. We had a bunch on around calving time. Mostly we was working on fixing the winter damage. Ain't like you bring bison into the barn when they're calving. They was all the regular crew. Bunch of thieving Hoots and some old boys."

"They ask if anyone's been recently fired?"

"Yeah, and the answer is no."

"What about Cole Lassiter?"

"What about him?"

I stared at Grady.

"They didn't ask no questions about Cole," Grady said.

"I am. When was the last time Cole worked on the ranch?"

"Last big crew we had on, Cole worked."

"Good hand?"

"Better'n most, I reckon."

"He have any dealings with Mordecai?"

"Well . . . in the end he did, but it really weren't nothing."

"What wasn't nothing?"

"Well, Cole, he quit on accounta Mordecai half accused him of stealing."

"How do you half accuse someone of stealing?"

"Huh?"

"What did Mordecai accuse him of stealing?"

"Hay."

"On what basis?"

"I guess Mordecai saw Cole leave the ranch with bales of hay in the bed of his truck. But he couldn't have stole nothing."

"How can you be so sure?"

"Didn't we have to count every fucking bale of hay in the barn twice? Manhandling that shit for two full days!"

"And."

"Everything balanced out like. Mordecai watches everything, keeps lists and records to beat the band. He knows where every tool is, he could account for every bale of hay, every spool of bobbed wire, every goddamned fence post."

"Cole quit anyway?"

"Said no one was gonna call him no thief. He got all huffy and just walked out."

"When was this?"

"Two months ago."

"You friendly with Cole?"

"How do you mean, friendly?"

"Are you friends with him?"

"In a manner of speaking."

"What manner?"

"Share a place in town with him, an apartment."

"I thought you lived in the bunkhouse on the ranch."

"I do," Grady said, "but you can't never take no women back to the ranch. What if a guy wants to lay a little pipe? Sometimes you just gotta get away from the bunkhouse, buncha young guys grabassing all the time. Gets tedious."

"Cole ever ask you about the ranch?"

"No, he could give a shit less. He ended up landing a permanent job on another ranch."

"Do you ever talk to him about the ranch?"

"We ain't no paira women! 'How was your day?' " Grady asked in a falsetto voice. "Je-sus!"

"Grady, I'm going to ask you to think about something, and think about it hard before you answer. Do you think you might have mentioned, in passing, of course, that you delivered feed on such and such a day?"

Grady thought. Swallowed. "Might have."

"I want you to do me a favor," I said. "I want you to call Cole and get him to come over to Stacey's."

"Don't have to. He's already here. Least he was when we stepped outside."

"Point him out to me."

We returned to Stacey's and Grady pointed to a table. "He's sitting over yonder, wearing the jean shirt."

"Do you know any of the other guys he's sitting with?"

"Don't know 'em by name, but he works with those guys on the Lazy D."

"Duff's ranch?"

"I guess."

I climbed back onto the stool and ordered another Guinness. When I studied Mordecai's map and the dates, a pattern had emerged. The first bison was shot and speed butchered in the fall of the previous year. Each subsequent killing occurred approximately four to five weeks apart. The calves started dying six weeks ago, and the last three bison were shot at two-week intervals, the day after the supplemental feed had been delivered. Two weeks before the poisonings began Cole Lassiter quit working at the ranch. Mordecai had witnessed him leaving the ranch with hay in the bed of his truck and thought he was stealing. Yet after checking the inventory the count was accurate. There were no bales missing.

I weighed my options. On one hand I could take action. Lassiter sat a few feet away from me. We could have a pleasant chat. Or I could patiently wait, reflect on the new information Grady gave me. Action versus patience. I chose action, with patience on the side.

Lassiter walked into the parking lot just after midnight. He climbed into a new Chevy truck and drove to an apartment complex. He drove slowly and carefully and after he stopped he sat in the truck for a few minutes. He might have been listening to a song on his radio. When he stepped out of the truck I met him with a solid punch into his stomach. Lassiter dropped to one knee and then rose suddenly, whistling an uppercut toward my chin. I stepped in and hooked him with a solid left to his chest, staggering but not dropping him. Lassiter circled, threw a jab, missed, but followed with a right that caught me on my stitches.

Tucking my chin into my chest I stepped in again, this time sending half a dozen short punches to Lassiter's chest and stomach. He backed into the side of his truck, throwing a few halfhearted punches. He tried to hold me in a clinch.

Breaking the clinch I stepped back, prepared to throw another flurry of punches, but Lassiter held up his two hands and shook his head. "What do you want?" he asked.

"Want to talk," I said, between gasps.

"You got a funny way of asking a fellow to talk."

"Depends on the fellow."

"I know you," Lassiter said. "I saw you sitting at the bar at Stacey's and I was wondering who you were, because you looked familiar. You work for Lather, right? Heard you get paid to kiss his ass."

"And I know you, too, Lassiter. You work for Brewster Duff and I heard you get paid to poison livestock."

"Fuck you, man. You ain't the police. I ain't got to talk to you."

"You're right, you don't," I said. I hit Lassiter again and this time he was unprepared for the punch. He dropped to his knees. I pulled him to his feet and pushed him back into his truck.

"But the police will be here. If not tonight then tomorrow, and then you will talk. And they'll want to talk to you about murder, you being an accessory."

"I had nothing to do with Mordecai getting killed."

"But you did. That's where you're wrong. You see, your actions contributed to his death."

"Bullshit."

"Mordecai had it all figured. You weren't stealing bales of hay from the Carved L, you were swapping them. Take one out, bring one in, and put it back in the barn. Mordecai thought you were stealing, but the count squared. He questioned you about it, probably when you had a bale in your truck and you quit. The hay you brought back to the Carved L was poisoned."

"I didn't know that!" Lassiter said. I slapped Lassiter. I was nearing an edge where I would have trouble controlling my own violence. "I swear I didn't. "

"Talk to me or I'll beat on you all fucking night."

"They told me they laced the hay with a laxative, keep the bison's weight down."

"Who told you?"

"Two fellows said they was from the Cattlemen's Guild. Said they was acting on behalf of all the ranchers who wanted to get the bison out of the valley."

"They pay you?"

"Sure they paid me. Hundred dollars each bale. Made me a thousand dollars."

"How did it work?"

"Like you said. I'd take one or two bales of hay and load them up in my truck and drive out. Met one of the fellows and we'd swap. He always had two bales."

Nailed it with my first guess. Or deduction.

"Names?"

"No names, except for Benjamin Franklin, and I got to meet him ten times. Never asked them their names neither."

"One of the men wasn't Brewster Duff, was it?"

"No, I work for Mr. Duff."

"Ebon Jones?"

"That fucking moron? No. Listen, I don't know their names. You could list everyone in the guild and I still wouldn't know who they were. Know their faces if I saw them again."

"How did you come to work for Duff?"

"Hey, I'm a top hand. Got me that job straight up."

"Coincidence? You poison the Carved L livestock on behalf of the Cattlemen's Guild and suddenly you're hired on your own merit by the president of the guild? Think."

"Nobody promised me nothing. Told me to go see the foreman on the Lazy D when it was all over."

"Mordecai caught you, right?"

"No. He said he saw me leaving the ranch on three separate occasions with hay in the back of my truck. I told him he must be mistaken. He called me a thief and a liar. Man can't take that."

"Especially when it's true."

"Weren't true. I didn't steal nothing."

"I'm sure you've rationalized everything, Lassiter. You probably convinced yourself that you did nothing wrong. You might even bullshit yourself into believing that what you did was somehow the right thing to do, get rid of the bison.

"So a few calves die, big deal. Today somebody killed Mordecai Shames. Murdered him while he was trying to find out who was killing his livestock. You ever stop and think how I knew to come to speak to you? Mordecai knew you were involved, had your name written on a sheet of paper found near the body. The police have that paper now.

"You helped kill a man, Lassiter. I'm sure it didn't start that way, but that's how it ended."

"I'm telling you, the poisoning had nothing to do with Mordecai getting killed. I know it. Whoever's shooting the bison, that's who's responsible."

"Wrong again. Who did you talk to about the feed schedule?"

"What do you mean?"

"You know what I mean. Let's start with this apartment. Rooming with Grady, that wasn't your idea, was it?"

"No."

"How did it work? They rented the apartment for you, right? All you have to do is tell them the dates and location of the supplemental feedings and the money keeps coming in?"

"How do you know that?"

"Because it doesn't make sense for you and Grady to be out here playing bachelor ranch hands. Grady just about told me you knew when the bison were fed. Probably just came out in normal conversation."

"Sure, sometimes. Asked him about what he did on the ranch that day. Mordecai would give the hands copies of the feeding schedule, complete with the GPS location. Grady'd keep it in his shirt pocket."

"How did you inform your pals at the Cattlemen's Guild?"

"On my answering machine. I'd record a message, say, 'It's a fine day. You reached Grady and Cole at . . .,' and the telephone number would be the GPS location."

"You ever see the men from the guild after you left the Carved L?"

"No."

"How do you get paid?"

"Three hundred cash dollars at the end of the month. Comes in the mail."

"Let's go back and talk a bit about swapping the hay. What kind of truck did they drive?"

"No kind of truck. Drove a van."

"Describe the men."

"Only met the one fellow once at the first meeting. Fat fellow, sweated a lot. Wore sunglasses and a baseball cap. Talked like he was real educated. The other fellow is about your size. Weight lifter type. Sounded like he was always pissed off about something."

"Tattoos?"

"Not that I could see."

"Tattoos here?" I pointed to the area between my thumb and forefinger.

"Wouldn't know. He always wore leather work gloves."

Suddenly I felt tired, drained. Without saying another word I walked to my truck and drove back to my cabin. I had been certain that the poisonings would lead back to Brewster Duff. Instead that road led to the Montana Patriots. The physical descriptions matched

Dalrymple Ferris and Axel Jackson, with Ferris holding himself out as a member of the Cattlemen's Guild. This I had not anticipated.

The headlights illuminated the stairs and porch of the cabin. Agent Sully Feib slept in a rocker I kept on the porch. The lights woke him.

"I was beginning to think you didn't care," I said by way of greeting.

"Your door is locked," he said by way of greeting.

"Yes," I said, "given the events of the past few weeks I have taken to locking my door."

I unlocked the door and we walked inside.

"You might want to wipe the blood on the left side of your head."

Lassiter's punch had opened the cut, but Dr. Patel's sewing still held tight. I wiped my head with a wet paper towel.

"Get you something to drink?"

"Coffee would be nice." Feib sat on the couch and read the letter from Zed that I had left on the coffee table. He stared at me. I poured coffee left over from the morning into a cup and placed it in the microwave.

"I'm deciding whether or not to arrest you," Feib said and yawned.

"Out of curiosity, what would be the charge this time?"

"Charges, actually. Obstruction of justice, for one. Impeding a police investigation. We found your fingerprints on the thermos and cooler in Mordecai's Jeep. Also on the sheet of paper he had tucked under the cooler."

I brought Feib the coffee.

"Thank you," he said.

I removed the copy of the supplemental feed schedule from my shirt pocket. "You mean the paper that looked like this?"

"Yes." Feib regarded me carefully. He examined the dates I had written on the reverse, then turned the page over and pointed to the LASS? notation. "What's this?"

"That would be Cole Lassiter."

"How do you know that?"

"Your computer technician obviously hasn't opened the payroll file in Quick Books."

Feib reached into the right outside pocket of his suit coat and laid a plastic badge on the coffee table. The badge read JUNIOR FBI AGENT, DEPARTMENT OF JUSTICE.

"Congratulations, Dahlgren," Feib said, "you made the team."

CHAPTER 19

LET THE GAMES BEGIN

When the Bozeman Police reported that Cole Lassiter and his Chevy truck had vanished, Agent Feib reconsidered arresting me, adding new charges. Aiding and abetting and conspiracy. All in all, though, it had been a good night for Feib. He had a sample of Zed's handwriting to deliver to the profilers. He confirmed his hypothesis that the poisonings and the recent shooting of the bison were somehow connected. Moreover, he knew the identity of the poisoners and how they monitored the supplemental feed schedule.

"You going to arrest Ferris and Jackson?" I asked.

"Not yet," Feib said. "We would like to make a clean sweep when we do and arrest the shooter at the same time."

"Any ideas on the shooter?"

"Ideas and suspicions aplenty. Hard evidence, no."

"Did you question Duff about the Sharps?"

"Horace did. Duff said the Sharps had been stolen."

"How convenient."

"Yes, quite a coincidence. Horace asked him when it had been stolen and Duff said he wasn't sure."

"Did he report the theft?"

"No," Feib said. "Claimed he exercised his Second Amendment rights by not reporting the theft."

"Rather obtuse logic. I still think Duff has something to do with all this."

"Why?"

"Mordecai. When I asked Mordecai if he thought Duff might be behind the poisonings he more or less indicated that it was a possibility."

When Feib asked me how I arrived at that conclusion, I recounted my last meeting with Mordecai, the evening I drove him back to Stacey's following his arrest.

"Talk about obtuse logic," Feib groaned. "'Yes, your honor, he shrugged.' A judge would not allow that as evidence of Duff's complicity."

"He's involved, all right."

"Up until this point you have been lucky, but we will take over the investigation from here. Because of your 'help,' a material witness has disappeared, one who had a little blood on his fingers. You frightened him into becoming a fugitive."

A car drove up my driveway and Agent Feib departed.

"Remember," he said, "you stay out of the way. Leave it to the professionals."

"I hear you," I said.

At the ranch the next morning I exchanged my truck for the Travelall and drove out to the meadow where I had found Mordecai the day before. A police car and a truck with a horse trailer were parked at the northern edge of the meadow. The bison were gone.

I parked the truck and walked into a stand of pines marked with yellow crime scene tape. Horace and A. J. Eaglefeather stood sipping urn-sized 7-Eleven coffees.

"Morning, gentlemen," I said.

"What the hell you doing up here?" Horace asked.

"Haven't you heard?" I answered. "I'm the new ranch foreman. Merely looking out for the best interests of my employer, Horace."

"Fred must have lost his mind. Hey," Horace said, snapping his fingers, "I just remembered that I'm supposed to be pissed at you for running Lassiter out of town."

Horace and A. J. continued their discussion. A. J. retired from Fish & Game a few years ago, retired as A. J. Eagleton. His reputation as the department's best tracker helped him launch a second career. Though he worked primarily for law enforcement, A. J. tracks anything from missing pets to lost hikers. "Changed my name to Eaglefeather," he reasoned, "because people think Indians are fabulous trackers, all mystical and such. Won't hurt business none if folks think I'm part Indian. Who knows, I might be anyway."

A. J. mounted his horse and rode off, one hand on the reins and the other still holding his coffee.

"The amateur sleuth," Horace said. "Sneaking around pretty good, aren't you?"

"Keeping myself busy."

"Now that you're the new ranch foreman, I suspect that your days as a detective are over."

"Feib warned me off last night. I heard the message."

"I know you've heard the message," Horace said, "but did you get the message?" He held up a hand. "Don't answer, because I don't want you lying to me."

"Honestly, I've got work to do in the barn, and then I have to drive into Big Sky."

"What are you doing in Big Sky?"

"I ran out of incense," I said.

"Don't you just hate when that happens?"

The ranch hands were not happy with my initial instructions as foreman. I wanted the first three lengthwise rows of hay and the first two rows on each side carried outside and laid in the yard as single bales with enough room to walk between them.

"Goddamn it," Grady complained. "That seems like busywork. You're talking about hauling 250 hundred-pound bales."

"Your roommate swapped bales of hay, replacing them with poisoned bales. We've been poisoning our own stock."

"Then we ought to check the whole lot."

"And we might have to do that, but let's try it my way first."

With nine dead calves found at five locations with five separate supplemental feed deliveries, I figured that at most five contaminated bales remained from the ten Lassiter said he had swapped.

Grady drove an ATV into the yard, pulling a trailer with twelve bales of hay in six stacks of two. I inspected the first bale he manhandled to the ground.

"What's this?" I asked, pointing to a blob of orange paint on one end of the hay bale.

"The Hoots mark each bale with paint."

"Why?"

"Identifying marks so they know what hay gets delivered to what ranch. Orange paint for the Carved L."

"Is there any difference between the hay?"

"I don't think so, but Mordecai did. This here hay is organic. No chemicals. Yield is less and we pay more for it by weight, but it's supposed to be better."

"How do you mix in the vitamins?"

"Spray it on. Let's say I check the schedule and know we have to deliver food tomorrow. Well, I'll lay out the number of bales we're going to deliver, usually ten, single row, like you're making us do now. Then I mix the vitamins by formula in distilled water and use the spray canister to lace the bales."

"Line up the bales so that the identifying marks are all visible on the same side," I said. "You can stack them three high as well, if that would make the job easier."

Grady nodded.

The first swapped bale we identified stuck out like a sore thumb. While the Carved L ranch bales were marked with neon orange, the markings on this bale were a flat orange.

"Could you look at something, Grady?"

Grady, sweat pouring off his face and soaking his shirt, and covered with dust and bits of hay, examined the two splotches of orange paint.

"Hell, yes!" he said, pumping his fist into the air. "Different as night and day. I gotta admit I thought you had a screw loose asking us to ruck this hay, but Goddamn!" Grady moved the bale with the flat orange marking to the side. "Look here," he said. With his fingers he pulled some of the orange paint away and revealed flecks of white paint. "Someone tried to cut out the original markings and then they covered it with the orange paint."

When the hands finished moving the hay we had found a total of four of the swapped bales. I had figured at least five bales of the poison-laced hay had already, and unwittingly, been delivered to the herd.

"Cole said he swapped ten," I said.

"Could be we delivered two bales in one delivery," Grady said. "Could be we got them all. How about we do one more row across and one more in on each side? We know what to look for now."

"Good work, Grady."

"Thank you."

I ignored the crime scene tape and walked into Mordecai's trailer. I studied the Charlie Russell watercolor as I talked with the chief of police.

"Horace," I said, "you need to come back out to the ranch. Think we found the poisoned bales. I'd bring a truck if you plan on taking them."

"I hardly think I'd drive out there just to look at them. Sounds like a job for Officer Andrew."

"Then I'd make sure to tell him not to eat any of the hay himself."

"Dahlgren, I appreciate this. I really do. But I thought we agreed you'd be retiring from the detective business."

"These are my hands on my ranch," I said.

"In a manner of speaking," Horace said.

"In a manner of speaking," I said. "We don't want any more of our calves poisoned, so we decided to inspect our feed."

"But you're still aiming to go to Big Sky?"

"Is PETEM really part of this investigation?"

"According to Feib, no."

"Then I'm not interfering."

"However, they are part of another ongoing investigation. You would do well to recall they also made a death threat against you. It's Feib's opinion they are not involved. Me, I'm waiting until the tracker finishes his work."

I drove to Big Sky, the county seat for Californicators. Way too many coffee shops and art galleries, and the only town in a hundred miles where you can buy patchouli incense, frangipani bath beads, and healing crystals.

Before I entered The Newest Age, I walked into the alley behind the shop and found the green Volvo. I pierced each tire with the knife blade, further adding to my list of uses for my Leatherman. Pinch a barb on a fly, trim tippet, slice cheese, tighten loose screws, and deflate four reasonably new tires. Pointless, needless, spiteful vandalism sometimes soothes the soul as effectively as patchouli incense and frangipani bath beads.

Chimes tinkled when I entered the shop. After making sure that I was the shop's only customer, I reversed the sign to "Closed" and locked the door. I slapped the Buddhist prayer wheel as I walked to the counter. Generic Windham Hill music played softly in the background. Straw Fields stared at me, then reached for the telephone.

I took the telephone from his hands. He looked at me and blinked.

"How rude. Making a call when you have a customer in the shop."

"I had nothing to do with it," Fields whispered.

"I haven't accused you of anything yet," I said.

"You will. I just know it."

"Where were you that night?"

"What night?"

"The night Zed and I had our little chat."

"Who is Zed?"

"Don't insult my intelligence. You know who Zed is. He's only the most famous animal rights terrorist in the world."

"Activist, animal rights activist."

"When I hear activist I think of Mother Teresa. When I think of Zed I think terrorist, maybe even sociopathic terrorist. Now, how about you answer my question. Were you there that night?"

"The night you and Zed allegedly met?"

"Yup."

"No, I wasn't there."

"But your car was."

"I reported my car stolen. I was fortunate to get it back."

"How lucky for you."

"Indeed."

"The reason I asked if you were there that night was to see if we could save a little time. Zed made a series of outrageous demands that evening. Demands he expected me to deliver to Fred Lather. By the way, I did deliver them. Fred, predictably, refused to knuckle under to the demands. So Zed had someone deliver a nasty note to my cabin last night. The letter threatened my life. I've never even received so much as a Christmas card from Zed before, so I figure he doesn't know where I live. You, on the other hand, know exactly where I live."

"I fail to see how this affects me. Do you think I delivered this threatening letter?"

"What does this do?" I asked, picking up a pyramid-shaped crystal.

"It channels positive energy through a prism and it helps you achieve harmony and inner peace."

"You think it can channel positive energy up your ass? Because that's where you'll find it if I have to come back to this shop again.

"Straw, I've got a lot on my plate right now, not the least of which is dealing with serious problems on the ranch. Somebody's shooting and poisoning our bison, issues that actually resonate with PETEM. Dealing with empty, extortionate threats is counterproductive. You and I are going to make a deal. You're the regional director for PETEM, so I know you can agree to my demands.

"No more death threats, no more bullshit demands regarding the Carved L ranch. Tell Zed to go fuck himself, Fred isn't playing his game. Knowing Fred, he would probably spend a fortune hiring manhunters to find Zed. Simply put, Fred will get to Zed before Zed gets to Fred. As for you, no more late-night unofficial deliveries of the mail. In exchange I will not deliver putrefying bison calf carcasses to the front door of The Newest Age. I will not collect roadkill and hide it in the backseat of your precious Volvo. You get the picture?"

"I hear the ravings of a man whose life spirit has been filled with the toxins found in eating the flesh of his fellow creatures."

"Please, Straw, no speeches. You don't have an audience to impress. The FBI knows that Zed is operating in Montana and they know he'll try to shove his monkey wrench into the works somewhere this summer. But the Carved L is off the list of targets."

"If I can deliver the message, I will. That's no guarantee that Zed will accede to these ludicrous demands."

"Then you should prepare to see carrion flying over your store and vehicle." I tossed him the crystal. "And don't forget, positive energy flowing right up your asshole."

Horace called with the news that A. J., faux Indian status notwithstanding, had come up against the modern tracker's insurmountable enemy, a paved highway. A. J. reported that the shooter appeared to head north on 191, but there was no guarantee that he hadn't doubled back.

"Said the perpetrator wore Cabela's Black Duty Boots, size 10," Horace said. "Figures him to be about five-ten to six feet tall, weight two forty-five. There was another man with him, shorter, went about two hundred pounds."

"What did they eat for breakfast?" I asked.

"Huh?"

"In the movies, the tracker usually can tell what his quarry ate for breakfast."

"Very funny," Horace said. "Another thing. Got a call from the sheriff down in Big Sky. Seems somebody vandalized Straw Fields's car. Slashed all four tires with a knife. You wouldn't happen to know anything about that, would you?"

"Terrible thing. All four tires, you say?"

"Told the sheriff I'd ask, but I never said I would actually investigate. Last item on my list. We released Mordecai's body to the funeral home this afternoon."

"Were we right about the Sharps?"

"The wounds were consistent with a fifty-four-caliber Sharps rifle bullet. We'll find what's left of the slug in the engine to confirm Cord's findings."

"So the round came from one of the original Sharps rifles, not a reproduction."

"Looks that way."

"Doesn't that make Duff's story seem even more far-fetched?"

"Far-fetched or not, I can't go traipsing into his office with allegations and not a shred of proof," Horace said.

"What about Lassiter working for him? Just another coincidence?"

"He said that he never met Lassiter. Couldn't identify him in a lineup, he said. Ranch foreman does all the hiring."

"Could be his stolen rifle is on the business end of the shootings. We know his ranch hand is part of the trio that poisoned our livestock. Mordecai thought Duff had something to do with the poisonings, and then him offering to buy the Carved L every other day. Seems like a hell of a lot of coincidences."

"And not even a shred of circumstantial evidence. I can't accuse him of anything."

"But I can," I said.

"Dahlgren, you are not heeding our advice. Stay out of this investigation. Bad enough you stampeded Cole Lassiter. If you screw up something with Duff and it turns out he might have something to do with all this, there might be formal charges."

"Do you honestly believe that Duff had anything to do with Mordecai's murder?" I asked.

"No, I do not."

"Neither do I, but I do believe he's involved with the poisonings. Even if he's charged with that crime, do you think he'll be convicted and serve any time? For killing bison? Remote, unlikely, a frigging miracle if he served one day."

"Get off with a steep fine, most likely," Horace said.

"And not even a blemish on his reputation. He would be the poster boy for every cattlemen's association in the West. I'm convinced that Duff holds the key that's important to this case."

"The only key he may hold is the one to your jail cell."

Next I called Agent Feib.

"Any chance your computer technician could just copy the hard drive on Mordecai's computer? I need it to run the ranch."

"That is a reasonable request," Feib said. "I will see what I can do."

"One other thing. You mentioned that the Montana Patriots are facing financial difficulties."

"Yes, they are desperately short of cash."

"When did they first start feeling the pinch?"

"Three or four months ago. Somehow they are still squeezing by."

"That could be one reason for the change in the pattern for the bison shootings. Every two weeks now instead of the four- to five-week interval we saw earlier. Subsistence hunting."

"When we raid the compound we'll be sure to keep our eyes open for buffalo roasts," Feib said, hanging up. The FBI does sarcasm well.

The final piece of the puzzle fell into my lap when A. J. Eagle-feather visited late in the day.

"Figured you'd be at the ranch," A. J. said, when I answered his knock on my door. "Seeing as how you're acting foreman and all."

A. J. was taking this Native American thing a bit far for my taste. He was dripping in turquoise jewelry and he had a feather tied in his hair. "Operative word there is 'acting,'" I replied. "Right now I don't feel like acting like a foreman. Want something to drink?"

A. J. made a show of kicking his boots against the doorjamb before entering the cabin.

"Wouldn't say no to some coffee." I made a fresh pot and poured us each a cup.

"Something I need to tell you," A. J. said. "I found another print near the meadow. Thought you would like to know."

"Did you tell the police?" I asked. Horace hadn't mentioned a third set of prints.

"No. It's only one boot print and it's old."

"How old?"

"Months old, maybe older. A miracle it's still visible. Not too clear at this stage, though I'd guess it came from a handmade pair of boots. Given the size I think it's a lady's boot. Narrow and tiny. Again, because of the age and condition of the print this is only a guess, but I'd say size five in a man's boot. Reason I didn't tell Horace, I figured it might belong to that Hollywood gal, Sally."

"You're probably right, A. J. Thanks for your discretion."

"Nothing, really. Like I said, the print's too old to be of any real use."

The director of the funeral home called and we worked out a schedule. Mordecai's funeral was scheduled for Tuesday. "We would not want to bury him on Memorial Day," the director said. "The funeral might interfere with many of the mourners' long-weekend plans." The Department of Health permitted the burial on the ranch.

"With your permission we would like to send a pair of cemetery landscape technicians to the ranch to prepare the final resting place," the director said.

"You mean grave diggers?" I asked.

"We prefer cemetery landscape technicians."

"Of course."

"Naturally." A long pause, then a small cough. "May we?"

"May you what?" I asked.

"Send the technicians?"

"Of course."

"Oh, of course. I see, yes. We would further recommend that you consider a reception following the service. Something tasteful, reserved. Again, we would be honored to make the necessary arrangements."

"Thank you, but no. I believe we'll handle the reception."

"As you wish. There is the matter of Mr. Shames's clothing."

"I'll bring that by this evening."

"Fine. The viewings are scheduled for tomorrow and Monday, with your approval."

"Of course," I said.

"Of course," the director said.

Of course, Tuesday was shaping up into a busy day. Mordecai's funeral and the reception in the afternoon. I had also decided to attend the evening meeting of the African Brothers Society.

CHAPTER 20

PATRIOTS GAMES

I spent Sunday evening with Mordecai. My only consolation was that in life, he had been only slightly more voluble. I had fished earlier in the day, floating the seven miles of the river on the ranch property, avoiding the holiday crowds. I didn't even see Sarah Kleinsasser, my favorite Hutterite poacher, whose Sundays were taken up with worship on the Bozeman Trail Colony.

Mordecai's viewing did not draw many mourners. The few people who did come probably wanted to see what he looked like without his hat. None of the ranch hands came to pay their respects. I attributed that to their relatively tender ages. They didn't know they were supposed to make an appearance. A few people sent flowers, including a modest spray from Stacey's. I sent two large wreaths in Fred's name, positioned at either end of the casket. Sally, the most recent former Mrs. Lather, sent a plant.

Mordecai didn't look natural and he didn't look peaceful. Mordecai looked dead. Waxy, his face and hands caked with heavy makeup, he looked uncomfortable. He wore a white cowboy shirt with pearl buttons and a bolo tie.

At times you learn things about people in death that surprise you. Given Mordecai's penchant for silence, his past was unknown to most. The *Chronicle*, in addition to covering the second lurid murder on the Carved L, also printed an obituary. Mordecai was fifty-five years old, had been born and raised in Bozeman, the only child of schoolteacher parents. He served three tours in Vietnam as a member of the elite Green Berets, earning the Silver Star and a Purple Heart. He graduated from Montana State University, attending on the GI Bill. He married the former Annabelle Sue Matthews. They had no children, and she died in 1979 of cancer. He had worked on ranches his entire life, most notably as foreman of two of the county's largest spreads, the Lazy D and the Carved L.

The talk of the town on Monday was the FBI's predawn raid on the Montana Patriots' compound. Assisted by agents of the Bureau of Alcohol, Tobacco and Firearms and local police, all fifty-eight members of the Patriots, fifty-two men and six women were in custody and being questioned regarding the murder of Mordecai Shames and other crimes.

As the evening wore on, rumors replaced facts. More people attended the viewing on Monday evening, merely to claim an attachment to the bizarre events of the last few weeks.

"Heard they found plans to blow up the police station."

"This is the gospel truth. My brother's girlfriend's uncle's son works for the police department. Not a policeman, he sort of cleans up at night. Well, sir, he heard those militia boys were fixing to take over the ranch. Kidnap old Lather and his guests and hold 'em hostage."

"Well, I heard the ATF found hand grenades and a missile launcher."

"You think them black helicopters were ours or do they belong to NATO?"

"They say the Patriots killed that California feller, that rich pal of Lather's."

"Oh, sure. Me and Mordecai talked about 'Nam all the time. I was a cook, but one night, when Charlie attacked our base, I grabbed me a machine gun and . . ."

". . . found a list with the names of fifty people on it they was fixing to kill when the revolution started."

"Supposedly six people were killed, two agents and four of them militia men. The federal agents are covering everything up; they don't want another Ruby Ridge."

Horace stopped by and told me what really happened. We sat in the chapel with only the mortal remains for company.

"They attacked the compound just before dawn. About fifty agents, special assault teams from the bureau and ATF, backed up by the local agents. We had about ten of our guys out there to help with prisoner logistics and transportation.

"The only guard was asleep. Never fired a shot, not even a teargas round. The women gave us the most trouble, kicked one of my people in the nuts as he was helping her into a prisoner van. Ferris and Jackson were loaded into the ATF helicopter, same one you took a ride in, actually. You should have heard Ferris screaming.

" 'The troops of the New World Order are going to assassinate us! They're going to torture us and throw us out of this helicopter. You Patriots are witnesses. Remember us, men. We are martyrs in the great struggle.'

"The great struggle," Horace continued, "was loading his fat ass into the helo. Him sweating and all, it was like trying to catch a greased pig at the county fair. Jackson, now, he approached things a bit differently. He shouted 'I am a political prisoner! I am a political prisoner!' over and over."

"Did you find the Sharps rifle?"

"We did. Found it in Jackson's room. His prints are all over the weapon and it has been fired recently. We found the slug in the Jeep's engine block. It's pretty mangled but enough markings are visible to make a match through ballistics.

"Found a bunch of other weapons as well, including a case of stolen military issue M-16s. That will help us immensely."

"How?" I asked.

"Ferris and Jackson have refused to speak. They demanded that an attorney be present when they are questioned. Ferris hired the same guy who represented Randy Weaver. So it's unlikely we'll make any progress on that front.

"The other Patriots? Now that's a different story. With federal weapons charges hanging over their collective heads, a few have already expressed an interest in cutting a deal in exchange for testifying against Ferris and Jackson."

"So much for solidarity and belief in the cause," I said.

"Don't get me wrong," Horace said, "most of the Patriots have refused to talk. Others can't wait. There's a Louisiana doctor who lost his license to practice medicine. I believe you made his acquaintance. Well, he's talking a blue streak.

"I also found out that the FBI has several hundred hours of audiotapes. The arrests came as a result of a conversation between Ferris and Jackson late Friday evening. According to Sully, Jackson says something like 'I've got good news and bad news.' Anyway, the bad news was that they didn't have any meat. He killed the bison but he was unable to butcher it and carry out the meat. The good news was that he killed Mordecai. 'Now Lather will give us that land,' Jackson says on the tape. 'Be so scared he may give us more.'

"Apparently Ferris did not share Jackson's enthusiasm. Jackson argued that he only continued what Ferris had started when he had Elderberry killed."

"Wait," I said, "you mean Jackson believes that Ferris actually did murder Elden?"

"So it appears. Sully says the tapes are filled with references to Elden's murder, but they're sufficiently vague as to be useless. Sully also is adamant that the Patriots had nothing to do with the first death. Ferris, however, was quite successful in selling his story to the Patriots."

"It sounds like Ferris is the star of the tapes."

"He is. Guess where they had the microphone planted?"

I shrugged. "The Bunker?"

"No, the Rottweiler's collar!"

"Himmler?"

"The dog's name is Himmler?" Horace asked. "Sick bastards. Ferris brought the dog in to see a vet a couple months ago, worming, distemper, routine stuff. The FBI wired his collar. The dog's at a secure government location now, kind of a canine witness protection program."

That meant that Feib not only knew the Montana Patriots had kidnapped me, but he also had a transcript of the entire meeting.

"I know what you're thinking," Horace said. "On the night you were kidnapped the FBI had an assault team in place and at the ready. In fact, the team leader was just about ready to give the 'Go' order, right after Jackson hit you with the steel baton. Evidently you fired back with a verbal salvo that allowed them to abort the assault.

"There's nothing on the tape about poaching or poisoning on the ranch, other than Jackson bragging about killing Mordecai. Based on initial interrogations, Sully said that buffalo meat started showing up on the tables about a month and a half ago. It was widely known throughout the compound that Jackson shot bison on the Carved L. He brought another Patriot with him to help carry out the meat. Never the same guy twice. They were able to carry out about three hundred pounds of meat. Someone in the compound witnessed the murder. We've got the forensics teams analyzing each pair of boots, looking to match soil or plant matter found on the Carved L. Problem is, everyone in the camp wore the same Cabela boot.

"We also found tansy ragwort at the compound. The toxicology screens from the necropsies show traces of pyrrolizidine alkaloids present in the calves' systems."

"What is a tansy ragwort?" I asked.

"A plant that happens to be quite toxic for ruminants. Supposed to be unpalatable, but if it's mixed in with hay or other feed, an animal will eat it. The way I understand it, the toxicity is a matter of body weight, which is why the calves died but the adult bison did not. Also explains why some of the adult bison appeared to be losing weight."

"How did you get the toxicology reports before we did?" I asked.

"Sully called and spoke to the vet. The results will arrive in tomorrow's mail. Problem is, it ain't exactly illegal to own a plant, but we'll analyze the bales of hay you gave us to see if the plant is present in the hay."

"Where do you stand with Ferris and Jackson?" I asked.

"They've been charged with possession of stolen weapons, the poisonings, and poaching. Murder charges against Jackson are pending, and when we file those we'll also name Ferris as an accessory."

"Something bothers me."

"What?"

"You said that buffalo meat started appearing on the menu at the compound six weeks ago."

"Right."

"We lost ten bison to poachers, and the shootings started back in mid-October, last year."

"You're thinking someone else is responsible for those shootings?"

"I am. Six of those bison can't be accounted for."

"Could be your garden-variety poacher," Horace said. "You've told me yourself you lose a few elk every year to poachers."

"No, I don't think so," I said. "The intervals were almost like clockwork, four to five weeks apart and always in the middle of the month. These were done in a systematic manner. The Patriots started killing and butchering our stock at the same time they started the poisoning. Lassiter told them the location of the herd based on the feed deliveries."

"Any other poaching is going to get our lowest priority. So far as we're concerned, the book's closed on this one."

"You're right, the book may be closed. Let's say someone else was responsible for the first five or six bison. The Montana Patriots are arrested, charged, and take the fall. That someone just breathed a big sigh of relief, figuring that he's home free. He's been presented with an opportunity to get away clean."

Horace stood, took his Stetson from the seat of the chair next to him, and threw me a half salute. "See you tomorrow at the funeral," he said.

Fred was as good as his word. His jet landed an hour before the funeral service was scheduled to begin. He wore a black suit, a white shirt, and a dark tie.

"I expect to be wheels up for New York in two and a half hours," he said.

"You're a pallbearer," I said as he climbed into my truck.

"Awww," Fred groaned. He pushed himself deep into the seat of the truck. "Fuck me."

"You told me to take care of the details and I did. Might make up for you ignoring your other obligations."

Fred fumed.

"Here's the latest," I said, giving him the details of my visit with Straw Fields, the arrest of the Montana Patriots, and the toxicology report.

"Still nothing about Elden's murder?" he asked.

"No," I said. "Feib insists that the Patriots had nothing to do with that murder."

"And I don't have to worry about the animal rights knuckleheads?"

"For a little while, maybe. You might see protestors when your guests arrive, especially the anchorman."

"That reminds me—there's been a slight change of plan. I'll be back Sunday morning. Susi's coming in on Monday to do the deal. She wants to go fishing."

"You're kidding."

"And . . . she also asked if you would be spending the night at the ranch," Fred said. "I find that mighty unusual, yes sir, I do."

I hazarded a quick glance at Fred.

"You're leering," I said.

"Just wondering about the nocturnal habits of my river keeper."

We turned into the ranch and drove to the house.

"Shit!" Fred exclaimed. "There's got to be fifty cars here."

"Yeah, a good feed has a way of bringing everyone out."

"What feed?"

"The Game Chef is catering the affair."

"What's this here shindig going to cost me?"

"It's a funeral, not a shindig, and it should set you back about sixty."

Fred laughed. "Excuse me. For a second there I thought you said sixty."

"I did."

"Sixty thousand dollars?"

"About. The casket alone was nearly forty thousand."

"Hell, that's more than his trailer is worth!"

"I wouldn't bet on that." I described the books and art in Mordecai's trailer.

"The man was always a fucking enigma." Fred sighed.

An Anglican minister conducted the service, the vicar of the church that Mordecai attended, well . . . religiously. As a result of his death, my knowledge of the ranch foreman had grown immensely. Fred's assessment was quite accurate.

Brewster Duff was among the mourners, accompanied by his hulking bodyguard, Ebon Jones. Jones carried a thin pink scar that ran from his forehead to the bridge of his nose, a memento of his encounter with Mordecai. When I caught Jones's eye, I scratched my forehead and winked. His brow furrowed, and then he scowled when he understood what I meant. He flexed his muscles during the entire service.

Agent Sully Feib and Chief of Police Horace Twain also attended. Officer Andrew thought it would be a great idea to copy down the license plate numbers of the guests; something he had obviously seen in a movie. It didn't seem to matter that the murderer was already in custody. Foremen from local ranches, ranch hands, waitresses from the diners in town, and a representative from the Bozeman Trail Colony came to pay their respects.

Everyone seemed surprised with the music that played while Mordecai's beautifully carved casket was being lowered into the ground. The funeral director had commented that he couldn't recall anyone else using Willie Nelson's "Mama, Don't Let Your Babies Grow Up to Be Cowboys." There has got to be a first time for everything. As we walked back to the ranch from the cemetery, "Streets of Laredo" played in the background. A fishing guide's idea of a cowboy's funeral. I think Mordecai would have been pleased.

"I get a lump in my throat every time I hear that song," Duff said.

"Willie Nelson's song?" I asked.

"No, the other song. Fred," he said, turning his full attention to the owner of the Carved L Ranch and away from its putative foreman, "I just came by to offer my condolences. Sorry I can't stay, but the pressures of business. I'm sure you understand."

"That's too bad," I said. "We're barbecuing a heap of fine buffalo steaks. I understand that's your favorite meal."

Duff stopped dead in his tracks. "You still have that wicked sense of humor, Dahlgren. I am sure that it will help to enliven this otherwise somber occasion. Fred." Duff tipped his hat and left.

"Dahlgren," Fred said, "you were perfectly rude to our guest. Mordecai's funeral is hardly the proper moment to display poor manners."

"That little shit is guilty of something," I said.

"We are all guilty of something. Ah, our dear friends in law enforcement. Good day, Horace. Afternoon, Agent Feib."

"Nice feed," Horace said, balancing a plate covered with a thick steak. "And, of course, my condolences."

"Thank you, Horace," Fred said. "I was just telling Dahlgren that we are all guilty of something. Do you agree?"

"I am certainly not guilty of anything," Feib said.

"Oh ye without sin!" Fred replied. "Now don't go bending down to pick up any stones, Agent Feib. Those of us who are not as righteous might be forced to make for the exits."

We all politely laughed.

"I'd like to thank both of you for what you've done for the ranch and me."

"We charged Jackson this morning," Horace said through a mouthful of meat. "First-degree murder. One of the other Patriots came forward and said he witnessed Jackson shooting Mordecai. Boots matched the prints we found at the scene."

"And you've resolved the poaching and poisoning on my ranch?" Fred asked.

"Yes," Horace said, fork poised in midair.

"Because my acting foreman is not convinced that the poaching issue has been completely resolved."

"He has made that clear to both of us," Feib said.

"Duff has something to do with this," I said.

"Even if he did," Horace said, "the likelihood that you'd receive any satisfaction from it would be remote."

"Like I was saying," Fred said, "we are all guilty of something. We all have our secrets, right, Dahlgren? We have all done things that we later regret having done. Like boinking widows."

Feib's eyes darted from Fred to me. "Wallace," he said, "don't tell me that you had sex with Elderberry's widow?"

"OK," I said, "I won't."

"I am serious," he said, pulling me away from Fred and Horace, his hand tight on my elbow. As we walked away, I glanced over my shoulder. Fred laughed, Horace stared, his face wrinkled in confusion.

"Confession is good for the soul!" Fred shouted.

"Wallace," Feib said, "did you have sex with Mrs. Elderberry?"

"How is my personal life your business?"

"Your personal life becomes my business when it directly affects an ongoing investigation. Let me give you a hypothetical. If you slept with Mrs. Elderberry before her husband's death, it could cause us to reexamine your role in the murder investigation. Maybe you are infatuated with her or maybe you want her money."

"I see your point," I said. "I did not sleep with Susi before the murder."

"That's a relief. But you did have sex with her?"

"Agent Feib, why are you still involved in the Elderberry murder investigation?"

"There are federal aspects to this case."

"Like what? Fred's stock market chicanery?"

"No. While Mr. Lather's actions stretched the limits of insider trading, he technically did not cross the line. He violated no securities laws."

"So?"

"Wallace," Feib said, "I cannot and will not share with you exactly why the Elderberry murder is still a matter for the FBI. In that context I will ask again. When did you have sex with her?"

"The evening of the day her husband was murdered."

"Quick work. Comforting the widow in her time of need, no doubt."

"I did not initiate the . . . ah . . ." Suddenly I was at a loss for words.

"She approached you?" Feib asked.

"Yes." Without divulging any details, I told Feib what had happened.

"In your opinion, was this an aberration?"

"Absolutely. I rarely receive the attentions of fabulously wealthy former beauty queens."

"Not for you. For her."

"What do you mean?"

"What do you think I mean? In your opinion, was this a response to her grief, an isolated event, or was Mrs. Elderberry practiced in these matters?"

"How the hell should I know?" I glared at Fred, who continued to watch Feib and me with interest. Horace was bent over his plate.

"Goddamned Fred," I muttered.

"Why did Mr. Lather see fit to expose your tryst?"

"I don't think he knew for sure that I had slept with Susi. He does now. He can't stand being out of the loop on anything. He mentioned that she will be back next Sunday and that she asked if I would be spending the evening at the ranch."

"Ahhh."

"Ahhh, what?"

"I believe Mr. Lather is jealous, or at least a bit bent out of shape that you . . . well . . ." Suddenly Special Agent Feib was at a loss for words.

"That's bullshit. Fred asked me to spend the night because he thought it would be inappropriate for him to stay alone at the ranch with Susi."

"Yes."

"Fred invited Elden to the ranch with the explicit purpose of buying part of his company. When Elden died, he knew he would have to deal with Susi."

"Yes."

"He intends to buy half her interest in VideoComp. There's no way he would jeopardize the deal."

"I am not suggesting that he would."

Fred shook hands with Horace and walked to my truck. He opened the door, climbed in, and started the motor. He waved again. Shit, I thought, he's driving himself to the airport and I would have to get somebody to run me out there to retrieve my truck.

And that's when it hit me. Fred's request to lend propriety to the evening. Feib's questions. The guarded comments of VideoComp's interim chairman, Brigham Briggs, regarding the Elderberry marriage. Briggs had said, "Some guys do, and some guys don't. Elden definitely did not."

But he had said nothing about Susi Elderberry.

Maybe Fred had asked me to stay because he had heard rumors. Elden and Susi, San Francisco's Mormon power couple. No children, though she wanted them. Susi's solo appearances on the society pages. Elden writing the checks to support her philanthropy. Elden's interest in the Mormon forgeries and his obsession with the Golden Plates. Susi's odd behavior at dinner the night of her husband's murder. Her even odder behavior later in the evening.

Misdirection. The murder of Elden Elderberry had nothing to do with Fred Lather and the Carved L Ranch, and never had. It was never about the Montana Patriots and their land grab. It was never about PETEM and their demand to turn the ranch into an animal sanctuary. And it was never about Brewster Duff and his obsession to own the Carved L.

The murder of Elden Elderberry had everything to do with Elden Elderberry.

CHAPTER 21

HE AIN'T HEAVY, HE'S MY AFRICAN BROTHER

Ever since the poet Robert Bly published *Iron John,* groups of men have taken to the woods to pound on drums, gripe about their mothers, and explore their maleness under the auspices of what is known as the Men's Movement. Men learning how to be men. Somehow scratching your nuts and baying at the moon releases the inner man in some men.

As I sat hidden in the woods, dressed in the modified RealTree ghillie suit I normally wear while turkey hunting, watching the African Brothers Society, I attempted to categorize the bacchanalia. The African Brothers Society is the illogical blending of the Men's Movement and the Safari Club. Robert Bly meets Robert Ruark.

Many of the entirely Anglo-Saxon members of the society also held membership in the Gallatin County Cattlemen's Guild. The remaining members were wealthy professionals or business owners who met the stringent membership requirements. A prospective member must have killed his game on safari in Africa, then had it professionally mounted by a taxidermist and displayed in his trophy room. Naturally, he would have a trophy room. An existing Brother sponsored the prospective member, and entrance was allowed only if during the secret ballot not a single negative vote was cast.

I fell back on my Deep Reconnaissance and sniper training to get within ten feet of the gathering. In Kuwait we once got so close to the enemy camp that a member of the Republican Guard urinated less than three feet from my head. I could sit still for hours, ignoring changes in the weather, insects, or my own need to take a leak.

By the time I had crept into position the events of the evening were quite advanced. No one had started stumbling yet, but some were merely a few sips away. Each member wore blackface, a sleeveless safari shirt, and a kilt. They walked about barefoot and congregated around a large bonfire. Turning on a spit was a roasting buffalo haunch. The Brothers cut chunks of meat from the haunch that they then ate with their hands, grunting.

Tatum O'Neill tended bar, incongruously clad in formal wear. Tails. He served generous portions of liquor in cut-crystal glasses.

Tatum had arrived at the ranch immediately after Fred borrowed my truck for his drive back to the airport. Tatum leaped out of his car and hastily attached a clip-on tie to the collar of his dress shirt. I had disentangled myself from Special Agent Feib and was busy performing my duties as the host.

"I hope I'm not late," Tatum said.

"No, you made it just in time to eat," I said.

"Not a total loss then."

Tatum and I walked through the buffet line and filled our plates. We sat together at a small café table.

"I need another favor, Tatum."

"What do you need, teammate?"

"Where do the African Brothers hold their meetings?"

"No can do. That's top secret."

"Tatum, this isn't a matter of national security."

"No, it's a matter of my financial security," he said. "I usually make a couple of hundred dollars tending bar for the society meetings. It's a good gig. Pour nothing but straight shots of the finest."

"I don't intend on crashing the party," I answered. "I need to get close and observe is all."

"If you get caught it'll be my ass. I need that money, Dahlgren."

"I won't get caught."

"These fellers are big-time hunters. They might spot you lurking around."

"These guys hunt in zoos. I could walk up to the bar and order a drink and I doubt anyone would notice me."

"They do some weird shit," Tatum said. "Stuff they don't want anyone to see."

"You see it."

"Yeah, but I signed what they call a nondisclosure agreement saying I won't tell anything I know to an outsider."

"Tatum, I really need this favor."

"All right." He told me the location.

After I finished eating, a young Hutterite approached me. Clean shaven, a bachelor, he took notice of the waitresses and the young women on the catering staff.

"Mr. Wallace?" he asked, his German accent faint, but noticeable.

"Yes."

"I am Heinrich Kleinsasser, Luther's nephew," he said. "You can call me Henry. My uncle asked me to offer his condolences. Mr. Shames was a friend of the colony. We enjoyed working for him."

"Thank you. Please give your uncle my best."

"I will."

"May I ask you a question?"

"*Ja*, of course."

"Do you know that our ranch buys hay from the colony?"

"*Ja*. I help my uncle with the farming. One day I hope to be farm boss."

"I understand that you identify the hay bales with paint."

"To make certain we know to what ranch the hay will be sent."

"And the Carved L—"

"Neon orange!" Heinrich laughed. "I bought this paint. Very cheap, too. The paint store could not sell this color. Everyone laughs at me; they think I am a hippie. It's too bright, not suited for the brethren. I tell them the price, and suddenly I am shrewd."

"Does Mr. Duff buy hay from the colony?"

"*Ja*, the Lazy D Ranch. White."

"What?"

"White paint. That's how we mark the hay for the Lazy D. White."

"Your uncle also told me that Ferris, the fat man who is the leader of the militiamen, also visited the colony."

"He did. He comes the first time with Herr *Runt der Sanfte*."

"Duff brought Ferris to the colony?"

"I think so. Herr . . . Duff, he introduces *Der Milizmann* to my uncle. He buys hams, I think. They talk about the land."

"Do you know how often Ferris visited the colony?"

"Not many times. Two or three times. The last time he comes, my uncle becomes very angry."

"Yes, Luther told me. Ferris lied to your uncle. He told him that he would soon own land on the Carved L Ranch."

"The land we wish to buy for the new colony?"

I nodded. "Did Ferris ever buy hay from the colony?"

"*Nein*. I don't think he has any livestock. He is so big maybe he eats the hay himself!"

"You know that he has been arrested and that it was one of his men who killed Mordecai?"

"Yes, my uncle tells me this."

~

Later that evening I watched grown men drink out of crystal, eat buffalo with their hands, beat on drums, sing, recite their own dreadful poetry, and generally act like asses.

I knew I had connected the dots from Duff to the Montana Patriots, and I also knew that no one else really cared. C. Brewster Duff IV would not be arrested or convicted. But I had moved from mere suspicion to circumstantial evidence.

Carrying a large percentage of Scottish blood, I knew a thing or two about kilts. Kilts don't have pockets, so there's no place to store your keys or wallet. Hence the sporran, or purse, that hangs around the waist. The sporran is usually made with the head and skin of a badger, or other skins like ermine or seal. The sporrans worn by the members of the African Brothers Society would not have passed muster with any self-respecting Highlander.

The sporrans were made of the skins of exotic African game animals, with several notable exceptions. Duff's sporran was made of the woolly fur found on the head of the American bison. Several of his Brothers wore similarly adorned sporrans.

The final rite performed at the meeting occurred at midnight, when even Tatum had been banished. Duff marched at the head of the line. Walking barefoot, he was easy to recognize, even shorter because he lacked the advantage of the lifts in his shoes. The other men followed behind in single file, hands on the hips of the man ahead. The last time I had witnessed anything like this was at my high school senior prom, when we formed a conga line for "I Heard It through the Grapevine."

Duff carried a papier-mâché head of a bison. The Brothers chanted *Tatonka*!, followed by a grunt. This was the Lakota Sioux word for bison. After several sinuous laps around the bonfire, Duff halted. Once again the Brothers shouted *Tatonka*!, and Duff hurled the head into the bonfire. The bison head immediately burst into flames.

"When will we hunt *tatonka* again, Headman?" asked a Brother.

"When we run Bwana Fred off his land, then we shall hunt *tatonka*," Duff said. "And we will have a great hunt, like the buffalo hunters of the 1800s, we will take many skins!"

Where were the People for the Equal Treatment of Every Mammal when you needed them? Duff, operating under the delusion that he would still someday own the Carved L, fantasized about wiping out Fred's bison herd. I felt like walking into the clearing and choking the little dweeb. When I chose between action and patience on this occasion, patience won out.

I waited for the Brothers to depart before I left.

On Wednesday morning I dressed for success. My other blue blazer, blue button-down shirt with a yellow tie, khaki trousers, and a pair of cordovan loafers. Damn, I almost looked preppy.

I drove to the Lazy D Ranch and parked in front of the ranch house. After Duff III died, Brewster razed the century-old ranch house and replaced it with a sprawling reproduction of South Fork, the Ewing house from the television show *Dallas*. Local contractors called it "Duff's Last Erection."

A maid answered the door and appeared to have every intention of keeping me in my place on the doorstep.

"Morning, ma'am," I said. "I'd like to see Brewster, please."

"I believe that Mr. Duff is not receiving visitors at this time," she said in a thick Scottish burr.

"Please tell him that Dahlgren Wallace is calling and that I have important news about the sale of the Carved L Ranch."

She closed the door and locked it. This in country where you only lock your door after being physically assaulted and threatened with death on multiple occasions. When the door opened a second time, Ebon Jones was behind it. He flexed his muscles.

"Hello, Ebon," I said, stepping through the door, "I didn't expect to see you here. Doesn't Mensa meet on Wednesday mornings?"

"Come with me," he said. "Mr. Duff is expecting you."

We met in his trophy room. Duff stood behind an aircraft carrier–sized desk, gleaming with oil and decorated with bronzes. He held a freshly lit cigar in his left hand and offered his right to shake. "Cigar?" he asked as I crossed the room. "A Fuente Fuente Opus X Chateau."

I accepted the cigar and declined the right hand. As I clipped the end from the cigar and lit it, rolling it gently over the flame from an expensive butane lighter, I looked around Duff's trophy room. Cape buffalo, grizzly bear, an extraordinary elk, an African lion, a number of antelopes, and, in a Plexiglas case, mounted in a diorama, the world-record dik-dik.

"I see you are admiring the dik-dik," Duff said. "World record you know."

"Brewster, anyone who has known you for more than five minutes is aware of the world record."

"He stands nineteen and three-quarter inches at the shoulder and weighed in at thirteen pounds seven and a quarter ounces."

"A monster," I said.

"He truly was," Duff said. He hadn't taken his eyes from the animal since we had started the conversation.

The cigar was wonderful. "For a guy your size, it must have looked as big as that elk there," I said.

Ebon advanced from his guard dog position at the door of the vast room, instinctively sensing danger long before Duff, still lost in reverie, did. "Brewster, get rid of Ebon. What I have to say I'll say in private."

Duff shook his head, as if to clear it of the pleasant memories and reluctantly return to the present. "Ebon," he said. "I think Dahlgren and I will be fine alone."

"I'll be right outside the door," Jones said. "If you need me, Mr. Duff."

A little popcorn fart of a man, Duff had arranged his world to give himself every advantage. A platform had been built on the floor behind his desk, elevating him from the rest of the room. When he sat down at his desk, he somehow looked down at me.

"Take out your checkbook," I said.

"I think I am going to enjoy this," Duff said, opening a ledger checkbook that sat on his desk. "The amount?"

"Fifty thousand."

"That seems like a rather modest down payment."

"It's not a down payment."

"Ah, I see," Duff said. He wrote with a fountain pen. "A bit of *bak-sheesh*, a little taste for Dahlgren. I like that."

"For the time being, let's leave the payee blank."

"All right." Duff capped the pen and sat back in his chair.

"Fred would rather donate the ranch to Buffalo Commons than sell to you."

"Then why did I write this check?"

"We'll come to that. I am here to deliver a simple message, Brewster. You will never own the Carved L Ranch."

"Don't be too sure. Do you like the cigar, by the way?"

"The cigar is wonderful," I replied. "And as far as the ranch goes, I have never been more sure of anything in my life."

"My family has been in this valley for more than a century, and we will be here a century from now. Your employer is the worst kind of parvenu, a carpetbagger. He has no roots in this land."

"He does, however, own the deed to the land."

"A mere legality."

"Legalities, yes. Let's talk about legalities. Tell me, Brewster, did you personally kill the first bison on Fred's property last October, or was it one of the other African Brothers?"

"Excuse me?"

"The first bison we lost was back in October, last year. Then we lost another every four to five weeks thereafter, until the Montana Patriots began their little reign of terror."

"I understand that members of the militia group have already been charged with poaching and poisoning Fred's bison."

"They have. My point is that they began their open season on our bison about six weeks ago. Somebody else rightfully deserves the responsibility for the first six bison."

"And how can this possibly concern me?" Duff asked.

"Because you did it."

Duff laughed. "Even if that were true, it would be impossible to prove."

"It is true, and no, it isn't impossible to prove. Mordecai would have nailed you to the wall. You can't believe how thorough he was. Or maybe you can.

"Mordecai recognized patterns in the poaching and eventually the poisonings. He kept highly detailed records. The first six bison were shot, as I mentioned, on regular intervals, four to five weeks apart. Of course, these are estimates, because Mordecai recognized that he might not have discovered the dead animal on the very day it had been shot. But you don't spend forty years on ranches without learning a few things, like estimating how long an animal has been dead.

"He finally understood that the bison were shot and butchered the week before the monthly meeting of the African Brothers Society."

"Coincidence," Duff said.

"I don't believe in coincidence," I said. "Mordecai also noted that there was a difference in the manner that the bison were butchered. On the first six the poacher took only a haunch and some of the head wool and hide. If the bullet did not pass through the animal, it was removed. The butchering was also quite expert, done with a meat saw and sharp butcher's knives.

"The last four bison were butchered more efficiently and less carefully. A small chain saw, actually. As much meat as two men could carry, three hundred pounds or so. No interest in the head wool or any other trophies.

"The butchering methods alone speak to two different poachers. The last four, as we know, were the work of Axel Jackson. The first six are your handiwork."

"Me, personally?" Duff asked. He had forgotten about his cigar.

"My theory, Brewster," I said. "Although I can prove some of this, the rest is conjecture, though I don't think I am far from the mark. Somehow you got it into your head to do a little neighborly poaching. The African Brothers Society always resented Fred's ban of hunting on the Carved L. Maybe you went in with the idea of taking an elk. Instead you stumbled onto part of the bison herd.

"There you were, an original Sharps rifle in your hand, the most lethal instrument of death on the Great Plains. That very rifle might have been owned by one of the legendary buffalo hunters, someone who sent hides by the railcar-load to the East and left bones and meat. What an opportunity to relive the past. And you do it; you shoot the first bison. Someone was with you, one of your hunting buddies or Ebon, and he does the heavy work, the butchering and carrying the meat out. You take the haunch to the next African Brothers Society meeting and you all decide that this would make fine sport.

"You pass the Sharps around, member to member, from one poacher to another, and for the next five months the Brothers get the thrill of a real buffalo hunt. At each meeting you roast a buffalo haunch.

"Mordecai gets close on the fifth and sixth bison. He's figured out the initial pattern and he starts monitoring the herd. But the herd is spread out over the property. You know it's only a matter of time before Mordecai gets lucky and catches one of the Brothers.

"About this time, you also decide that you, Brewster Duff, should be the laird of the land. Perhaps you think that because the poaching has been relatively easy that the ranch is poorly run. You make your first offer and Fred doesn't even acknowledge that he received it. Owning the ranch becomes an obsession.

"You decide to change your tactics. Things are moving too slowly for you. Time to up the ante. You meet with Ferris and you work out a new plan. The Montana Patriots are nearly penniless. What did you offer them—the ten-thousand-acre tract they wanted, or was it just cash?"

Duff did not answer. He no longer looked at me; his eyes fixed on the view from the floor-to-ceiling window at the far end of the trophy room.

"The Patriots are desperate. You give Ferris the Sharps rifle and a plan. The Patriots can take as much meat as they need, but again you want quicker results. You want to decimate the herd, and you decide that poisoning the herd will achieve that end. The calves die and some of the adult bison get sick and lose weight, but they are tough, rugged creatures that survive under the harshest conditions.

"Then you send death threats to Fred. Not you, directly; probably the Patriots acted as your proxy, using like-minded militia groups around the country. You designed a well-orchestrated campaign of poaching, poisoning, and threatening. Your only direct contributions to the pressure are the annoying and frequent offers to purchase the ranch.

"The Patriots aren't hunters, they don't care about fair chase. They are interested in the meat. You lead them to the herd by learning where the supplemental feed will be delivered. Cole Lassiter, like the Patriots, can't rub two nickels together. He owes money all over town and the repo man is sizing up his truck.

"Ferris approaches him under the guise of being a member of the Cattlemen's Guild and bribes him to swap bales of hay, replacing the Carved L hay with bales that have been laced with tansy ragwort. Suddenly Lassiter has money and an apartment that he conveniently shares with one of our hands. He's been told that when his temporary employment at the Carved L ends, he'll be hired full-time on another ranch. He finds gainful, full-time employment at the Lazy D.

"You're a careful cuss, Brewster, so I figure you met with only Ferris. I believe you made the proposal to Ferris when you two visited the Hutterite Colony together. Ferris is nobody's fool either. I'd guess he got you to agree to pay for his legal expenses if he ever got caught.

"When Elden Elderberry is murdered, both you and Ferris, who started running his own game, seize the opportunity. The threats escalate along with the poaching and poisonings, and the demands become more strident.

"No one expected Mordecai to be killed. You thought you had all the angles figured, but Axel displayed initiative. He actually believed that Ferris masterminded the plan and executed Elderberry. When he saw Mordecai in those Creedmore sights, he didn't waste the opportunity.

"There's blood on your hands, Brewster. You supplied the hay, the Sharps rifle, the money to first bribe Lassiter and then pay the rent on his apartment. Hell, it was your plan. All the pieces came together because of you."

"You can't prove any of it," Duff said, his voice lacking its normal bluster and confidence.

"I can. There is a cast of a footprint taken on the ranch that will probably match your hunting boots. The Hutterites color-code the hay and I found flecks of white paint on the bales that were exchanged. White paint is the color code for the Lazy D. You and Ferris were seen at the colony. You introduced Ferris to the farm boss. You also used the same syntax in the threatening letters that you did with Mordecai the night he threw you out of Stacey's. And, I would bet that if the police questioned them, a couple of the African Brothers would break ranks and admit to playing a minor role in this debacle.

"Can I prove all of it? No, but what an interesting talk I could tell around town. Imagine the crowds I could draw at a chamber meeting or at the next guild luncheon. You could sue me, of course, and then we would march into court and let a judge and jury examine the story. Even if I lost, what would I lose? A couple of fly rods and a truck. Even if you won, you'd lose your reputation and good name."

"What do you want from me? This check, is it to buy your silence?"

"No. I'm not interested in blackmail, Brewster. I don't want you as a friend and I also don't want you having something to hold over my head.

"There are two conditions you must satisfy to ensure our little discussion remains in this room. You will write a letter to Fred withdrawing your most recent offer to purchase the Carved L ranch. Furthermore, you will agree never to make another offer to buy the ranch."

"Even if Fred decides to sell the property in the future?" he asked.

"Especially if Fred decides to sell in the future," I countered. "Why don't you write that letter now? I'll hand-carry it to Fred."

Duff opened the center drawer of his desk and removed a sheet of paper and an envelope, both displaying the ranch brand and address. He wrote a brief letter and covered both points we discussed.

"Now the check," I said. "We lost eleven adult bison and nine calves. After examining the last two years' sales the ranch averaged twelve hundred per head sold. So we lost approximately twenty-four thousand dollars in future sales. We'll consider the other twenty-six thousand a frontier version of punitive damages."

"Should I make the check out to Fred personally, or to the ranch."

"Neither. Fred's a billionaire, what's fifty thousand to him? No, with this check you have an opportunity to do some good, Brewster. Make the check out to the Gray Wolf Foundation."

"Are you insane?" Duff snapped, recovering a bit of his bluster.

"No."

"Do you realize what a donation to this group would mean?"

"Yes; that you support the efforts to reintroduce the gray wolf back into its native range. It's a noble gesture."

"They are killing machines, Dahlgren. I'd be cutting my own throat. Wolves prey on cattle!"

"Let's not quibble. The government reimburses ranchers for losses to wolf predation. Besides, ranchers are notorious for overestimating the impact of the wolf."

"Do you realize that this donation will make me the laughingstock of the Cattlemen's Guild? This goes against everything I believe."

"Brewster, don't act like a dik-dik. Write Gray Wolf Foundation on the pay-to-the-order-of line. Remember, things could get worse. And if you put a stop payment on this check, they will get worse."

Duff finished writing the check, tore it from the ledger, and handed it to me.

Without saying another word, I left. I only wish I had had the foresight to take another Fuente Fuente Opus X Chateau.

CHAPTER 22

SON OF A SON OF A DANITE

The only consolation was that I hadn't started fishing yet. The beeper buzzed and vibrated. I put aside my rod and reached inside the waders, found the insistent device and stared at the number, cupping my hand over the display to cut the sun's glare. A 406 number and one I did not recognize.

When I called, Sy Schwartzwald answered.

"*Oy*, you are a difficult man to contact," he said.

I mumbled a reply, still baffled that the owner of The Cowboy Vey Deli had plucked me from the banks of a trout stream.

"First I tried your house, then the ranch, then Horace, who finally gives me Fred's number," Sy said. "I explained to half a dozen *goyim* that I have an emergency, and finally Fred comes to the telephone.

"So here I am."

"There you are," I said.

"You must come to the shop immediately."

"Sy, what could possibly be so earth-shattering at The Cowboy Vey Deli that it takes me off a trout stream?"

"Dahlgren, you must hurry into town, that's all I can say. Trust me."

Reluctantly I removed my boots and waders and drove into town. Another busman's holiday interrupted. I was beginning to feel put upon.

As I parked I saw the van from the Bozeman Trail Colony in front of the hardware store. The van cruised the streets on Saturday, disgorging Hutterites with business to do or personal needs. Mostly the colonists came into town to shop, spending their meager allowances on sundries and trinkets.

The bell tinkled over the entrance to the bagel shop as I entered. Midmorning customers crowded the shop, lounging over a coffee, a bagel, and the newspaper. A few people stood at the register, deciding what to order. Sy's young helpers, a couple of kids from the university, including Aaron wearing his knitted yarmulke, assisted the patrons.

When Sy saw me he waved and then ushered me into the back of the shop. Waiting in the backroom, warm, close, and damp from the recent boiling and baking, were Luther Kleinsasser and his granddaughter, Sarah.

Luther and Sy were actually old friends. Sy had taken a sabbatical a decade earlier, and the former professor of comparative religion had lived, along with his wife, for six months at the colony. "The world gained the definitive text on modern religious colonists and I gained twenty-three pounds," Sy often said, summarizing his stay with the Hutterites. "Those people know a thing or two about noshing."

So it didn't surprise me to see Luther in the backroom of Sy's shop. Sarah, however, was a complete surprise, especially given that the little imp held a six-hundred-dollar fly rod in her hand.

Susi's rod.

Luther extended his square, strong hand and we shook.

"Dahlgren," the farm boss said, "I do not know where to begin. Last evening my son, Sarah's father, comes to see me. He brings Sarah and this fishing stick. At first Sarah is very stubborn and silent. Then she admits that she found this stick. Finally she tells us a remarkable story. I pray about this and decide that I must speak with you. You will know what to do."

"Me?" I asked.

"*Ja*," Luther replied. "We want as little to do with this world as possible. With the computers and all this science, we must come into the world more frequently than our ancestors. But we are not experienced in this world. You are. So I leave this to your judgment.

"Sarah, she steals this stick. It is expensive, *ja*?"

"Quite expensive." In addition to the rather steep price of this rod, the reel was of equal value. Add it all together and you have a number that more closely resembles a couple of mortgage payments.

Sarah held the rod out to me and I took it, examined it, and then leaned the outfit against the wall.

"Sarah," I asked, softening my voice, "where did you find this rod?"

"It was in your boat, *Herr* Dahlgren, and nobody was around. I worried someone would take it, like *Der Fische Mann* did with the lady's sweater."

"Fisherman," Sy explained.

"You saw a fisherman take the lady's sweater," I repeated. "What sweater?"

"The sweater, like you wear," Sarah said. "Where you keep the boxes with your lures and where you attach all your little machines."

She meant my vest.

"I was fishing down the stream," Sarah said. "I see you and the man and the pretty lady come in the boat. So I hide. I think this is a good time to eat. Sometimes when I am fishing, *Herr* Dahlgren, I forget to eat!"

The child was a marvel.

"I watch you and lady fish. I do not see the man fishing in the side river where you bring him. That was where I wanted to fish. There are many fish in that side river. I am a little angry because the man spoils the fishing for me."

"How?" Sy asked.

"*Herr* Sy," Sarah patiently explained, "you cannot fish in a place after someone else fishes there. That would be foolish.

"I eat my cookies and my pear and I watch. You leave the woman for a time and when you come back, she is catching a fish. You take her rod and the fish is gone! The lady hits you. I think she is angry because she wanted to catch that fish. It was a big fish, too big for the pan!"

I knew I should have let Susi catch that fish before I told her about Elden.

"Then you and the lady leave. This surprises me. You place her sweater and the rod in the boat but you do not get into the boat. You walk up the stream, away from me.

"When you are gone *Der Fische Mann* comes." Sarah looked at Sy. "He is not *Der Fischer*, *Herr* Sy but *Der Fische Mann*."

"I'm lost," I admitted.

"Not a fisherman but a fish man," Sy said, shrugging his shoulders.

"He is not dressed like you do when you are fishing," Sarah explained. "This man wears a *Gummiklage* and glasses that press into his face."

"A rubber suit," Sy said. "The man was wearing a rubber suit."

"It sounds like she's describing a diver's wet suit," I said. "Sarah, this—?

"*Gummiklage*."

"*Gummiklage*," I said. "Does it have sleeves?"

"*Ja*, and hands too, rubber hands. Rubber head. All in black. And the funny glasses."

"What did this man do?"

"He walks to the boat and he takes the lady's sweater. Then he walks downstream. I am hiding now and he does not see me. Soon he turns around the bend in the river and he disappears.

"I am afraid that he will steal the fishing pole. I say to myself, 'Sarah, surely he only forgets the pole and he will come back and steal that too!' So I take it. To keep *Der Fische Mann* from stealing it. I was going to tell you that I had it, but it is so beautiful that I wanted to keep it for a little while."

Sarah looked up at her grandfather, a hint of defiance in her eyes.

"I do not steal the fishing pole," she said. "I protect it."

"I think sometimes a little *Teufel* lives inside you, Sarah," Luther said.

"Devil," Sy explained, continuing in his role as translator.

"Thank you for protecting the rod, Sarah," I said.

"You are welcome, *Herr* Dahlgren," she said, flashing her grandfather a look of triumph. "It is a pretty fishing pole, but it does not work very well."

"I'll teach you how to work this rod," I said, "if you promise to continue to protect it. Will you do that for me?"

Sarah, her triumph complete, her larceny vindicated, beamed.

"Sarah," I asked, "you did not see the other man, the one who got out of the boat with me?"

"*Nein*," she answered. "I saw you walk with him to the little side river. When I take the pole, to protect it, *Grosvater*, I am scared. So I walk down the river also. My shoes and dress are very wet. Then I run back to the colony."

"Thank you, Sarah," I said.

"Sarah," Sy said, "let's go into the shop and you can eat a nice thick slice of bread with some jam."

"Dahlgren," Luther said, "I am no fool. Sarah did not take that rod to protect it."

"Of course she did, Luther. Anyway, it's not important, the rod is hers. I make her a gift of it."

"You are rewarding bad behavior."

"No. I am relieved that a murderer walked past your granddaughter and did not see her."

"This fish man, he kills the other man?"

"Yes," I answered. "And Sarah saw him take the lady's fishing vest from the boat."

"He is stealing?"

"No, he is hiding something."

Luther left, and in a few minutes Sy returned to the backroom and found me sitting in a chair.

"Ah, you look like the Montana version of Rodin's *The Thinker*," Sy said as he handed me a cup of coffee.

"Sy, what do you always tell me about my chess game?"

"My boy, you have all of the characteristics of a fine player except one," Sy said. "The best players have focus, the ability to not only concentrate on the game, but also to see all the permutations, the possibilities, the alternatives available to their opponents. The true masters can see the entire game in a single move."

"Since Elderberry's murder," I replied, "I have focused on the game. You convinced me to play. Having the shit kicked out of me a couple of times had some effect too. But now I realize I've been playing the wrong game."

"Explain."

Sy and I talked for nearly an hour, and he listened as I discussed everything that had happened in the last few weeks.

"I don't disagree with your conclusion," Sy said.

"Everyone believed that Elden was killed to somehow get to Fred."

"Or they wanted to believe that," Sy said. "In some cases, they needed for this to be the case for their own purposes."

"Right; it's like that old saying, 'Just because you're paranoid, that doesn't mean someone's not out to get you.' "

"I prefer another adage: 'A paranoid is someone who has all the facts.' In some cases people wanted or needed to believe the Elderberry murder was connected to Fred."

"Horace?"

"I am not so sure that he is as much in the dark as you believe."

"Feib knew the game from the beginning, and he was able to deflect our attention from the truth."

"This Feib would make a superb chess player. For him not to play chess would be tragic. You think you know who killed Elderberry?"

"Not necessarily who, but how. What I don't know is why."

"Though you have a good idea."

"Yes. Money."

"Always a fine motive."

"But not enough. I think that there must be something else."

"Because you think the wife is involved?"

"Susi's part of this, in some way."

"And you want her murderous intention to be somewhat ennobled by a motive less base than money?"

I winced.

"I am not disagreeing with you," Sy commented. "Often the simple solution is the correct one—but not always. Why would Susi want to kill her husband?"

"Divorce?"

"California is a community property state," Sy said. "Even in divorce she remains one of the wealthiest women in the country."

"Not if she signed a prenuptial agreement."

"Suppose she did sign an agreement. Don't you think that any resulting settlement would be less than generous? And you're not even certain that a divorce was imminent. Divorce is very unusual among Mormons."

"But not unheard of?"

"No," Sy sighed, and shook his head. "This explains your recent interest in the Latter-day Saints."

"Yes."

"We discussed earlier that if you wanted to silence a Mormon proselytizer, merely ask him about polygamy."

"I remember."

"There is another way to achieve the same result. Ask, who are the Sons of Dan?"

"The Sons of Dan?" I asked.

"Wait a minute," Sy said, leaving the backroom and returning with a Bible. He put on a pair of reading glasses, opened the book, and said, "Here. Genesis, chapter forty-nine, where the tribes of Israel are named. Verse seventeen. 'May Dan be a serpent by the way, an adder in the path, that biteth the heels of the horse, so that its rider shall fall backward.' "

"And?"

"In the 1830s and 1840s, the Gentiles hounded and persecuted the Mormons, literally ran them out of town on several occasions. They decided not to turn the other cheek. Instead they formed their own army, a militia, that they called the Sons of Dan. When the group disbanded, a dozen or so of the Danites, as they were also known, swore absolute allegiance to the First Presidency. In time, they became almost legendary bogeymen.

"You spoke earlier of Elderberry's interest in the Mormon forgeries. In the early days following the bombings, rumors ran wild that the Danites committed the murders."

"You make them sound like hit men," I said.

"Dahlgren, this was the American frontier, the wild, wild West. People faced violence as an everyday occurrence. They fought to keep what was theirs and to take what they felt should be theirs. Is it any different today? In business, for example, in corporate takeovers, the battles may be less bloody but still profound in human cost.

"The Mormons sought their Zion, free from the persecution of the Gentiles."

"That's the second time you've mentioned Gentiles," I said.

"They consider themselves descendants of the Israelites. The Book of Mormon, though debunked by every major university in America, is still a wonderful fable, thought-provoking and entertaining. A marvel, really, and as I said, uniquely American."

"How does this all fit with *Der Fische Mann*?"

"Our discussion? It may not fit at all. We began with a conjecture about divorce and meandered to the Danites. What you know, based on the fortunate observations of young Sarah, is that a man in a wet suit probably killed Elderberry. Was he lying in wait, actually in the river? How did he do this?"

"The how may not give us the why, the motive."

"Perhaps not. How do you think the murder took place?"

"I don't see the murderer lying in wait. That would mean that he would be submerged in water with a temperature in the low fifties. Even with a wet suit, you'd be hard pressed to leap into action at a moment's notice.

"And a moment's notice is what he would have had. In fact, he couldn't be completely sure that I would leave Elden alone. This was an opportunistic murder."

"Yet highly premeditated and carried off by a plan. Several things bother me," Sy continued. "First, how does the murderer know that you will stop in that precise location?"

"I stop in pretty much the same holes on every float. You get to know a river when you fish it as much as I have. There are places generally guaranteed to surrender fish, even to the novice angler. It's also the second or third place I'll stop on any trip. Common knowledge."

"Yes, common knowledge, but only to those who have fished the ranch before."

"Right, but remember, I took Elden and Susi out the day before."

"That hardly makes them experts."

"That's true."

"Here is my point. Are there other places on the river that present an equally attractive opportunity for murder?"

"That's a great question," I said. I thought about the river in a vastly different fashion. Where could someone lie in wait and hide from any witnesses? And it had to be water where I would feel comfortable leaving a novice alone to fish so that I could attend to another novice. Actually, a few bends might make likely ambush points, but the possibility of discovery on those were greater. The murderer had found the best place on the river to commit murder.

When I told that to Sy he then asked, "How does the murderer get to the ambush point?"

"That's easy. There's an old section road and a fire road that gets you within a quarter mile of the river. Any four-wheel or all-wheel-drive vehicle can negotiate either road without a problem."

"Now, how does the murderer become familiar with the terrain?"

"A topo map," I said, "or a DeLorme atlas, GPS—it's never been easier to find your way around."

"And you also assume that the murderer is not a local man?"

"Yes. If Susi's involved, then it stands to reason that whoever helped her doesn't live in the county."

"And you can further assume that he didn't just drop in for the day," Sy said. "By that I mean he must have spent the night somewhere."

"How do you locate a hotel guest in Bozeman or Gallatin Gateway who also happens to be a murderer?"

"Good point. You would need a name at the very least," Sy reasoned. "The search could be narrowed if you could cross-reference airline reservations or car rentals."

"They could have just driven into town," I countered.

"The killer may or may not have flown into town, may or may not have rented an automobile, may or may not have stayed in a hotel. The only certainty is that he did commit a murder. And me, speculating like a Jewish Sherlock Holmes, and on the Sabbath no less."

The next day Fred arrived, accompanied by Billy Sherman and several bankers. Neither Billy nor the bankers expressed a desire to fish and Fred begged off. We met for lunch at the Gateway Café.

"Can't concentrate," Fred said. "I'm focused on this deal to the point where I almost forget to breathe."

"Susi wants to fish," I said.

"I doubt that's all she wants to do," Fred said. "I think she wants to spend some quality time with you."

"I haven't properly thanked you for including Special Agent Feib in what I considered a very private and personal matter."

"I had to take you down a peg, son. You got to feeling morally righteous about my decision to allow Feib to arrest you. You were damn near smug about it. Can't let the bottom rail on top, especially on my own ranch. By the way, you are most decidedly not spending the night tomorrow evening. Pass the Tapatio, please."

"I had no intention of spending the night," I said, handing him the hot sauce.

"Do I smell a whiff of that moral superiority returning, Dahlgren?"

"You do not."

"Besides, I think there's something wrong with the world when my river keeper is getting more quality sack time than me, and in my house with my guest. It's galling!"

"Fred, you asked me to spend the night."

"I do recall that, yes."

"You didn't want to be alone with the recently widowed Mrs. Elderberry."

"True."

"Any reason?"

"These things are not discussed in polite society."

"It's OK to broadcast my peccadillo, but we can't discuss the Elderberrys. Why? Because they're rich?"

"The lady has a reputation. Let's leave it at that."

"How'd you learn about this reputation?"

"Dahlgren, I do own the world's premier twenty-four-hour news station."

"And because you want to purchase an interest in VideoComp, you didn't want to complicate the transaction by discovering if the reputation was well deserved."

"Exactly."

"When does Susi arrive?"

"This evening. We sent the jet out for her and her team."

"Her team?"

"Estate planning attorney, corporate counsel, and get this . . . a personal bodyguard. Susi said that Church Security insisted that she travel with protection, a bodyguard, until the deal is signed."

"Why?"

"Protecting their investment."

"The ten percent they already own?"

"Well, there's that stock. But no, they are concerned about the tithe from the proceeds of the deal. Susi intends to tithe ten percent of the profits to the church."

"And how much will that be?"

"Elden's basis, what he paid for his stock, is pennies a share. Susi will profit handsomely. We offered a billion seven."

"Ten percent . . . one hundred and seventy million dollars?" I asked.

"Give or take those few pennies. Hence the bodyguard, who, by the way, goes with her everywhere. He will be joining you on the float tomorrow morning."

"Does this bodyguard have a name?"

Fred reached into his shirt pocket and removed a folded sheet of paper. He held the paper at arm's length and squinted.

"He does. Fellow name of Rockwell. O. P. Rockwell."

CHAPTER 23

"A" IS FOR APOSTATE

At the eighth hotel I checked, I found my man, and his accomplice.

When I finished my conversation with Fred, I now had a name: Rockwell. I concocted a simple ruse and began my hotel-to-hotel search. While it would have been easier to use the telephone, I felt that I would be more successful in person. I was driving the ranch Travelall around town because I figured that Feib still had a tracking device on my truck. Since I had been repeatedly warned off the investigation, I didn't want him knowing that I had decided not to heed his warnings.

"Hello," I said, introducing myself to the desk clerk at Embassy Suites. Her nametag read, KYRA, LOS ANGELES.

"Good day, sir," the attractive woman replied. "Do you have a reservation?"

"No," I answered. "I work for Fred Lather, and I was wondering if you could do us a favor."

Fred's name usually worked magic.

"We would be delighted to assist you and Mr. Lather in any way we can."

"Thank you, Kyra, because it's an embarrassing situation for us. You see, we had guests at the ranch last month . . ." I gave her the dates. "They had an assistant who did not stay at the Carved L. We didn't find out about it until recently. Of course, Mr. Lather would like to pay his bill."

"I understand. Do you have the name of the guest?"

"I do. Mr. O. P. Rockwell."

Kyra tapped a few keys on her computer. "Yes, sir," she said. "Right here. Mr. Rockwell drove in from Salt Lake City." She gave me the dates. Rockwell had checked in two days before Elden's murder and left the day following.

"That's some drive," I commented. "His employers flew, naturally. I hope that he at least had a comfortable car."

She checked the record, and laughed. "He came in a Pontiac Montana minivan."

"Life is more exciting in Montana," I said, quoting the television commercials that promoted the vehicle.

"Will you be paying for Mr. Rockwell's associate as well?"

"Sure. That would be Mister . . . uh . . ."

"Lee. Mr. John D. Lee."

Kyra gave me the amounts on the bills and I said that I would send a check.

"When we receive the check," she said, "we'll go ahead and make adjustments to their American Express cards."

My next visit was to The Cowboy Vey Deli. A few patrons sat over late lunches.

"Dahlgren," Sy said, "you look like you could use a pastrami sandwich."

"And some advice," I said.

"I can handle both."

Sy carried the sandwich to a sofa and easy chair near the front window of the shop and far away from his other customers.

I told him about Susi's bodyguard and my discovery that Rockwell and his associate, Lee, had been in Bozeman at the time of Elden's murder.

When I mentioned the names, Sy laughed.

"Arrogance!" he snorted. "Yesterday I told you about the Danites."

"I remember."

"Among the most famous of the Danites were Orrin Porter Rockwell, John Doyle Lee, and Bill Hickman. Rockwell's life is truly the stuff of legends. He himself was illiterate—a pity, really, given the Mormon predilection for keeping journals and diaries. It would have been interesting to read the private thoughts of a man who was known as the Avenging Angel or the Destroying Angel of the Mormon Church.

"Rockwell was one of the earliest converts to the Mormon religion and he was fiercely loyal to the Prophet. He was rumored to have assassinated a former governor of Missouri at the bidding of Joseph Smith."

"Smith, what, ordered a hit? Like a Mafia chieftain?"

"Oh, my friend, it's better than that," Sy said. "He prophesied that Lillburn Boggs, the former governor and avowed enemy of the Latter-day Saints, would die a violent death within the year."

"And Rockwell killed him?"

"No. I used one of the precise definitions of 'assassinate.' An unknown assailant shot Boggs. The gun was fired through the window of Boggs's study, wounding him. His daughter was playing at his feet and the child, fortunately, was not injured. The suspected assassin was Porter Rockwell.

"Rockwell was also thought to be one of the 'White Indians' who preyed on emigrants, and not just Gentile emigrants."

"This all seems, well, a bit bloody."

"And it was bloodier still in Utah. When Joseph Smith was murdered in Carthage, Illinois, Rockwell transferred his allegiance and fierce loyalty to Brigham Young. Then there is the matter of his friend and fellow Danite, John Doyle Lee."

"Lee's Ferry?"

"Correct. The only man punished for the Mountain Meadows Massacre. Cold-blooded murder in the name of religion. Dahlgren, there is a third discussion that you may have with a Mormon that could lead to a one-way conversation. That would be the concept of blood atonement.

"The Mormons believed that certain sins were so grievous that the crucifixion of Jesus Christ could not redeem the sinner. These sins, including murder, adultery, and sexual congress with Negroes, to use the vernacular of the times, would prevent the sinner from entering the Celestial Kingdom. Redemption was possible, though it came at a high price. Someone would have to kill you. 'Your blood spilt on the ground as a smoking incense to the almighty.' "

"You're joking."

"I am not. Those Mormon forgeries? Hofmann's father believed in blood atonement. He believed that if his son had committed the murders, then the only way for him to enter the Celestial Kingdom would be to face a firing squad."

"Capital punishment?"

"Yes, but not just any method of capital punishment. The electric chair or lethal injection, even hanging, would not work in this case. Blood must be spilled on the ground."

"Is that why they still have a firing squad in Utah?" I asked.

"Yes."

"But what does this have to do with Elden Elderberry? I'm fairly sure that he wasn't guilty of any of the crimes you mentioned."

"There was one other sin that could lead to the unfortunate necessity of blood atonement. Apostasy."

"What's that?"

"There are times I find it astounding that you have a university degree, Dahlgren. Apostasy is when one abandons or renounces his religious faith. These apostates were quite dangerous to the Church, especially in the early years."

"Why?"

"The most dangerous defectors, if you will, were those privy to the inner workings of the Church. Eyewitnesses to the events of an embryonic religion, they did not know the Prophet from a sanitized catechism. They knew the Prophet personally, knew him as a man, not myth.

"We Americans have always feared cults and dealt with them using rather extreme methods. The witches in Salem, the Masons in the early ninteenth century, and more recent examples, Jonestown and Waco. The Mormons were hounded and vilified, persecuted and driven from three states. Apostates published lurid, and sometimes specious, denouncements and exposés of the Church."

"Like the tabloids?"

"Exactly. They were the equivalent of *The National Enquirer*. What people don't understand, they demonize. Dahlgren, there are still people who believe that Jews sacrifice and devour Christian babies."

"But what has this got to do with Elden?"

"You mentioned that Elderberry might have had a crisis regarding his faith. Think."

"One of the most successful Mormon businessmen wants out of the Church."

"Yes, a paragon of a church that preaches and promotes secular success as well as an afterlife where a priestholder may become a god."

"And one hundred and seventy million dollars." I explained Fred's purchase of half of Elderberry's stake in VideoComp. "At a later point the entire company may be sold. When Susi sells the remaining shares of VideoComp stock, she'll tithe another ten percent. The church also owns ten percent of the company outright."

"When all is said and done, how much money would the Church make?"

"Don't know, but it could be maybe a billion dollars."

"Men have been killed for less."

"Sy, you're suggesting that the Church is responsible for Elden's murder."

"That is one conclusion, yes."

"And the other?"

"The one that you have been avoiding."

"That Susi had something to do with it."

"Yes."

"That she is somehow responsible for the death of her husband."

Sy was silent.

"She didn't kill him. She couldn't have. She was fishing in the river."

Sy remained silent.

"I know," I said.

"I believe that you do know. Now, to the problem at hand."

"That is?"

"Tomorrow morning you are going fishing with at least one murderer. Maybe two. Perhaps it's time to tell Horace about your discoveries."

"No," I said. "I've been ordered to keep my nose out of the investigation."

"Instead you have been the buttinski, a real busybody."

"Not only that, but I am hiding evidence—Susi's fly rod. I know someone, Sarah Kleinsasser, who may have seen the killer. Then I spend all afternoon lying to hotel desk clerks all over town until I get the information I need. That hardly qualifies as letting the professionals work the case."

"So what are you intending?"

"I think I'll just go fishing."

"*Meshuggeneh!*"

"What's that mean?"

"Crazy," Sy said. "You're crazy is what you are."

"Sy, think about it. The river's got to be the safest place in the world. Do you think that they would kill me on the same river where they murdered Elderberry?"

"I admit that the scenario may stretch credulity. Then again, murder itself is absurd. 'Who knows what evil lurks in the hearts of men?' "

"'The Shadow knows,'" I replied.

"How is it that you know about the Shadow?"

"The Alec Baldwin movie."

"*Oy*, I know nothing from Alec Baldwin. I know the Shadow from the original, an old radio program, Dahlgren. Before your time. Me, I'd march over to the police station and have a nice long chat with Horace. How can it hurt?"

"It could hurt if I'm wrong. If I tell Horace that I think Susi is involved in the murder, then he'll pass it along to the FBI and she'll be questioned. It could have the effect of derailing Fred's purchase of VideoComp stock. And that's if I'm right or wrong. Either way I could be a loser."

"How?"

"If I'm wrong, and she had nothing to do with the murder, she could take umbrage—"

"A fine word, 'umbrage.' Perhaps you truly did attend a few classes at MSU," Sy interjected.

"—and refuse to sell Fred the stock. If I was right and she's arrested for murder, then she might not be in a position to sell. The authorities could freeze the assets pending the results of a trial. That's why my plan is to go about my business and do the one job tomorrow I was actually hired to do—fishing guide."

"And you will be careful."

"I'll be extremely careful."

"What is the plan for this investigation of yours?"

"I'm about out of ideas on how to proceed. I only know certain things and don't have the resources to do much more. I can't examine telephone or travel records. I can't look into the background of our two born-again Danites. If this does lead back to the Church, I doubt that my questions would be answered in Salt Lake City. I think I now understand the motive."

"Or motives."

"True enough. I think I know the motives, but proving them would be impossible."

I managed a few hours on the creek, caught the evening hatch, and returned to my cabin. Once again I had slipped back into the habit of leaving the door to my cabin unlocked. With the Montana Patriots enjoying the hospitality of prison while they awaited trial, and the zealots at PETEM at least temporarily neutralized, I saw no need to take that simple precaution. But that was before Sy had raised the specter of Danite bogeymen, complete with aliases honoring their earliest—and apparently, most ruthless—members.

The lights in the cabin were on, weakly reaching out through the gray dusk. My scalp bristled in anticipation of receiving a love tap from a steel baton, or worse.

With relief I saw Special Agent Sully Feib once again had selected my couch to catch up on his sleep. He awoke when I opened the door.

"I have half a mind to arrest you right now," Feib said.

"Don't they teach the social graces at FBI school?" I asked. "Would it be so hard to say 'Good evening, Dahlgren. I have half a mind to arrest you right now?' "

"Academy, FBI Academy. Located in Quantico, next to The Basic School."

"And this is the gratitude I receive."

"For what?" Feib asked.

"For providing you with a place to actually get some rest, Agent Feib," I answered. "It seems that every time I see you, you're comatose. My sofa, my truck, my rocking chair out there on the front porch."

"Power naps."

"Right. That first night you were damn near drooling."

"I never drool."

"You probably didn't drool when you were a baby. I'm having a drink. Would you like one?"

"No." Then as an afterthought, he mumbled, "Thank you."

"Was that so hard?" I opened a Black Dog and sat in the easy chair.

"What have I done this time?" I asked.

"Two hours ago the San Francisco field office received a visit from Susi Elderberry."

I said nothing.

"Mrs. Elderberry expressed serious concerns about you."

"Me?"

"She claims that you are making unwanted overtures toward her. Furthermore, she claims that you are obsessed with her and that it started the first day you met, the day before the murder. In fact, now that she's had time to reflect on it, she thinks you might have killed her husband. She even remembers a comment you made to Mr. Elderberry. Something about BYU football and making it off the river alive."

I held out my hands, palm down. "Cuff me . . ."

"I may. She says that you have been calling her, an average of three times a day."

"I have never called her, not once. Surely you checked my phone records."

"We did," Feib said. "The numbers she gave us are all from public telephones. She has caller ID and made it a practice to write down any 406 numbers."

"How helpful."

"Approximately seventy calls," Feib continued.

"Obviously my passion knows no bounds," I said.

"Apparently you were quite persistent. After the first few calls she refused to talk with you, and instructed her staff to tell you she was not available."

"But I continued dialing, hoping to win the widow's hand."

"She also confided to my colleague that you made sexual advances toward her, both before and after her husband's murder."

"She arrives at the ranch this evening. Fred told me that she asked if I would be spending the night at the ranch."

"You mentioned that at Shames's funeral. Susi also discussed that identical issue with my counterpart. She said that she asked Fred that very question because she was afraid that you would be spending the night. She feared a repeat of the 'unfortunate incident' that occurred on the evening of her husband's murder."

"Now it's an unfortunate incident."

"Yes. You pressed yourself against her in the hall and tried to force yourself into her room."

"This is rich," I said.

"No," Feib said, "she is rich. And in a case of 'he-said-she-said' money and beauty, combined with a sincere story full of graphic details, usually carry the day."

"What graphic details?"

"She used a quaint phrase. What you would expect from a devoted, demure wife, now widow. I believe that she said 'Mr. Wallace was fully aflame, his member in a heightened state of arousal.'

"The Special Agent who spoke with Mrs. Elderberry suggested, quite strongly, I might add, that we interrogate you, at the very least. Mrs. Elderberry presented a persuasive and cohesive set of facts. You are attracted to her. You made sexual overtures toward her; you even tried to force yourself on her sexually. Then you embark on an energetic and persistent telephone courtship. Harassment, really. She's worried that you'll be in residence at the ranch to prey on her again. Oh, and yes, you might have killed her husband."

"Can you prove I made the calls?" I asked.

"Can you prove that you didn't?" Feib countered.

"Funny, I thought this was America. Don't you guys have the burden of proof?"

"Sexual harassment is the modern witch hunt. Accusations are enough."

"So I'm in the unenviable position of trying to prove a negative."

"Not really."

"Oh?"

"I compared some of the calls with your known whereabouts."

"Are you having me followed?"

"No, but we do know where you are most of the time. One of the calls was made when you were visiting with Zed and PETEM. Another was made during Mordecai's funeral. So unless you can be in two places at once, that clears you."

"Completely?"

"Legally. That's not to say you didn't make the other calls, but I would bet you didn't."

"You'd win that bet."

"May I have that drink now?"

I brought him a beer mug and a Black Dog. He poured the beer, studied the head, and then took a sip.

"You might take this opportunity to tell me what you know," Feib said.

"Why?" I asked, quickly adding, "that is, assuming that I actually know something."

"You are being set up. Someone has gone to great lengths to cast you in the role of Elderberry's killer. Frankly, you're made to order."

"A patsy."

"Yes. You have a history of violence toward Californians. Low-grade assaults, but in the hands of a skilled prosecutor, these minor scrapes could be inflated into much more. Anyone who knows you knows that you also bear ill will toward Mormons."

"Just the football team at BYU."

"There's a newspaper article from the day of your injury that paints a less than flattering picture of the BYU program. You intimate that the Church uses missions for the BYU players as a steroid-laced two-year training table. You called the leaders of the Church hypocrites."

"I didn't say any of those things!" I protested.

"Nonetheless, they are in print and in the public record. By your own admission you had a drink on the morning of the murder."

"A wee dram. Hair of the dog."

"You entered the side channel with the victim. The only witness is Mrs. Elderberry. Two men wade into the side channel, one man wades out. You show up at the ranch with a split lip. Did I forget to mention that we found the murder weapon in your drift boat?"

It would have been easy to tell Feib about the man that Sarah Kleinsasser saw. The men who drove from Salt Lake City in a van. The men who had taken rooms at the Embassy Suites in Bozeman. The man who removed Susi's vest from the McKenzie boat. But I didn't.

"Then there's the night of the murder. On one hand we have a fishing guide who has acquired expensive tastes and habits. On the other hand we have a beautiful, wealthy widow."

"Agent Feib," I said, "she came to dinner in a little black number that would have turned heads on Rodeo Drive in Beverly Hills."

"At your trial she'll wear an ankle-length, long-sleeved, high-collared dress that will make her look like she just walked off the set of *Little House on the Prairie*. That same destitute fishing guide later boasts that he bedded Mrs. Elderberry. He tells his employer and an FBI agent, and the conversation is overheard by the police chief."

"I didn't brag," I protested.

"I'm just telling you how it will play out in a courtroom. Meanwhile, the widow is on the record with another FBI agent claiming you mauled her. Then she finds she has a stalker on her hands. Scores of intrusive and unwelcome telephone calls."

"Based on all this, I guess I won't be taking Susi and her bodyguard fishing tomorrow."

"Oh, but you are."

"How do you know that?"

"She told my colleague in San Francisco that she intends to go out tomorrow, accompanied by her bodyguard. She wants to successfully complete the transaction with Mr. Lather, so she doesn't want to cast a shadow over the deal with a display of pique. And she intends to lay a wreath at the place her husband died."

"That is so fucking California," I said. "Maybe she can pass out ribbons for us to wear on our lapels. I wonder what color is available."

"Which is precisely the reaction they want and expect from you. All of this, however, is speculation. It doesn't really matter because there won't be a trial."

"Damn straight. You know I didn't kill Elden."

"There won't be a trial because you'll be dead."

Despite their recent frequency, I hadn't become inured to death threats. Both the Patriots and the People for the Equal Treatment of Every Mammal had threatened me with death. But when a Special Agent of the Federal Bureau of Investigation alludes to your demise, speaking with confidence of the event's immediate occurrence, well, that troubles a man.

"What the fuck are you talking about?" I asked.

"No one knows what I know, Dahlgren," Feib said. "No one knows about our previous discussion regarding Mrs. Elderberry. I did not file a field report about that interview. No one knows we are talking now. In effect, as far as anyone else is concerned, no one knows that I know, with absolute certainty, that you did not kill Mr. Elderberry.

"The scenario that I laid out is what the real murderers of Elden Elderberry will put forth. The way to ensure that their story is accepted as fact is to have only one side told."

"Their side," I said, barely above a whisper.

"Correct. If you are dead then you would be unable to defend your good name, to offer your side of the story."

"And who are *they*, Agent Feib?"

"You know who *they* are. You know much more than you've told Horace or me. I'm suggesting that now would be an excellent time to tell us what you know."

"You know everything that I know."

Feib paused, finished his ale, and then smiled. "I know more than you think I know, Junior FBI Agent Wallace, though I suspect that you have a detail or two that would assist in closing this investigation.

"You sit squarely on the horns of a dilemma, Dahlgren. You want to believe that Mrs. Elderberry's involvement in the murder of her husband is somehow tangential.

"A couple of weeks ago you called Horace and asked him if he had found a telephone among the items in Mr. Elderberry's vest. Naturally, he told me."

"Elden didn't have a phone in his vest."

"No, because we believe Mrs. Elderberry had the satellite telephone in her vest," Feib said. "The vest that went conveniently missing. While we don't have an exact time of death, we have, based on your interview, a rather narrow window. The records show that just before the murder someone made a two-second telephone call to an 801 number. For your information, that's the area code for Salt Lake City."

"What can you possibly say in a two-second telephone call?"

A car drove into the front yard.

"You don't have to say anything," Feib said. "The call was a signal. To go forward with the plan to execute her husband." He reached into his pocket and took out a tiny Ericsson wireless telephone. "I pushed a button and the telephone automatically dialed a preset number. After the connection was made, I hung up. The driver and car magically appeared. Easy.

"If you want to talk, call me. Otherwise, good luck tomorrow, Dahlgren. You're the best Junior FBI Agent I've ever worked with, and I hope that you're alive when I make the arrests."

CHAPTER 24

TIGHT LINES

I chose not to call Special Agent Feib, in part because I took him at his word that he actually knew more than I suspected he knew, and that he would steer me out of harm's way. The only details he could not possibly know came from Sarah Kleinsasser, and I remained determined to keep both her and the Hutterite Colony out of the investigation.

Feib's conjecture, however, had sobered me. If I were to be ushered into a less than celestial kingdom, the river, where I once felt safe, now loomed as the perfect setting for the final act of the drama. That night I mentally prepared myself as if I were going on a Recon mission.

My sudden apprehensions heightened at breakfast. Fred's table was full with panting financiers and lawyers, all eager to work out the final details of Fred's stock purchase. Two had even fired up their laptop computers and pounded keyboards in between bites of the buffet breakfast.

Susi smiled when I entered the dining room. I returned the smile and waved. Rockwell sat next to her, a man in his mid-fifties.

Everything about him, except for his height, was average. He was as tall as I am. He had average features, a nondescript haircut, salt-and-pepper hair, and alert blue eyes. Rockwell blended in. He sat to Susi's right.

"Good morning, Susi," I said as I took a seat across the table from her. "Ready to go fishing?"

"I am!" she answered, color rising in her cheeks. "This is Porter," she continued, tilting her head toward the bodyguard. "He'll be joining us this morning."

"Morning, Porter," I said. Rockwell nodded. "Have you ever fly-fished before?"

"Yes, I have," he answered, in an average voice, devoid of accent, "though I won't be fishing today."

"What a shame. Most anglers would give their left . . . anything to fish this river."

"Perhaps on another occasion. I am here to provide protection for Mrs. Elderberry. I won't have a fly rod in my hands, I won't row the boat, and I won't carry any gear."

"I hardly think Susi would require any protection on the river."

"I am sure that Mr. Elderberry thought that he was perfectly safe as well," Rockwell said, staring at me, "yet here we are." He spread his hands out in front of him.

"Indeed," I said, "here we are."

Rockwell raised an eyebrow.

"Are you former Secret Service?" I asked, as I started eating my breakfast.

"Pardon me?" Rockwell said.

"I'm curious. How does one become a bodyguard? In that movie, the one with Kevin Costner, well, he was a former Secret Service agent."

"Navy SEAL, though I have been trained by the Secret Service and the FBI."

"Vietnam?" I asked. Rockwell looked to be about the right age.

He nodded.

"Susi, how have you been holding up?"

"Fine, thank you," the Widow Elderberry answered, "though these past few weeks have been hectic."

"They do say that staying busy helps deal with the grief."

"It has, though I miss my husband, Dahlgren. I truly do. My only consolation is that I know I shall see him again in the Celestial Kingdom." Susi's eyes moistened.

"But you have had more tragedy here at the Carved L," she continued, "with the murder of the ranch foreman."

"Yes, though his killer is in custody."

"I don't think the police are any closer to solving Elden's murder now than they were a few weeks ago."

"Really?"

"Of course, we heard that you were arrested," she said. "It was all over the TV."

"The police asked me a few questions and I was released the same day. They did not charge me."

We finished breakfast and walked to the river. I carried Susi's gear bag and fly rod. She put on her waders, boots, and a new Patagonia vest. Rockwell also pulled on waders and a pair of Aqua Stealth wading boots. Most boots have felt soles, but the Aqua Stealth boots have a rubber sole designed to provide better traction both in and out of the water. Rockwell fastened a belt around his waist. Attached to the belt were a Folstaf wading staff and a pistol.

"You won't need that," I said.

Rockwell's hand touched the pistol as if to confirm that it still hung from his belt. "I hope that I won't need it," he said.

"Not the weapon. That. You won't need the wading staff. It won't be that difficult wading."

"It's on the belt now," Rockwell replied. "No sense in leaving it behind."

When I had checked the boat before breakfast I found the wreath. MY LOVING HUSBAND was written on a scroll across the top, IN MEMORIAM on the bottom.

"I intend to place the wreath where Elden died," Susi said.

"We can place it atop a boulder, near where I found him," I said.

"And, I hope you don't find this too morbid, Dahlgren," Susi said, "but I'd like to fish that water again."

"I don't think it's morbid at all." In my mind it was a more fitting tribute than a circle of flowers and leaves.

"If you don't mind then, I'd prefer it if we made that our first stop of the day."

I rowed. Susi sat in the front of the bow, facing downstream, hands on her knees. Rockwell sat behind me. In the few times I was able to look at him, I saw that in addition to watching me, he studied both sides of the river.

Vigilant. Alert. The model bodyguard.

I opposed the oars, spinning the McKenzie boat, and then pulled hard on both oars, driving the boat into the gravel bar that separated the main river from the side channel. I jumped into the water, tied the boat to a tree, and set the anchor in the sand and gravel. I helped Susi out of the boat and handed her the fly rod. I carried the wreath.

"Porter, please stay at the boat," Susi said.

"Ma'am," he said, "the instructions from Church Security are explicit. You are not to be out of my sight."

"This is a private moment, Porter. Surely you understand that."

"He'll be there," Porter protested, referring to me as if I wasn't there.

"I know Dahlgren," she answered. "He was also quite fond of Elden."

"I'm sorry. I can't do that."

"And I am afraid that I must insist."

"Insist all you want, ma'am. My orders came directly from the First Presidency."

They arrived at a compromise. Rockwell would stand at the downstream end of the gravel bar. We crossed to the side channel and walked along the gravel bar. Susi and I waded into the river just downstream from the boulder. I held her left elbow with my right hand, using my body to create a small lee for her to walk across. The current was not as strong in the channel as in the main river, and the water level had dropped since the Elderberrys' last visit in mid-May.

"Porter creeps me out," Susi said, when we were alone but still under Rockwell's scrutiny. "I truly resent the church's insistence that I travel with a bodyguard. I have no privacy. Last night he slept in a chair outside my bedroom door! Can you believe it?" She glanced downstream and then drew closer to me. "Is there any way you might be able to spend the night at the ranch? I'd like to see you again."

"No," I answered. "Besides, what good would it do with him guarding the door?"

"I would find a way, Dahlgren. Trust me, I would."

We stood at the boulder, in the calm, flat water behind it. Fish that prowled the edges of the foam line scattered at our approach. Rockwell walked downstream, stopping only about twenty yards behind us, but well beyond the range of any of Susi's backcasts. I could throw eighty feet of line with no problem, and briefly considered tying on a streamer, a Woolly Bugger tied with a lead wrap, and sending it into his forehead.

"Susi, I think that it would be best if we kept our relationship on a professional basis."

"Dahlgren, you're a fishing guide, not a doctor or lawyer. You didn't keep it on a professional basis the last time I was here."

Failing a quick rejoinder, I held out the wreath. Susi had an odd way of honoring the memory of her husband.

"Place it anywhere," she said, a hint of petulance in her voice. "Say a few words if you want."

"Me?"

"Sure, why not?"

I placed the wreath on the top of the boulder. The current pushed water into the upstream face of the rock and droplets of water and spray began to cover the wreath, beading on the waxy leaves and the carnations.

Clearing my throat, I searched my mind for an appropriate phrase or quotation. At Mordecai's funeral the vicar had quoted Teddy Roosevelt, so I made my start there.

"Teddy Roosevelt once said something like all death is a tragedy. I didn't know Elden Elderberry long, but we fished together for a couple of days and you get a good measure of a man when you fish with him. I think he would have made a fine fisherman, and the tragedy is that people he trusted, and perhaps once loved, took so many years away from him."

"How odd," Susi said when I finished. "You act as if you know who killed poor Elden."

Taking Susi's rod from her I tied on a Yellow Humpy. I smeared Gink on the fly to aid its buoyancy and cast the line, watching my backcast while sneaking a glance at Rockwell, still positioned like a sentry. He stood in the channel, the water breaking against his shins.

"Why are we fishing this way?" Susi asked.

"When we fished here last month we used nymphs," I explained, "and we fished downstream. I thought we'd try a dry fly, upstream, a more classical approach. Do you remember what we discussed about casting?"

"Some of it," Susi said. I helped her through a few casts, casting to the right of the foam line.

"You're back in the groove," I said. "Let the fly drift downstream until you feel that the line is taut. I want you to use the surface tension of the water to make your forward cast. Let's see if you can put the fly just inside that foam line."

She did, and the fly bounced in the turbulent water upstream of the boulder until a large rainbow trout nearly leaped from the river to take it. Susi raised her rod and stripped in line, setting the hook. The rainbow had other ideas, bolting upstream.

"Ease up on the line," I instructed. "Let the fly line slip through your fingers." The trout continued to take line, now working against the drag on the expensive reel.

"Let him run. Try some side pressure."

Susi bent the rod to the right and then the left, attempting to turn the trout's head. The veins in her hand stood out.

"If he turns and runs back toward us, you strip line for all you're worth. You have got to keep the line tight. Any slack at all and he'll be off."

And that's when I realized that I had not been careful. Instead I had allowed myself to get caught in the moment, assisting a novice fly fisher in landing a big fish. I remembered Sy's admonishment. Focus, see the entire board, and anticipate the next move.

I measure my time on the water not in hours, but in days and weeks. My livelihood depended on my ability to read water, to understand what the river tells me. Two trout swam past me, bullets in the water heading upstream. Driven upstream. Something had forced them to abandon the relative safety of their lie to swim directly past Susi and me.

Instantly I regretted my decision to fish upstream. I knew without looking behind me that Rockwell was on the move. He had driven the fish upstream. If Susi had been fishing downstream I would have seen changes in the water from the tiny insects and silt dislodged from the river's bottom by someone wading.

"Strip, Susi!" I shouted as the trout turned and made a downstream run toward us. I reached behind my back and found the handle of my net, pulling it clear from the clasp that fastened it to my vest.

The sound of the water behind me changed, a subtle, almost imperceptible change. A shadow broke over the water to my left, nearly hidden by the current.

As I ducked I heard a spring release. Something hard creased the top of my head, sending my baseball cap into the river. I swung the net hard into Rockwell's right leg. The wooden frame of the net cracked and Rockwell's leg buckled slightly, enough to alter his downward swing with the telescopic steel baton. I brought the net up into his face, the wooden frame catching him under the jaw. He staggered, but managed to bring the baton around with a backhand stroke that caught me on my left shoulder. My left arm instantly went numb. I drove the wooden frame of the net into the bridge of Rockwell's nose. It exploded into a crimson blossom on his face and he fell back into the water.

I fell on top of him, raising my numbed left arm into his throat, forcing his head under the water. His hands, acting purely by reflex, sought to move my arm away from his neck. I groped and found the buckle of his belt, pressed the tabs in to release the clasp, and slid the holster and pistol from the webbed belt. Kneeling in the river, I yanked the pistol from the holster and edged away from Rockwell as he struggled to regain his balance.

Susi screamed during the brief struggle. Hysterical, hyperventilating gasps. She struggled to control her breath, to push out coherent words. “Kill him,” she finally rasped. “Kill him.”

I stood and moved away from Rockwell, easing my feet behind me as I sought the solid ground of the gravel bar. He was a former Navy SEAL. I knew that he didn't need a pistol to kill me.

“They made me do it,” Susi shrieked. “They made me kill my husband.”

Rockwell kneeled in the river, his hands on his thighs. Blood poured from his shattered nose, spraying from his lips as he exhaled sharply, yet I saw calculation in his face. He measured.

"Shut up!" he barked at Susi.

"Susi," I said, "walk over to me."

Like a sleepwalker, Susi shuffled her feet through the water.

I raised the pistol and aimed it at Rockwell. He stood, gathering his strength. In his right hand he held a knife.

"Ever kill anyone before, Wallace?" he asked.

I didn't answer. I had. I could drop Rockwell with a double tap before he started his next sentence. Two in the forehead.

"Birds don't count. Deer don't count. Elk don't count." His voice was hypnotic. He moved toward me. "Killing a man is very different."

It was, but I wanted Rockwell alive.

"Kill him. Kill him. Kill him." Susi's words sounded like a chant, without panic, without emotion. She still held her rod, the line trailing downstream. When she reached the bank she almost walked past me. I caught her elbow and drew her tight against my left side.

"Once I get within twelve feet of you, you're dead," Rockwell said.

"Kill him. Kill him. Kill him."

"Listen to her, Wallace. She's giving you sound advice, best to just kill me." I continued walking backward, losing in my effort to maintain the distance between us, until I was stopped by the cold muzzle of a pistol pressing against the back of my head.

"Give me the gun," a voice behind me commanded.

"Kill him," Susi said. "Kill him and let's end this thing." As she tried to wrench herself away from me I pulled her sharply around so that she stood in front of me in a half embrace. I cocked the hammer of the automatic pistol and jammed it under her chin. The fly rod clattered to the ground.

"Decision time," I said.

"Drop him," Rockwell commanded. I felt the pressure of the muzzle against the back of my head ease.

The air exploded, shattered by the gunshot. The man behind me slammed into my back, knocking both Susi and me to the ground.

As I landed heavily on the gravel the air whooshed out of my lungs and my chin smashed into a rock. A wet heaviness pressed against my back.

As I struggled for breath, as I struggled to retain consciousness, a pair of black boots entered my collapsing field of vision. As if in a tunnel I heard angry, insistent voices and the soft *whump,whump, whump* of a helicopter. The weight on my back disappeared and a pair of hands grabbed my shoulders and turned me over. Before I lost consciousness I saw the smiling face of Special Agent in Charge Sully Feib.

CHAPTER 25

THE SCOTTISH PATIENT

"If I were you, Mr. Wallace," Dr. Patel said, "I would swear off women. Three broken ribs, eleven stitches on your chin to go with your other set, and a hematoma that covers half of your back. A remarkable collection of injuries given the circumstances."

Once again I had enjoyed an evening at the hospital compliments of the federal government. I had offered Dr. Patel a version of the truth; I had fallen while out fishing with a woman. During his morning visit, the good doctor gave me instructions on what I could expect to face as a result of the injuries.

"Return here in one week and I shall remove the stitches," he said. "Once again I performed masterfully, though you shall have a manly scar that will be quite attractive to the sort of woman you seem to favor. The ribs, six weeks. Try not to laugh, cough, or sneeze. Here is a prescription for Vicodin. Take them as needed."

Grady picked me up from the hospital in the Travelall and drove me out to the ranch. He looked over at me during the drive, regarding me with part awe, part raging curiosity.

"How'd it feel?" he finally asked, as he turned the Travelall into the ranch.

"How did what feel?"

"Well, having a feller die right on top of you?"

An FBI sharpshooter had killed the man, later identified as John Doyle Lee, who had been standing behind me. I felt the impact of the bullet in my own back and chest, as if I had been hit with a sledgehammer. The force of the shot had sent the man, Susi, and me to the ground. Susi had been uninjured, thrown clear and landing on her backside, breaking only her fly rod. My body absorbed the full weight of the dead man.

"To be honest, Grady," I said, "I don't remember much. At first I thought I had been shot."

"I heard they found the bullet in one of your fly boxes."

After the bullet passed through Lee's body it also had gone clean through my leader wallet that contained a thick collection of leaders and mini lead heads. Then the bullet penetrated a Wheatley fly box, its energy finally spent. Both had been stored in the back pouch of my vest.

"Lucky, that's me," I said. "The fly box cost me a hundred dollars."

"Mr. Lather would like you to stop in for breakfast," Grady said, as he stopped the Travelall in front of the ranch house. He braked hard, and I gasped as my chest pressed into the shoulder strap of the seat belt. "Sorry," he mumbled. "When you're done with breakfast I'll drive you home."

It seemed like it took me half an hour to climb the stairs to the porch of the ranch house, lifting first one foot and then the other to each step, shuffling like an old man. When I entered the dining room, Fred jumped to his feet and announced, "The man of the hour!" He held a chair for me and I gingerly lowered myself into the seat. "Does it hurt?"

"Only when I breathe," I answered.

"What do you want to eat, son?" Fred asked. "Anything—eggs Benedict, scrapple, haggis, you name it."

"Toast and poached eggs," I answered, "if it wouldn't be too much trouble."

Chief Horace Twain and Special Agent in Charge Sully Feib sat at the table, empty plates in front of them bearing the evidence of hearty, if not healthy, breakfasts.

"'Course," Fred said, "I've still got a good mind to fire you."

"Deal fall through?" I guessed.

"Yes, sir," Fred said, "and the stock exchange halted trading in VideoComp. All we needed was Susi's signature on the stock certificate, one little signature, which of course she can't do at present, seeing as how she's under a federal indictment for murder."

"And racketeering charges," Horace said. "I'm sorely disappointed in you, Dahlgren. Not only did you fail to heed my advice about staying clear of the investigation, but also when you actually discovered crucial information, you never even bothered to tell your old gin rummy partner."

"I'm the only person standing between you and obstruction of justice charges," Feib said. "You came close to derailing a long-standing FBI investigation."

"Let's not forget, gentlemen," I replied, "that I came close to finding myself on a metal table in Iggy Cord's morgue."

"Our sharpshooter had to take the shot," Feib said. "We felt that the man who called himself Lee was seconds away from pulling the trigger."

"So you knew about Rockwell and Lee?"

"Yes," Feib said. "We've been investigating one of the General Authorities of the Mormon Church for eighteen months. This man controlled a rogue element of Church Security."

"The Sons of Dan," I said.

"I knew you knew it!" Feib said. "Rockwell and Lee . . ."

"Aliases. Sort of a warped tribute. They took the names of two of the original Danites."

"I'm duly impressed, Dahlgren. Rockwell and Lee had complete operational covers, an entire set of forged documents, including passports. We suspect that this element is responsible for at least three other murders and a number of other crimes, including blackmail and extortion.

"The Elderberry murder was by far their most ambitious operation. Elderberry had sought legal counsel in anticipation of filing for divorce on the grounds of infidelity. It also appears that he intended to leave the Mormon Church, the culmination of religious doubts that had plagued him since graduate school."

"Are you familiar with the concept of blood atonement?" I asked.

Feib smiled again, and nodded his head.

"I'm quite familiar with the concept of blood atonement," Feib said. "I'm a Latter-day Saint."

"One who's quite fond of Black Dog Ale," I said.

"I'm also partial to Coca-Cola and coffee," Feib replied. "I'm not perfect, Dahlgren. In my own mind I rationalize my transgressions as necessary subterfuges."

"Lying for the Lord," I said. "Elden told me about that. And I'm guessing that in Elden's murder, blood atonement became the rationalization for the true motive—money."

"We disagree on that point," Feib said. "The member of the Quorum of Seventy who put all this into action sincerely believed that he was saving Mr. Elderberry's place in the Celestial Kingdom. To him the money was secondary."

"And in Susi's case?"

"Mrs. Elderberry herself has been silent on the subject. She had signed a prenuptial agreement that would have given her ten million dollars in a divorce. I believe that money was her only motive. Her attorney, however, steadfastly maintains that she was coerced into assisting in her husband's murder. That she herself was threatened with death, and being a deeply religious woman she felt obligated to listen to those who controlled the church."

"Yesterday, in the river, she said something about how *they* forced her to kill her husband," I said.

"Quite calculating, our Mrs. Elderberry."

"How did they expect to get away with this? Wouldn't it have been highly suspicious to kill me at virtually the same place Elden was murdered?"

"Rape. You would have died from injuries as a result of Rockwell strenuously protecting Mrs. Elderberry from your sexual assault. Actually, the beating you gave Rockwell would have added credibility to the story."

"What will happen to her?"

"Maybe nothing."

"How is that possible?" Fred asked.

"The Quorum of Seventy member committed suicide yesterday," Feib said. "As a courtesy, the SAC in Salt Lake City informed the First Presidency that we intended to make an arrest. He was dead from a self-inflicted gunshot wound when our agents arrived to take him into custody. We expect the church to offer little in the way of assistance. They are already stonewalling our investigation.

"Rockwell refuses to talk. Personally, I think Mrs. Elderberry masterminded the entire operation. When she learned or suspected that her husband planned to leave both her and the church, she made inquiries that eventually led her to Church Security and the Danites.

"The visit to the Carved L proved fortuitous. Remote location along with the possibility that the death might be ruled an accident. If ruled a homicide, the murder could be laid at Dahlgren's feet. Every step, including the accidental punch, the stalker calls, even your tryst, was carefully planned."

Fred snorted in vindication.

"We think that she selected the side channel as the perfect location for the death to occur. We suspect that she fixed the position with a handheld GPS device. Rockwell and Lee were already in town, in residence at Embassy Suites with their customized Montana minivan."

Feib looked directly at me. "But you know all this, right?"

My turn to smile and nod.

"When Fred told me the name of Susi's bodyguard," I said, "I checked hotels in town until I found where Rockwell had stayed." I turned to Fred, wincing in pain. "I told them that a ranch guest's assistant had booked a room and that you wanted to pay for it."

"Your fictitious generosity almost got you killed last night," Horace said. "The FBI had listening devices in Lee's room and we overheard an interesting conversation between Lee and Rockwell."

"Because they used encrypted satellite telephones," Feib said, "we only heard one side of the conversation. When Lee checked in at six o'clock last night the desk clerk—"

"Kyra, from Los Angeles?" I asked.

"Yes. Kyra not only remembered him from his previous visit, but also informed him that all his charges would be paid by Fred Lather. She mentioned Dahlgren's visit to the hotel earlier in the day. She even asked if Mr. Rockwell would be checking in!"

"An efficient girl," Fred said. "Maybe I ought to hire her."

"Lee was all for killing you last night, but Rockwell vetoed the idea. The plan hinged on the rape scenario, your accidental death as a result of Rockwell's overzealous defense of Mrs. Elderberry, and the subsequent revelation that you killed Mr. Elderberry. Regardless, we had a four-man team assigned to watch you until you got to the ranch this morning."

"What I can't understand," Fred said, "is why they used the same names twice. A fishing guide tracked them down!"

"Hubris, arrogance—call it what you want," Feib said. "I call it a fortunate lapse of judgment."

"And you think Susi might not be convicted?"

"She may never be indicted," Feib answered. "We have developed a vast amount of circumstantial evidence, including travel records, telephone records, and audiotapes, but without direct testimony an indictment could be problematic. We had directional microphones and video equipment and recorded everything on the river yesterday morning. A defense lawyer will argue every word on the transcript because of the ambient noise, the river and the wind. Makes it difficult to pick up nuance and intention. The video is ambiguous as it relates to Mrs. Elderberry's actions."

"When I first heard Susi say 'Kill him,'" I said, "I thought she meant for me to kill Rockwell."

"And Rockwell counted on you being unable to shoot him in cold blood," Feib said. "He also knew that Lee was hiding in the brush on the gravel bar. He basically herded you into position. When Rockwell ordered Lee to 'drop him,' I released the sniper. I had no choice. I didn't know if they meant to shoot you or knock you unconscious. I knew there was a possibility that the bullet would pass through both of you."

"It nearly did," I said.

"Dahlgren," Fred said, "you'll be dining off that story until you do die. Wheatley fly box dented by a bullet, what a yarn!"

"Why didn't you take Rockwell and Lee down earlier?" Horace asked.

"We wanted to catch them in the commission of a crime," Feib said. "Wading a river and sitting on a gravel bar are not crimes."

"Trespassing is most certainly a crime!" Fred blared. "That pissant Lee drove that Goddamned minivan on my section roads and entered my river illegally. You could have arrested him for that."

"Ever the Montana landowner carping about river access," I said. "Fred, they shot and killed the man, that ought to be punishment enough for trespassing and entering your river illegally."

"I guess," Fred said, without conviction.

Feib continued. "By the time Rockwell got close enough to assault Dahlgren, we didn't have a clean shot. I intended to take Rockwell down after the first blow. Then Dahlgren decides he's back in Force Recon and he drops Rockwell. Later, when Lee appeared, as I mentioned, we had the same problem. We never had a clear field of fire."

"That minivan Lee was driving," Horace said, "unbelievable."

"What we know at this point in time is that it was customized by a specialty vehicle company in San Marcos, California. The company makes mobile command posts and surveillance vehicles for law enforcement. This van had sophisticated surveillance equipment, an arsenal, and a telecommunications suite. Invoiced to and paid for by Church Security. A strong piece of physical evidence. We found a wet suit and a small rebreather that we think were used in the Elderberry murder.

"I'm curious, Dahlgren. How do you see the sequence in the Elderberry murder?"

"I had Elden fishing downstream with a streamer," I said. "The water level was slightly higher then than it is now, just above his knees where I had positioned him, upstream and to the right of the boulders in the middle of the run. He was a decent wader, good balance. I waded back to the main river to help Susi. When she saw me she must have signaled with the satellite phone that Rockwell could proceed."

"Rockwell is a former Navy SEAL. The reason we never found any footprints along the bank was because he entered the river far upstream from the side channel and left far downstream. He was probably hiding in the brush on the gravel bar. When he received Susi's signal he slipped into the river. With the current pushing him, and by pulling himself along the bottom, he could have reached Elden in a few seconds.

"He used the steel baton first to disable Elden. The blow to the knee and then another to the back of Elden's head. Even if Elden had

had the time to scream, I wouldn't have heard him in the main channel. Agent Feib, you said that Elden had a small amount of fresh water in his lungs. After the initial blow to the head, Elden fell facedown in the river, and that's when Rockwell used a river rock to crush his skull. That would also be where he lost his glasses.

"Here's what I think happened to the rod. Like a lot of beginners, Elden had a lazy backcast. His loop would widen, the cast would fall apart, and the fly and leader actually fell into the water. Elden hooked Rockwell, and hooked him deeply. When Elden came forward with his cast he broke the tip section of the rod.

"The other damage occurred when Elden was facedown in the river. He fell on the rod. His reel came off, and Rockwell wound the line on backwards and tried to put the reel spool back on the seat. He's left-handed, and my guess is that his reels are set up for a right-hand retrieve, because that's how the line would be wound on a reel set up that way. Elden's injuries were too excessive for his death to look like an accident. Maybe after taking a moment to think, Rockwell realized that winding the line back on the reel was a useless exercise."

Feib made a note.

"Then Rockwell arranges the body, still hoping to sell the murder as an accident. Elden's body and his outfit looked staged when I first saw them. The physical hydraulics of the water could not have caused Elden's injuries. No way he could have fallen and sustained those injuries; he would have had to dive into the rocks, and even then, it all appeared a bit overdone.

"Rockwell watches us, observes. It's too risky to make his escape while we're still around. He sees me dump Susi's vest in the boat. After we leave he takes the vest. The vest contains the satellite telephone Susi used to give him the signal. Then he makes his way downstream and leaves the river."

"Thanks for the detail about the reel," Feib said.

Horace and Feib rose and shook Fred's hand, then mine.

"Spot me twenty-five points a game," Horace said. "That's your sentence for treating your old friend like a mushroom—keeping me in the dark and feeding me bullshit."

"Dahlgren," Feib said, "thank you."

"Agent Feib—" I began.

"Please, call me Sully."

"Sully," I said, "Sully. Since I met you I've been knocked cold, stunned into paralysis, broken three ribs, damn near shot, and my head has more stitches than it takes to hem a pair of pants."

"I know, you don't know how to thank me. Semper fidelis, Junior FBI Agent Wallace."

Fred and I sat alone in the dining room.

"No chance you can take Brokaw out on Friday, I guess," Fred said.

"Dr. Patel says six weeks."

"Shit."

"I think four or five."

"That's still shit," Fred lamented. "Had you and me entered in the one fly contest in Jackson Hole. Got the Senate majority leader coming next week and the chairman of Citibank the following week. If these were just plain old guests I wouldn't insist, but these folks, these folks, they deserve . . ."

". . . the Royal Fucking Treatment!" we both said.